OBLIVION'S ALTAR

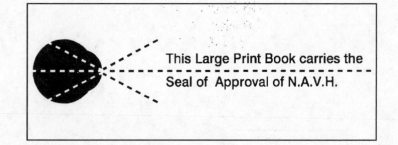

OBLIVION'S ALTAR

A NOVEL OF COURAGE

DAVID MARION WILKINSON

THORNDIKE PRESS

A part of Gale, Cengage Learning

GALE
CENGAGE Learning®

Detroit • New York • San Francisco • New Haven, Conn • Waterville, Maine • London

GALE
CENGAGE Learning®

LIBRARY OF CONGRESS CATALOGING-IN-PUBLICATION DATA

Wilkinson, D. Marion.
   Oblivion's altar : a novel of courage / by David Marion Wilkinson. — Large print edition.
     pages ; cm. — (Thorndike Press large print western)
     ISBN 978-1-4104-6482-8 (hardcover) — ISBN 1-4104-6482-2 (hardcover) 1. Cherokee Indians—Fiction. 2. Whites—Relations with Indians—Fiction. 3. Large type books. I. Title.
   PS3573.I44185O27 2013
   813'.54—dc23   2013037093

Published in 2013 by arrangement with Goldminds Publishing, LLC

Printed in the United States of America
1 2 3 4 5 6 7 17 16 15 14 13

For my sons,
Dean and Tate,
With love and hope,

And for Kah-nung-da-tla-geh,
With respect and admiration

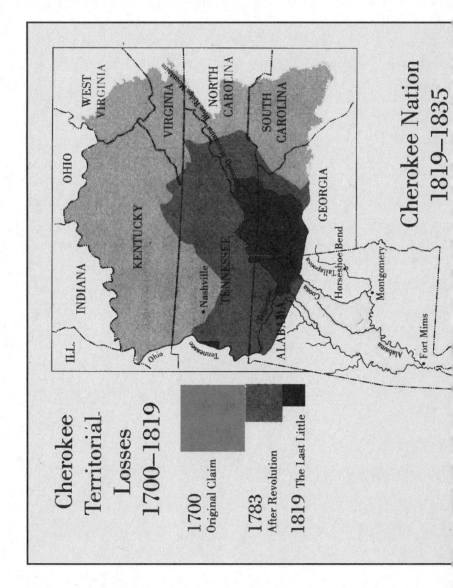

Cherokee Territorial Losses 1700–1819

1700 Original Claim

1783 After Revolution

1819 The Last Little

Cherokee Nation 1819–1835

ILL.

OHIO

INDIANA

WEST VIRGINIA

KENTUCKY

VIRGINIA

TENNESSEE

NORTH CAROLINA

SOUTH CAROLINA

GEORGIA

ALABAMA

Nashville

Ohio

Tennessee

Blue Ridge Mountains

Coosa

Tallapoosa

Horseshoe Bend

Montgomery

Fort Mims

Alabama

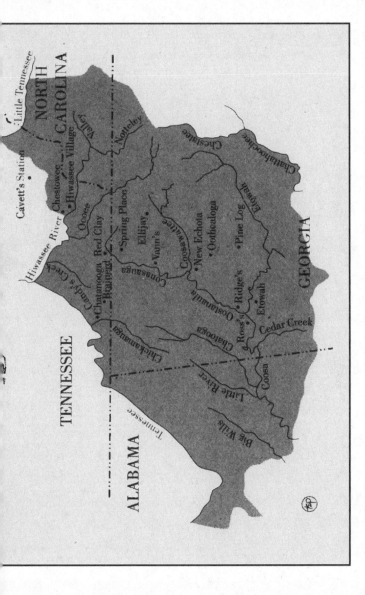

I admit that there are good white men, but they bear no proportion to the bad; the bad must be the strongest, for they rule. . . . They would make slaves of us if they could, but as they can't do it, they'll kill us.

— Buckongehelas, Delaware chief

For [the Indians'] interest and their tranquility it is best they should see only the present age of their history.

— Thomas Jefferson

[The Cherokee] are not inferior to white men. John Ridge was not inferior in point genius to John Randolph. His father, in point of native intellect, was not inferior to any man.

— Sam Houston

In truth, our cause is your own.

— Cherokee Memorial to the United States
Congress, December 29, 1835

[Americans] are, in effect, trapped in a history which they do not understand; and until they understand it, they cannot be released from it.

— James Baldwin, *The Fire Next Time*

PROLOGUE:
JUNE 22, 1839

Kah-nung-da-tla-geh always watched his backtrail. He drifted like mist from underneath the cool shadow of towering cottonwoods, sycamores, and sturdy hickory trees, their limbs woven together by tangles of wild grape and other vines he could not yet name. Red buds, sassafras, chinquapin, and dogwood saplings reached upward straight and thin, hungry for the sparse sunlight filtering through the larger woods. At their feet, pokeberry and blackberry bushes dug their pale roots deep into flinty soil. This was truly beautiful country, but it was not his. He knew his people would learn to love it, this land of their banishment. For him, there would be no time.

His horse shied when the sun blinded its black eyes. *Kah-nung-da-tla-geh,* known to the whites as the Ridge, felt the warmth on his face. Below him ran the sparkling waters of Little Branch, also called White Rock Creek, a stream of quartz etched into banks of white limestone twisting west through the hills of the Indian territory to join Barren's Fork. The world seemed lush in that morning light, and he found some comfort in its quiet beauty, a brief respite from the burden he had carried for close to forty-five winters.

He let loose the horse's reins, allowing the blood bay gelding to drink its fill, nodding to the slave boy, Joseph, to let his mount do the same. Ridge breathed deeply, drawing in the last of the cooler air the sun was driving to the bottoms, and listened to the grace of silence. In the Arkansas hills, one mile east of the boundary that marked the beginning of Cherokee Nation West, he knew that he, the hunted, would be safe.

Ridge had intended to make this journey to the town of Van Buren alone. A few days before he'd sent a wagon with Daniel, another slave he'd captured in the Creek War thirty winters before, to purchase oats for his general store. Word reached his ears that Daniel had fallen deathly ill with a fever, and Ridge, who felt he had failed so miserably as a shepherd for his people, wished at the very least to care well for those under his roof. Against his wife Sehoya's protests that it was far too dangerous to travel alone for any reason, he saddled his horse in determined silence.

"I won't be alone," he told her. "Joseph is going with me."

"Have your own way then, you stubborn goat," Sehoya said, washing her hands of the whole affair as she marched back to their home. She paused before reaching its threshold, then turned and ran back to him. For all of the silver hairs on her head, Sehoya was still spry. She threw her arms around his neck and said, "I love you, my stone-headed husband."

"There's only one who kindles the fires of my heart," he said, smoothing her soft gray hair with his fingers. "The wind blows cold when I'm apart from you. But think what it would be like to be sick and alone."

"I think about it every day," she said, squeezing him tighter. He felt her fingers dig into his back. "I beg you not to go."

"This is a thing I've got to do," he said. He had kissed her forehead and peeled her arms from around him and left her standing there as he mounted his horse. When he'd turned back to offer her his best attempt at a smile, she'd already gone inside. He flicked the reins and rode on, fording Honey Creek, then turning east to catch the Old Line Road that cut south through the Arkansas Ozarks for Van Buren and a sick slave.

Ridge shoved the rifle that always lay across his waist back into its beaded scabbard and rested his wrists on the saddle's pommel. Joseph had been a wise choice for a travel companion. The boy was bright and respectful, and understood the value of quiet contemplation. Ridge decided he would send Joseph to Miss Sophia's school back at Honey Creek. No inquisitive child of any color under his charge would remain ignorant if he had his way — and he would. He must strive to do right by the children. They were the future, and in them lay the last of his hopes. For himself, he had none.

His horse popped its head up from the creek, locked its front knees, and pinned back its ears. Slobber trailed from its lips to the stream as it cocked its head west and nickered in alarm. Ridge bristled, cutting his gaze sharply in the same direction. Joseph's horse spooked. Ridge grabbed its harness to still its nervous agitation.

When all grew quiet again, he heard them. The rustling of brush, the cracking of twigs beneath quick feet and bent knees, the flutter of broad green leaves being parted by nervous hands for a better view. Ridge heard their whispers, the clicks of cocking hammers, a lone horse whinnying over the ridge. They were here, waiting.

His first impulse was to dig his spurs deep into the horse's ribs and bound out of the bottoms of Little Branch for safety. But what about Joseph? Could he leave a child to fend for himself in the woods? Ridge exhaled in resignation. How did they know where to lie in wait for him? Which of the few friends who knew of his journey had betrayed him to his enemies? And what good would it do for him to run? Must he surrender his pride along with everything else he had sacrificed? Why put off the inevitable for another day? The feud would end here, in this lonely place that belonged to neither faction. *So be it.*

His next instinct was to fight them, to let them pay dearly for his blood. He grasped the slender throat of his rifle stock and slid it halfway out of the scabbard before he thought better of it. His precautions had been foolish; to defend himself now would be even more so. He was ready for his agony to end, and had been for some time. Now that his enemies had gone to some trouble to confront him, he understood that this journey had never been about a sick slave. Sehoya must have sensed it, too. Ridge had traveled far to arrive exactly at this stream — this finger of a great river — where he now stood. He removed his hand from the stock. His fingers were trembling until he made a fist. *Steady,* he begged himself. *What are you afraid of? This is the beginning as well as the end. Show your people who you are.*

Ridge calmed the frightened Joseph with a forced look of assurance. Then he bade the boy to put a step or two between them, and then upon another moment's deliberation, two steps more. Once he was certain the boy was clear, he turned back in their direction,

15

to the bone-colored lime stone bluff above him, where he knew dark eyes were already fixed down the sights of blued barrels aimed in hatred at his heart. He spread his arms from his chest, and called out to his killers in their shared tongue.

"Before you stands *Kah-nung-da-tla-geh,*" he said, drawing breath deeply from his lungs. "The Man Who Walks the Mountaintops, the Ridge, once a warrior and chief among you. He stood alone on the barren peaks, studying both slopes carefully, knowing each direction would be a journey of pain."

Ridge let the hills absorb his words, waiting to see if his murderers would show themselves. They loathed him, but they were also willing to listen. If not, he'd already be dead.

"The Ridge had no counsel," he continued, finding his rhythm. "The old ones were dead. The chiefs of his own time, once both brother and friend to the Ridge, closed their ears to the truth."

He paused, and gathered himself. He found strength in his conviction that his executioners owed him his say. "Yuh!" Ridge yelled so loudly that his voice spooked Joseph's horse. Such a grunt was the traditional manner by which all the great orators of his day accentuated their speeches, and this one was most likely his last.

"It's said the Ridge betrayed his Nation," he shouted, the weight of years lifting with the last of the morning haze. "He was, in fact, their salvation. The Ridge alone saw the future. And then, with love in his heart for the Cherokee, he picked their only path."

He waited. The cool breeze washed over him, chilling the beads of sweat on his brow. The horse strained against the bit. Ridge, listening to the stream, let his arms fall. His hunter's eye discerned his assassins' crouched forms behind the brush, their white orbs blinking behind the rifle sights, their cheeks still hollow from the suffering of their forced journey, their fingers still pressed against cool triggers that they could not yet pull. He had more time than he expected. What was to prevent him from saying his peace?

"You young warriors think you know why you've come to murder your chief," he said. "You don't. The truth is never as simple as a killing. The Ridge knows you consider your cause just, but he will not die in silence. You walked the Trail of Tears, but you don't understand why it happened. If you can't abide the whole story, you had best shoot the Ridge where he sits. Otherwise, he'll tell you exactly what brought us to this awful place, how it all started."

Ridge focused again on the running water. "And then you," he said, "who squat behind bushes in judgment, must decide how it will end."

■ ■ ■ ■

PART ONE:
THE DARK AND
BLOODY GROUND

SPRING, 1776 — 1796

■ ■ ■ ■

CHAPTER ONE

"We begin and end with the rivers," the old man said in a fatigued and raspy voice, as if each word would be his last. He pointed at the Hiwassee River flowing below their grassy perch as a prime example. "The streams that emerge from the mountains are trails to the underworld. They flow into the rivers that mark our time and place, and then run on to join the ocean that is the universe. The earth beneath our feet is but an island that floats on this great, infinite sea. The streams pass from one world to the next, connecting us to all that has come before us, and to what will come. Water is sacred to us. We begin and end each day bathing in the rivers, not only to cleanse our bodies and purify our souls, but also to remind us that all was once water. And water all will be again."

Nung-noh-hut-tar-hee could not get past his first impression that this *adawehis,* a shaman or conjurer, was distinctly odd. Nung-noh-hut-tar-hee sat naked, river water dripping from his curls after their predawn devotions together. At his mother's bidding this day had begun earlier than the rest, with daybreak still an hour away. He watched the old fool prance about in supple deerskin leggings the color of his teeth, fanning his face with the wing of a sizable bird the boy could not name.

The old *adawehis,* called Waesa, the Cat, chanted prayers and songs in some dialect Nung-noh-hut-tar-hee did not understand. He watched him stop before the fire, which he had called Ancient Red, and toss in pinches of powders and herbs as an offering to the flames. Then, knees creaking, Waesa squatted beside Nung-noh-hut-tar-hee in silence, so quiet that the boy could hear the crackling of the limbs consumed by the fire, notice the pulsing of white coals in its bed, and the gushing sound of its rising vapors. A fire was a thing alive, shot to the earth as lightning by the Thunders to warm the people who before then had known only coldness, and the boy watched the flames breathe in silent wonder. Waesa, grandfather of all conjurers practicing around his home village of Hiwassee, studied only him.

"I see sadness in your lines, boy," the *adawehis* finally said. "Has there been tragedy in your family?"

"I'm my mother's fourth son," the boy said once he recovered from his reverie. How the flames had held him. "The three before me died before they saw one winter."

"I can see your mother's tears in your eyes. She worries about you, too."

"She cries at night sometimes. Her face grows dark when I cough."

"You are called Nung-noh-hut-tar-hee," Waesa said, changing the subject. "He Who Slays the Enemy in the Path. Too strong a name for a child, I think. Obviously your father's notion."

"It's just a name," the boy said.

"Well, a name defines you — tells people who you are — and your mother thinks you need another one. Hence, my young friend, we share this early hour together." Waesa gripped him by the chin to pull his face to him and peer into his eyes. "Hmmm. By looking at you, I don't get a sense of anything better. Do you spend your learning time alone in the woods?"

"Each day," the boy said. With only seven winters on his head, *Nung-noh-hut-tar-hee* was encouraged by his mother's brothers to fast in the morning and walk through the woods all day without food or water. Tradition taught that hunger would keep his desires high and his senses keen. He practiced stalking deer, turkey, and buffalo. He soon learned where they fed, and where they bedded. He tracked bears to their dens, their paw prints easy to follow even in dry times by the indentures their claws left in the rich, black earth. He practiced mimicking the bleat of the deer fawn, or the bark of a fox squirrel, to lure them within range of his blowgun. He sent his darts true for fifty paces or more, always begging his quarry's permission before he sent a projectile flying in its direction, for the ancient people had once killed wantonly, which caused the beasts to curse man with disease. The plants rallied to their rescue, offering the powers each possessed, but even they weren't strong enough to undo the curse, and the boy knew better than to thumb his nose at his prey.

Nung-noh-hut-tar-hee learned to pound the root of the buckeye to a pulp, and gather it into a basket he would set in a stream. The juice would seep out into the water, stunning the fish, which the boy would gather in quantities large enough to feed his family for seven sleeps. He let Ancient Red's flames lick his moccasins to protect him from the fangs of the water moccasin and copperhead. At sunset, he would go to water again and recite the ancient prayer: *Give me the wind. Give me the breeze. Yuh! O Great Earth Hunter, I come to the water's edge where you rest. Let your stomach cover itself in a single bend, and may you never be satisfied.* He knew also to return naked to the rivers at dawn and to faithfully offer up the hunter's sacred prayers as he

24

waded into the currents. Water might be the beginning and end, whatever that meant, but it was also a guardian spirit, and *Nung-noh-hut-tar-hee* didn't need an *adawehis* to tell him that the rivers were forever tied to his people.

Even at his young age, he'd become an adept student of nature's mysteries and secrets. He delighted to spend his days alone, watching, listening, learning. All of this he frankly revealed to the *adawehis,* chattering away about every notion that popped into his head, just as his mother had told him to do, for she had explained to him that he had come to stand before the threshold where boys begin to become men, and that she had picked this strange old man to guide him through it. He understood that his mother had sent him here to learn of his life's purpose. At least, that was how she had put it to him.

"Good," the conjurer said. "Then you're acquiring patience along with learning the language of the woods and the virtue of silence."

"I guess so," the boy said. He hadn't thought much of the reason for his adventures. He just knew he loved them.

"It's self-understanding that you need now as we search for a better name," Waesa said. "Is there an animal you admire above others?"

"Not really. They're all special in their own way."

"Ah." The *adawehis* laughed. "I couldn't agree with you more." He looked long at him. "You're quite stout for your age. I think maybe you eat too much."

"I eat well, but only at night."

"And how do you travel when in the woods? Do you keep to the paths made by others or move along the edge of streams?"

"I like the mountaintops best."

Waesa cocked his head. "Hard walking, no?"

"Sometimes, but I'm small and the trouble's worth it. You can see more if you walk the ridges."

"Ah, there we have it," Waesa said, sharply clapping his hands. "That particular habit in such a young boy says a lot. We'll call you Kah-nung-da-tla-geh. The Man Who Walks the Mountaintops. Or maybe just the Ridge for short."

The boy contemplated the pronouncement and decided he liked it. He nodded his head.

"All right, then," Waesa said. "We're done here. Leave an old man to his foolishness. Greet the dawn alone in the river and be sure to thank the Provider for all the blessings he's bestowed on such a bright-faced, healthy young boy. After that you can put that blowgun to use and put some fresh meat on your mother's smoke rack."

Ridge started to leave, but something held him. Was he supposed to just walk away now? Certainly not. Not after Waesa had gone to such trouble on his behalf. He turned toward the old conjurer and raised his arms. Waesa smiled in turn, and bent over to receive the boy's embrace. A musty smell hung about the old man's body. His back was humped like a buffalo bull; his skin felt rough and scaly like a skink lizard. And yet Ridge felt more attached to him than he did to his own father, Agan'stat'. Waesa had warmth, and Ridge was drawn to it.

"You know what's best about you?" Waesa said. "You have a caring heart to go along with a smart head. Those two qualities together in such a young boy tell old Waesa that you have a great future before you."

Waesa released him, and gently shoved him down the path that led through the brambles and canebrakes to the dark and powerful Hiwassee. "To the river now, Man Who Walks the Mountaintops," he said. "Your life will be different from this day hence. Your river is finding its own course. Everything will change now. You wait and see."

Ridge squatted in his mother's lodge, lashing thistle blooms to his blowgun darts of yellow locust wood while he thought about his experience that morning with Waesa. His mother's house was built in the old way, a

27

series of upright poles that supported a skin of interwoven leaves of dried cane smeared with a thick coat of red clay, grass, and loose hair from the whitetail deer. Cracks in the walls were patched with wads of tree moss and broom sage. The structure was sound enough to keep them dry when the spring rains came, and Ridge felt content under its roof listening to his mother sing ancient songs, the meaning of the repetitive refrains forgotten. Tobacco leaves and pumpkin slices hung from the rafters to dry. Beside them dangled ears of seed corn, their husks braided together. Corn and purple-speckled beans stood in baskets woven from river cane, ready to cook whenever his mother wanted.

She had already singed the hair from the fox squirrels he'd killed that morning. Ridge watched her scrape away the last of the auburn hide with fine ashes, thinking about how he'd heard the males barking at each other from the ridge above. He'd dropped down quietly like a fog until he was level with them. Busy with their squirrel squabbles, the first thing they heard of Ridge was the gush of air from his lungs that sent his darts true. Soon he'd smell the meat roasting on a chestnut bark shake beside the fire. His mother would catch the grease drippings for cornmeal gravy, leaving just enough in her clay saucer for Ridge to pour over fresh watercress. Such a meal was fit for a chief.

His family was poor, he knew, but they ate well enough and slept under a sound roof. Just the same, Ridge was unsettled by his neighbors' disturbing gossip about his father. As a hunter and warrior, Agan'stat's skills were adequate, but his accomplishments were said to be behind him. Agan'stat' had turned his back on the position of war chief with only a few scalps to his credit and half his warriors killed in an ill-conceived alliance with the French fifteen winters before. His own father, the great civil chief Ada-gal'kala, had steered the Cherokee toward the bosom of the British for King George's promise to stem all white encroachment on the land the Cherokee had left. Though the Cherokee did not love the English as they'd loved the French, their reluctant allegiance still lay with the British as their sworn protectors, and it was said that Agan'stat's spirit walked two steps behind his body after his people's confidence had abandoned him.

All of this had occurred before Ridge's time, yet he couldn't help but notice his father's withdrawn demeanor and the perpetual darkness of his mood. Agan'stat's gait was stooped, his stare distant, and a cloud of sorrow hung over him wherever he went. Ridge seldom saw him smile. If a fire once burned in his father's heart, only cold ashes remained. It bothered Ridge that Agan'stat' took so little interest in the education of his sisters' sons, an obligation enthusiastically undertaken by Ridge's own maternal uncles. Already, the neighbors whispered, Agan'stat' had placed what remained of his hopes and ambitions on his eldest surviving son, quite a burden on the shoulders of such a young boy. While Ridge's doubts about his father remained unspoken between them, as did almost everything else, he was aware that most considered Agan'stat' a failure.

Ridge couldn't accept their opinions. The gossip just didn't describe the quiet man he knew. He studied Agan'stat' as he wove the last of the reeds of his newest fish trap, wondering what taboo his father had transgressed to become the target of such slander. Agan'stat' regarded him blankly as he tested a series of knots, and then stepped outside to visit with his few remaining friends by the communal fires.

Ridge's stomach gurgled at the smell of roasted venison, deerhorn mushrooms frying in tallow, and fresh bean bread dumplings boiling in the iron kettle in the nearest neighboring lodge. These were times of plenty in Hiwassee village. His people, busy with their day-to-day chores raising crops and children, seemed occupied.

But they were also worried. Tension hung heavy in the air like smoke. Rumors of war wagged on the tongues of the old men. It was known that the whites, the Americans, were in revolt against their English father, King George III. Old Adagal'kala, the Leaning Wood, known to the British as "the Little Carpenter" for his craft at "joining" a treaty, insisted that the Cherokee maintain ties to the Crown. As a reward for the Cherokee's loyalty, the British promised to drive trespassing Americans east of the Blue Wall, the Unending Mountains. Now that the English were at war with their rebellious children, few doubted which side the Cherokee would take.

In a rare display of opinion, Agan'stat' admitted that his father's alliance was proving beneficial to the Cherokee. Even he was aware that the Americans were the real enemy. But Ridge's father understood also that they knew the ways of the woods and Indian warfare. When provoked, he said, the Americans were formidable adversaries. He cautioned that while the British were probably the safer bet, an ocean lay between them and their rebellious children. It made little sense to him that an island nation should rule a continent. The British had the means to destroy the Americans, but did they have the will? The contest would boil down to whose fire burned hotter. Would it not be wiser for the Cherokee to maintain neutral, leave the whites to their shameful winter wars, and approach the victor with assurances of peace and mutual prosperity?

Cherokee warriors scoffed at his father's supposed wisdom, late in coming now that his war blades had rusted. Sensing opportunity for a preemptive strike, war parties soon carried death to any whites they could find along the Catawba River settlements. But Agan'stat' brooded that the Cherokee would soon see a darker day, and so did many other of the elders and beloved women. At the beseeching of the British, Cherokee warriors hot for honor had drawn first blood. Now there was nothing to do but wait in strained silence to learn how the Americans would vent their outrage. Agan'stat' claimed they would not have to wait long.

Ridge ate his fill, kissed his mother, and then started for the cleared fields to watch a game of anetsodi, the fierce ball plays that prepared young men for war. Ridge longed for the time when he could run alongside the war trails and win the honor his father had been denied. Ten more winters apprenticed to the hunt and the day would come when Ridge would prove who he was to the gossips and redeem his family's ailing reputation. He'd taken only a few steps when he saw Agan'stat' and his friends cease their disgruntled discussions. Ridge sensed a stillness sweep over the village, a disruption of all normal activity, just like browsing deer when they caught the first scent of the stalking wolf pack. Soon he heard the criers shout in the distance. Barking dogs and whickering horses. The thunder of hooves by horses at full gallop crashing through the underbrush. An unseen woman screamed. There was no mistaking the sharp lines of agitation in Agan'stat's face, the fear in his wild, rolling eyes.

"Where were your scouts?" he shouted to Suyeta, the war chief who had supplanted him. "You were out looking for war when it slips in behind you! Many will die today because of your arrogance!"

"Now is not the time, Agan'stat'!" Suyeta said. "Help me hold them back!"

"I'll see first to my family," his father snapped. He snatched Ridge by the waist and carried him like a log into their lodge. "Come!" he cried to Ridge's mother, stripping the dried meats and vegetables from the rafters and stuffing them into bulging wicker baskets. "To the river!"

"What's happened?" his mother cried.

"The whites have come just as I said they would! Hundreds on horseback! Take what we can carry and run for the river."

Ridge heard the yells of Suyeta's warriors hurling themselves against the horsemen to buy their families a little time. Ridge and his brother, Oo-watie, stuffed baskets with food, blankets, and weapons. His father herded them to the Hiwassee, where hundreds of poplar log dugouts waited on the muddy banks. They frantically loaded what they could as the other families were doing, and his father launched them into the currents.

Ridge turned back to look at Hiwassee town. White soldiers thundered into the village, their reins gripped in their teeth, indiscriminately firing their long rifles. Ridge saw the glint of their long knives in the sun. The whites looked as fierce as any warriors Ridge had ever seen. Men, women, children, horses, and cattle all fell screaming in crimson pools. Some of the soldiers dismounted to scalp the dead and dying, while others tossed torches on their homes and fields. Hiwassee village was immediately shrouded in smoke and blood.

Ridge lurched when he saw Sehoya, his favorite among the girls of the village, scrambling alone across a bean field. She stumbled and fell facedown, helpless. He'd known her all his life, and hadn't felt any more for her than he did any other girl up until the point when they had encountered each other at Ridge's preferred stream. Ridge wasn't about to swim elsewhere and neither was she. Before long, they had played together in the water until their stomachs ached for food. They dried off in the sun, gorging themselves on Old Terrapin's strawberries. As odd as it was, Ridge discovered that he enjoyed the girl's company as much as he did that of his friends. Sehoya was special to him. Certainly he could not leave her alone now to be slaughtered.

"Stop!" he yelled to Agan'stat'.

"Don't be foolish! We're running as fast as we can!"

Ridge didn't wait another instant. He bailed out of the dugout, worked his toes into the ooze of the river bottom, leaned against the currents, and started for the bank. His mother shouted. Agan'stat' struggled to hold the dugout in place. Ridge ignored everything but the lone little girl who had become his friend. Before he reached the bank, he saw Sehoya's father emerge from the woods, gather his daughter in his arms, and scramble to the river. Ridge helped him launch a spare dugout, locking stares with Sehoya as her father's paddle plunged into the water. A bullet whined over his head, and then another. Ridge dove under the depths and swam to his family's dugout. Agan'stat' pulled him aboard by the seat of his breechclout and slapped a paddle against his chest.

"Was that wise?" Agan'stat' asked him.

"She needed help," Ridge said.

"They all need help," Agan'stat' said between clenched teeth, resuming his fierce paddling. "You listen. Agan'stat' ran the war trace for twenty winters, ten as Kalanu, the Raven, war chief of his people. When you see Agan'stat' running, stump-stubborn boy, it's time to run."

"I'm not afraid of the whites," Ridge said as he crawled to the stern of the dugout and stabbed his oar deep into the river.

"That's good," Agan'stat' snapped, "because they may catch us yet, and it didn't help your family's chances to wait for you. Even the grizzly runs from a battle it cannot win, especially if she has cubs. Today was not our day, and that's my last word on the matter."

Ridge watched the muscles of his father's back bulge with effort. His mother held his sister close. Oo-watie paddled, too, and between the three of them the dugout swam faster than the Hiwassee's currents, leaving only stillness behind its stern.

As they rounded the first bend, Ridge turned back to look at his village. He could see nothing but hungry yellow flames and black smoke swirling angrily overhead like a tornado. He could no longer bear to listen to the clamor of destruction. He clapped his hands over his ears when he heard his father's muffled voice.

"Paddle, now! As fast as you can!"

Spent lead balls skipped across the water to bury themselves with a dull thud in the Hiwassee's muddy banks. Women and children ducked down in the dozens of dugouts plunging downriver. Sweat poured from men who paddled as though the water were in flames. The rest of the Cherokee scattered into the thickets where the horsemen could not follow.

Ridge had pledged himself to help his father paddle. But after only an hour or so, his arms ached so badly they felt as if a bear had ripped them from his shoulders. His legs and shoulders cramped. He skimmed a little water from the river to pour down his parched throat.

"The night will soon hide us, boy," Agan'stat' said as stroke followed deep stroke without complaint. Ridge watched the little eddies dissolve in the muddy water rolling past. "You can rest for a while."

Ridge was so exhausted he sank to the bowels of the dugout and immediately fell asleep next to his little brother and sister while the bilge swept against his cheeks.

His eyes opened again at dawn the next day, and Agan'stat' paddled still. Ridge sat in awe of his father's stamina. Where were his detractors now? Who among them could paddle for two days without sleeping?

Agan'stat' followed the Hiwassee until it merged with the Tennessee. They turned in to Sequatchie Stream toward the mountain that fed it, and there his father let the dugout coast into the soft bank. "Here," he said, unloading their scant supplies, "we'll be safe." There was comfort and assurance in his voice, and Ridge clung to it as he helped his father pile rocks into the dugout to sink it.

He couldn't stem the tears that first night off the river in strange country. But when dawn came, the work began and there wasn't time for despair.

As much as his muscles ached and his stomach growled from the days of deprivation, Ridge felt the burn of his rage far stronger. His gaze met that of his weary father, and Ridge knew the very same indignation simmered in Agan'stat's heart. Together they would fend for their family. But soon, very soon, Ridge resolved to seek his father's blessing to run the war trails against the murderers of his people. Watching his mother gather reeds and moss for makeshift beds for his whimpering brother and baby sister, he vowed that he would not rest until his people killed enough whites to account for every Cherokee lost at Hiwassee. Revenge was about balancing the natural world. As soon as he was old enough, he would have a hand in setting things right.

CHAPTER TWO

"The blood in your veins is a river," Waesa said once he'd herded Ridge out of voice range from his group of naked initiates. "It connects past and future. You belong to the Ani-yunwi-ya, the Original People, known to all other nations as Cherokee."

Old Waesa's speech seemed a little rushed to Ridge, especially out of place in this lazy time of the summer, Tsa lu wa'nee, the month when the corn sprouted its tassels, in the white man's numbered year of 1783. Under this June moon Ridge would at last become a man. At least, he would once he was done listening to Waesa's jabbering.

Over the rise, waiting beside the river, sat all the elders of Sequatchie Mountain, along with their honored guests, the celebrated war chief Dragging Canoe, who would do the honors himself, and Ridge's fire brand cousin, Doublehead, whose pine branch was already thick with fresh scalps. This evening was the most important one in Ridge's life.

Everything was going beyond his anxious expectations until Waesa pulled him aside.

Eight winters had passed since Ridge had last seen the old *adawehis,* and the years had not been kind to him. Waesa had seemed old when Ridge was a child. He looked positively mummified now, his eyes clouded, hair white, blue-spotted arms as brittle as the limbs of a winter-killed pine tree.

Ridge wondered why Waesa had carted him away from his friends, White Path of Ellijay village, and Alexander Saunders, the mixed-blood son of a trader whom Ridge had known from Hiwassee, and all the others who had come to manhood in exile from their ancestral homes. Anger was the bond between them, and Ridge, like the other boys of his youth — reared in the wilderness, hardened by war and hunger, deprived of familiar places and extended clan, far too accustomed to grief, usually on the run and always wary — was ravenous to vent his bilious hatred against those who had cast them out. Ridge possessed the sturdiest frame in a lean generation willed by the Provider to be born in blood. At last, he was old enough to raise his tomahawk against the enemies of the Ani-yunwi-ya, if he could endure this evening's torture.

He knew the old *adawehis*'s unfortunate appearance was at his mother's request. She was adamant about maintaining the old traditions, remarkable given that she'd reared her family in makeshift shanties hidden at the foot of Sequatchie Mountain rather than in the center of a thriving village. Ridge admitted to himself that he probably owed Waesa a degree of respect as one who had always had a special interest in his upbringing. Ridge struggled to feign an outward appearance of interest, yet his mind continually dwelled on the promise of pain to come before the sun rose tomorrow.

"Now the boy I named is a man, soon to be a warrior," Waesa said summoning the old charisma that sadly remained out of reach. "There are things you must understand about your people, and about yourself, before your stream flows on to join the greater river that is the course of your life. I'd suggest you listen carefully."

"Of course," Ridge said. What was there to do but humor the old witch.

"Your mouth says one thing," Waesa said sharply, "your eyes another. You think Waesa is some old cob to be tolerated. Well, that's all right. Waesa was born different from other Ani-yunwi-ya. He has always walked a narrow path. His flesh has withered and his bones are frail, but his mind still soars. Waesa has knowledge that he wants to share with you. He'd like to link your time with all that has come before you, because if you don't understand the past, Ridge Walker, you cannot prepare for the future."

"I'm sorry if I've offended you, Waesa," Ridge said apologetically. "My heart is impatient for this special night, but my head reminds me that you are not only my elder; but also the best teacher I've ever had. Of course I'll listen to everything you want to tell me."

Waesa clucked his tongue. "If you'll shut up, we'll get started then," he said. "You understand that your blood ties you to the ani-kawi, the deer clan. You are the grandson of Ada-gal'kala, the greatest of Ani-yunwi-ya chiefs, who once crossed the great waters to sit in council with the British Father. Before him walked the ancient ones, whose tongue I still speak." The *adawehis* closed his eyes. "Let me tell you, young yunwi, who you are."

Waesa repeated his version of the old legend. There had been a time when hearing a gifted storyteller recite it left Ridge almost shuddering with wonder, but he no longer saw what the past had to do with his people's present humiliation at the hand of the whites. Yet Waesa had grown irritable in his old age, and Ridge didn't want to provoke his ire a second time.

Waesa explained that long ago the Original People had abandoned their villages in some distant, forgotten land, crossed the oceans on a bridge of ice, and wandered for generations through a strange country of snow, rugged

42

mountains, fierce beasts, and continual night. Many perished along the way. Those who survived went in search of the rising sun for a place where they could prosper. They found it well to the north, and their numbers increased until there were too many.

"Your ancestors were among those with the courage to leave their homes and wander again," he said, gesturing passionately with his hands. "They settled near Otter Peaks, where the cycle repeated itself. The Original People quarreled when their children cried for food, and the grandfather of your great-grandfather led his kind south and west. His cousins, who became the Iroquois and Delaware, went their own way. Your people crossed over these mountains you see before you, the peaks born on the wings of the Great Buzzard back when Turtle Island was flat and muddy, the very same place where you and I now sit."

Old Waesa tipped back a gourd half-full of water. Ridge watched his Adam's apple bob up and down like an acorn floating in the river. Waesa set the gourd aside, ran his forearm across his mouth, and squinted his cloudy eyes as he looked back at the waiting river.

"This land of ours is rich in plants and game, and others wanted it," he said, his stare returning from the heavens to focus on Ridge. "We fought our cousins the Iroquois, the Catawbas, the Creeks, and the Shawnee, but none were strong enough to take it from the Ani-yunwi-ya. These fields of corn, squash, beans, and melons, and also the hunting grounds to the north, the Gan-da Giga-i, the Dark and Bloody Ground, are all fertilized with the blood of your ancestors. They won it by conquest for you."

The *adawehis* studied how the smoke hung in the air above them. "When at last we earned our peace," he continued, "the elders fasted for many days to celebrate. All signs were good until the last day, when they heard strange sounds coming from the eastern shores. A great chief among us decided to go in search of their meaning. For thirteen moons, the Ani-yunwi-ya heard nothing from him. On the fourteenth he returned, saying the prophecy had been fulfilled. The Ani-yonega, half-faced white men, had come as the ancients foretold."

"What was the prophecy?" Ridge asked.

"It was this: Once the Ani-yonega have come among us they will become our teachers. Our ways will change. But in the end these changes lead to our undoing. Our teachers soon become our masters, and when there are enough of the whites to overpower us, they will point our feet westward, never to return."

"If anything, Waesa," Ridge said, "the Americans have become our killers."

"For now," Waesa said, closing his eyes. "The wars will end in time. And when they do another battle begins where few bleed but many die. The whites are most dangerous when they are friendly toward the Cherokee."

"What does *that* mean?" Ridge asked, impatient with the *adawehis*'s riddles.

"It means we will wander again, for when the wind blows ill, what can the blades of grass on the bare slopes do but bend?"

Waesa fell silent as Ridge pondered his words. What did all this have to do with running the warrior's path? His father, Agan'stat', always said that conjurers were more witch than sage. How much longer would Ridge have to humor this one? There were more important things at hand.

"Do you have courage, boy?" Waesa asked.

"I'll prove that soon enough," Ridge said.

"I believe you will," Waesa said. "My time comes soon, I think. Before long, I'll float down the dark river — remember where we all end — until the currents carry me to my ancestors' village somewhere beyond the Sky Vault. But you must face the gathering storm." He drew his knobby knees to his chest. "You have a tinge of the white blood, do you not?"

"A little," Ridge admitted. He was not proud of it. The Cherokee had been crushed by the whites just a few winters before his birth in the French and Indian War, and after the humiliating treaty terms and land cessions had been stuffed down their throats, the whites still poured in around them. Blood ran again as the Americans rebelled against their British father. The Cherokee remained loyal to the Crown and they paid dearly for it. Ridge was troubled by the notion that he shared the blood of his people's enemy. But suddenly Waesa had his attention. Realizing that he had underestimated the *adawehis*'s abilities, Ridge opened his heart to him.

"It haunts me," Ridge admitted in a whisper after he looked over his shoulder to make sure they were still alone.

"Why?" Waesa said. "Is this not the way the Provider in his wisdom made you? Besides, in your case, it's a good thing. I've already told you that you belong to us. I'm telling you now that the Ridge Walker was born to lead the Cherokee. But you were also born with the blood of two worlds, and the eternal river hurls you at the rapids where they collide. You will rise above the tumult to see when other chiefs remain blind."

"What will I see?"

"You will see what *is.* This is your gift as well as your burden. And after a journey of pain and disappointment, you will come to understand which path the Cherokee must choose."

Ridge was growing frustrated by Waesa's continual equivocations. "I don't follow your meaning."

"Yours is not to follow, Ridge Walker," Waesa said. Ridge saw the old spark return to his eyes. "You must lead in a time when the world is out of balance. The ancient cycle repeats itself. The season of fire and blood returns and our path once again divides. Oblivion stalks the Cherokee, and great men must rise and slay it at all costs. Do you see?"

"No," Ridge answered. He felt even more unsettled as fascination gave way to uncertainty.

"You will," Waesa said. "What I'm telling you is too much for a young man of your years. But you won't forget it, and by the time you've seen one-third as many winters as I have, you'll understand the importance of what was revealed to you tonight. Then you must summon the courage to act. I'm not here to teach you how to be a warrior. I'm here to teach you how to be a chief."

"If your goal was to enlighten me, Waesa, you've failed. I'm more confused than ever."

"One can teach another to do a task, Ridge Walker, but one can't teach another to understand. The Provider, however, chose to bless you with the proper soil, and all I have to do tonight is plant the seed. Time will do the rest."

Waesa touched his temple and then pointed at the stars. "I see far, Ridge Walker," he said. "And so will you. Take heart. Keep to your mountaintops. Look long before you choose our way. Your ancestors will be watching. When the time comes to make great sacrifices, remember that you were chosen for this difficult path. And never forget, when the loneliness of leadership overtakes you and only bitter winds blow, that you are loved by many of the living *and* all of the dead. You will always be loved by the living spirit that is Ani-yunwi-ya. On your darkest night, it will never abandon you."

Ridge sat in silence, the peaceful night around him in stark contrast to the turmoil churning within. He wished he were anywhere but here, listening to nonsense spoken by an old witch who was neither his kin nor clan. Why would his mother want this disturbing experience for him? And how soon would he be free of it? He figured he'd wait just a few minutes longer before he'd try to crawl off and leave the old man to his gloom. Dawn would find him a warrior with more important things on his mind than prophecies. Ridge was ready to rejoin White Path, Saunders, and the others on the verge of manhood. A nod from Waesa that he was finished and then Ridge could be mercifully off to the next step.

In the last light of the coals, Ridge saw a single, crystalline tear stream down Waesa's cheek. He turned away again, wrapped his arms around his knees, and stared blankly at the stars. How much longer?

"I see what's coming," the old man finally said. "Soon, so will you. Remember that change is inevitable. Manage it as best you can. We are not white men and our culture is in no way inferior to theirs. For some reason, the Provider has decided that they will overwhelm us by sheer numbers alone, but that doesn't necessarily mean they must destroy us. This is where your choices matter most. Pick and choose among their methods as best suits the needs of your people, while you shun all ways that will corrupt them. Keep the Cherokee rooted to our traditions. Never let them forget who they are. Tell them the legends that I've told you."

Waesa rose on his wobbly knees and poured out the gourd on the dying fire. The coals sputtered and dulled to lifeless charcoal. Steam rose and then drifted back to the earth until the night wind dissolved it.

"The final challenge," he said as he turned his back on Ridge, "is to endure. You will never achieve it with a gun or a tomahawk. Once you realize that, your battle has only just begun. Waesa doesn't envy your burden, Ridge Walker. His only consolation is that he won't live long enough to watch you struggle under its crushing weight."

Waesa patted Ridge's bare shoulder and then wrapped his trade blanket tight up around his skinny neck. "Above all, you must endure," he said, nodding his head in the direction where the others waited, and then he began walking away. Ridge watched him go, and even listened to his footsteps once he'd disappeared. He shuddered, as if attempting to shake himself free of Waesa's warning. He cast his stare toward the rhythm of the drums near the river and knew he must join the dancers without further delay.

"Gatlun hi a-sga si-ti!" Dragging Canoe barked to the Ridge. "I will make you dreadful!"

Ridge had never heard another Ani-yunwi-ya say such an evil thing. Cherokee was a musical language used by a handsome race to describe wondrous things. He was stunned to hear his own war chief vow to make him ugly. Ridge was sure he didn't mean it. At least, he hoped he didn't. Ridge was proud of his looks as they were. Tsiyu Gansini, He Is Dragging the Canoe, son of Ada-gal'kala, and Ridge's uncle, threw his head back so violently that his earrings clanked against his necklace of wampum and shells. The blood between them seemed no advantage tonight. Dragging Canoe treated his nephew as coldly as he did the rest of the anxious initiates.

Though the war chief's militant demeanor unnerved him, Ridge admired his elaborate dress, a mixture of red for success and triumph and black for death — the colors of war. Dragging Canoe wore a raven's skin around his neck, a blood-colored buckskin shirt that reached his hips, red breechclout to the knees, and a cap of otter skins adorned by white crane feathers on his head. Raccoon-skin sleeves covered his powerful arms as he lifted them to the stars above on this still, warm summer night. His dark eyes mirrored the flare of the flickering torches.

"Speak to this young warrior," Dragging Canoe prayed. "Fill his head with cunning. Ignite his heart with courage. Make him worthy to walk like a man among the Ani-yunwi-ya."

Ridge watched as Dragging Canoe's attention returned to secular matters. Before all the elders and warriors his father had invited to witness the ceremony, the war chief pulled the thigh bone of a wolf from his pouch and snapped it in two. Wolves were sacred among Ridge's people, and only those rare few who had observed a conjurer's strict regimen of prayer and fasting were allowed to hunt them. How Dragging Canoe had come by this bone, Ridge could not say, but he had seen the scars on the young warriors enough to know what his uncle was about to do with it. Apparently, so did White Path, who appeared more than happy to allow Ridge to go first.

Dragging Canoe burned Ridge with his stare, and Ridge knew better than to glance aside for a moment, even though the night wind blew his eyes dry. The war chief ran his thumb across the bone's jagged end to test its sharpness. Then he cut seven fine points into its tip with the razor-sharp blade of his knife. Ridge had heard that sometimes timber rattler fangs were used for the ceremony. Either way, the procedure wouldn't be pleasant. His jaw tightened with the anticipation of pain.

Ridge's random thoughts abruptly ended when Dragging Canoe snatched his hand and jabbed the bone deeply into his open palm. Ridge clenched his teeth, but he had long before resolved to reveal no outward sign of his suffering. The chief raked the bone up the inside of Ridge's arms to the shoulder and across his chest, ending at the opposite arm. Then he carved three more until there were four parallel wounds gushing with fresh, warm blood. Next Dragging Canoe dropped to his knees and gouged the Ridge's heel, ripping his skin up the length of his leg to his back, across his shoulders, and down again to the tops of his feet. The muscles of Ridge's temples quivered and he ordered them to be still. Then Dragging Canoe began again, starting with the back of Ridge's hand across to the other until blood covered every inch of his firm body.

Four and seven were the Cherokee's sacred numbers. But as the Original People expected much from their warriors, the blood must run from four times seven wounds. The most powerful number under the Sky Vault was twenty-eight, and thus all new warriors and ball players proudly displayed twenty-eight scars. Since the earliest days in his memory, Ridge had marveled at the healing scabs of young initiate warriors and athletes. He'd never understood what they'd endured to earn them until now. His skin screamed as if he'd suffered the stings of a thousand yellow jackets.

Ridge stood firm as the night air chilled him, denying the tears of pain welling up in his eyes, hearing the blood drip from his fingers in pools to the earth below. Dragging Canoe started to carve the same pattern on White Path's body, and then Saunders, and the others, while Ridge waited in silence. A conjurer whose name he did not know scraped bloody soil into his fingers, wadded it into a ball, and pressed it hard into Ridge's fist. "This earth, and the Ridge Walker's blood, form one spirit, forever joined. Separate one from the other and both will die."

Ridge clenched the wad of bloody earth in his fist. The conjurer's wild eyes seemed to burn through him.

"This night," the conjurer said, "you would become a warrior for your people — a protector of our ways, a defender of our land. Would you, the Man Who Walks the Mountaintops, lay down your life for the Cherokee?"

"Willingly," Ridge replied abruptly in his deepest voice. Agan'stat' had reluctantly coached him to answer this exact question without hesitation.

"This one has chosen," the conjurer said, and he backed away into the night. Dragging Canoe reemerged to face him again, but said nothing. His countenance burned hotter than Ridge had ever seen it. His uncle must have terrified his enemies.

"Do you waver, boy?" Dragging Canoe said.

"I do not," Ridge cried.

"Does the sight of your own blood make you faint? For you will see it many times if you follow me."

"The Ridge would bleed to death before he'd ever run from his enemies."

"Dragging Canoe would have this one by his side in battle," he said. He looked to the elders to approve of Ridge's performance, and then went on down the line to each of the bloody bodies. The elders nodded unanimously to each of the supplicants, and when at last it was over the war chief winked at Ridge. Ridge, in turn, looked immediately at his father, who stood with his arms crossed as if he weren't concerned with Ridge's success one way or the other. But Ridge saw pride in the lift of his father's nose and the brightness of his eyes as he feigned disinterest for his detractors. Ridge exhaled in relief that Dragging Canoe's wink had signaled that his kinship at last had a little value, but before he'd taken another breath, his uncle abruptly shoved him backward into the river to wash the blood away.

Ridge spun gracefully and dove headlong into the onyx waters. He heard White Path splash near him, and then several more as the others were flung off the bluff. The river felt cool on Ridge's stinging skin. He screamed, knowing no sound would reach the old men waiting on the bank, until his lungs ached for breath, holding fast to the bloody dirt gripped in his clenched fist. Crimson clouds swirled around him, dissolving into the great river. Then he planted his feet in the river muck and pushed hard for the surface, breaking the water's plane with a forced smile on his face, and together with White Path, swam strong for the bank where the elders waited in judgment.

Once on the bank, Ridge cocked back his thick shoulders and stood straight among them, and allowed the mixture of water and blood to drip from his body onto the earth he had sworn to protect. He had intended to add his fistful of bloody soil to his medicine pouch that dangled beneath his breechclout. The little buckskin bag included a hawk's claw, a piece of mica he fancied as one of the scales of the Uktena, the Keen-Eyed, a mythical horned serpent from ancient times, and a small crystal that had revealed itself to him while he was hunting. But when he opened his hands he discovered that the river currents had leached all of the mixture away. This was a night of triumph, but Ridge was beside himself with disappointment. White Path regarded him.

"What's wrong, brother?" White Path asked. "What have you to mope about? We're warriors now."

Ridge didn't answer. He had held on to this symbol of his purpose with all his strength and had emerged from the river with none of it. While his elders slapped his back in congratulations, Ridge only stared at his empty hand.

CHAPTER THREE

Sehoya

I grew up in a different age than my mother. In her time, young women were taught to make the things our people used each day. They wove river cane into baskets, fired clay into glazed pots and beads, stitched turkey feathers into beautiful, warm cloaks, and knotted hemp into carpets they painted with plant dyes. I still sleep on the cane splitter mattress crafted by my mother's own hands. My brothers slept under blankets of bearskin in the hopes that they would absorb the beast's power and courage, but she wove one made of buffalo calves for me. My bed has a buckskin canopy and curtains along the sides to keep out the winter winds, but I've always liked the privacy of it most. On cold mornings, I lie under those soft skins, too warm and comfortable to move. My mother would call three times for me to get up and begin my chores, but I'd ignore her. Finally she'd throw back the curtains and skins and toss a gourd of springwater on me to drown me out. At first I'd be angry. But then she'd look down on me and laugh at my laziness, and I couldn't help but laugh, too.

The wars reaped only hardship for us. In my mother's time, each family staked out a little plot in the communal gardening grounds. We planted enough to see us through the winter and spring and then by the time we gathered at the Green Corn Dance in summer, we knew we'd soon have enough to see us through another year. The men hunted while the women tended the gardens. Together, our people usually had enough.

These days we've been on the run so often. We barely have time to work our soil, and even when we do, we may not be around when it comes time to harvest our crops. I've seen my family's freshly cleared fields burned three times. We lose everything but our lives, and that's still better than many others less fortunate than we. In spite of all the misery we've known I always feel like we have plenty. The Provider gave us everything we need to live if one knows where to look for it. When the whites destroyed our fields of corn, beans, and pumpkins, we needed only to go into the woods in search of our meals. My grandmother taught me to look for all kinds of edible roots and berries. Some we boiled and pounded into meal. Others we stewed and ate whole. We pulverized persimmon pits in stump mortars, kneaded it into dough, and formed little cakes that we grilled over open fires. We dried peaches and apples in late summer, and in the fall we gathered chestnuts, walnuts, and whortleberries, which we sweetened with fresh honey. Everything was there for us if we knew where to look for it and how to prepare it. The old ones did, and my mother learned from them. I learned from her. Even if she had to flush me out of my bed on cold mornings, I observed everything she did very carefully. In my family, we lived as the ancients did. We took from the earth only what we needed and left the rest alone. Extra peas and pumpkins were something one gave away. We never sold the Provider's blessings for money. Why would we?

It was not until the whites — Scotch traders and missionaries — came among us that some began to wonder if our ways were not good enough; if our lives were somehow incomplete. My father explained that we needed their guns, lead, and powder in order to protect ourselves, but my mother didn't see where we needed the iron kettles they sold us, or those scratchy wool blankets. We didn't need their money to live. We certainly didn't need their whiskey. No one understood the religion that the black robes kept harping about. We had one God, as they did. The men just knew that tanned buckskins bought fine rifles and trade goods, so they killed many more deer than they could ever eat, and for the first time in our memory, the game grew scarce. My father said that when the whites infected us with smallpox and measles, they also infected us with greed.

Some of us full-bloods could see right away that things were out of balance. In response, we were encouraged to shun the whites and their ways. But we could see also that these first traders had grown fond of us. Many of them took Cherokee women for wives, and little blue-eyed, fair-skinned, half-breed children began to sprout up all over the Nation. They spoke two languages. They lived two ways. They were the undesired link between red and white. The family of the boy, Ridge, was one of these.

My mother and father were always leery of these mixed-blood offspring, especially when so many rose to positions of wealth and prominence among our people. They were the first who began to farm huge fields to raise crops far beyond what they could possibly need, selling them to white people for money and other goods. To us they seemed greedy, although mixed-bloods were still the children of Cherokee mothers, which meant they were born with a clan affiliation that made them as Cherokee as any full-blood. But from what I could see, they were usually not treated like one. Living in two worlds, they belonged to neither.

I knew Ridge was only one-quarter white, but he was still different, although in his case I mean special. His mother was ani-kawi, deer clan, and therefore, so was he. I was ani-sahoni, the blue people, so when my heart was drawn to him I did not have to resist it. Nor did I want to. I could not mention my desires to my father, who felt mixed-bloods were more interested in hoarding money and fine clothes and in claiming bigger fields and pastures than any one family needed. Dogs slept outside of our lodges. Mixed-bloods had cats sleeping inside of theirs. My father and brothers hunted deer, buffalo, and bear in the thickets. Mixed-bloods kept fat cattle and hogs behind pine fences. I always felt that my father was jealous of them. They had plenty of money and food and always seemed to know how to acquire more, and this set them apart from common Cherokee, who were always struggling with the unwelcome changes the whites had brought to our lives. "While our blood appears to mix well," my father said, "our cultures do not." This was supposed to be the end of our discussions.

"Agan'stat' lives just as we do by the hunt and by the bounty of his fields," I said. "How is his son any different from us?" My father's stare almost burned holes through my body. My mother is a willful woman and he saw that I would grow to be the same.

61

"Half-breeds have a little different way of looking at the world," he said: "Time has proven that the Cherokee way is good and right. Why should we let thoughtless mixed-bloods who don't know who they are change it?"

What was the point of arguing with him? My mother knew I cared for the little mixed-blood boy, the Man Who Walks the Mountaintops, and she kept my secret to herself.

She always told me that I was young, things would change, and that I would grow fond of many boys along the path to womanhood and cast all of them aside as I went. "One day a special man will come to my lodge," she said, "and lay a fresh-killed deer at your father's feet. Be patient. You have not met this one yet." But I was sure that I had. Only I couldn't let him know it. The Ridge was unbelievably handsome. His skin was every bit as dark and smooth as mine, but his bear-black hair was unnaturally curly, a rare mixed-blood feature. I loved the way the locks fell across his shoulders, which had already grown broad. Ridge was stout for his age, had a chest as thick as a red oak that tapered down to a sapling's waist, and he flashed his bone-white teeth in an easy smile. His stomach muscles were defined and hard like the underside of a turtle's shell. I liked the way he walked with assurance among our elders, the tender manner in which he cared for his baby sister, and his custom of offering extra venison to those who did not have enough. I could have done without his strutting whenever he was around those of his own age. But more often he was well mannered, quiet, and deep in thought. People watched him with wonder. Everyone said that Ridge, mixed-blood or not, was marked for greatness.

But I didn't care about any of that. The boy just made my heart sing, and whenever he was around me I felt drawn to him in a way our language cannot describe. For me, seeing his face was like watching the sunrise. From the very first moment we locked stares, I wanted to tie my mother's blanket to his. I didn't care if we had to live in a cave. For me, it was only a matter of waiting for the proper time, while never letting him know how much I loved him. My mother taught me that, too.

We jumped a wide valley toward that day after he was accepted into the warrior's ranks. His initiation was a ceremony for men, of course, but I knew all about it. Dragging Canoe himself performed the rites. I knew Ridge wouldn't flinch while they scratched him. People gossiped that his father walked apart from his soul, but Agan'stat' had once been a warrior, as were all his kin and the ancestors who came before him. I didn't worry much about Ridge enduring what was expected of him. The warrior's way was in his blood.

After it was done, they applied a salve of bear fat, crushed oak bark, black willow, and wild grapes to his cuts. For seven days thereafter, Ridge was under gaktunta, taboo. He could not associate with women in any way. He could not even allow his mother to touch him. The flesh of a rabbit was forbidden, because it loses its wits when the panther comes near, as was that of the frog, because its bones are so brittle. Ridge was instructed to live wild among the bear and panther until he possessed their cunning and courage. He was to sleep under the Sky Vault and each dawn greet the Great Apportioner, the rising sun, as naked as the day he was born on Turtle Island.

What he did for these seven days is anyone's guess. But I know what happened on the eighth because Ridge told me. Dragging Canoe crossed the stream on the log Ridge had used as a bridge. When his uncle found him, Ridge was reclined on a bed of yan utse'stu, "the bears lie on it," ferns the beasts favored for their summer naps. His sores were scabbed over and healing well. Dragging Canoe carried a gourd with him, and Ridge said he could smell its aroma long before he saw the man carrying it. Yet as hungry as he was, he could not shame himself by reaching for it. He waited for it to be offered, because he had to demonstrate his hard-won discipline, and he'd always known that among the Cherokee, good manners were everything. A moment of hesitation was all it took, and Dragging Canoe passed him the gourd. Ridge poured the corn mush down his throat. He dug out the roasted partridge breast with his fingers, and tore into it with his teeth.

"Consume the partridge's ways as you consume its flesh, Ridge Walker," Dragging Canoe had said — Ridge later proudly repeated every word. "This bird relies on patience and stealth while on the ground, yet its wings beat like thunder when at last it flies. So it must also be for you. Creep quietly toward your enemies until you know their manner. And when the time is right, let them know it's the Ridge who has come for them."

I roll my eyes when I hear this kind of talk, but young men seem enamored by it. Tradition says this is how hunters and warriors are made. Cherokee women aren't taught any of this. We are never pampered. We harvest our crops with babies strapped to our backs. But I'll tell you this: When the Ani-yonegas went to scalp our dead after the massacres of our villages, they found many Cherokee women dressed in battle regalia who died with tomahawks in their hands. We can feed hundreds from what we find in the wilds, but when we must, when our families are threatened, we can fight as ferociously as any man.

We just have better things to do in the meantime than brag about it.

I was on my knees picking blackberries when I saw him trotting up from the bottoms. He wore only his breechclout, his chest muscles bouncing with every step of his bare feet, and his dark, smooth skin glistening from a thin coat of sweat. I sighed at the very image of him. This was no longer a boy who emerged from the wilds. My basket was half-full of the morning's gathering, but I chose to toss it aside when he approached me. He wanted to startle me and I didn't want to disappoint him. At closer inspection, I noticed that his body was covered in scabs. He looked drawn and pale from want of food. I didn't want any blood on my new calico dress, so I backed off a step or two.

"It's done!" he cried. His passion waned a little when I appeared not to be all that interested in the news. Ridge had forgotten his wretched condition. Even his curls were terribly matted.

"What's done?" I asked. "And don't scare me like that unless you want your head cracked open with a hickory stick."

"I'm a man now."

"Oh," I said with a smirk. "You don't look any different than the last time I saw you. Actually, you look much worse."

"Joke if you want, Sehoya. Soon I'll win honors, and when I do, I'll be tying my blanket with yours."

I glanced over at my mother and aunts grooming bushes in the fields above me. My youngest uncle, Swimmer, stood watch over us armed to the teeth. "Hush, now. If my mother hears that kind of talk, she'll drag us all across the Father of Waters."

"I'm not good enough to be your husband?" he said, as if I had shamed him.

"You're not old enough, Ridge." I knelt again and parted the limbs of another thorny bush. Ridge dropped to his knee beside me, plucked a ripe berry, and popped it into his mouth.

"I have a gift, Sehoya. Waesa told me that I can look far in the distance. And I have to tell you that I see you and me together."

"It must've been foggy that day, Ridge," I said moving away from him. "Best look again if you think my father will let me be some half-breed's wife."

Ridge gasped, brow rumpling, mouth agape, as if I'd punched him in the stomach. I'd hurt his feelings. I hadn't meant to.

"I'm three-quarters Ani-yunwi-ya by blood but whole in spirit," he said in his deepest voice. "Dragging Canoe himself anointed me into the warrior class. Once proven in battle, I'm good enough for any woman."

"Don't go beating your chest around me," I said, pinching a little white thorn from my finger. "Like I said, it's a problem for my father, not for me. When I'm ready, I'll pick who I want."

His chest deflated. "My heart is yours, Sehoya. Don't toy with it like this."

"I really don't want it just now," I said, my attention returning to my berry bush, but actually I was flush with excitement. I'd always thought that he felt that way, but he'd never been bold enough before to say the words. I couldn't help but wonder what it would be like to sleep beside him, my bare skin next to his, that first night alone in our own lodge when I'd use his chest for my pillow. A woman could do far worse. "Shouldn't you be off in the woods tracking a skunk or whatever it is you people do?" I said. "I have to work for my meals."

Ridge scoffed. He knew I enjoyed my games. I paused to stare at him. The breeze swept a strand of hair across my face and I raked it back just so with my fingers. Ridge sighed. Someday we would make beautiful children. I glanced back at my gawking relatives and then leaned over and pecked him on the cheek. I didn't care what they thought. This boy would be mine. I needed to show him just enough affection to make him think of me first, just as he had this day, the most important in any young warrior's life.

There were obstacles to our marriage, youth only the first of many. Our union had to be handled in a certain way, but I knew I could manage it with some discretion and a little craft. Ridge must win honor; then he'd win my father, and then he'd win me. I'm patient. I expected the same of him. I couldn't have him buzzing around me all the time like a horsefly. People talked, and my father listened.

"Now, shoo," I said, back to picking my berries. "I'm busy. Marriage can wait ten winters."

"It'll wait four," Ridge said, flashing those teeth. "And then I'll come for you." He puffed up his chest and cut a lean gaze toward Swimmer. "And there's nothing that little man over there can do about it."

"That's not the man you need to be worried about," I said.

"I won't live my life as your father dictates," he said. "And neither should you."

"I don't think I'd put it quite like that when you two get a chance to talk," I said. "*If* you get a chance to talk, rather."

"I don't see the point," he said. "Especially if he talks in circles like his daughter. So many words come out of your mouth, most of which are meant to ridicule me. But you never say the ones your heart wills you to say."

"Like what, exactly?"

"Like you want me as much as I want you."

"Oh, Ridge," I said. "You take such leaps when small steps would be wiser."

"I take leaps when I must, but I look long and hard before I do so."

He glanced at my family. Then he smiled and reached down and cradled the back of my head, lifted it to him, and pressed my lips against his. "Grow up, little girl," he said, still holding me, our noses still touching. "Your husband is waiting for you to become a woman."

Then he left me kneeling there, feeling like I floated in the summer-warmed waters of a still river. I looked back at my mother, and she slowly shook her head, her lips taut at my impropriety. My aunts stood frozen with their mouths hanging open like knotholes in an old snag. I wish a bee would've happened by and stung their soon-to-be flapping tongues. I grabbed my basket and crawled to another bush and halfheartedly rummaged through the fuzzy limbs after I wiped the sweat from my forehead with the hem of my skirt. Uncle Swimmer, his arms latched across his chest, stared coldly in Ridge's direction. I was in for a hot time when my father heard about this.

And I couldn't have cared less.

Chapter Four

For two summers, Ridge hunted the verdant slopes and sharp ravines of Sequatchie Mountain, Where the Opossums Grin. He perfected the art of making weapons and honed his skill at sporting games. He sat at the feet of old men listening to tales of times past, walked just a step or two behind blooded warriors, and led those of his own age into the wilds after deer, bear, and elk. But at dawn and dusk Ridge waded alone into the Tennessee River to pray.

He also helped his mother tend his family's fields. She worked so hard, her sorrows were so many and her pleasures so few, that Ridge felt an obligation to assume some of her burden despite the fact that Sehoya's father claimed women's work demeaned him. Already Ridge's prowess as a hunter outweighed his invectives, for Ridge brought more fresh meat to the lodge than most of the Sequatchie men. It mattered far more to him what Sehoya thought of his interests anyway, and she seemed pleased that despite his standing as an young warrior, Ridge still loved to spend time alone with his etsi, his mama.

He willingly crawled on his knees beside his mother, watching her long, slender fingers tighten around an interloping weed, wrap a strand of graying hair around her petite ear, or straighten her long spine while she massaged away the ache in the small of her back. There was a warmth to her eyes that drew Ridge to her, a grace to her movement that he strove to imitate, and a ring in her lyrical voice that always soothed him. Her paunch was a little swollen after giving birth to so many children, her gait was a little stooped from her labors, and her cheeks were drawn from constant worry and the occasions when she'd gone hungry, but none of these signs managed to diminish her air of confidence and well-being. She was still a beautiful Cherokee woman, and despite all the tragedies she'd endured in her life, she still loved living. If only Agan'stat' could have been half as resilient and courageous as she.

"Go on," she would say. "There's better places for young men to spend their days than in these dusty fields."

"No, there's not," Ridge answered, prying another weed from the soil with the blade of her mallock. "I'm where I want to be."

"It's all right, son," she said more emphatically. "I can finish just fine."

"What's wrong? Can't you abide a son who loves to garden?"

She stopped cold and draped her dirty fingers across his cheek. He could smell the fresh earth. "You've never done a single thing to disappoint me, Ridge Walker. I love having you here. It's just that with age comes responsibility. I'd like to see you enjoy the free years that you have left."

Ridge examined the purple lines on the firm green hulls. They were warm to the touch. "I guess I'm free to pick a few of these peas," he said. "They're ripe now."

"Sehoya doesn't know how lucky she is," his mother said.

"Sure, she does," Ridge said. "I've told her several times."

"You might grow into a good man if you don't trip over your vanity," she said. Her little slight was worth the laugh that followed it.

Ridge filled that basket and two more with fresh peas before he walked beside his mother on the path back to her lodge. She went on to start the cooking while he drifted off to do as he pleased. His back ached from carrying three awkward baskets as he sat quietly before the flames listening to the old men tell their stories of the hunt and of war while they smoked their soapstone pipes. Most of all this evening they spoke of peace, of the "talking leaves" the chiefs had signed with the Great Father, Washington, who had defeated their allies, the British. The Treaty of Hopewell it was called, a paper promise to end the bloodshed.

The Cherokee's war with the Americans had gone so terribly wrong. The hapless British could not protect the Cherokee as they had promised. Ridge's people stood alone as Virginia, Georgia, and the Carolinas joined forces for a series of punishing raids that lasted for four winters. Their backs again broken, the Original People were driven west to scratch out a hard living with bounties on their scalps. By the time the chiefs signed a treaty with the fledgling American Congress, fifty Cherokee towns lay in waste, including Ridge's home village of Hiwassee.

Even the peace all of his people had prayed for had come at a price. The Cherokee forfeited more of their hunting lands, their Dark and Bloody Ground, and also what remained of large tracts to the east of the Blue Mountains. The Nation was a land diminished by three-quarters of what the Cherokee had owned in his grandfather's time, as were the spirits of those who still called what remained of their country home. Ridge stewed in indignation as he listened to the hard terms the Cherokee had received under the heel of the Americans. When he'd heard enough, he scaled Sequatchie to watch the sun set and slept under the stars.

At dawn the next day, Ridge rose and swam naked in the river, saying his prayers beside its smooth bank. When he returned still dripping to his mother's lodge, his parents were stuffing their beans and pumpkins into fat reed baskets. Others were already bulging with their skins and blankets. His father's weapons and his mother's tools were stacked neatly outside beside the mortar and pestle and all her clay pots and greased skillet.

"Where are we going?" Ridge asked, irked that his parents had decided to relocate without consulting him, the oldest son, the hunter who brought fresh meat to the hearth and still picked blueberries for their dessert.

"Home," Agan'stat' said, obviously irritated by his son's abrupt tone. These days, father and son were always one breath away from an argument. "Where we belong."

"Hiwassee?" Ridge asked. His father nodded. The new treaty left Hiwassee to the Cherokee, but Ridge couldn't see the wisdom in camping under the nose of the Americans. "Is it safe?"

"As safe as here."

"I'd like to see that for myself before we go to all this trouble," Ridge said, spreading his feet shoulder width before he planted them.

Agan'stat' stopped his packing and straightened his back. "I've already made the decision."

"I'll have a say in deciding where my mother and siblings live," he said. "You eat out of my hand, Agan'stat'. And still you treat me like a child." Ridge no longer felt comfortable calling his father Edoda, the familiar Daddy.

"Don't disrespect your father," his mother said. "The war's over. I want to go back home as much as he does."

"He disrespects himself," Ridge said.

"Enough," his mother snapped, wagging a finger of warning in his face. "Returning home is a thing to celebrate." She slapped a basket of dried corn against his chest. "Now get busy. You can argue with your father some other time."

"I'll go," Ridge said, "but only because I don't trust him to look after you or little Oowatie and that sweet little girl over there who follows me everywhere."

"Ridge," his mother said, "I told you wrong yesterday. You have disappointed me when it comes to how you treat your father. You don't understand what he's been through. It's not your place to judge him. We're going to make a new start in Hiwassee and at the same time I expect you to make a new start with Agan'stat'."

She arched her eyebrows once she'd fallen silent, which alerted Ridge that she was demanding a vocal response. Instead, Ridge carried the basket out the door without another word. He'd battle his father as long as Turtle Island hung from its four stone cords, but he would never have a cross word for his mother. He'd bite his tongue around Agan'stat' only because it pleased her. Once outside, he heard Agan'stat's muffled voice, though he couldn't make out the words. But his mother's response rang clearly.

"His spirit stirs," she said. "It's the same for all young men his age. Don't dwell on it."

They carried load after load to strap on the backs of his father's horses. His family had accumulated too much to paddle their pos-sessions upriver by canoe. Sometimes he brushed shoulders with Agan'stat' but he never looked at him.

Sehoya emerged from the woods with a bundle of freshly cut reeds in her arms. She saw Ridge packing his father's horses and stopped cold. Ridge handed his animal's reins to Oo-watie and trotted over to her.

"I'm so glad I saw you," he said. "Someone must've poured live coals into Agan'stat's bed last night. He won't wait another day."

"Everyone's talking about going back east," Sehoya said. "But I thought we'd have more time."

"Where will your family go?"

"My father wants to settle near his brother at Tellico. Mother wants to return to Hiwas-see. But we won't do anything until the crops are in."

Ridge gripped her hand. "Send word to me if you're not coming to Hiwassee. If I don't hear from you in two moons, I'll come back here to check on you. For now, I want you to know that just because you and I will be separated for a little while doesn't mean my plans for us have changed."

"Nor mine," she said.

Ridge frowned and looked at his feet. "It's not a good time for me," he said. "I'm not a boy anymore, and yet I'm not a man. I don't like Agan'stat' leading me around like one of his mules, but I can't imagine breaking loose from my family."

"I'm pretty sure what you feel is normal," Sehoya said.

"This can't be normal. Nothing feels right anymore, least of all leaving you."

"Don't worry, Ridge Walker," she said, pressing her lips against his. He felt her fingers thread through the curls on the back of his neck. "I'm yours. You're mine. And nothing's going to change that."

"Ridge!" Agan'stat' hollered. "We'd like to make some time before nightfall."

Ridge closed his eyes and grimaced. What was the blessed hurry? He hugged Sehoya tightly, kissed her forehead, and then let her go. He took the reins from Oo-watie and led Agan'stat's pony down the path. At the crest of the last hill before the first hard bend in the river, Ridge looked back at Sequatchie and the village that had been his makeshift home for so long. Sehoya still stood with her back to the sun, her face a shadow, reeds scattered about her feet, watching. Ridge decided he'd carry that image of her with him through these uncertain moons apart — her standing there alone, awaiting his return.

Ridge's family traveled overland along a narrow, twisting path toward Hiwassee town, with Ridge sometimes usurping his father's place in the lead to demonstrate to Agan'stat' that he was no longer a child. Though they had been gone for eight winters, the country passing slowly by seemed much the same as Ridge remembered it.

What was different were the ax blazes on the hickory and oak trunks, marking the new trails cut by white men. Here and there, Ridge saw their blood red survey stakes. He had assumed the whites had abandoned their claim on Cherokee country, as the old men claimed they had agreed to do under the treaty's provisions. Yet as his family neared Hiwassee town, they came across cleared land and fresh soil churned by the white men's plows where impenetrable thickets once stood. Fresh sap oozed from the pine logs stacked into houses larger than any owned by a Cherokee. Newly hewn shakes cast the rain off pitched roofs and into waiting barrels for fresh drinking water. Fences stretched deep into the woods, marking the boundary of fields several times larger than the communal gardens for a whole Cherokee village.

The war years had taught him that the Americans were every bit as aggressive and fierce as the Cherokee in battle. But seeing how they'd conquered the mountain terrain, Ridge realized that they were also equally tenacious. Ridge saw much to admire in the way they lived — the magnitude, of their labors and the bounty it had earned them. They were not afraid of the wilderness. They were not afraid of work.

But there was nothing about their appearance that redeemed his low opinion of their culture. Ridge collected the inevitable scowls from every bearded man and plain woman and dirty-faced child as his family passed them by on their journey over the hills to Hiwassee. The Americans' rifles were always near them. Their eyes were full of hate and distrust, always watching. And as far as Ridge was concerned, they were right to do so.

"Did Chief Otter not say that the Americans had agreed to remove the squatters from our land?" Ridge asked Agan'stat'.

"He did," Agan'stat' replied, his eyes always forward, watching the road ahead. It irked Ridge that his father's answers were so cryptic. Agan'stat' spoke to him as Cherokee spoke to white men — as briefly as possible.

"They don't look like they're leaving to

me." In fact they hadn't covered a single league on this trail without hearing the thud of ax blades or the gnawing of saws.

"We'll see," Agan'stat' said.

Their pace quickened as they crested familiar hills and views of the river. Ridge reached landmarks that told him Hiwassee lay just ahead. He herded Oo-watie along to catch up with their parents, certain that the next hill would be their last. When they reached it, his mother was weeping against Agan'stat's shoulder. The old settlement of Hiwassee, once home to maybe five hundred of Ridge's neighbors and kin, still lay covered in ruin and ashes. In the eight winters since its destruction not even one family had attempted to move back.

One glimpse of his boyhood home and Ridge remembered the screams of the dying on that terrible day when they'd left it. Such an image unsettled him more than the scorching glares of the stubborn white settlers who still refused to leave the Nation. Without a word, Agan'stat' turned and led them back west toward Chestowee, the Rabbit Place, the closest living village to the one that had died. There, Agan'stat' pledged, Ridge's family would start again.

And so it came to be. Ridge cast off all doubt and apprehension as he plunged in with his parents to construct a new lodge, this one larger than any they had known before. The work went quickly, and soon a young fire burned in the hearth. Ridge felt its warmth on his body, but he was comforted more by his mother's songs in his ears. In his spare time, Ridge reacquainted himself with the hills and streams of the old country. Nothing had changed, and he found comfort in the fact that nature was immutable.

The journey back to the Hiwassee River valley had been hard, just as Waesa had forecast the night when Ridge became a warrior. But the last few days of toil restored hope to his heart. It felt good to begin again in peace near the very same place where his countless ancestors slept. When Ridge went twice each day to the water to begin his devotions, he had a sense that the departed watched over him and encouraged him to aspire to great things. At the end of his prayers, he always thanked his ancestors for their interest in his young life, promising them that the Man Who Walks the Mountaintops would not disappoint them.

Ridge's blood may have been mixed, but his identity was as pure as a winter stream. The slim white percentage coursing through his veins was insignificant, like a mountain brook that merged with a rushing spring river. The Ridge was Ani-yunwi-ya like rock was mountain, tied forever to the proud hunters, warriors, and chiefs who had come before him, to ani-kawi, the deer clan, the link that connected him to his mother, and through her to a vine of blood relatives that spread throughout every remaining Cherokee village and valley, and to the soil beneath his bare feet the Original People had won by conquest back in the dark days when the mountains walked. The Man Who Walks the Mountaintops was of his people and pledged himself to live only for them. All he hoped for now, in the event that there were those who doubted him, was the opportunity to prove it.

CHAPTER FIVE

The Ridge stared at his reflection in the waters of the Hiwassee River. His sister had shaved his head as smooth as a river stone, save for a small scalp lock, to which he tied red feathers, their tips dipped in white dye. He painted his face with vermilion, the color of blood. He circled one eye in white, the other in black. He smudged the shape of a skull across his chest with charcoal he'd scraped from an oak that had survived a lightning strike. Each ornamentation had a symbolic purpose, and as he attached them to his body, he felt his power grow. In the distance, he heard the songs of dancing warriors and the steady beat of drums. He laid his red-and-black war club before him and sank to his knees to pray for courage and honor, just as he had for the three previous nights.

"Hay-ee!" he prayed. "Yuh! Listen! Now I have lifted up the red war club. Quickly my enemy's soul will be without motion. Under the black earth, there his soul shall be, never to reappear. I cause it to be so!"

He heard moccasins crunching the dry summer grass behind him. He paused to listen without opening his eyes. This was no time to be bothered. He didn't want to rush through this very private ritual. Perhaps the intruder would understand the sanctity of the moment and go away of his own accord.

"Let me shield myself with the red war whoop," he prayed. "Cause not my soul to break in two or be severed from this earth, but let it rise white like snow to the seventh heaven long after the hair on my head is gray. So shall it be. Yuh!"

"You're to go with them, then?" the encroacher asked.

Ridge sighed and rubbed his numb head until he found his scalp lock. He gave it a little tug, thinking that the answer to Agan'stat's question should be obvious.

"With your mother and I both sick?" his father said. "Your brother and sister hungry, and you, our eldest and only hunter, on the war trace?" Ridge rose to his feet and squared off with Agan'stat'. The old man looked smaller, as if he'd withered over the last few years like an uneaten piece of fruit. "How else are we to avenge Old Tassel's murder?" Ridge said smugly.

Other men his father's age were preparing for war after this latest outrage. As far as

Ridge was concerned, their reaction was late in coming. The Americans had never honored the Treaty of Hopewell. They squatted wherever they pleased on land that belonged to the Nation. They sold whiskey to young warriors and then robbed them once they were drunk. Property had been destroyed. Fields and corn cribs raided. Women subjected to abduction and rape. Lone Cherokee had been found out on the roads with their throats cut.

Increasingly frustrated warriors had just cause to take up the tomahawk again, but Old Tassel, like Ada-gal'kala' before him, cautioned the Cherokee to remain at peace. He was on his way to remind American leaders of the promises they'd made at Hopewell only to be shot dead under a flag of truce. Dragging Canoe's militant western Cherokee, known as Chickamaugas after the village that lay at the defiant heart of their remote country, planned to answer with blood, and Ridge hungered for it.

"Is that your only reason?" Agan'stat' asked.

"It's the only one I need. Our cause is just."

Much to Ridge's annoyance, his father clicked his tongue and shook his head. "And if you kill one white man," Agan'stat' said, "have you not learned that fifty more will come and kill a hundred Cherokee? Walk among the ruins of Hiwassee town if you've forgotten."

"I've forgotten none of it!" Ridge snapped.

He was so tired of arguing with this wasted man. "And if my youth has taught me anything, it's that it's time to kill the whites before they take everything we have. What do the Cherokee gain by signing the talking leaves if our peace chiefs are murdered before the ink dries?"

"The question," Agan'stat' said, "is what do we lose? Doublehead, Pumpkin Boy, and the other Chickamaugas poke sticks in the hornet's nest like children as a point of honor. But it will be the innocents who get stung. I beg you to stay clear of hotheads and help care for your family."

Ridge expected such talk from his father. What their neighbors said of him was true: Agan'stat' owned a frog's spirit. Toss a pebble into his little pond and he'd dive for the depths. He regarded his father with spitting contempt.

"And do what?" Ridge said. "Run?"

"Live." His father's aging body heaved in a fit of coughing.

"That's not living. I'd rather die than live another day like a rabbit."

His father dismissed his passions with a wave of his hand. "Go, then, Ridge Walker," Agan'stat' said. "By all means, win your honor. Rant and rage with the young men. I did when I was your age. But I'll tell you that the whites are no winter season. They don't come and go. They are like the waves breaking on the beach. Only a fool would try to hold them back with a tomahawk. I've spent my last years searching for another way. I hope before too much longer you'll join the search with me."

Ridge angrily stripped his leggings away and tossed them aside. He stood in his breechclout and leaned over to stretch his muscles. Then he picked up his club, gripping it so tightly that the knuckles on his fist turned white. Ridge swung the weapon in circles over his head to check its balance. Everything felt right except this conversation he was having with Agan'stat'. "There was a time," he said, "when a father would've been proud to see his son follow the war trace."

"There was truly such a time," his father answered. "That's what I'm trying to teach you, my son. Everything's different now. I would've hoped the Man Who Walks the Mountaintops could see that for himself."

What more was there to say to such a coward? Ridge broke off eye contact with his prideless father and fastened his patch of dried cornmeal to his breechclout, his only rations until he'd won more from his enemies. He was truly glad that Ada-gal'kala's blood ran in his veins, as well as that of Dragging Canoe, Old Hop, and Doublehead, Chickamauga war chiefs who wanted to take the fight to the Ani-yonega. The blood of Agan'stat', who should be leading his oldest son into battle rather than trying to talk him out of going, was worthless.

Ridge would waste no more time justifying his intentions to a man of no honor. He turned his back to his father to insult him while he gathered the rest of his weapons, and marched off toward the sound of the beating drums.

"Kiss the tears from your mother's face before you go, Ridge Walker," Agan'stat' said dryly. "She may not last long enough to see yours again."

Ridge flicked a spotted tick from his forearm as he lay in wait, hidden in the tall grass that framed the grove at Setico, Big Fish There, long ago abandoned by the Cherokee.

"Have you noticed how the whites plant their fruit trees in neat rows like British soldiers?" White Path whispered.

"Ssshhh," Ridge hissed. "Doublehead said to be quiet."

"It's odd to me is all I'm saying," White Path said. "Yet look how their limbs sag with the bounty of fruit. My family hasn't had much luck with apple trees."

"The whites baby them like their children," Ridge said, his curiosity piqued. "I've seen them do it, working dead foliage into the soil around their roots in winter and clipping the weaker limbs."

"One shouldn't have to go to such trouble

for a tree to grow," White Path said. "But just the same I think I'll give it another try when I get home. I love the sweet taste of apples and peaches as much as any white man."

"That's why we're here," Ridge said. "When the soldiers come for these, they die. At least, they might if you'd quit your jabbering."

White Path shrugged. "No one said we couldn't visit on this raid."

"Would you shut up!" Ridge said. His irritation stemmed from his grumbling stomach as much as from his fraying nerves. As was the custom, he'd fasted the first day on the war trace. After that he was expected to thrive on one cup of cornmeal each day. But he, too, could smell the sweetness of ripe fruit, could almost taste its crisp, tart flesh on his thick tongue. Once he and Sehoya had established a lodge of their own, he'd acquire a few of those trees and care for them as the whites did.

Below the orchards stretched fields of corn, beans, tomatoes, melons, and squashes, enough crops in this one location to feed his village for one whole winter. What a luxury that would be, especially in February, Gaga lu'nee, the month of the hungry moon, when the children cried from want of food. Ridge had felt such pangs before, too. Did the whites ever hunger? No wonder so many were fat.

A hand clamped down on his shoulder.

Startled, he knocked it away and threw back his tomahawk to strike.

"Easy, cousin," Doublehead said, his dark eyes drawn to the edges of the woods bordering the orchard, a hunter waiting for his prey. "I see you're anxious to use that thing. You'll get your chance soon enough." Ridge collected himself as Doublehead shoved Ridge's tomahawk aside with thick, sinewy arms. His shaved head jutted from a powerful neck, chest and back muscles taut and as well-defined as the ridges on rough bark. With his slightest movement, they flexed. His haunches were beefy like a bull elk's, his gait equally assured. When he spoke, the veins throbbed against his bare, painted temples as if they too commanded attention.

Doublehead resonated with intimidation. Like the dominant hunter beasts of the wild, he held power and rage composed. Doublehead did not assert his authority; he wielded it naturally like yet another mastered weapon for others to recognize and behold. Warriors whom Ridge quietly feared automatically deferred to Doublehead as he walked among them, positioning a few men here and a few more there, organizing a mass of fiercely independent warriors to strike together like one great coiled copperhead. The simple fact that this Cherokee champion shared his blood caused Ridge to stand straighter and draw more air into his lungs. What Doublehead was, Ridge aspired to be.

Doublehead reached into his pouch for a wafer of bean bread and showed it to Ridge and White Path. He snapped it in two and gave one half to each. Despite its staleness, the bread was far better than the cornmeal. Ridge could still taste the hint of bear grease and the flavor of hickory coals.

"When this thing begins," Doublehead said, "I want you two to hang back for a while. Let the older warriors engage the soldiers. Your task is to guard the rear and cut down any stragglers who may wander this way. There should be great confusion among the whites once we attack them. I expect the Cherokee to keep their heads."

White Path nodded and so did Ridge.

"Now," Doublehead said to White Path. "You move away from us a little and cease your chatter." White Path looked at Ridge and then crawled off.

"Agan'stat' came to see me when I was in Chestowee," Doublehead said, running his thumb over his knife blade. "He worries for you."

"The Ridge will do what's expected of a warrior," Ridge said.

"No one doubts you, my cousin. Doublehead sees the hunger in your eyes, the very same he once saw in Agan'stat's." He shoved the dagger inside his sash. "You see, your father once led Doublehead on the war trace as he now leads you. You didn't know that, did you?"

Ridge shook his head. All those nights he'd begged Agan'stat' to tell him of his youthful adventures and still he knew nothing but the image of his father's distant stare.

"He was the equal of Dragging Canoe in battle," Doublehead said. "Many men fell before him. I walked in his tracks for moons without end and was proud to do so."

"He won't talk about it," Ridge said.

"I don't know why," Doublehead said. "These days our opinions differ and that pains me. He thinks it's useless to war against the Americans, and I'd rather kill them than eat." He patted his fingers against his forehead. "Agan'stat' doesn't believe the Provider blessed Doublehead with a chief's wisdom. Maybe not. Perhaps that is why the Provider gave me a warrior's heart. It's an even trade, no?"

Ridge nodded.

"Is there anything you want to tell me before we are seared by the flames of war?"

"No," Ridge said, swallowing hard. He wasn't really sure how he should've answered that.

"Well, there's something I want to tell you," Doublehead said. "I think that you doubt yourself because you're a mixed-blood."

Ridge started to protest when Doublehead held up his hand.

"This is between you and me, cousin, and I say what I feel. It gets me into trouble sometimes when I'm around my village, but here on the war trace, where proud men live one day and die the next, there's no time for discretion. Out here we bare our hearts to one another like children without shame. There are no secrets between us. Say what you want. The soldiers are coming and you may not get another chance."

Ridge thought about that and then slowly nodded his head. "I've been shunned since I was a boy and it gnaws at me," Ridge said. His mouth felt as if it were full of dust. "I am what the Provider made me, a son of good people in this time and place, and yet some of my own kind don't trust me because I'm not full-blooded. My friend White Path has no idea what it's like to be born in suspicion. I came here to fight for the Cherokee so that they will know that I love them enough to lay down my own life."

"Good enough," Doublehead said. "I know your blood is red like mine, and for me — simple man that I am — that's enough. You stand your ground in this encounter. Live or die like a brave man this very day and Doublehead — war chief of all war chiefs who answers only to Dragging Canoe himself — will shout from the highest peak that the Man Who Walks the Mountaintops is first and foremost Ani-yunwi-ya. And woe to any man

94

who disputes me." Doublehead rammed his fist against Ridge's chest. "Make it so, Ridge Walker! Make me keep my promise!"

Ridge gasped for breath. "At the very first opportunity," he said with a cough.

"I see your situation thus," Doublehead said. "The Provider gave you just enough white blood for you to know what they're thinking as you lift the scalp from their heads! You, my cousin, are a very dangerous Cherokee! Foolish men may doubt you, but don't you ever doubt yourself."

Doublehead snapped his head toward the sound of horses splashing into the Little Tennessee River. His eyes glazed over and a thin grin emerged on his lips.

"Ah," he said. "The moment that makes men. You won't need your brain for this, Ridge Walker. This is the time when instinct rules. There's nothing a warrior can do but give himself to it. And when you do, no bullet will ever touch you."

He reached down and yanked Ridge's ear hard. Ridge almost screamed, certain he was about to rip it off.

"That is the last pain you'll feel today, my cousin," Doublehead said. He released him and started to slip away, his stare drawn to their approaching enemies. "Make it so."

Ridge crawled beside White Path and sank down beside him in the tall grass, his heart pounding against the earth. His first test was about to begin. "What was all that about?" White Path said.

Ridge pressed a finger against his lips. Soon the whites emerged from the thick bottoms and rode straight for the rows of trees. Ridge recognized them as militia, fathers and sons of the people who took land that did not belong to them, white men who looked upon the Cherokee with contempt. Most dismounted and laid their long rifles aside to rip an apple or two from the lower limbs. He could hear the apples crack as they bit into them with their brown teeth.

Doublehead signaled for some of the warriors to slip between the orchard and the river to cut off the soldiers' escape. Once they were crouched in position, Ridge heard a war whoop, and everywhere around him barked Cherokee rifles. Six soldiers fell as the acrid smoke drifted over them. The rest remounted and fled, plunging headlong into the warriors, who greeted them with another thunderous blast of powder and ball. The Cherokee erupted in war cries and turkey gobbles and rushed them from behind, blades flashing in the morning sun, and Ridge's blood rose with theirs. He couldn't keep himself from running headlong into the heart of the struggle, shouting with his war club poised over his head, White Path three steps behind him.

Ten more whites died in the booming cross fire, the white survivors spurring their horses back into the river to make their escape. Ridge unsaddled a frightened man who swung near him, smelling the stench of his breath as they both crashed to the earth. Ridge knocked him senseless with repeated blows of his fists. And then he stood, feeling no pity as he pulled his tomahawk from his breechclout and split the soldier's head open to the bridge of his nose.

Ridge dove in after the others, swam the currents, and crawled up from the slick bank to battle the soldiers hand to hand. One walloped two Cherokee with the butt of his rifle and then came at Ridge. Ridge picked up a spear and hurled it into the soldier's chest, skewering his body to a sweet gum tree. The soldier screamed, then choked for breath as blood bubbled from his nose and mouth. Ridge jerked the spear from the man's dying body, and kicked him facedown in the dirt. He whooped his war yell, and searched for another to kill just as White Path hurled his tomahawk into a soldier's back. Ridge heard a distinct thud, and then the soldier slipped from the saddle, his body crashing against a thick pine.

By then, what remained of the whites had cleared the steep riverbank that trapped them. Ridge heard them crashing through the underbrush in which no soldier could hide from the Cherokee trackers. Many of the soldiers left blood trails on the black soil.

The warriors could easily run them down in the thickets and kill them all. Ridge turned to see if the war chiefs were regrouping for pursuit, but they were busy collecting uska-na-gili, their enemy's hair. Ridge stood in disappointment, listening to the last of the horses bound through the deep brush.

"You are outa-cit-e!" Doublehead praised him in a voice that shook the brambles. "Man-killer! My cousin succeeded where two others had failed! Take what is yours!"

Ridge pulled his knife from his breechclout and plunged it under the soldier's scalp, running the blade against his skull until the warm, slick flesh came free like filleted fish. Then he dropped the body to rot under the sun so that its soul would never enter heaven.

Doublehead lifted Ridge's bloody hand with his for all to see. "Did you see what this man did?" he said. "Who among you would not have the Man Who Walks the Mountain-tops by your side? This is my cousin! A Cherokee warrior!"

The war chief wrapped his arm around Ridge's neck, pulling him against his chest, sweat and blood gluing their bodies together. Ridge felt Doublehead's heart pound against him, echoing his cousin's courage throughout his body. Ridge tightened his chest to trap it inside him. This was the moment Ridge had always wanted — trial by fire beside warriors bound by blood, his enemy's hair hanging from his sweating hand.

"Give me one hundred Ridges," Double-head said, "and I'll drive the Americans into the sea."

By now the Cherokee were gripped in a fever, and Doublehead did nothing to cool it as they fell against the bodies of the slain. For many warriors, a scalp was not enough. Bear Paw hacked off a white man's head with his tomahawk, dug his heart out with the blade of his knife, and spilled his intestines onto the bloody earth. Others cut open the stomachs of the dead and cast their bowels upon the waters of the Tennessee. All of this, Ridge knew, was not done simply to avenge Old Tassel's murder. Ridge hoped the mas-sacre would satiate the warriors' rage and serve as a warning of what the Americans could expect if they did not leave the Original People in peace.

Ridge knelt at the riverbank and washed the blood from his body. How quickly the currents dispersed the thin red clouds. Agan'stat' thought wrong. War was the only way to send the message. Other tribes equally powerful had battled the Cherokee for this country and failed. What chief could gaze upon this shocking carnage and think it wise to send his warriors against them?

Ridge left the river to cut down a branch of green pine, tying the fresh scalp to its limber tip. Already the warriors were singing of what

Ridge Walker had done in his first battle. In just one encounter, he'd won honor. He knew he would soon win more.

"Enough now," Doublehead said. "Gather your weapons and let's take up their trail. The rivers will ice over before the Cherokee break off the hunt."

Ridge was among the first to fall in behind his distant cousin and resume the war trace when Doublehead planted his feet and motioned for Ridge to overtake him. They ran in single file as tradition dictated, following the hoof prints into the brush. An enemy waiting in ambush would meet the fiercest of the Cherokee first, and Ridge proudly claimed that place of honor as he led them onward into the dark and angry woods.

Behind him came others who spoke his name.

CHAPTER SIX

Ridge wavered in exhaustion, struggling to listen to Bob Benge's offer to the defenders trapped within. Four winters of killing and he saw no end in sight to promise there would not be a fifth. Wave after wave of soldiers and militia swept across the Blue Mountains, answering blood with blood. The men of Virginia, the Carolinas, Tennessee, and Kentucky joined the hunt for the Cherokee and slaughtered them on sight. Dragging Canoe had died in his bed. The half-breed John Watts emerged to lead the Chickamaugas, now a distinct and separate tribe from the Cherokee, who had suffered so many white retaliations that they wanted no more part of Dragging Canoe or his war.

By remaining with the Chickamaugas in defiance of the many Cherokee chiefs who had sued for peace, Ridge was a man apart from his people, apart from his family, and apart from the woman he loved. At night sleeping on a bed of pine needles, listening for the sound that would signal his last violent encounter with the whites, he tried to imagine Sehoya's face. After four winters on the war trace, he could no longer see her clearly. No word had reached his ears of her fate during the repeated white raids. He had no idea if she had given him up for dead and taken another to her lodge. These misgivings constantly gnawed at him.

Furthermore, Doublehead's relentless warfare had sucked Ridge's soul dry. Agan'stat' was right in his assessment that Doublehead lacked the chief's head. He lived from one battle to the next, with no vision beyond that tainted by tomorrow's blood and hatred. Doublehead thought of killing and nothing more.

Dragging Canoe's death gutted what remained of Ridge's flagging resolve. In his opinion, John Watts lacked Dragging Canoe's genius for war. Watts, a charismatic half-breed who wore a turban and a Cherokee hunting shirt over English breeches and boots, envisioned an Indian army that marched in ranks and fought in formation, a force to be admired and feared by their American enemies. He was weary of the cut, slash, and run tactics of a hundred scattered, independent war parties. The Chickamaugas needed a great victory to turn the tide, and so he led a thousand former Cherokee, Creek, and Shawnee north toward Knoxville, which they planned to reduce to ashes to prove that the Americans were not yet masters west of the Smoky Mountains and that even their cities were not safe.

They'd passed over a dozen smaller settlements and blockhouses on the trail. Doublehead and his brother, Pumpkin Boy, were incredulous that Watts wouldn't lay waste to them, as well. He and many other lesser war chiefs had grown accustomed to killing whites where they found them. Watts wanted Knoxville, and refused to forfeit the element of surprise by engaging insignificant targets. The issue had become a running argument as the Chickamaugas swept north. By the time they reached the family-owned Cavett's Station, John Watts could no longer hold Doublehead back.

"Enough of your schemes," Doublehead said. "Let's make war." He cut a hundred loyal warriors from out of the main body to stalk Cavett's blockhouse just as dawn was breaking in the east. Others followed, and Watts's "army" was cut in two. Ridge saw the half-breed's face flush in frustration, but he knew Watts couldn't afford to split his forces if he wanted to see Knoxville fall.

"Make it quick then," Watts said, and a thousand warriors swarmed the lone station. A young boy feeding horses spied them drifting through the early mist and fled screaming behind the walls. Some warrior fired a shot, which thudded into one of the pine logs. The blockhouse's gate slammed shut. Ten or so long rifles appeared through slits in the closed portholes. Ridge saw the fire spit from their bores and five Cherokee tumbled from their horses.

One of them was Pumpkin Boy, who died screaming in his brother's arms. Doublehead climbed out from under Pumpkin Boy's body and flew into a wicked rage. His lungs forced malignant oaths through his gaping mouth loudly enough to ring Ridge's ears.

"Before the sun rises," Doublehead vowed, "those within will fall under my knife." Then he flung his warriors at the walls.

But those inside Cavett's Station had other plans, and laid down a withering fire that sent Chickamaugas bounding for the bushes. Even Doublehead was driven back. The shooting went on until the sun rose above the treeline without accomplishing much of anything, and finally Watts couldn't stand it any longer.

"Let's finish this," he said to Bob Benge, his half-breed lieutenant.

"I wonder how," Benge said. "Doublehead's damned determined."

Watts hastily tied a white rag on Benge's rifle barrel. "I'll handle Doublehead. You go and talk to those people. Tell them if they surrender we'll trade them for Cherokee prisoners. If not, we'll burn them out and let Doublehead have his way with them."

Ridge and others circulated around the warriors, telling them to hold their fire while Benge arranged his parley, and hoping they could still go on to Knoxville as Watts had planned. Ridge noticed a calm descending as Benge approached Cavett's waving his flag. Ridge's ears pounded from all the yelling and shooting, but he could still hear Double-head's angry footsteps as he cut a swath to Watts.

"What's this?" he demanded, pointing to Benge and his white flag.

"There's no more time," Watts said. "If they'll come out, they'll live."

"I didn't agree to this," Doublehead said.

"You're not in command," Watts said.

Doublehead's answer was to spit on Watts's boots in defiance. "I'm not some slave at your beck and call. My warriors follow me." He looked at Ridge, who took another step closer to Watts and crossed his arms. Ridge wanted Doublehead to know that he had come to know his cousin's heart and wanted nothing more to do with it.

Watts placed his hand heavily on Double-head's shoulder. "My brother, try to calm yourself. I tried to tell you that the prize is Knoxville. This," he said, pointing to the blockhouse, "gains us nothing. We've run the war trace together for so long, Doublehead. Let's make our struggle mean something."

Doublehead pointed to his dead brother.

"Tell that to him," he said.

"I did," Watts said. "He didn't listen." His stare narrowed. "Will you?"

Doublehead deliberated. Ridge watched his eyes shift until his stare fell on Benge and an opening gate. "As you wish, my chief," he said. And then he walked over to his brother's body and smeared his fingers with his brother's blood. He smudged his cheek first, and then that of his most loyal warriors, pacing back and forth like a panther, waiting.

Benge finished his discussions and returned to Watts.

"They'll take you at your word," he said. "They're comin' out."

Watts looked at Ridge and White Path. "You, Ridge Walker. Pick twenty warriors and take those people to Holston," he said. "And don't go anywhere near your cousin." He scribbled words on a piece of paper and handed it to Ridge. "Keep them safe in the woods and go alone under a white flag to see Sevier. Give this to him and await his answer. If he agrees, deliver the prisoners to him with my regards. You understand?"

Ridge wondered how he would conduct himself once he was face-to-face with John Sevier, the Tennessee leader who had burned so many Cherokee villages in the war. Ridge had long dreamed of killing him in battle to avenge his people, but now they would meet on other terms. "It will be done just as you say," Ridge said. White Path nodded his head in agreement.

"Good," Watts said. "Then we're finished here. We're going on, and soon."

Ridge kept an eye on Doublehead as Watts addressed his other war chiefs. "Who knows, my brothers? A little mercy shown here in this hopeless situation followed by a big victory in Knoxville, and maybe we'll come to terms with the whites. Now let's get mounted and ride six abreast, just like we were before all this started."

The blockhouse gate squealed open. A bearded man of perhaps fifty winters emerged first, followed by nine men and boys and three women. They held up their empty hands.

"Come, Ridge," Watts said. "Set down your rifle. Let's make our introductions as civilized men."

Before Ridge had taken his first step he heard the war cries. Doublehead looped his leg over his saddle and, swinging his tomahawk above his head, bore down on the helpless whites. Without hesitation, his warriors followed him. The Cavett women screamed in terror as their men frantically herded them back inside the blockhouse. Doublehead's horse rammed against the closing gate and it flew open. Ridge heard Cavett's skull crush like a melon thrown against a stone as Doublehead buried his tomahawk in his head. Blood sprouted from the gaping wound, covering the flanks of Doublehead's horse as the enraged war chief turned on another victim. The women fell to their knees, pleading for their lives. Doublehead's warriors hacked them into pieces. Watts was too stunned to move.

Ridge dashed into the compound, hoping to save anyone he could. He scooped up a young boy in his arms as Doublehead lurched toward him. Ridge stepped back until he was pinned against the wall.

"Spare this one, cousin!" Ridge cried. "I beg you!"

Ridge's body shuddered from the blows as Doublehead buried his tomahawk into the boy's neck until his head was attached by a thin strip of skin. Doublehead's eyes were as dead as slate as he swung and swung again, until he and Ridge were drenched in the boy's blood. In horror, Ridge let the body slip from his arms to coil on the ground.

"Why?" he asked. But Doublehead was beyond all reason, glaring past him with crazy eyes, blood running down his face like tears. He raised his tomahawk yet again and Ridge braced himself for the blow. White Path dove his warhorse between them, driving Doublehead back. Watts gathered a young boy, the only living Cavett, and whisked him away into the woods while Doublehead screamed obscenities at him. White Path dismounted and wrapped his arm around Ridge's neck and pulled him, too, beyond the reach of Doublehead's rage.

"There's nothing you can do," White Path said. "He'll kill you."

"He's crazy," Ridge said, wiping angry tears from his face.

"His hatred rules him. Don't let the same happen to you."

Doublehead whooped, pulling his hunting knife from his sash, and began to scalp their victims. His men chopped off heads and gutted the dead, stringing their entrails on fence posts. Ridge broke free of White Path's grasp, his stomach churning so that he thought he would vomit. He looked again at the vile image of possessed men mangling bodies, and then he turned his head away in shame. Doublehead's warriors looted the station and then set fire to everything that would burn.

Ridge turned his back on the searing flames and walked away. The breeze on his face felt cold. He untied his horse in silence and lifted a heavy foot in the stirrup.

"Where do you go?" White Path asked him.

"I want nothing to do with this," he said. And then he rode out alone as the flames rose behind him. He looked at his scalp branch, the symbol of his many personal victories, dangling from his scabbard. He yanked it free and pitched it to the ground. He turned south and did not look back.

CHAPTER SEVEN

Oo-watie

I am the ancient one, younger brother of Kah-nung-da-tla-geh, the Man Who Walks the Mountaintops, best known as the Ridge. Let me tell you what I know.

I don't really remember Ridge ever being a child. My earliest recollection is his quiet, solemn bearing, quite advanced for his years, as if he carried the weight of Turtle Island on his shoulders. Ridge was born powerful. Sometimes he would flex his muscles to show off. I hit them with my fist as hard as I could. They were like stones. But my brother's mind was as agile as his body.

My father was a poor man, and for us living came hard. I think Ridge was embarrassed by our station in life. Even as a boy, my brother wanted better for us. I was in awe of him when he left home against my father's wishes at only seventeen winters of age. Life was miserable without him. I had no big brother around to protect me from bullies. I did not have his skill at the hunt, so I often came home from days in the woods with only excuses to face an empty meat rack. I had no knack for gardening when my mother was too sick to tend to her plots herself. I had no one to talk to as I lay in bed at night. While Ridge was away I'd lost my friend as well as my teacher. I felt half of what I was when he was beside me.

For four winters, Ridge remained on the war trace with the Chickamauga war chiefs Dragging Canoe, Doublehead, Pumpkin Boy, and John Watts. He returned home once in all that time, and only then to urge my father to move south to Pine Log, a wilderness settlement between the Oostanaula and Etowah rivers. There Ridge felt we stood a better chance of avoiding American reprisals. Whole villages were abruptly abandoned, and when at last the soldiers did attack the Nation, they encountered three thousand armed and angry warriors — not the old men, women, and children they'd expected. One of them was my brother.

We had our successes. Dragging Canoe defeated General Martin at Lookout Mountain, and after his death, John Watts, nephew of the slain Old Tassel, harassed Sevier's column as he marched through the middle towns of the Nation. After that, the Chickamaugas turned again against the white settlements along the Blue and Smoky Mountains. They burned John Gillespie's fort to the ground and laid siege to Houston's Station and White's blockhouse.

Ridge told me that things fell apart after Dragging Canoe's death, but we all knew that the Chickamaugas' efforts were not without result. The Great Father Washington had heard of our troubles and claimed he understood our anger. His council, Congress, assured us through General Martin that the terms of the Treaty of Hopewell would be enforced. All white squatters would be forced from our country. This is all we ever wanted.

John Watts withdrew his remaining warriors to wait out the winter at Flint Creek and see what would come of the promises. We did not have to wait long. In Unu la ta 'nee, the Cold Moon, January, Sevier surrounded our exhausted warriors. By all accounts the battle was tooth and claw.

Flint Creek was the first Chickamauga defeat in that winter of blood. Maybe a hundred and fifty warriors died in the battle. Many more left blood trails in the snow for the soldiers to follow. When we heard this news, I worried that my brother would be among the dead.

But Ridge returned home alone in his twenty-first winter. I expected to see his scalp branch thick with trophies. He never said what became of it. He seemed impatient

when the older warriors praised his name.
They even sang songs about what he'd done.
Words do not express the pride I felt in this
man, and in what he accomplished at such a
young age. But Ridge only tolerated their
celebrations in the very same manner he did
when our great-aunts doted on him when he
was a boy. He always pleased others ahead of
himself.

He was thinner when he came back, his
gaze detached and more distant, his mood
sullen, his grave expression surprising given
the honors of war he'd won. My sister and I
ran up to hug him, which embarrassed him
some, I'd guess. He was a warrior now, tough
like a pinecone, and he shrugged off our show
of affection.

"Where is Agan'stat' and Etsi?" he asked in
such a way that told me he sensed he would
not like the answer.

"A fever came while you were gone, Ridge,"
I told him. " 'Doda and Etsi rest with those
who came before them."

I didn't mention that the *adawehis* felt the
hardships of a winter relocation had led to
their demise.

The blood drained from his head until he
nearly swooned. He buckled and immediately
began wailing as I'd never heard him do. I
held his head against my shoulder and whispered into his ear.

"Was it your fault that we were at war with

the whites? Many others in our village are alive because you came home to warn us. Draw from that what comfort you can."

Ridge collapsed where he stood, crying into his hands. "Please, Ridge," I said. "Let's go into our lodge and mourn in private."

"You have no idea," he said, "how it pains me that my last words to Agan'stat' were said in anger."

"Enough of that," I said. "You did what you thought was right, and I promise you that regardless of what Agan'stat' said to you he was proud of your accomplishments."

Over the next few sleeps, Ridge came to grips with his situation. I think he came to understand that he was now responsible for our welfare. The Ridge Walker believed in our traditions, especially when it came to the preservation of our clan. As the eldest son, he held more authority over us than even our father, for mother and children were of the same clan, and always a father's clan was different. Ridge knew that if our family's seed was to survive, he would have to put down his weapons and plow our fields for the spring. This he did with his usual determination in spite of his grief. He made no effort to see Sehoya. And she, knowing he chose to remain in mourning, did not come to him. I felt sorry for both of them.

Ridge tilled our fields alone with Mother's mallock, which he prized above the fine weapons he had won in the wars after his return. Once the soil was turned, we all went with him to sit in its center and pray to Selu, Mother Corn, with our noses full of the smell of fresh earth. We begged Selu to give us a good crop, as there was no time when we needed it more. Then we made a small grid of mounds in the field, planting seven kernels in each. My mother had usually planted only four, but seven was considered magical, the most spiritual of all.

Ridge drove the tomahawks into the earth, their blades facing each of the four winds to break up the storms of early summer. We planted our beans and squash in a similar fashion and then prayed for the nurturing rains of female storms, when clouds would squat over the hills and rain gently for days, seeping into the soil. Male storms were violent, with thunder and hail and rains severe enough to drown the sprouting grains; sometimes they were all bluster and wind and too little rain. That first summer we were lucky, and each morning when Ridge led us all to water to prayer, we remembered to thank the spirits for their kindness to us.

Once the fields were planted, Ridge Walker took to the hunt. He brought home young buck whitetails, their antlers coated in velvet, their flesh far more tender than it would be in the fall running time, the rut. Their antlers were hard as bone then, and their necks swollen. Ridge killed turkeys and rabbits, and once even a buffalo on which we feasted until our stomachs swelled.

My sister and I did our part, too, collecting wild grapes and muscadines, strawberries, wild plums, and apples. We climbed the mountains in search of huckleberries. In the bottoms we hunted for stands of persimmon ripe with bitter fruit. In the fall, after the first hard freeze, we'd know where to find them, ripe and sweet for the picking. We'd rub them on our calico shirts until the hazy golden skin nearly glowed, and then, laughing at how we'd cheated the bears out of their favorite meal, we'd eat them on the spot. With my older brother watching over us, we knew everything would be all right.

I expect Ridge was proud of the manner in which he cared for us. The burden was not easy to carry, and often my sister and I were sick with fevers. This must have worried him to no end. At such times he called upon the *adawehis* to attend us, doing precisely as they prescribed even if it meant bathing us naked in mountain streams or blowing tobacco smoke into our aching ears. He hauled our vomit and cleaned our soiled clothes without one word of complaint. Ridge cared for us as well as our parents ever had, and we loved him for it.

But some times were harder than others for Ridge. On occasion he buckled under the burden of his family. He was most strongly affected when he watched the other young warriors prepare for the raids. He understood the purpose of the violence — that we were fighting for our land. But after Doublehead's conduct at Cavett's Station, Ridge wanted nothing more to do with war. I knew that he had sworn an oath to lay down his life in defense of the Nation when he'd become a warrior, and this promise kept him at odds within himself. He stood in silence as painted warriors left the village in a single line. After they had gone and we were alone within the confines of the lodge he had built himself, he would break down in tears. He told me that at night he kept seeing the young boy he held in his arms as Doublehead hacked him to a pulp. The image haunted him. I, sharing his sorrow, cried with him, wiping the sweat from his troubled brow.

I knew something had gone out of him after his return. He still had the heart of a warrior, but his gaze was drawn to the destruction all around us — the burned lodges and fields of our friends and clansmen, the fresh graves of our mothers, elders, and chiefs, the half graves of children. About then, Ridge began spending his free time alone on the mountains, where he said the rainbows touched his shoulder, looking far in the distance, seeking.

The wars ended at Etowah in the summer of the year the whites call 1794. General

Sevier came with seven hundred soldiers and annihilated our warriors and left what remained of our homes cloaked in ashes. The men who were not slain were flogged unmercifully. Almost all of the Cherokee chiefs gathered at the Tellico blockhouse to beg for peace. The People's delegation met with Great Father Washington himself, and appended their marks to the talking leaves. The Cherokee were humiliated, but at least with the treaty we could live, as Little Turkey said, so that we might have gray hairs on our heads.

At dawn the very next morning, I went to the river with my elder brother, and together we bathed in the cool currents. He spent the balance of that day praying alone in the woods. And then, under the light of the harvest moon, he buried his tomahawk and pistols in the same fields where we grew our corn, beans, and melons. Near our father's grave, he built a great fire and sacrificed to Ancient Red the clothes he'd worn on the war trace. Together, we watched them burn. And then he rose and took me by the hand and said, "Come, Watie. We're done with all that."

The next day we rose early and tended to our fields. The harvest was good that year. We had to build new cribs to store our corn. Ripe pumpkins and full baskets of beans bulged in the corners of our lodge. Combs full of rich honey stood in fat jars beside them. Fresh venison hams were cured over hickory coals. We stitched feather beds from empty sacks of seed and crawled beneath soft, warm trade blankets to sleep on cool nights. I was tired from all the work, but my stomach was always full.

"Look at us, Ridge," I said. "Wouldn't our parents be proud? We're orphans, but we have plenty."

"Next year we'll have more," he said.

As always, I believed him. I have never heard my brother speak a lie. He was our sun in those years. Others took notice of his resourcefulness and wisdom, as well. The elders and *adawehis* sat and smoked and said that the Man Who Walks the Mountaintops would rise among us, and I, Oo-watie, the Ancient One, believed that, too.

Ridge saw that our sister spent much time with our aunts. "What can I teach a young girl?" he said. I knew our mother would be pleased with the way Ridge raised her. He made sure I hunted with him and my uncles and sent me to the merchants to trade our surplus grains, so that I, too, would be educated in the ways of our world. He gave everyone what he felt they needed. Yet he deprived himself of redemption after the way he'd left things with our father.

I tried my best to console him whenever I saw the sadness creep into his eyes, saying that their lives had followed a similar path.

Agan'stat' had been young once, I told him. He of all people would've understood why his son had answered the warrior's call. I reminded my brother that Agan'stat' loved him. Had Father lived, he would have forgiven him. But when I spoke of any of this to Ridge, he abruptly cut me off.

"I made my choice," Ridge said. "It's my burden to live with it. I listened to Agan'stat's detractors behind his back and mocked him to his face. He offered me wisdom and I called him a fool. He gave me love and I hated him for it. When my family needed me I was out destroying the lives of innocent people. I was not even here to comfort him in his last illness. I was not given the opportunity to tell him that everything happened as he predicted it would. I can't tell him how sorry I am or ask for his forgiveness. The grave's forever, Watie. There's no way back."

Regardless of his accomplishments, his guilt always gnawed away at him. He wanted to suffer with the same passion that he'd run the war trace. Once he gave himself to his grief, there was no turning his head. I knew then that peace had come to all the Cherokee but the one I loved most.

We came home from hunting one afternoon, a fat doe hanging from a pole suspended on our shoulders. Ridge was taller than I, and I griped about carrying most of the deer's weight. I could tell my brother was about to shove a pinecone down my ungrateful throat when we heard a woman wailing in the woods above us. We dropped the pole where we stood and I followed Ridge up the hillside.

We came to a young woman cradling three small, dirty-faced children in her arms. She scooted away in fear as Ridge reached out to soothe her.

"Don't be afraid," Ridge said. "We can help you."

"There's nothing you can do," she said. "I've got no husband and no family. My children and I will waste away."

"What's happened?" Ridge asked. There was no war going on that we knew about.

"My husband accidentally killed his friend while they were hunting," she said. "His kin came to our home last night to claim their right under the Blood Law. Knowing that we couldn't survive without him, my husband fought them. In the scuffle that followed, our house was burned to the ground. They dragged him out into the woods and shot him anyway." Ridge untied the scarf around his head and handed it to her to wipe the tears from her face. "I didn't even have the strength left to bury him. Nor could I bring myself to drown my children. All we can do is sit here and wait for death to take us."

Ridge knelt down beside her and picked

the youngest child out of her arms. He handed him to me and reached for another.

"Do you see down there?" he said, pointing at the deer. "I've got plenty of meat for all of us. Near my home, I have rich fields. You are all welcome to be my guests until your grief passes. After that, we'll see about building you a new lodge."

"I couldn't," she said, sobbing. "That's too much for me to ask of a stranger."

"You didn't ask," Ridge said. "I offered. Besides, you'd be doing me a favor. There's a man I wronged. He's gone now and I've lost the chance to make things right between us. Perhaps if you'd allow me to help you with your troubles, I could help myself by making peace with him. Think of it as a trade."

He held his hand out to her. "What's your name?" she asked, rising.

Ridge told her as he wiped the tears from her eyes. They walked together down the hill. He made a fire near the trail and we grilled the doe's backstraps on green hickory spikes. I've never seen children inhale meat like those starving kids. I don't think I'd ever seen my brother more content watching them do it.

"I hate the Blood Law," Ridge told me when we went to dig her husband's grave. "It makes no sense to kill innocent people for an accident. Look what it's done to that young woman."

"It's the ancient way," I reminded him. "We

shouldn't question it."

"The ancient way is wrong," he said. "I'll question it from now on."

We spent the next week building a lodge for that woman and her children. Whenever we returned from the hunt, Ridge delivered fresh meat to her door. When we harvested our crops, Ridge laid full baskets of squash and beans at her feet. Better yet, when eligible young warriors sought out Ridge to rekindle their bond to one another, my brother made sure they accompanied him on his visits to the family who had come to depend on him. Soon she tied the blanket with one of them and moved away. But before she left to begin her new life, however, she gave him a hand-beaded sash as a token of her gratitude. It was the finest in our village. Ridge wore it proudly wherever he went, but I never heard him boast to another person how he'd come by it. My brother was like that. He'd do some great, noble thing and never mention it to another soul. I think he inherited his pride from Agan'stat'.

The work never ended. One morning when we were weeding our fields, Sehoya appeared. I remember how the morning breeze lifted the tails of her calico skirt as she waited for him on a hill at the edge of the woods. She had come as far as she could.

I had often begged Sehoya to speak to him, but she said she would come only when

Ridge asked for her. I knew he'd never do it as long as he had to care for us and the other family. So I went to her at the Green Corn Dance. "If you still want him," I said, "come and get him. Otherwise, you run a great risk. Many women orbit around him. Sooner or later he'll reach out to one, and then what good would your pride be to you?"

She said nothing at the time, and I thought their relationship was for some unknown reason hopeless, another casualty perhaps of the wars. But when I saw her standing there that morning, the sun on her golden face, her body slender and her legs long, I knew things would return to normal.

Ridge went after those weeds like he'd once gone after white men, sweat pouring from his face and coating his bare chest and back, and teeth gritted, threatening our corn not to thrive. Finally he looked up at me, standing there leaning on my mallock with a foolish grin on my face.

"Do you think you'll feel like eating this winter?" he said, back to chopping away.

"Everything you bring me," I said. "In fact, I'm hungry now."

"It's going to be a thin year for you, little brother, if you don't get busy."

He looked up again to see if I was working, and, of course, I wasn't.

"Why do you have that stupid look on your face?" he said, and by now he was angry. I nodded toward Sehoya and watched as he turned his head. He couldn't make her out until she stepped from the shadows. Once he did, he instantly threw down his mallock and ran toward her, mashing every melon in his path between her and him. I followed him to share in his joy. He slowed to a walk as he neared her, uncertain as to how she'd react. But then she opened her arms to him and he lifted her over his head.

"I'm sorry," I heard him say. "I was buried under a mountain of grief. I didn't know what to say to you, and after I'd waited so long I didn't think you'd care what I said. I'm so, so sorry." The tears streamed down his cheeks. In one instant, she released him from his guilt. I hope I find a woman someday who loves me like that.

"Speak of it no more," she said, her palms pressed against his face. "We've wasted enough time. We'll just start over like none of this happened."

He glanced over his shoulder at me and his expression withered. He sat her down and turned his back on her. She cocked her head and looked at me for answers. I had no idea what he was thinking.

"I'm still not free, Sehoya," he said. He pointed at me. "I'm responsible for him and my sister. To pursue my own happiness is to deny theirs. I won't take a wife until I see them married."

I crushed a dirt clod in my fist and flung it at him.

"Do you know how that makes me feel?" I shouted at him.

"You're just a thoughtless kid," he said. "I know what my obligations are to my family. I stood over Agan'stat' and Etsi's grave and promised them I would do everything I could to raise you right. I'll keep my word regardless of what it costs me."

He turned back to Sehoya and wiped the tears from her face. "I'm sorry," he said. "My heart sings to see you but you shouldn't have come. I can't marry for four more winters. You must choose another."

I don't think Sehoya was as angry as she was heartbroken. She turned around in silence and walked back down the trail with her eyes to the ground.

"Agan'stat' was right," I told him. "You're a stubborn fool."

"Shut up and get busy," he said.

I threw my mallock at his feet. "No," I said. "I don't want to be around you today."

I stormed off, leaving him to his labors, and caught up with Sehoya. I begged her not to give up on him. I was sure he'd change his mind.

"I don't know what gets into him," I told her.

"I do," she said. "And I don't ever want it to get out. In a day or two, after he calms

126

down, tell him I'll wait for him. He made a promise to his parents and I'd never ask him to break it. But he made a promise to me, too, and I won't release him from that one, either. You tell him that for me, won't you, Oo-watie?"

I assured her I would do as she asked. Two nights later, as I lay beside my brother waiting for sleep to take us, I made good on my word. He didn't say a thing in response and I was troubled. But in the moonlight I saw the glint of his teeth and I knew that in spite of every obstacle he'd laid between himself and happiness, he'd one day lead Sehoya to his lodge.

I'd help him build it.

CHAPTER EIGHT

The Ridge cursed his cow-hocked, pin-eared, broom-tailed pony along with every other dingy possession he owned. The nag's yellow molars were worn smooth, its back slumped low, and its pale cream color and mangy coat made it appear plagued — which it was. What little silver landed in Ridge's hands went for seed and used farm equipment for his family's growing fields, and a few manufactured items like iron kettles, fustian fabric for winter shirts and kersey worsted for blankets, DuPont gunpowder, bullet molds, and lead stock for his free days on the hunt. In the wars with the Americans, he'd won fine horses. In peace, he was stuck with this one.

As bad as his horse looked, Ridge knew his own appearance fared worse. His clothes were old, torn, and dingy from fieldwork. Moss and river sand would not scrub the grit from his calluses. He'd never owned cloth fine enough for a turban, which his curly locks would defy anyway. The small silver medal and gorget he'd inherited from Agan'stat' were scratched and tarnished — meager adornments, indeed. His appearance was wretched, and there was nothing he could do about it. Nor could he do anything about the elders of Pine Log choosing him to represent them at the tribal council at Oost-anaula.

Ridge had only twenty-five winters behind him, and was poor as a wood rat besides. Yet he'd given his word to the elders that he would do his best. Now, as he tethered the slack-jawed, wall-eyed cob to a hickory sapling with cracked leather reins before the curious gaze of wealthy, graceful warriors, elders, and chiefs, Ridge lost his resolve. He looked down at his miserable attire and butted his forehead against the hickory in shame. When the callers cried, "All who have a purpose here enter now," Ridge could delay no longer. He shook the rain off his coat and plodded toward the seven-sided council lodge, representative of the Nation's seven clans.

He'd just ducked his head to cross beneath the threshold when three young mixed-bloods barred his way. He didn't know them, but he knew who they were — moneyed Cherokee who knew enough of the white world to mimic their grand estates, complete with grand fields and slaves to work them. Fine silver rings hanging from their ears, silk turbans wrapped tightly around their close-cropped heads. Fast risers in fast times with arrogance the foremost flaw among many.

"This is the National Council, bumpkin," one of them said. "Have you no respect?"

"I am Kah-nung-da-tla-geh," Ridge said. "Sent here by my village."

"For what? To gather firewood?"

"To speak for Pine Log."

"Not dressed like that, you won't. Ride home if that horse will live long enough and tell your elders to send a man of property to speak for them."

Ridge struggled to remain calm, though his temper simmered. He knew what he looked like, but that had nothing to do with what he was. And since when was it a crime for a workingman to be poor? He'd been away at the wars while these few mixed-bloods of the merchant class grew wealthy. Most Cherokee reaped corn while they acquired silver. Had they bothered to inquire before they'd judged him, Ridge would have informed them that he had come of age as an orphan, and still others ate from his hand. Could any of these peacocks have managed as well under the same circumstances?

Ridge stared at uncaring eyes. He was certain they meant business. His face flushed. His temples throbbed. Had he been two winters younger, he would have entered by virtue of a well-placed war club against their arrogant heads. But the war trace had depleted his tolerance for violence, and he was no chief. Nor was he fit to be an elder, as he had repeatedly explained to the council at Pine Log. Ridge sighed to vent his humiliation and spun on his heel.

Little Turkey caught his arm and jerked Ridge tightly against his chest as a father would do to a long-absent son.

"Come inside, Ridge Walker," the principal chief said, magnificent in his hunting breeches and calico shirt. Silver rings hung from his earlobes, and a silver medallion hung from his neck. Little Turkey possessed power like sunlight. One scowl from him dissolved the young councilmen's resistance. "This house is proud to have you among us."

Little Turkey continued to frown at the errant elders. The Cherokee considered it rude to stare a man in the face, and these boys clearly didn't want to offend. "This is the warrior Man Who Walks the Mountaintops," Little Turkey said. "Grandson of my beloved friend, Ada-gal'kala. He's known to me and many others as a man of courage and integrity. Welcome him as you would me."

"They're all talk," Doublehead said. The war chief slumped in his seat in the deer clan section, his head resting against the white wall, his disinterested gaze fixed on the ceiling. "That's all we do here." He yawned, and then addressed the young mixed-bloods. "Let

131

him in or perhaps we'll need to do something else today."

With some reluctance, the stunned young councilmen took Ridge's hand with a limp squeeze. Others greeted him warmly as Little Turkey hustled him inside, and introduced him to the ani-kawi clan mother, who hugged him as if she'd given him birth herself, then offered him a place of honor directly behind her with the oldest and wisest of the deer clan. Ridge nodded to Doublehead but did not take his hand.

Once inside, Ridge took in the Oostanaula council house, one of the few built in the ancient seven-sided scheme — one for each clan — that had escaped destruction in the wars. Bleachers lined the entire structure, with each clan sitting along one specific side. Below them was a bench for the elders, and in front of that, a single stool for the clan mother, of which there was only one to represent her extended family. Ridge held his palms out toward the fire of seven sacred woods that roared directly in front of three white high-backed chairs that by custom faced east. Little Turkey sat between the speaker and his assistant principal chief. The sacrificial post where a captive would be tied was still standing, as were the tethers to bind him in place until the clan mothers, who always had the last word in any discussion, pronounced his fate.

This hallowed structure had been the home of wisdom and communal reason. For Ridge to stand under the same roof as all the great chiefs and heroes of his youth was to bear witness to his living heritage and tradition — a dip in the river that ran from the dark, forgotten times to where the sun stood this very day. He had never anticipated that such opportunity would come his way when he was so young. Ridge couldn't stop the smile that emerged on his face. He forgot all about his broken-down horse.

"Sit quietly and learn," Little Turkey whispered in his ear. "Your time will come." The principal chief took a step or two and paused, summoning Ridge with his index finger. Ridge leaned close and turned his ear to Little Turkey. "I have some things that will fit you," he said. "Come by my lodge when we're through here."

"I will," Ridge said. "And I'm grateful. But we'll have to hurry. I have some hunting to do."

"Hunting?" Little Turkey said. "There's plenty of meat in my smoke house if you're hungry."

"Your meat won't do," Ridge said.

After the meeting, he followed the principal chief to his home, making small talk as they went. Once they'd reached Little Turkey's lodge, Ridge refused his invitation to come inside. He waited until the principal chief emerged with a shirt finer than any Ridge had ever owned. He folded it neatly and stuck it in his saddlebags and left Little Turkey standing there wondering while Ridge rode into the woods with his long rifle resting across his thighs. An hour before sunset he had what he needed in his sights.

Like many Cherokee, Sehoya's family had relocated south in the wars, residing in a small village not far from Oostanaula. Family and political affairs had kept Ridge away from Sehoya more often than he would've liked. Despite their promises to one another, they had once again drifted apart.

In a practical sense, Ridge told himself that the distance between him and Sehoya was the principal cause for their estrangement. But it occurred to him that perhaps there were other factors as well. Sehoya had grown up to become a beautiful young woman, and Ridge could not have been the only young Cherokee man to notice. He agonized over many sleepless nights that he might lose Sehoya to another. With the success of his fields and his new position at council, together with the fact that he felt his brother was now old enough to accept greater responsibility for his own life and that his sister had already married, Ridge felt the time had come for some plain talk with Sehoya and her family.

He wiped the blood from the nose of the freshly killed doe and washed it clean with river water. The deer would make a fine meal for five families. He stood at the threshold of Sehoya's parents' lodge, leaning against that shameful pale horse. He waited so long, he felt certain his feet had sprouted roots. Finally the door opened.

"Si-yo'. Dto-hi'-tsu?" Ridge said in greeting, discovering his mouth was dry as dust.

"I'm fine," Sehoya's mother said crisply. Ridge smiled and gestured proudly to the deer that proved he was a great provider, in case these people had not already heard it elsewhere. The woman stared vacantly at it, and then finally at him. "So you've finally come, have you?" she said. "Sehoya always said you would, but we were all beginning to wonder."

She turned back in to the house and called her sons. They appeared and, with one point of their mother's finger, eagerly dragged the deer off his horse and hauled it to the meat rack. Without another word, they began to work the hide from its flesh with quick strokes. Ridge watched the torchlight reflect off their busy blades when he heard Sehoya's mother slam the door.

Ridge waited, perplexed, swatting at gnats, listening to the muffled voices within.

"Who?" he heard the father ask. "Oh, him. Sehoya's still seeing others, isn't she?"

"I believe her heart has chosen this one," her mother said. Ridge cringed at her apologetic tone.

"Yes, but I was hoping that her mind might get involved."

"Ssshhh," she hissed. "He's waiting outside."

"So he is," the man said. Ridge started when the door flew open, and he met a discerning glance. He was glad that at least he was wearing Little Turkey's shirt, even though the cut was a little small for Ridge. There was a fresh bloodstain or two, as Ridge had gotten a little careless hauling the deer. But no one could deny the shirt's quality. "Go away, Ridge Walker," he said. "Such a big decision doesn't happen as quickly as you'd like."

"Oh," Ridge said just before the door slammed in his face. What was quick about it? he wondered. He'd waited ten winters. He'd won honors. He'd met all of his family obligations. The deer was fat. And though one didn't buy a wife, it was wise to offer gifts when coming to ask for her hand. Ridge had promised Sehoya long ago that he would abide by their traditions, and this was the result? Before Ridge could turn away, the door opened again.

"Thanks for the deer," Sehoya's father said, shutting it again. The wreath of white feathers, symbolizing a happy, healthy home, teetered slightly.

"I was hoping we could talk," Ridge said to

weathered planks, steadying the wreath with his hand.

"Now's no good," her father said from inside the lodge.

Ridge led his horse away in confused silence toward the river, desiring to end a troubling day with his prayers. He dragged a stick alongside him as he rode, making his trail easy to follow should anyone wish to find him, not really certain if anyone would. The journey proved a lonely ride.

Fresh from the river, Ridge perched on its edge, tossing pebbles while he waited for the moon to rise. He'd say the last of his prayers and return home to an empty lodge. His sister had her own home now. Oo-watie was three weeks out with a hunting party up north. Ridge's prospects for beginning his own family didn't seem all that promising, especially if Sehoya wasn't strong enough to make her father aware of her desires. It was also possible that the problem lay elsewhere. Perhaps her coals had grown cool and her parents' rudeness to him was by her design.

Nevertheless, he planned to confront her about her intentions just as soon as he caught her apart from her family. If she no longer wanted him, she'd have to tell him herself. She owed him that much after taunting him for a lifetime. He was about to kick at the root of a defenseless mountain laurel when he saw Sehoya's younger sister ambling down the path toward him, poking at tufts of weeds with a stick.

"Will you come to our house for a late dinner this evening?" she asked. She was a bright-faced child, as sweet as her sister.

"What are you having?" Ridge asked, recovering his dignity. "I'm a rich man with plenty to eat."

"No, you're not," she said, giggling. "And we're having fresh venison."

Ridge clapped his hands. "Yuh!" he cried in joy. "Success!"

"Not so fast," the girl said. "My father said to tell you there's another stream to cross before my sister is yours."

"Isn't there always?" Ridge said, shoving her along. "Tell your father the Ridge is a strong swimmer."

Two weeks later, Ridge found himself sitting with Sehoya beside a roaring fire, anxious to get past this one last hitch. He had not been allowed to see Sehoya after their short family dinner until the moon phase was right for the conjurer's reading.

Ridge observed the *adawehis*'s strange ceremony. This conjurer prayed to the Provider for wisdom and insight, tossed pinches of herbs and tobacco dust upon the vapors, and then clasped each of their hands in his as his eyes closed. Everything fell silent save the rush of hungry flames. Ridge fidgeted. No blessing, no marriage.

Suddenly the old man let go of their hands and faced Sehoya's mother.

"All signs are good."

Ridge beamed like a full moon upon first rising.

"Let them join blankets after the harvest-time."

The old man took Sehoya by the arm. "Make children with this man," he said with authority. "There's greatness in your shared blood."

Ridge whispered in Sehoya's ear. "I promised to abide by the conjurer's decision," he said.

She slapped his eager hand. "After the harvest," her father said sternly. Ridge wanted to ask him what the difference was between now and a few weeks later. Had they not waited long enough? And her father was mistaken if he thought he could continue to look down his nose at him. Ridge was about to declare that he'd run the war trace for too long to be treated like a child when his new father-in-law embraced him warmly.

"Welcome to our family," he said, smiling. "If Sehoya loves you, so do we. We're so proud to have you among us."

Ridge's anger left him with his next breath. "I'll live for her," he said.

"I know you will," his father-in-law said. "But you can't live *with* her until *after* the harvest."

"Of course," Ridge said, smiling at Sehoya. "I wouldn't have it any other way."

Marriage balanced Ridge. All sense of urgency left him. He built Sehoya's lodge to the best of his ability and tended her fields as he'd once done with his mother. His domestic labors complete and crops rising, he left on daily sojourns to walk the mountaintops again, thinking about his people, learning to look far ahead as Waesa had charged him. As the voice of Pine Log, he found most of his deliberations centered on the Nation's affairs. It was good, also, that he'd acquired patience, a quality a man who rode a sorry horse to council meetings and everywhere else was forced to learn. The Ridge sat listening at this latest gathering of chiefs and elders, wearing Little Turkey's shirt that he'd boiled for at least an hour and the same rear-laced breeches he'd worn the year before. Outside, tied to that same hickory sprig, grazed the same ugly horse, no doubt gumming away on the closest fodder. Some old chief droned on about a return to the old ways, and the wisdom of the ancients. Ridge had already learned that most council sessions closed in this predictable manner to no avail, but the old bull dragged on. He took no notice of the elders nodding off or the muffled yawns of the young men. No Cherokee of breeding would dare interrupt an elder while he spoke.

Ridge had said nothing for the entire gathering, as Little Turkey had suggested the year before. But for some time he'd been troubled by one of the ancient laws, and when the old man finally shut his mouth and the entire assembly started to empty out of the council, Ridge rose.

"While the Ridge agrees with his uncle about the wisdom of the ancient code," he said, "let this house remember that even then the law was a living thing, growing as circumstances dictated. The whites claim their laws were brought to them by a prophet set forth in stone by the Great Provider. Of course, they don't abide by them, so the source failed to make an impression."

Ridge paused to allow for their laughter.

"The Cherokee are not so rigid," he said. "We alter our law as we see fit. The Ridge believes one of the ancient codes has outlived its usefulness."

"Which one would that be?" Leaper asked. Little Turkey resumed his seat out of interest, motioning for the others to do likewise.

"If a man should meet an accidental death," Ridge said, "the law allows his relatives to kill the one responsible. If a murderer flees the Nation and the punishment of this council, his relative dies in his place. These laws claim innocents for reasons that no longer make sense. Cherokee blood is precious, and we have lost so many to the wars and diseases brought upon us by the whites. Let this council, in its wisdom, set aside the killing of our own people. Forgive your offender as if his blood ran in your veins."

Silence gave way to murmuring. Who among the elders could not agree that their losses had been great? Why did the old laws demand innocent blood?

"We see your point, Ridge Walker," said Dawnee, clan mother of the anisahoni, the blue people. "But in these days of rapid change, the Cherokee are reluctant to set aside more of the old ways."

"They will if their chiefs pledge themselves to it," Ridge said, "and make an outlaw out of any who would kill an innocent man. Who, in these times of change, would risk being shunned by his own people?"

"And who will enforce it when a warrior tests a chief?" one of the young men asked to mock him.

"I will," Ridge said. "I've been tested by young warriors before and still I stand here."

Again the old men laughed and the young elder, flushed with embarrassment, sank to his seat. After a moment's deliberation Dawnee nodded, as did Little Turkey and the other chiefs.

"What say the other clan mothers?" Little Turkey asked.

They put their heads together near the fire. Soon they disbanded and resumed their seats.

"What the Ridge says is good," said Naki, clan mother to the ani-tsisqua, the bird clan. "Enough killing."

"So be it," Little Turkey said, taking Ridge by the hand. "This council agrees to set the Blood Law aside. Send the criers out to every village and make it known. And let those who would oppose the measure know they will come face to face with our brother, the Ridge."

Ridge was adjusting his tack on the swayback when Little Turkey and a few others walked out to him. "It's true what they say," he said. "You have the gift of leadership."

"Thank you, my uncles," Ridge said.

"Use it wisely, won't you?" Little Turkey said.

■ ■ ■ ■

Book Two:
The New and
Dangerous Path

1801-1814

■ ■ ■ ■

CHAPTER NINE

The years had smiled at him. Like a few other progressive Cherokee, Ridge had begun to borrow from the Americans whichever of their ambitious methods he felt best served his needs. Ridge opened his eyes, absorbing all. From traders, he learned the power of gold — that money was a living thing, a servant to do his bidding. From large farmers, he learned the potential of cleared fields and improved lands. From the half-breeds, he learned to generate income from river ferries, timber, and toll roads, and with his proceeds, he learned to buy slaves as he could afford them to work his holdings.

The Cherokee had always kept captives to toil for them. The humiliation of such servitude was one reason no courageous warrior would allow himself to be taken alive in battle. Captured enemy women and children were raised as slaves. Some were ultimately adopted by the Cherokee. Some were traded back to their tribes. Some were never released from slavery until the grave. Though most Cherokee neither kept slaves nor aspired to, ancient tradition generally accepted the practice. When Ridge experimented with the plantation lifestyle practiced by his Anglo neighbors in Virginia, the Carolinas, and Georgia, he experimented also with its accepted form of labor, and no Cherokee he knew thought twice about it.

The concept of managing land for profit was entirely alien to him; however, he could not deny the sense of accomplishment and contentment that emerged as a direct result. For a man who had known hunger, it felt good to reap plenty. He beamed over recently cleared patches of pumpkin, squash, muskmelons, sweet potatoes, cabbages, and beans. Stalks of green corn, speckled with morning dew, thrived in the dark earth of the larger fields. The morning mist settled at the edge of the woods that surrounded him. An hour more and the sunlight would burn it away.

Already his seven Negro slaves sang on their way to attend the peach and apple saplings. The boy, Pleasant, had already seen to milking the cows and was now churning the rich cream into butter. Later that afternoon, Ridge would slaughter one of the hogs, fat on river bottom acorns and walnuts, and hang its hocks over hickory coals in the smokehouse.

Ridge surveyed his holdings, proudest of the Anglo-style split-log home and stone chimney he had built for Sehoya, warmed by the knowledge that he had prospered by walking the new path. Hunting grounds within the Nation were communal. The fields he worked belonged to him and Sehoya, and he stood proud over what they had accomplished together.

Ridge caught the occasional barb from those who felt tradition doled out only as much land as one needed to feed his family. But the agents and missionaries among them had long urged the Cherokee to abandon their towns and villages and spread out to new fields to raise crops for profit. The Great American Father Washington had promised a place in his new confederacy for all his red children who would surrender the hunt for the plow. Washington reached out to the Cherokee, and Ridge, astounded by the Great Father's generosity toward those his nation had crushed under their heel, was among the first to take his hand. Ridge discovered that he had it within him to farm like white men, especially if the practice still allowed him to live like a Cherokee with his nation intact. The Ani-yunwi-ya were *allied* with the Americans, not ruled by them, at least not within the borders left to them forever by the treaties. And all Ridge had to do was farm. Agan'stat' had believed there was a way to live in peace with the white man. Ridge believed he had found it.

Seeking suitable land for this purpose, Ridge had brought Sehoya to the Oothcaloga Valley, which he shared with the mixed-blood chief William Hicks, who read English books, and two cousins, Black Wat and Red Wat Adair, whom Ridge had known from the days of war. Together they were trying the white man's trail, especially if the journey would put them on par with the whites, as Washington's first Indian policy promised.

In one generation, the Cherokee would leave savagery behind and stand beside the Americans as equals. Ridge saw the new path opening to him, just as Waesa had promised he would when he was a boy. Before long, Ridge hoped his brother, Oo-watie, would follow him to this place of abundance, where tangled, impenetrable slopes were giving way to rich fields and green pastures, where darkness was surrendering to light.

Ridge heard the jostling buckboards and jingling tack of an approaching wagon. Soon he could see the odd black robes flapping in the warm summer breeze. Ridge couldn't understand why any man would choose to wear such an absurd outfit. How could one stalk a deer in even the slightest breeze with all that commotion of cloth? A brush against the first brier and he'd be hopelessly entangled. How could such impractical people bring hope to the Cherokee? The Moravian missionary tugged back the reins and stalled in front of Ridge's house.

"A most admirable structure," the young priest pronounced with his thick tongue. The missionaries butchered the Cherokee language, but at least they had bothered to learn it. This fact swayed the divided council, who just this season, the American year of 1801, had agreed to allow the Moravians to build a mission in the Nation. For Ridge, the decision was yet another victory, another step closer to winning his country without war.

The black robes selected Spring Place, where three streams bled from the limestone bluffs, a league or so east from the Conasauga River and only a day's travel north from Oostanaula, home of the National Council. The Moravians spoke of bringing a new religion to the Cherokee. Their primary purpose, as Little Turkey and the other wary chiefs had made quite clear, was to instruct the Cherokee in the language of the talking leaves. The mission was to be considered a trial.

"Did you bring it, my friend?" Ridge asked in Cherokee.

"I did," he said, patting the musty oilcloth that covered his load. "But first I'd like to take this opportunity to thank you for your grain and hogs, and also for the use of your slaves."

"Yes, yes," Ridge said. He was happy to support the missions, at least up until the time they could support themselves. He'd soon reap crops enough to replace that which he'd given away, but if the mission succeeded, he felt the Cherokee would reap much more. Understanding the white man's books was the key to understanding the white man. It wasn't enough that Chief Hicks and a few other mixed-bloods could read. When their Great Father Washington walked among the Cherokee, he would be delighted to find their children's noses pointed at open books. Ridge wanted the Great Father to know that the Cherokee had taken him at his word, and were faithful to their part of the bargain.

"Sehoya!" Ridge called. "Come and see your new, uh, thing." Sehoya appeared, rubbing her stomach. Very soon, the time for her birthing would come. Ridge proudly yanked the canvas free of the wagon.

"It's yours, my wife."

Sehoya screwed up her face. "What's that contraption?"

"A spinning wheel and a loom," he said with a radiant smile. "The finest in all the Nation."

"What's it for?"

He nodded to the missionary and took Sehoya by the hand. Together they went to the fields, where Ridge yanked a green bulb free. He broke it open, felt the moist whiteness in his fingers as he pressed the bulb into his wife's hand. "For this," he said. "When it blooms, we make our own cloth. And the cloth will be worth more than a full year's hunting."

Sehoya looked puzzled.

"Don't worry, woman," Ridge continued. "If you'll only listen to this bird's prattle, he'll teach you how to use it. Then it'll be your task to teach others."

Sehoya's fingers reluctantly explored the machine's levers, pedals, and wheels, when Ridge noticed that the Negroes were arguing with some Cherokee who had emerged from the thickets. He left his wife with the missionary, who had already begun her instruction. Ridge mounted his horse and rode out to see what the trouble was. A smile came to his face as he recognized an old friend.

"Will you not share with us, Ridge Walker?" White Path asked. Ridge knew none of the people accompanying his old comrade, but he saw that they were full-bloods from the remote mountains, poor and hungry, and confused and disgruntled about all the changes being forced upon them, just as his own father had been.

"If you'll learn with me," he said, and they all nodded politely, except White Path, who looked around him with a sneer.

"What's all this about?" he said.

"It's a farm," Ridge said.

"For one man?"

"For many."

"Madness," White Path said. "You'll never eat all this before it rots."

"I intend to trade it," Ridge said.

White Path snorted. "To whom? Me?"

"To the whites, my friend. As always, you're welcome to take what you need. My only request is that you'll consider growing your own crops in such abundance."

"We're grateful for what food you can spare," White Path said, "but we Cherokee of Ellijay don't care to live like white people."

"Neither do I," Ridge said. "I only want to eat like them. Why not move from the towns and try your hand at this? There is plenty of land. Raise your crops and cattle, plant your fruit trees, and hunger no more. Before you," he said, spreading his arms to his burgeoning fields, "is a better way."

"We thank you for your vegetables," White Path said, "but we don't like your advice. We'll take only a little for our journey home to Ellijay, where the Cherokee are content to live like Cherokee." He pointed down the length of Ridge's fields. "Is this what we fought for, Ridge? So that you could fill your purse along with your stomach?"

Ridge, incredulous, blinked his eyes. "You insult me, White Path, while you eat from my hand?"

"Oh, yes," White Path answered, "because you take from ours. The whites know it takes less land to live as the Ridge wishes. No need to hunt, no need for hunting grounds. We full-bloods may be ignorant, but we aren't blind. Year by year, the chiefs sell more land to the Americans so that they grow fat while we go hungry. Shame on you and all your kind. And I say this to you, Ridge Walker: All that you grow here this year, and in all the seasons that follow, will never stem the white man's hunger for our country."

"What chief sells land for his own profit?" Ridge asked. He felt his jaw tighten.

"Doublehead's done it three times," White Path said. "He houses his fine horses while we sleep hungry under the rain. Before your corn ripens, he'll do it a fourth time for more slaves and coin sacks. We elevated this so-called chief to speaker of the Nation and the first thing he does is whisper into the Americans' ears. Little Turkey is too old and weak to stop him. Doublehead will sell every hill and valley, and then where will the Cherokee go?"

"Take what you want," Ridge said crisply, his thoughts drawn from the abundance of his fields to Doublehead's alleged abuse of power. "You're welcome to stay as my guest for as long as you like. We have much to talk about."

"We'll only argue, Ridge," White Path said, picking a cantaloupe from the vine. "You mixed-bloods see the world differently."

Ridge sighed and shook his head. "After all

we've been through together, I would've hoped that my blood no longer made a difference."

"Whose fault is that?" White Path answered, again spreading his arm across Ridge's holdings. "It's not what you are, my brother. It's what you do."

"I don't want to get into this right now," Ridge said. "I've got this Doublehead matter to look into. If he's betrayed us, the council will hear of it."

"Go then," White Path said. "The council will soon see my dark face, too."

"One more thing before we part," Ridge said.

"And what would that be?"

"That cantaloupe isn't ripe, you fool. Pick another that's more golden." Ridge pointed to a melon near him as a better choice and wheeled his reins without another word. Agitated, he walked his horse back to Sehoya, who was still fumbling with the contraption. She slapped away the Moravian's helping hand whenever it pestered her. When Ridge passed her, he whipped the reins across the horse's flank until the beast was at full gallop. Ridge had to learn whether Doublehead persisted in illegal cessions of tribal land. Always Doublehead! Find trouble and discontent, and he could bet Doublehead had a hand in it. In the struggle to merge old and new, Ridge and the other progressive chiefs walked in the shadows of their people's suspicions. Doublehead's greed tarnished their best efforts, eroding the people's faith in their leadership at the crucial moment when they must trust it most.

"Ridge!" Sehoya yelled. He rode on. Ridge had warned the National Council at the time they had passed the laws forbidding individual sale of land that the measures needed teeth to have import. If Doublehead had truly defied them, Ridge had grounds for recommending that the law be amended with the harshest imaginable punishment. If it were true that Doublehead had betrayed his people to fatten his purse, Ridge swore that his cousin would be the first bitten.

"Ridge!" Sehoya called again. He pulled up the reins, exhaled, and looked back. Sehoya, hands planted on her hips, stood in the road with her nose lifted. There was no mistaking the anger in her voice. Gone were the days when he could think of his needs first. He walked the horse back to his wife.

"What trouble takes you from me without a word?" she said when he was near enough.

"I fear a chief has strayed, Sehoya. My thought was to confront him about the rumors to see if they are true."

"You stray yourself if you feel you can leave me to manage all this madness without any discussion." She swept her arm across the fields and pastures, across arguing slaves and strange Cherokee, across bawling cattle and barking dogs and a bland, black-robed foreigner. Last, her hand rubbed her ripening stomach. Ridge slumped over his saddle and stared at the dirt. "And to respond in anger doesn't require much thought at all. Is someone's life at stake if you wait a sleep before you act?"

"No," he said. "I don't think so."

"Then come inside and talk to your wife of your troubles. We'll reason together as wise couples should, and then, when you know exactly what you must do and I know exactly where you're going to do it, you can ride out of here as fast as you want."

Ridge slid out of the saddle without another word. Sehoya reached for his hand. "Come, Ridge," she said. "I'll draw you a cool drink from the well and you can tell me what's made you so angry."

"And the loom?" the Moravian asked. "The skill requires instruction, and I've traveled far."

"Forgive me, but my husband needs me now," Sehoya said. "Chief Ridge and I look forward to your visit another day."

CHAPTER TEN

Two children in three winters and still he was not accustomed to the worry that walked along with a parent. Ridge gently pulled the babe from Sehoya's listless arms and handed the child to the midwife. Sehoya had been up most of that night and the one before it, trying to get the feverish infant to nurse. She was exhausted, as was their elder child, Nancy, two winters old but wanting to help her mother. Nancy already displayed Sehoya's qualities — she was warmhearted, loyal, and stubborn as a mule. Ridge would lose both of them to exhaustion, too, if they didn't rest. Ridge fluffed up the tick mattress, covered Sehoya and Nancy with blankets, kissed their foreheads, shooed the meddlesome midwives and conjurer out the door, snuffed out the candles, and tiptoed out of the room, pulling the door closed behind him.

Ridge was used to the tragedy of stillborn children. He'd known many to live for only a few months. But the boy trembling with fever in his arms was his only son, born seven moons ago.

"What can we do?" Ridge whispered in desperation to Dazizi, the greatest *adawehis* of the mountain Cherokee. His appearance at this late hour had cost Ridge plenty. "He'll waste away to nothing."

Dazizi probed the listless child Ridge cradled in his arms. The *adawehis* peered into his eyes, cupped his hand around his head, and pulled back the cloth to inspect the belly button. He pressed his nose close to the boy's mouth to test his breath. Last, he ran a long, trembling finger across the lesions that had formed rough and raw like a turkey's neck on the child's hips and thighs within seven sleeps of the day he was born. Local conjurers came and went, shaking their heads in frustration as the disease grew stronger, until now, when it threatened to snuff out the child's light.

"I've seen this before," Dazizi said. "In my opinion, it's cousin to the coughing sickness that destroys the lungs. The skin lesions are obvious. What you can't see is the swelling of the joints."

Ridge folded the cloth over the child's body and cloaked him under his coat next to his bare chest. "Can you save him?"

"If we can break the fever this very night, Chief Ridge, he has a chance. But . . ." His glance fell to the puncheon floor.

"But what!" Ridge demanded. "Spit it out."

"The pain must be unbearable. I'm also afraid that the damage has been done. Even if we get the fever under control, in cases where it's run its course there's a good chance he'll be lame."

"Paralyzed?" Ridge said, his heart sinking.

"No," Dazizi answered. "I mean crippled. The swelling often damages the hips. If so, the child probably won't be able to run. He may walk, but only with a pronounced limp." The conjurer's voice grew quiet. "You have to understand, Ridge, that while I can control this disease, I can't cure it. There'll be times when the fever and lesions will return with a vengeance and he'll be bedridden for weeks at a time. It's possible that he'll outgrow it and live to adulthood. I've seen this happen. But I have to tell you that in my opinion it's far more likely that sooner or later, the disease will overcome him."

"One worry at a time," Ridge said. "For now, let's treat the fever before he gets any worse."

"If that's what you choose."

"And what would my alternative be?" Ridge said, struggling to govern his rising anger.

Dazizi took a deep breath and swallowed hard. "To leave this one in the mountains for the Great Provider to reclaim."

"No," Ridge answered sharply, as certain as a rifle shot.

"My friend," Dazizi pleaded. "I beg you to

listen to me. This child will never possess your strength. He'll never be a warrior. I've mentioned that he may already be lame, but what I didn't say was that it's possible the fever has left him simple, as well. Are you and Sehoya prepared for such a burden while you're young with your best years ahead of you? Your daughter is a healthy, beautiful child. You'll have others strong and bright like her. You're known to be a man of vision. Consider the longer view and your family's happiness."

Ridge shook his head. "I could never do such a thing."

"You must speak of it to Sehoya. The decision is hers."

"I don't have to ask her to know what she'd say."

"What I'm suggesting is no crime," Dazizi said. "We Cherokee take refuge in our traditions when we're faced with hard choices, and life these days is difficult enough for a healthy child. Invest your love and faith in a sound body and mind."

"It's too late," Ridge said. "I've invested everything I have in this one." He clenched his fist. "The fever will pass. The disease will pass. And the Ridge Walker knows that gone are the days when Cherokee fathers hope for warrior sons."

He passed the baby to the midwife, Naki, and turned back to the conjurer. "Please," he said. "I beg you to do all you can to save him. I know his body's sickly, but when I first laid eyes on him I saw a strength in his spirit that's greater than any disease. This one — the only son of the Man Who Walks the Mountaintops — was born to serve his people."

The *adawehis*'s expression clouded. "You're asking for too much. Didn't you hear my warnings?"

"I heard, but I don't believe. Look how he stares at us. As sick as he is, do you not see the light shining in his eyes? If he lives, he'll be a warrior of the mind."

"All right," Dazizi said, rummaging through his deerskin pouch for his roots and herbs. "Who can argue with that? What good are traditions in these times anyway? You people in these Lower Towns pay them no mind whatsoever."

"If that were true," Ridge said, "then why would I send for you?"

"Because you're as wise as they say, Ridge Walker," Dazizi said as he set out his clay pot and pestle. Then he pulled his crystal from a buckskin pouch and held it next to the candle. He studied the refracted light as if in a trance before he broke free of it and set it down and began his ministrations. Ridge reached for the crystal to examine it, but Dazizi brushed his hand away. "Don't touch that," the old man said. "The stone serves only me. I'll be buried with it."

Ridge apologized for his curiosity and watched Dazizi grind a dried ginseng root, a plant known to the Cherokee as the mountain climber. "For the colic," the *adawehis* said with newfound confidence and ambition. "Sassafras to purify the blood. Black willow for the skin lesions. Goldenseal to calm the stomach. Snakeroot for the chills. Mint to clear the lungs. And last, from my own personal experiments, a touch of elm-berry tea to smooth the elixir's rough edges. That's seven ingredients. We'll give the boy four doses between now and dawn."

"And then what?" Ridge asked.

" 'And then what' is a question for the Great Provider," Dazizi said. "The now is my only concern."

Ridge's expression must have darkened. Dazizi glanced up at him and ceased his preparations. "Worry not, young chief. I'm gifted in my art. Seventeen *adawehis* from all the blood clans walked Turtle Island before me. And know that I'm the most powerful of them all."

Ridge watched him grind the leaves and roots into dust and then sift them into spring-water until the cloudy mixture was nearly the consistency of honey. Then Dazizi let the concoction ooze from his smallest finger into the baby's mouth. An hour passed before he got the full dose down the child's raw, constricted throat. After that, the conjurer patiently spooned water into his mouth, blew tobacco smoke over the lesions, and held his ear to the child's feeble heart.

Ridge paced the puncheon floors as the *adawehis* threw back his head, closed his eyes, and spoke the ancient formula:

"Yuh! Listen! I am a great conjurer. I never fail at anything. I am the greatest of my kind. I surpass all who came before me.

"O Red Woman, you have caused this child to suffer! You have put the intruder under him. Release its grip from his bones. Relief is accomplished. Let it not be for one night alone."

And so Dazizi perpetually chanted, ceasing only to administer another dose of herbs and springwater. Ridge slumped in Sehoya's new pine rocker, mesmerized by the cadence of the words until he drifted off.

He saw himself floating, swept along in a clear mountain stream by cool, powerful currents. He soon tired and thought he would swim to the bank to rest. But the current overpowered him, forcing him instead downstream. Once exhausted, Ridge began to sink into the depths. He waited to reach bottom, when he would thrust upward on his powerful legs. But he sank deeper into dark, bottomless water. When he looked around him, he noticed the river was red with his own blood.

Instead of panicking, he grew calm. With his release, he no longer wanted for breath. He waved his hand, dispersing the crimson clouds that swirled around him, drifting along with the river as it diluted his blood, carrying him farther and farther away from his troubles until his body dissolved and his life force merged inviolate with the power of the river, rushing together headlong into a warm, fathomless, waterless ocean. His blood, his spirit, running on with the currents. Running free. Around him, only expanding space and the distant shimmer of uncountable stars. He felt the unmistakable sense of belonging.

He snapped awake when a baby's cry reached him in the remote regions of sleep. The dream was so wondrous, the vision so stark and reassuring, that he hated to leave that world behind. He shot out of the rocker and rubbed his eyes with the palms of his hands. Through the window that faced east he saw the maroon and golden crescent of the burgeoning dawn. Dazizi radiated even though the infant had soiled one of his better hunting tunics with the first stream of urine Ridge had seen in three sleeps. Ridge sighed in relief.

He slapped the conjurer on the back. "You've done it!"

"Indeed I have," the conjurer said proudly. "I'd say it was a miracle if I weren't so good at my trade." He pointed to the urine trail on his shirt. "This cost extra, make no mistake."

"To the river?" Ridge said, dabbing his finger in the pestle's leavings. He'd had a cough lately. Just this morning there'd been a catch in his throat. If the *adawehis*'s brew could do that for a nearly dead infant, Ridge wondered what it could do for him. The medicine tasted like green walnuts, curdling on his tongue. He preferred the cough.

"Ah, yes," the *adawehis* said. "The river will do the rest." Dazizi knocked his hand aside a second time. "Don't take medicine that's not prepared for you."

Ridge was miffed to learn that the smaller streams around Oothcaloga would not do. Dazizi insisted that only the Coosawattee's current was strong enough to release the fever's grip on the child's body. They scrambled between the heath and hemlocks, around pepperbushes and shrub alders, weaving through stands of chestnuts and white pine, the babe's cries grower louder with every hurried step. Naki could stand it no longer, and she tried to wrestle the child from the conjurer.

"Have we beaten back the fever to let a chill take him?" the midwife complained.

"He's fine," Dazizi said. "Let him scream. It's good for the lungs."

The sun was not yet up when they reached the banks of the Coosawattee, so thick with rosebay rhododendrons that Ridge had to kick a path through for the others to follow. Without hesitation, Dazizi stripped the clothes from the baby's body and waded into the dark river with the child in his arms just as the sun, Une' lanu' hi, the Apportioner, appeared above the stark eastern ridge. To see his naked son crimson with rage in the middle of a river in the arms of an old conjurer who understood the ancient ways brought a calm to Ridge that he had not known since the child arrived in this world. Ridge watched as Dazizi, chanting some prayers that Ridge could not understand, immersed the screaming child again and again into the shimmering currents.

It was obvious to Ridge that Cherokee were born for the water. The baby did not attempt to breathe when dunked under. Nor did he choke when Dazizi brought him up for air. Instead the boy wailed like a mountain cat as the sharp chill of the morning air washed over him. This one — the warrior for a new age — would live. Ridge thanked Une' lanu' hi for his light and Long Man, the river, for his powers of healing and renewal, and, for good measure, he thanked the thousands of spirits who occupied the hills and valleys of his living world. Today it was good to be Cherokee.

Across the Coosawattee, in the narrowing shadows, Ridge caught movement. All other interest stopped until Ridge spied the dark form of a missionary, robes flowing as he heaved with his back to the wind, poking at tufts of weeds with his cane to flush a potential snake. Ridge relaxed his vigil. From the man's girth, clumsy stride, and shocks of coiled gray hair, Ridge reckoned the man to be Father Gambold, the Moravian missionary who ran the school at Spring Place. He'd heard the baby's screams and rushed toward them, although not quickly enough to risk snakebite from the water moccasins that lay coiled under rotten stumps and on overhanging limbs.

"By the grace of God!" Father Gambold yelled in labored Cherokee as soon as he caught his breath. Ridge understood him well enough against the roar of echoes. "Why do you torture that child so!"

Ridge had long since grown tired of explaining the ways of the Cherokee to these somber foreigners. He said nothing and impatiently waved him on. Dazizi was never once distracted from his ranting. Neither was Father Gambold.

"Don't you know he'll catch his death?" the missionary yelled.

"On the contrary," Ridge shouted back. "He's just been freed from it."

Father Gambold shook his head. "Chief Ridge!" he said. "I know you to be a highly intelligent and resourceful man. Do you honestly believe that by allowing this witch to immerse your son in that freezing mountain water that you can protect him from illness?"

"Without a doubt," Ridge said. "I witnessed the same this very night as I've witnessed it a hundred times in the mountains since I was first born."

"Nonsense!" Father Gambold replied.

"Nonsense?" Ridge said. "Let's talk about nonsense. I've heard what you've been teaching about your own religion. It's a running joke in the council. Your own god banished demons from the deranged, restored the dead to life, fed thousands with two loaves of bread and two fishes, and, my favorite myth of all, walked on water in the middle of a storm. You teach all of that as absolutely true to our children even after you admit that you'd seen none of it yourself. Don't speak to the Ridge of nonsense."

Father Gambold shook his head in disappointment. "We have oceans to cross before we can deliver your people from savagery," he said.

"The Cherokee do not cross oceans," Ridge said. "We flow into them, returning to whence we came in a cycle that never ends. What becomes of you strange people only the Provider himself knows."

"I am not dissuaded," Gambold said, "to find the most enlightened among the Cherokee still cloaked in ignorance. God will give me patience."

"The Ridge will give you a green switch

upside your arse if you don't make haste and leave us to reclaim the quiet of dawn. Now is the time of prayer and devotions. Respect it."

Father Gambold sauntered up the trails that had brought him to the river until the thickets absorbed his black robes. Ridge dropped to his knees, spread his arms wide, and sang the chant his favorite uncle had taught him as a boy.

"You gave my son life," he said in benediction. "He will repay you a thousand times over. I, the Man Who Walks the Mountaintops, swear it this day."

Then he waded into the river and took his son from Dazizi's arms. He kissed the boy's forehead before he raised him over his head to face the rising sun, the child's body glowing golden in its warm rays. The cries ceased. Ridge drew his son against his chest, holding him with gentle arms that would carry him home to his crib.

"Come what may," Ridge whispered into the child's ear as he made his way up the bank to fetch soft, dry blankets, "I will always love you."

CHAPTER ELEVEN

The Half-Breed

I am Alexander Saunders, born to walk two roads. My Scottish father saw to it that I was educated in the way of his people. But my mother insisted that I be raised to live and breathe like a Cherokee. Through her blood, I claim my clan affiliation. I am ani-wodi, paint clan. Because I am the son of a Cherokee mother, I am as Cherokee as any fullblood. Our mothers make us who we are.

I was ordered from the mouth of Black Fox himself to do this thing; otherwise I would've had no part of it. When Black Fox had risen to principal chief after Little Turkey's death, he swore to do everything within his power to protect the Nation's land. We all assumed that this included making a boy of his friend, Doublehead, who had become an abusive tyrant.

White Path's accusations about Doublehead's plot to sell tribal tracts proved true and then some. Knowing Doublehead would give them everything they wanted for money and slaves, the American agents sought him out to make agreements that affected all Cherokee. Doublehead was repeatedly warned by the National Council not to enter into any treaty without their consent. Instead of listening to the council's messenger, Doublehead flogged him, saying that as speaker of the Nation he had earned the right to do as he pleased. Other innocent men who stood in his way fell to his hand. Thus, for Black Fox to keep his word, he had no choice but to agree with the council that the time had come to make an example of a chief.

Ridge sat hunched over beside me, cradling his cup of water between nervous hands. I rolled my mug between my palms. It was warm to the touch, as was the stale air around us. Like me, Ridge hated these grog shops and the poison they served, idle surroundings for weak, idle minds. James Vann had been selected for this honor — after all, his sister-in-law had been murdered at this villain's hand. But Vann fell ill and the duty passed to my childhood friend, the Ridge, who accepted with grim silence. I promised the chiefs that I would do all I could to help him.

Some thought Ridge would have some reluctance about all this. Doublehead was his kinsman. We'd seen enough of Doublehead's treachery during the past few years to detest him. But owing to something that had passed between them during the wars with the Americans, I knew Ridge's hatred burned hotter than mine.

Doublehead was a war chief, a powerful and imposing man, and I'd have to admit that we both grew anxious when we heard the night rider approaching. Ridge stared sternly at the other patrons to remind them of our authority and why we had come. There were a few whites who could not have cared less. But the half-breeds and full-bloods nodded in respect. Ridge looked last at me, which I knew was to fortify me to act without hesitation, while he rubbed his medicine pouch that hung below his sash.

Doublehead barged through the tavern doors, kicked a chair out of his way, and sat at the first open table. Always aggressive, violent, and unpredictable, he seemed agitated tonight as well. Doublehead's hand was crudely bandaged with bloodstained cloth. Ridge sank back into his seat, content to bide his time in the shadows and let Doublehead drink his fill of fool's water.

"Whiskey," Doublehead snapped at McIntosh, and without hesitation the innkeeper delivered the bottle. He brought with him a lit candle, and placed it near the chief's face. I suppose he wanted us to be certain of our prey, and also to keep Doublehead's eyes from adjusting to the darkness.

"You have the courage to drink with patriots?" said John Rogers, a white trader who had taken a Cherokee wife. Ridge blinked his eyes and watched, no doubt wondering why Rogers would take it upon himself to anger an already belligerent man.

Doublehead scoffed. "Doublehead drinks with whom he likes."

"You disgrace the nation that bore you," Rogers said.

"And you, yours, white devil," Doublehead said. "You people live by sufferance among us. I've never seen you in council or on the warpath. Hush and interfere no more with me. You have no place among the chiefs."

Ridge wrapped his fingers around the walnut grip of his North and Cheney .69-caliber pistol and pulled the weapon from his hunting pants. He cocked the hammer, rose from the table, and drifted toward the drunken chief. He leaned over Doublehead's table and blew out the candle. "And neither do you," he said.

He shoved the pistol to the chief's head and snapped the trigger. The flint sparked as it fell against the pan, igniting the charge behind the ball with a thunderous blast. Doublehead's body crashed to the floor beneath billows of white, sulfurous smoke. Some of the sparks lit Doublehead's hair on fire, at least until the smolders were quenched by the chiefs pooling blood. The tavern filled with an awful stench.

Ridge stepped over his victim, the same chief who had first led him on the warrior's trace. He yanked Doublehead's knife from his sash, unfolded the death warrant signed by all the council chiefs, and impaled it against the wall for everyone to see. Then he slipped out the door with me close behind. We mounted our horses and pushed them far too hard. We both wanted to put distance between us and that evil place.

Runners swept in like a storm, disrupting the quiet. I heard their blowing horses pounding the moist earth. Ridge was already awake, leaning on one elbow, listening. Raised alone in the woods as hunters, we always slept lightly under the stars. We armed ourselves before we crept outside to see who had come for us. I broke out in a sweat. Doublehead was corrupt, but he had many clansmen and friends whose first thought would be to avenge his death. Though banished ten winters before, the Blood Law still lived in the distant hills.

Soon enough, I recognized two of Bone Polisher's clan. Doublehead had murdered Bone Polisher at a ball play a few hours before Ridge had shot him. Bone Polisher had nearly severed Doublehead's thumb before he fell, and hence the chief had shown up at McIntosh's with the bloody bandage on his hand.

"He lives," one of them said. I was shocked. What man could survive a wound to the head like that?

"Not for long," Ridge answered, and already he was saddling his horse. I figured I'd better attend to mine. "Where is he?"

"Black, the schoolteacher, is hiding him in his loft."

"Away, then," Ridge said to me with gritted teeth. I'd never seen him more determined. "Let's finish it."

We raced down darkened trails until we reached Black's house at dawn. Without a word, we drew our pistols and stormed into the house. Black and his wife, already dressed and warming beside the fire, backed away from us in terror.

"Be still!" Ridge commanded. "We aren't here for you." He stared at the dark rooms behind him. "Where is he?" he said, and Black looked up at the ceiling. Ridge and I and both of Bone Polisher's clansmen raced up the stairs to face the horrible vision of Doublehead, a festering bullet wound in his cheek. He was holding a knife and screaming the most unholy Cherokee obscenities at his would-be murderers. Bloody skin flapped around his mouth as he hollered, lending him the most macabre appearance. I froze. Ridge leveled his pistol and yanked the trigger. Nothing. I came to my senses and tried my piece next, and it misfired as well. Too long a journey in damp night air. I panicked. I guess Ridge did, too. We made instant eye contact, begging of each other, *What now?*

Doublehead threw back the blankets and leaped at Ridge, wrestling him to the puncheon floor. Though his wound was obviously severe, he still possessed extraordinary strength. Bloody drool seeped from his mouth as Ridge tried to strangle him. When that failed, Ridge pummeled him with is fists, but Doublehead absorbed the blows, slashing at Ridge's neck again and again with his dagger.

Fearing for my life and Ridge's, too, I ripped my tomahawk from my sash and, screaming like a beast possessed, buried it with one swift blow in the chief's forehead. Blood sprayed in brief pulses from the awful gash, covering my hands, clothes, and face, even the walls. Doublehead had a stunned expression on his face, as if someone had asked him a simple question and he couldn't think of the answer. He wobbled back and forth for a moment, and then fell hard. By the time Doublehead hit the floor, one of Bone Polisher's clansmen caved in his skull with a spade.

Ridge climbed to his feet and stared at the dead chief. He wiped the blood from his face, wedged his foot against Doublehead's neck, and yanked the tomahawk free. As the others bashed the dead chief's head to pieces, Ridge and I walked out of the house in silence. I still remember the hollowness of our heavy steps. Our task was done. Neither of us wanted anything to do with Doublehead's mutilation.

A crowd of Cherokee had gathered, mostly former Chickamauga, followers of Doublehead, shocked by the blood splashed all over our clothes, hands, and faces, and by the whispered rumors that their chief had been murdered in their midst. Their vacant stares begged the question: *Why was this awful thing done?*

"The war chief Doublehead sold your lives to the whites," Ridge told them quickly to hold them at bay. "For that reason, the Ridge claimed his. This act was done by the order of your council in accordance with your laws. A bad man is dead. Let that be the end of it."

Then he mounted and rode off alone. I'd have to ride hard to catch up to him, but my friend wouldn't spend another moment in that place. Doublehead's execution had been by the chiefs' decree, but I knew that for Ridge there was no honor in it, no pride. For all his faults, Doublehead was still Cherokee, a man we both had once respected enough to follow on the war trace. Whether it was the whiskey or his greed for riches that led to his death warrant, both faults stemmed directly from the Americans. Both Ridge and I felt that Doublehead had been corrupted by white encroachment that had pushed him to extremes. Had he lived in another age, the errant man would have lived a full life as a valued war chief among us. It's true that Ridge loathed his cousin. But he hated what Doublehead had become, not what he could have been. Now the complexity of our times forced Cherokee to kill Cherokee, and therein lay the tragedy that burdened the Ridge with the deepest guilt and self-recrimination he had known in thirty-six winters of life. I saw this in his face even before he pulled the trigger in McIntosh's Tavern.

The next time the council ordered the death of one of our own, the chiefs could look upon younger faces to kill for them. Ridge and I would have none of it from this night hence. Our hands were now bloody enough.

We ran the horses ten leagues or so before Ridge dismounted, deep lines etched into his sweaty face as he scrambled to gather kindling and dead limbs for a great fire he sparked in the road. He said nothing as he blew on the flames to give them life. Once they took, Ridge heaped on stacks of wood until the fire shot embers higher than the trees. He tore his bloody clothes from his body and tossed them onto the flames. Then, wearing only his breechclout, he grabbed the horse's reins, threw his leg over the saddle, and lashed his mount's hip with his quirt.

Our legends claimed that the spirits could hunt down and kill offenders, much like wolves ripped the throats out of running deer. Ridge's blaze was meant to be a barrier between us and them, and still he lathered his horse. I knew then that the council's talking leaves were not enough sanction for him. Regardless of the authority extended to Ridge by our new laws, he believed that by the purest interpretation of our ancient codes he had done wrong. And he believed enough in our religion that he feared the vengeance of the primeval spirits far more than that of Doublehead's clan or kinsmen. He didn't have to tell me why he built the fire. I knew.

Ridge left the road for a narrow trail through the thickets. I rubbed out our tracks on the road beyond the fire until I reached the point where he had split off. Once we were away from the fire's light, the darkness engulfed us. All I heard was thundering hooves and hard-breathing horses and the occasional grunts of a hard-riding, terrified man. Ridge splashed through a creek and waited for me on the opposite bank. When he saw me, he wheeled his mount and plunged ahead.

I kept my eyes forward as we raced on for daylight. Ridge was always looking back.

Chapter Twelve

Ridge drew disgruntled stares when he stamped his foot. He knew such rudeness was ill-advised, especially during the principal chief's speech at the National Council, now gathered at Ridge's rejuvenated boyhood village of Hiwassee. But his gut coiled so that he couldn't help himself.

"Steady," White Path said. "They'll toss us both out if you keep that up."

"I can't stand listening to this," Ridge said.

"You must," White Path said. "You'll get your say." He took notice of Ridge's new frock coat, rubbing the sleeve between his thumb and finger. "Do you think this would fit me?" he said.

Ridge jerked his arm free. The deer clan mother shot him a baleful look that implied that his behavior had reached her level of tolerance. One more infraction and a warrior would come and tap on his shoulder and point to the door. Ridge could do nothing but bow his head and bide his time.

Black Fox cleared his throat at the petty disturbance and continued his speech. "It's my wish that the Glass Toochalar and Tahlonteskee travel east to the Great Father Jefferson's house to finalize our ongoing discussions there." Ridge fumed at the mention of the names. These were the lapdogs of Black Fox. Had Doublehead's execution not tempered their greed and ambitions? The council fire illuminated the crow's-feet etched into the corners of the old chief's eyes. Ridge felt it appropriate that Black Fox's face bore the mark of nature's scoundrel.

"I have made our problems known to Jefferson," Black Fox said, "and then together we opened our hearts to a solution. Our game has disappeared, and I have come to the difficult decision that we have little choice but to follow it west. The Cherokee are Jefferson's friends, and we hope he'll grant our petition, which is to remove our people toward the setting sun."

What words were these? Ridge wondered. No chief who earned his respect would suggest his people move west, to the place where the sun died and dark spirits roamed the most desolate and inhospitable province of Turtle Island. The earth was suspended from the Sky Vault from four pillars of stone. The *adawehis* always claimed the western pillar was stained black — the color of death. The principal chief would have to do some talking

183

to convince Ridge's people to move anywhere near it. Ridge didn't expect Black Fox to be so blunt in his opinions and so sudden in his schemes, especially after what had become of Doublehead. From the expressions of the elders around him, they were equally stunned by the brashness of the statement.

"But we shall give up a fine country," Black Fox continued, "fertile in soil, abounding in rivers and streams, and well adapted for the residence of white people. For all this, we must get a good price."

He finally said the words, Ridge thought. A good price. This whole enterprise was about money after all. Ridge had already heard rumors that Black Fox had met with the American agent, Col. Return J. Miegs, and, like Doublehead before him, had accepted gifts and money to advance this bleak cause. Ridge scanned the faces of the appalled elders, many of whom murmured among themselves. Still no one spoke. No one had the gall to confront this hypocrite.

Ridge's chest heaved with anger and scorn as he fidgeted on the bench, waiting. Where were the wise words from the elders? When Ridge could no longer stomach their reticence, he rose from his place among the young chiefs and beloved woman of the deer clan, his hand resting firmly on the shoulder of his full-blooded colleague.

"My friends," he began, "you've heard this

astonishing talk of selling all we have and moving west, set forth by our own principal chief. As a man he has the right to his opinion, but as elders of this council we are not bound to his whim. Black Fox's decision was not made here, in the light of day before this body, but in some dark corner after Colonel Miegs whispered in his ear; the same as he did with Beats the Drum, the Glass, and Tahlonteskee — men Black Fox would have speak for the People. Yuh! Before you now stands the Man Who Walks the Mountaintops. He won't have these men speak for him."

The room fell quiet enough that he could hear coals crumble away from the heart of the council fire. Ridge nudged the embers back into the flames with the toe of his moccasin, letting Black Fox stew over what would come next. The principal chief's head sat back on his shoulders, a deep-set frown on his leathery face, waiting. The Glass and Tahlonteskee waited, as did all the chiefs and elders. Ridge drew a breath.

"In exchange for riches," Ridge began anew, "Black Fox decides to drag his people, without their consent, to the unknown land of the setting sun. I resist it here in my place as a warrior, as a chief, as a yunwi. I have the right, as you do, to be consulted in matters of such importance. The Provider gave us eyes to see, ears to hear, and a mind to think. Use these gifts to consider Black Fox's words and decide what's best for us all."

Ridge Walker paused to assess the crowd's mood. He knew he gambled to speak openly against a man of Black Fox's standing. If Black Fox held sway as he obviously felt he did, Ridge — a young chief — would be set aside in shame. But Ridge knew his people, and he knew right from wrong, and he'd rather be banished to the swamps than to condone such a grand corruption.

"I scorn this movement of a few to dislocate the many," Ridge said, pounding his fist into his palm. "Look around you at the face of this country — along the mountains, rivers, creeks, and woods. Behold the homes and fields of the many who prosper here. Are we to lose everything so that Black Fox alone may gain? Do we submit to his will or the will of the thousands who depend upon us? Are you free men who know your rights, or have you become the slaves of Black Fox? I pause to hear."

The council house erupted from every clan among its seven sides. Ridge nodded in warm approval and then turned to glare at Black Fox. The old chief scanned the crowd and gauged their solemn mood, knowing that a chief ruled only by his people's consensus, and also, Ridge hoped, that to persist in this endeavor in defiance of his people's will would most likely earn him a grave next to

Doublehead's.

In the time it took for a man to snap a twig in two, Black Fox stepped down and shrank from the center of the council house for the door. The Glass and Tahlonteskee followed him with their stares cast to the ground. Ridge's chest heaved with pride, but his expression remained stern. He had just broken three chiefs on the spot with his tongue, but it was the Cherokee Nation that had been aggrieved.

He stepped forward, careful not to stand too close to the principal chief's position. "My friends," he said, "who do we wish to send to Washington City to speak to the Great Father now?

CHAPTER THIRTEEN

The Ridge stood with his arms crossed before Thomas Jefferson, a gaunt twig of a man with cheeks the hue of a robin's breast. The chiefs wondered how one of such faint voice and sickly demeanor could rise to a position of such power among the whites. The chieftains of the Original People emerged from the warrior class. A leader must prove his courage before he was allowed to exercise his wisdom. And yet this skinny, quiet-spoken, ill-looking man ruled a nation that had crushed the Cherokee as they'd crushed the British Father before them. Truly, it was as Waesa had told him long ago. The world was out of balance. What remained for Ridge was to determine if his people could seize an opportunity in all the chaos.

Another thought occurred to him: If a man like Jefferson could rise among his people, perhaps Ridge's sickly son would also rise among the Cherokee. The changing times offered a different measure of a man, and encouraged Ridge about his son's prospects in a new class of leaders.

Jefferson sat quietly in this mountain of marble, still being built around him by a thousand pairs of hands in the Americans' year of 1809. Black men dragged slabs of white stone as smooth as the surface of still water across rolling, creaking timbers, where they were hoisted into place by a series of ropes and contraptions more complex than the most intricate spider's web. Above Ridge's head, on flimsy scaffolds higher than the most majestic pine, workers wrestled with a dome of glass and stone that fifty warriors could not lift.

The dome was the crest of this great house, like a snowcap on a mountain. *Magnificent,* Ridge thought. Next to the heavens on a moonless night and the Smoky Mountains at dawn, he'd seen nothing on this earth that awed him more than this great structure. There could be no mistake: The Americans were a powerful race. Clearly, the Great Father had arranged their meeting in his rising capitol rather than his grand white home to remind the Cherokee delegation of this fact.

Ridge pulled the lapels of his frock coat up around his ears to stave off the chill of the structure's cold heart. But he couldn't keep his fingers from trembling or calm his rapid breathing. The journey through the mushrooming settlements to the sprawling cities of Baltimore and Charleston and on to Washington City itself had been overwhelming. But none of his tours had prepared him for the stuff of myth he saw this day. Black men were building white mountains. And the frail voice of this sickly white man lorded over them all. While Ridge stood studying Jefferson's every detail from a distance as he'd once studied the black bear as a boy, the next stone set in place blocked out the morning sun.

The Great Father Jefferson must have been confused at first. Two different delegations, each with its own voice, answered his invitation to talk. Black Fox proved far from broken after his embarrassment in council. He rallied those loyal to him and persevered in his aims to cede land and move west. As expected, the former principal chiefs adherents had sent Toochalar to finalize the terms of removal beyond the Mississippi. If Black Fox's contingent were set on going, the council agreed to let them go.

The newly elected full-blood principal chief, Pathkiller, had summoned the most promising and enlightened of the young chiefs, of which the Ridge was one. This faction advocated holding fast to their land while they embraced the new ways. They strove to exist as a tribe, with tribal ownership of their own country — to merge the old with the new and still live as Cherokee — in the way they had been promised by George Washington and his secretary of war, Henry Knox. For Ridge, the issue before Jefferson was simple: Would the third Great American Father honor the words of the first?

Of course Stone Carrier, Woman Holder, the Crawling Boy, Chilcohatah, and many others from the Upper Towns had visited Jefferson some moons before on their own. Thus Jefferson was to hear three Cherokee tongues. This prior delegation claimed they wanted no part of Black Fox's Lower Town intrigue. Nor were they comfortable with the absolute position of Pathkiller's defiant young chiefs. They aspired to become farmers and asked the government to provide them with the materials to do so. But they were also interested in American citizenship and individual ownership of their family land. Jefferson encouraged them in their path toward civilization but sent them home to seek a consensus. Even before Ridge had scaled this mountain of marble, he sensed that if Jefferson knew anything about the Cherokee, he knew they were hopelessly fractured, like a wet stone set too close to a roaring fire.

Now Jefferson sat before them, his rust-colored hair streaked with gray, calmly saying this to one group and that to another. There were no soldiers beside him, no guards of any kind. Even the most elderly, feeble chiefs could leap upon him and slice his throat from ear to ear in one beat of their troubled hearts. But this skinny old man did not fear the Cherokee, or apparently any other nation for that matter, perched as he was in this house of winter ice. Jefferson knew he could speak a single word and thousands of soldiers would sweep across the Blue Mountains with blood in their eyes. The continual threat of total annihilation was left unspoken, but the menace ruled every thought and every action among the Cherokee leadership.

Ridge understood only a few English words. As Jefferson spoke, Ridge studied the Great Father's face instead, assaying the tone of the words floating airily between his thin lips. He listened carefully to the linkster translate the Great Father's words into their language. Ridge judged Jefferson shrewd, perhaps coldly analytical, as he'd observed other powerful white men to be. Jefferson rarely laughed in council. His oratory as translated seldom relied on natural allusions. Ridge found little passion behind his words. For if the linksters attempted to translate emotion, their efforts failed. Government for the whites was a thing apart from the natural scheme, and among them the spoken word was obviously not considered an art. If what they were saying didn't make the difference between life and death, their monotone addresses would've put Ridge to sleep better than any *adawehis*'s concoction. But Ridge sensed intelligence, warmth, and honesty in this man's face. And better yet, he caught a glint of compassion.

Jefferson had obviously read and considered the various addresses and proposals of all three Cherokee factions. When the Great Father spoke at last of his decision, Ridge appreciated the deep thought and prior reflection behind his words. "You inform me," the Great Father said through his linkster, "of your anxious desire to engage in the industrious pursuits of agriculture and civilized life, and that finding it impractical to induce the Nation at large to do this, you wish a line of separation to be established between the Upper and Lower Towns. And once this line is drawn, you wish to establish fixed laws and regular government."

Jefferson balanced the talking leaves on his knee and lifted his gaze above his eye crystals to scan the chiefs' expressions. He locked on Ridge's last and his countenance warmed. Ridge returned his regard.

"You have my blessing for all of this," Jefferson said, "provided the division you suggest is approved by mutual consent of both parts of the Nation. The next step is to divide the land among you — one equal parcel for each family — to be passed down forever by a father to his wife and children. This business of an uncle or some such taking possession of any tract after his sister's death will not work in our system. Reach beyond your traditions in this respect as you have in so many others."

"Can we not continue to learn your way while we continue to respect ours?" Ridge asked. The linkster went to work.

"Well, yes, you can — in part," Jefferson said. "But you have to think of how to administer your laws. So far, your success in this regard has been most remarkable, completely noncoercive with no requirement of police or courts, and living under no law but that of nature. This will change, however, as your nation merges with ours."

Ridge, listened as the linkster translated the words. The Cherokee word *merge* flashed the image of two streams meeting and flowing as one. Once joined, there was no longer any distinction between the two. This word did not suit what Ridge had in mind.

"Our intent, Great Father," Ridge said, "is to learn. We understand that our elder brothers have much to teach us, but the Cherokee must remain one people as we reach out our hand to you. We see no reason to divide the land, a little to each family."

"Ah, but you won't need so much, you see," Jefferson said, eyes sparking like freshly blown coals. "Small portions of land well improved are worth far more than extensive forests unemployed. The Cherokees, in particular, are most adaptive to civilization. Your progress these past twenty years has been astonishing. Once the northern European tribes came into contact with the arts and sciences of ancient Rome, it took sixteen more centuries to produce an Isaac Newton. I believe the Cherokee can adapt from their savage state to civilization in only one or two. Prove me right, my red children, for if you will not go west beyond the reach of my people, you must prepare to mix your blood with theirs. The ultimate point of rest and happiness for you is to let your settlements and ours meet, blend together and intermix, and become one people."

The linkster picked up where Jefferson left off. Ridge understood the words well enough, but he didn't understand what they all meant. He wondered how long it would take the missions to produce some Cherokee who could. He wished someone could explain Jefferson's comments to him in some detail. He knew the future was being cut straight to the bone for all eyes to see.

Jefferson must have sensed their confusion from the Cherokee delegation's collectively blank faces. He paused a moment, and began again in a more instructional tone, like an uncle teaching a boy to chip flint.

"I feel I'm among friends here," he said. "Let's speak frankly. The success of our system depends on the abundance of fresh, rich, and, most important, inexpensive soil.

You possess more land than you could ever farm. We possess more technology than you could ever require. My hope is to see you continue along the path to civilization while you organize a government much like our own. I'm proposing that the Cherokee gain experience with democracy."

Ridge absorbed every word of how the system worked. Elections brought the wise to office and there were no appointments. Laws were agreed upon and issued in writing for all to see, understand, and abide by. Enforcement and courts were established for those who could not bring themselves to follow. None of this would be difficult. The Cherokee had been talking about these things for years.

"The time will come," Jefferson said, "when you see with your own eyes that you no longer require so much land. But you will need so many other things. Then your land becomes a commodity, much like the corn and cotton and tobacco you raise now. Sell it wisely at a fair price and your people will have the money to buy their draft animals and livestock, seed, plows, and other improvements."

"No Cherokee chief," the Ridge said, "regardless of how powerful he is among us, can sell what belongs to all Cherokee without their consent. Others have tried. Some were killed. The rest were broken."

"Well, that's the problem, isn't it?" The

Great Father shifted in his seat, squaring off with Ridge alone. "I repeat the advice I've given you for years. Your path divides. If you wish to live in the old ways, the only solution is to migrate beyond the Mississippi with the chiefs of the Lower Towns. If you choose to stay where you are, you must adapt. It all begins, as I've tried to explain, with fee-simple ownership of your lands — one family, one farm, which will belong to them forever, and which the nation shall have no right to sell under their feet."

"This," Ridge said, "is what our chiefs don't understand. The treaties say we can keep our land as long as the rivers run. We see how well you people live, and the Cherokee know we can thrive in the same manner. But if we say we'd like to join you as one nation, the very next thing out of your mouth is that to do so, the Cherokee must give up their land."

"Exactly."

"Why? Our Great Father Washington led us to believe that if we took up the white man's ways we would be welcomed by the Americans without ceding more land."

Jefferson leaned forward, resting his elbows on his knees. "May I ask your name, sir?"

"Kah-nung-da-tla-geh," Ridge replied, and the linkster spoke the clunky English words in Jefferson's ears.

"Ah, yes. The Man Who Walks the Mountaintops. You are young to speak as a chief."

197

"I have seen thirty-eight winters."

"You remind me in some ways of myself when I was younger. I once sent a letter to the British Father about our grievances. It had your tone, I think." He cocked his head. "You appear to be full-blooded. Is this true?"

"No. My mother's father was from across the waters."

"Scottish, perhaps."

"I have heard it said so."

"I'd give a thousand English pounds to reunite you with your Highland cousins — to watch them touch your face, and for you to touch theirs. How proud they would be of you."

"I don't understand," Ridge said.

"Of course you don't," Jefferson said. "You're blessed with an ignorance of history and politics. You have no idea that civilization — what we call 'the white man's path' — is like a swollen river, powerful and destructive and beyond all human control. You, Ridge Walker, and all your kind, were cut off from humanity's flow for a thousand generations, left to roam free in this American Eden. I know there were wars, conflict, calamities, disease, natural disasters, and great human suffering beyond description. But this was still your golden age."

Ridge never broke eye contact with Jefferson as the linkster translated his words. Before he could respond in any way, Jefferson began again. "Now fate has thrown us face-to-face again, cousin reunited with cousin. I know in my heart that white people are no better than red in nature, intellect, and ingenuity. I look in your eyes, Ridge Walker, and I see my equal."

This time Ridge focused on the linkster as the words were translated. The conversation had taken a strange turn. The chiefs began to look at one another.

"But my mind tells me," Jefferson continued, "that even the Cherokee cannot catch up to us as quickly as you think you can, even though I know you will try. It will wrench my heart to observe the consequences of your determination and goodwill. The river runs wild for a few seasons, my red children. For an Indian to have a treaty in his hand in this country is not protection enough."

Ridge listened closely as the linkster translated everything. Puzzled, he looked again at the other Cherokee, who appeared equally confused. "Do any of you have any idea what this man is talking about?" he said in Cherokee.

"I was lost as soon as I shook his hand," Pathkiller said.

"My father told me that once these people turn gray," William Hicks said, "they go mad. Apparently it's the same with this one."

Ridge shot the linkster a stern glance. "Translate none of that," he said. "We're searching for balance in a rushing stream. Say to him instead that the Cherokee are moved by the power of his words."

"Moved?" Hicks said. "He shoved me aside right after he sat down. We were talking about plows and blankets and then suddenly the man's mind took flight."

Jefferson closed his eyes to compose himself. When he opened them again, his voice was weaker than before. "The Great Father Washington," he said, "had hoped there would be time enough to leave you alone in your own country without interference from our people so that we could bring you along with us over a period of several generations. Washington was a strong man, and even those who didn't agree with him dared not defy him, even when he built forts between our nations to keep us from harming you."

"We admired and respected him, too," Ridge said.

"Now I sit here in Washington's place," Jefferson said. "My position is weaker than his, and I honestly feel that's for the best. The stability of this democracy — and the success of this experiment — depends upon the constant expansion into new territory by an ever-growing population. We must grow to survive. Your Great Father, who is proud of your efforts and loves you as much as his own children, must not — and cannot — stand in the way."

"My friends," Hicks said in Cherokee, "it gets worse as we go along. Next he'll tell us why the stars drift across the Sky Vault or some such. We're wasting our time."

"He warns us," Ridge said, again threatening the linkster with a cold stare. "I can see it in his eyes."

"I can't make you understand," Jefferson said as he pushed himself up on the arms of his chair. Ridge saw the frustration on his face. And maybe the pain. "Go west with the Lower Town chiefs beyond the reach of my people. That's my earnest advice. If you choose to remain in your country, the storm awaits, the same faced by every tribal people on the face of this earth. Stay where you are and your time is now. Those who survive will live under our laws and mix their blood with ours. One day we shall all be Americans." He looked at his attendants with tired eyes. "That's all I have to say."

Ridge turned his ear toward the linkster in order to absorb every word and then measure it. Where was the foothold to dig in his toe and press upward? Would the Great Father honor the treaties or not? When would he send soldiers to drive out the squatters? What forms of assistance in terms of plows, seeds, and expertise could the Cherokee expect? Ridge wanted to ask him so much more.

Pathkiller stepped forward to speak the Cherokee's last words. "For too long, my people have been much confused and divided in our opinions. Black Fox and the others can move west with our blessing. The rest of us will settle our affairs and become one — the true Cherokee Nation. Tell your agent Colonel Miegs not to whisper in my chiefs' ears with promises or to bribe them with money and slaves. No one will listen to him. The Great Father Washington promised us we could keep our land for as long as the rivers run. All the Cherokee ask of you is to keep his word, and then maybe peace can shine down on both of our nations."

Pathkiller bowed his head as the linkster translated. Ridge rested his hand on the chief's shoulder to tell him he approved of his eloquence. There was no reaction for Ridge to read in Jefferson's face. It was as pale and blank as his stone walls. He wondered if the linkster had made it clear to the Great Father that the great mass of Cherokee intended to stay. Americans said so much and meant so little.

"Very well," Jefferson said. "The Cherokee and I have traveled far together — just not as far as I'd hoped. When you come again to Washington City another man will be sitting in my place. Hopefully he will continue what has already begun and help the Cherokee find their place in this new nation. It was my honor to reach out to you. Go in peace, my red children."

Ridge shook his limp hand, as all the other chiefs did in their turn. He watched Jefferson walk wearily out of the chilled room. His steps echoed off cold stone walls as he disappeared into the depths of his white cave. William Hicks tugged his cloak up tightly around his neck. Old Pathkiller shivered.

"Let's go before we catch our death," the principal chief said. "It's too dark in here for me."

CHAPTER FOURTEEN

"Hurry along now, boy," Ridge said whenever Skah-tle-loh-skee allowed his horse to graze so he could gawk at a spooked buck bounding through the thickets or study the patterns of frost on a dead leaf. Whenever Ridge cajoled his son, the boy jerked the reins and trotted the animal to catch up with his father, squirming like an unearthed grub worm in his stiff, new white man's clothes. There was no talking him out of wearing his moccasins, and Ridge didn't even consider ordering him to leave his blowgun and bow and arrows at home. Time would tell which skills the boy would favor and which world would belong to him. In the clearing ahead lay the new school. The boy's wondrous journey would begin.

"I'm sorry, Ridge," Skah-tle-loh-skee said. Ridge noted the grimace on his son's face as he adjusted himself in the saddle. Even this short ride had irritated his inflamed hip, yet the boy said nothing.

"Don't ever apologize for being curious, son," Ridge said. He feigned a yawn. "What do you think about resting under the sycamore yonder? I could use a little nap." Ridge reached over to pin his son's black hair behind his ear, pausing to test for fever. It was there, as it usually was.

"I'd rather ride on, 'Doda," Skah-tle-loh-skee said. "I spend plenty of time in my bed when I'm sick. Why would I want to nap on a beautiful day like today?"

"Spoken like a chief," Ridge said, his mind flashing to the countless nights he and Se-hoya had paced the puncheons, willing Skah-tle-loh-skee's fevers to break. Dazizi's concoctions and incantations had had little effect over the recent months. His son languished in his sweat-soaked feather bed for weeks on end. The inflamed hip joints prohibited him from fledgling attempts at ball play and the hoop chase. None of this had escaped Ridge's concerned eye. If he couldn't trick the boy into resting, he knew he should make him. But Skah-tle-loh-skee's nature was such that babying him would only bring him shame, and Ridge wanted no part of that, either.

"Let's ride on, then," Ridge said with great hesitation. "You must already know that when we get to the end of this trail, your life will change."

"Mother says it's my duty to do this thing.

She cried when she told me, but I'm not afraid."

"It would be all right if you were," Ridge said. "I'm proud of you."

Ridge regarded his son. He'd never really noticed how much of Sehoya was in the boy's face. Skah-tle-loh-skee was small for seven winters, rather thin, and fair-skinned enough to pass for an Ani-yonega — strange for a child who was only one-eighth white. He was graceful and articulate for his young age, the gift, Ridge assumed, of his mother's blood. But the wavy crop of crow black hair and the eyes in that boy's head — dark, bright, and piercing — had come from his father. Ridge Walker was certain of that. Sehoya, fascinated by the missionaries' teachings, had chosen a Christian name, Tsan. For a modern surname, the missionaries suggested the boy claim a piece of his father's mystique. So the child who focused on everything except the path ahead to the school was better known to English speakers as John Ridge.

John rode in tandem and in silence beside his father as they rounded the last bend. In the clearing ahead lay the school. Ridge hailed once they were in range and soon the missionary Gambold stepped out to greet them. John's eyes widened in awe of white people, as was his custom when he encountered anything he had not yet seen.

The morning breeze caught the skirts of

Gambold's black robes. Despite their absurd attire, Ridge was convinced that the Moravians were sincere in their promises and had nothing but good intentions in their hearts. Just the same, he planned to keep a close eye on this stumpy black bird.

"My son, Skah-tle-loh-skee," Ridge said, by way of introduction. "Called John Ridge. He speaks no English, but he's a quick learner." Ridge ruffled the curly tufts of John's black hair, motioning for him to sit tall in the saddle.

"He's a fine-looking boy, Ridge," Gambold said in thick, clunky Cherokee. "I'm sure we'll get along quite well."

The educated mixed-bloods who understood the talking leaves said that the Moravians were German or some such. Ridge knew of the French, the Spanish, and the English, and had warred plenty with the Americans. But this man was from yet another nation, another white nation, and Ridge wondered how many such Ani-yonega tribes there could be on the face of the earth, and why they were not satisfied with their own country. The few Cherokee who had gone west had done so only because they felt a pistol to their heads. Otherwise, no right-thinking person would ever consider leaving the Nation. Why were the whites so different in this regard?

Ridge turned from this line of thought to

the more pressing matter. "You have no idea how deeply I hope that your school will be successful," Ridge said.

"We hope as you do," Gambold said.

The missionary seemed pleased with his pupil, yet as John dismounted, Ridge saw Gambold's expression fade when he realized that his son walked with a limp. John flinched when the missionary pressed the back of his hand against John's brow.

"Is he well?" Gambold said, his own forehead rumpling in concern.

"Well enough," Ridge said, ignoring the Moravian's stare. He untied the bag of his son's belongings and handed it to Gambold. "We have an agreement?"

"Oh, yes," Gambold said.

"Teach my son your religion if you must. But his true purpose is to learn foremost the ways of the whites — their language, their history, their science, their law."

"We agreed to do as much before the council, Ridge. But please understand that education is a great experiment for the Cherokee. We have no idea how well your people will absorb our teachings. We made no promises but that we will do our utmost to enlighten your children."

"You'll be held to your oath, Black Robe," Ridge said. "The Nation watches what is happening here. Open your books before my son's eyes. He'll soon learn to understand them." He nodded to John to take his place inside the structure. "Soon my brother Oowatie's boy, Kilakeena, will come also. He's equally bright and well mannered. Instruct him as you would my son."

"You have my word."

John Ridge entered the shadow of the structure's threshold and paused to look back at his father. Ridge marked well the tear streaking down the boy's face. They'd fallen like rain from Sehoya's cheeks when they'd left their home earlier in the day. Ridge had to beg her to allow her oldest son to spend his days apart from her. He reminded his wife that John was marked for a higher purpose, and that sacrifices had to be made to prepare him for it. Sehoya acquiesced to her husband's will, mainly because she understood as he did that the Cherokee faced a new and threatening world. Education was the torch that would illuminate the Original People's path into the night that was their future. Like Ridge, Sehoya believed that John was born to bear it. She was brave enough to let her oldest son go.

But watching the skinny boy stand alone upon the school's threshold, Ridge's own courage faltered. What kind of times were these when a child must grow up under a stranger's roof? Ridge smiled with his lips pressed together, nodded to the missionary, and then tugged on his reins. The horse started to turn when Ridge dug his feet into the stirrups and waved the boy back to him.

Without hesitation, John scampered to his father, wrapping his arms tightly around Ridge's leg. Ridge reached down and pulled him up to his saddle, and hugged him to his chest.

"I love you, 'Doda," John whispered, his boy's voice as sweet and pure as the mockingbird's. "Don't leave me here."

"We don't want to, son," Ridge said. "You know that. But as hard as it is for your mother and I to bring you here, we must all do as we are bidden. You are the son of a chief, and a chief serves his people. It becomes your obligation to go inside that house and learn everything that man will teach you. It becomes mine and your mother's to make it happen. None of us have a choice."

"I'll be alone."

"No, you won't," Ridge said. "There are other Cherokee children inside, waiting to play with you. Your cousin is coming soon. Your mother and I are only a half day's ride from here. We'll come and see you often, and we'll bring your aunts and uncles and all your friends. And just in case you get lonely, step outside at night and look up at the stars. They are the eyes of your ancestors who shine down on you, their favorite, with undying love. You're never far from your family when you're under the stars." Ridge ran his fingers through the boy's hair. "Go now, young warrior."

Ridge let John slide down the flank of his horse. The boy rubbed his arm under his nose, looked darkly at Gambold, and walked slowly toward the door. He turned one last time to stare back at his father and then vanished into the darkness. Ridge pressed his hand into the Moravian's, and then he clicked his tongue to prod his horse.

"He may be too young for this," Gambold said. "Perhaps next year."

"We can't wait," Ridge said, pulling back on the reins. "He'll begin now."

"What shall I do if his fever returns?"

"It's more a matter of when. My son has to live with his disease, and so must you. Continue his studies, even if you have to bring his books to his bed. But watch him closely and use your judgment. If you fear for him in the least, send word to me immediately. His mother and I will come with his medicines and all will be well."

"I'll care for John Ridge as if he were my own," Gambold said.

"I believe you will," Ridge said. "Or else I'd never have brought him to you." Ridge put his heels to the horse's belly. "Keep your promise, Black Robe. The Ridge will keep his."

Before he had traveled beyond sight of the school, Ridge heard the voices of the children singing a strange song. The melody lingered in the woods until Ridge put enough thicket between himself and the mission school. The woods swallowed the sound of children's voices, leaving only the song of nature he had heard since birth. He still liked this one best.

CHAPTER FIFTEEN

Never had he seen such power and grandeur, this split-tailed spark of the Provider's distant fire, an omen of change.

Did the sign bode good or ill?

Ridge watched the comet blaze through the night sky while he sat among forty-five Cherokee delegates and linksters involved in lesser affairs. As Pathkiller's Cherokee ambassador to their southwestern neighbors, the Creeks, Ridge had ostensibly come to their capital of Tuckabatchee to negotiate an end to the horse stealing between the two nations. According to the oral traditions, the Creeks and Cherokee had once been close, and the Ani-yunwi-ya *adawehis* and silver heads still affectionately referred to the Creeks as elder brothers. But there had long been competition between the two tribes. Once blood was spilled, the Blood Law ran its course, and the Cherokee had been at Creek throats as often as they were with their powerful enemies, the Iroquois.

The Ani-yonega wars and a common enemy had quenched these long-smoldering tribal feuds, save for the escalating theft of horses by young and most likely intoxicated would-be warriors, which was more of a nuisance than a threat. Ridge planned to sort out the mischief once the spectacle of the comet was behind them.

Ridge got along well with the Creek chiefs, particularly Tastanagi Tako, Big Warrior, head man of Tuckabatchee, speaker for the Muskogee Creeks, and the most powerful and influential man on the National Council. Ridge admired him not only for his courage, wisdom, and formidable manner, but because Big Warrior was an advocate of civilization and tribal integrity. On this matter, they were of one mind. Normally on these diplomatic jaunts, Big Warrior — intelligent, jovial, and gregarious, his skin spotted like a bobcat — was the focus of Ridge's attention. But on this occasion a stranger held his interest.

Ridge had chosen his Creek visit to coincide with the appearance of the Kispoko Shawnee Tecumseh, who hailed from north of the Ohio. The interpreters claimed that Tecumseh's name translated to "Shooting Star" in his own Algonquin tongue, and given the brilliant comet overhead, he suspected that Tecumseh had chosen the timing of his visit carefully, as well.

It was known among all the nations that

Tecumseh had come south to deliver an important message — a final solution, the rumors went, to the American menace. The Choctaw, Seminole, and Chickasaw had also sent emissaries to hear it with their own ears. According to loose tongues, Tecumseh advocated a confederacy of all northern and southern tribes, and once the alliance was forged the Indians would wage a war of extermination against the whites. Survivors and refugees would be driven into the sea from whence they came.

Ridge had lived long enough to know better, but he couldn't think of a young warrior who didn't dream of destroying the whites in one fell swoop. He had once advocated that path himself, but his experiences in Washington City, Baltimore, and Charleston had convinced him that the opportunity to dislodge the powerful Americans had long passed.

The Creek agent, Col. Benjamin Hawkins, whom the Ridge despised just as much as the Creeks did, must have heard these whispers also, for he lingered about the council, too. For his part, Tecumseh said nothing as long as his voice was in range of the agent's ear.

Instead, he danced for seven straight sleeps. He was naked save for his breechclout and moccasins, his temples shaven smooth to the scalp, his plaited hair laced with two red-and-white crane feathers. He had smeared red paint under his eyes and across his broad chest, dabbing a single red dot on both of his bare temples. Bands of silver squeezed his carved biceps. Ridge could not deny that the young, bright-eyed, charismatic Shawnee was quite impressive. The young Alabama Creeks, who saw Hawkins as too aggressive and self-serving, and Big Warrior as too acquiescent to Hawkins's schemes, fell one by one under Tecumseh's spell. They painted their bodies and war sticks red, and danced Tecumseh's Dance of the Lakes with a growing fury. Ridge scowled as he watched all of this beneath the wonder of the great comet.

Hawkins, among other shortcomings, was no diplomat. Impatient with Tecumseh's games and reticence, the agent had broken camp and retired home. But true to his belligerent nature, he had decided upon his departure to inform the council that yet another government road would be cut through Creek country with or without their consent. Such a pronouncement was a wonderful example of the white man's arrogance. The young Creek dancers were a hairbreadth from slitting Hawkins's throat regardless of the consequences, and still he spit in their faces.

Big Warrior calmed his people as he almost always did, but Ridge estimated that there were at least five thousand worried, disgruntled, or angry Creek moderates who were suddenly very interested to hear what Tecumseh had to say. A lull swept over the dancers when the Shawnee broke out of the swirling circle and stood in silence before the council fire. Ridge rested his chin in his palm and listened.

"Once my parents sought shelter among the Muskogee, the people of the swampy ground," Tecumseh said through his Creek linkster. "Your kindness and generosity to them forever binds you to my heart. I came among you because I heard of your troubles — troubles shared by all nations north and south. Any one tribe is powerless to rise up alone against those who would squash us underfoot like a summer insect. I, Tecumseh, the Shooting Star, have come to speak of another way."

He tilted his head back and gazed at the night sky, thrusting his index finger toward the comet. "Behold the sign of Waashaa Monetoo, the Maker of Breath, who speaks through my brother, Tenskwatawa, the Prophet, to let his will be known. Let the wise pay heed. Each day the comet grows brighter and more powerful, and each day so do we. Join our alliance, my brothers. Let us rise up and take back what is ours, for if we do nothing, rest assured our kind will no longer walk the earth."

Tecumseh paused. Big Warrior locked stares with the Ridge, snorting as if he found the

Shawnee's speech amusing.

"Very soon," Tecumseh said, "guns will be fired in the north. When you hear their thunder and the blood begins to spill, waver not in your faith in me. Our friends the British will come to our aid, as will the Maker of Breath himself. He knows ours is a just cause, and he won't rest until we, his true children, put an end to the whites who would destroy us."

Ridge heard the rising murmur from the sweating warriors. They obviously placed a great faith in Britain's alleged support of their troubles, where Ridge's experiences in the disastrous American Revolution had taught him to invest none. The red nations knew war loomed again between the British and the Americans. The English in Canada could never protect their long southern border against American invasion without the help of the Shawnee and Iroquois, and so, once again, they had sent agents to their red brothers wagging silver tongues. Ridge knew how fickle the British could be in their alliances, and who had paid the price once they changed their minds. They threw drowning nations a vine of sand. The Cherokee knew better than to grasp it a second time, but were the young Creek warriors as wise? Tecumseh had already gathered his kindling. All he needed was to strike the flint.

"For now, be still," Tecumseh said. "Be at

friendship with the whites. Steal not even a bell from anyone of any color. Let the white people on this continent manage their affairs in their own way. Let the nations manage theirs, also. This I declare in the name of the British."

Ridge tapped his finger against his cheek as Tecumseh continued to urge the Creeks to cede no more land. To break corrupt and greedy chiefs who grew fat eating out of the white man's hand. They must turn away from the white man's road. Scorn his crops that must be planted in rows. Kill what clumsy beasts and stupid fowl of his waddled among them. Burn his looms, cotton cards, and noisy contraptions along with the talking leaves that spoke only of the white man's God. Teach their children the old ways and the oral traditions. Introduce them to the wonders created by the Maker of Breath.

"And while you do all of this," Tecumseh said, "prepare for one final, bitter war. It will come like a thunderstorm — quick, hot, and violent. When it's over, your country will once again belong to you."

When he at last fell silent, Ridge gauged the crowd. Like him, the old skeptics were unmoved. But there was a glint in the eyes of the sweaty young warriors and in that of the hillis haya, the medicine men, who shunned all white influence. Ridge knew the young hotheads pestered Big Warrior no more than gnats in their intratribal squabbles. If united in rebellion, however, they could become very dangerous. Ever since the comet appeared they'd prayed, danced, and fasted, waiting for the Shawnee prophet. The dancing had only heightened their resentments and their appetite for blood. For them, Tecumseh's temptation would be too great. But for Ridge, the most heartbreaking to witness was the glimmer of hope he saw in the anxious faces of the common Creeks.

Satisfied with the effect of his words, Tecumseh turned away from his new supporters, crossed his arms over his chest, and faced Big Warrior.

"What says the chief of the Creeks?" Tecumseh said.

"Do my ears hear," Big Warrior said, "that the Shawnee would have us burn our crops, and kill our meat animals, only to scrounge in the woods again for squirrels and nuts? Have our women abandon their looms and their weaving of blankets now, with the winter about to set in? I'm old enough to remember how the babes cried for food in the winter moons. I'll not hear it again."

Big Warrior turned from the Shawnee and addressed his people as a whole. "What difference does it make if a useful thing comes from white hands or red? If it serves the Creeks, the Creeks use it, and the thing becomes Creek. Do you think our ancestors first walked the earth with bows and arrows in their hands? No. They saw them used by some other nation, or had them used against them, and they knew at once that it was a thing they must adapt and make their own. The same was true in my time with guns and black powder, as it is now with the looms and plows this man would have you burn. I tell you, my people, that the Creek Nation is like a living tree. As it grows older, its roots sink deeper into our soil, accumulating greater branches and more leaves. The Big Warrior rests easy in its shade."

"And the whiskey?" Tecumseh asked, his lip curling in contempt.

"Not a useful thing," Big Warrior answered wryly, "but it amuses from time to time."

"It is poison, my great brother. As is the white religion and the white culture, as are the contraptions of their cluttered lives that you've allowed your people to depend upon — all of which destroys your people in both body and spirit. The Maker wills you to touch none of it and return to the ways of your ancestors."

"I'm confused," Big Warrior said, crossing a leg over his knee. "Do you speak for the Great Spirit now, Tecumseh, or for your friends, the British? If you have the blessing of the first why do you need the other?"

Tecumseh jutted his chin. Ridge could tell he'd not been rankled like this before.

"The British are white men," Big Warrior said. "Grandfathers of the Americans who would bring down the Americans' wrath upon our heads. We were once allies of the British in the Revolutionary War. When they abandoned us, the Americans took half of our land to punish us. What will be the cost this time?"

"The British," Tecumseh said, "are nothing to the Maker of Breath, nor to me. They are a means to an end."

"The end of the Creeks, I think," Big Warrior said. And then he faced his people again. "Consider this man's talk. Tecumseh says nothing about burning your guns and knives, yet did these not come from white hands also? He would have you keep the tools of war and destroy the comforts of peace. Any sensible man can see the inconsistency."

Tecumseh raised his arm over his head. "And how do you explain the comet that signals my arrival?"

"I've seen comets before, Tecumseh. But this is the first time a man has claimed kinship to one. Any fool could say the same."

Tecumseh seethed, the first crack in what had been a confident shell. "Your eyes are blind, Big Warrior," he said. "You've grown timid and weak. Hope stands before you and like a child you turn your head away. The white blood that flows in your veins cripples you."

Ridge shuddered and gritted his teeth. This was an old dig whenever a full-blood disagreed with the mixed-breeds. Suddenly a man's life and deeds meant nothing. In times of dissent, blood mattered more than the heart that pumped it. Ridge had heard such stinging words from his own people, yet he had never grown accustomed to them.

Big Warrior flared as he leveled a menacing stare at the Shawnee. "The Big Warrior," he said, shifting to the more formal third person, lest Tecumseh fail to comprehend that this was his final opinion, "has shed far more white blood than what little flows in his veins. His deeds of war speak well enough for him. Yet he is proudest of the wisdom of his years — wisdom you, Shawnee, do not yet possess. He has listened patiently to your words. He sees how the hearts of the young men stir as his once did. But Big Warrior sits in this place because he speaks for all of the Creeks, and now he offers his people these words: A war with the Americans is madness. They are more than the stars in the sky, more than the leaves of grass in the fields. In my time the Creeks fought them tooth and claw. The rivers ran red with blood. Much was lost, but we won our peace and what land we have left. Big Warrior will risk neither for the Shawnee. The Americans are here to stay; the whites in their country, the Creeks in ours. It is good. Let no Creek take up the war club against them, for you might as well pick it up against your neighbor, your wife, and your children. So speaks your chief."

Everyone grew quiet, save Tecumseh, who flew into a spitting rage. "I'll abandon this place governed by fools for the land of wiser men and remember well this warning: When I arrive there, I'll stamp my feet and the earth will shake until every house in Tuckabatchee crumbles! Then you Creeks will know far too late who among them spoke the Maker's truth."

With his Shawnee, Kickapoo, and Sioux in tow, Tecumseh stormed away from the council fire. When he came close enough, Ridge reached out and snatched him by the arm and jerked Tecumseh's ear to his mouth.

"Come among the Cherokee and speak these words, Shawnee," he said through clenched teeth, "and you'll speak no more."

Ridge allowed him space enough so that Tecumseh could peer into his eyes and understand that their discussion was a warrior's threat, not a stern warning from an idle chief. He could see the Shawnee consider whether or not to retaliate. Ridge tightened his grip to antagonize him further, hoping to make an example of this self-destructive foreigner in front of the young Creek warriors whom he would lead to their doom. All Tecumseh had to do was raise his hand in anger and Ridge would thrash him to a pulp.

Tecumseh must have sensed Ridge's intentions, for all he did was break free and stomp off into the woods. Ridge heard the brush snap as the mystics plunged deeper into the surrounding thickets. Behind him, he heard only the murmuring of confused and frightened Creeks. Above him, the comet burned hot.

CHAPTER SIXTEEN

A still, clear night during the month of U Ski'Ya, the snow moon, brought a knock on Ridge's door. He took a pistol with him to answer it. There were always white outlaws loose in the Nation. It was only a matter of time before they came calling on him for money or horses or whiskey.

"Who comes?" Ridge called quietly in Cherokee. His younger son, Walter, lay asleep beside Nancy, and Ridge hated to wake them unless it was necessary.

"Jefferson McCoy," a boy's voice answered. "I bear a message from Father Gambold at Spring Place."

Ridge uncocked his pistol, threw open the door, and invited the half-blood inside to shake off the cold beside a roaring fireplace.

"Is it the fevers again?" Ridge said, setting the gun aside. Not a day passed when he didn't worry that sickness would carry away his oldest boy.

"John's fine, Chief Ridge," McCoy said.

"You mustn't worry so."

"Then don't come banging on my door like that in the dead of night," Ridge said. "Let me show you something." He flung open the door and pointed to the bellpull Sehoya had ordered from Charleston. He gave the brass knob a sharp tug and rang the little bell that hung by the door. "I hear that and I know someone's come."

"What will they think of next," Jefferson said.

"No telling," Ridge said, rapping his knuckle against a glass pane for good measure. "Of course, you could stand in front of this and just let me look at you, too. We're trying out lots of new things around here."

Ridge noticed what a fine boy the half-breed had become as he took in Sehoya's porcelain chamber set that cut down on trips to the well to wash up and the whale-oil peg lamps they carried at night from room to room. Young McCoy was the son of an old Scottish trader who had taken a Cherokee for his wife, as Ridge's white ancestor had once done two generations before. His father schooled him as best he could, but Jefferson had never seen the things Sehoya had acquired for her home. In fact, neither had Ridge.

The boy handed Ridge the letter as he reclined on the English-made Hepplewhite mahogany sofa. McCoy ran his fingers across the carvings of feathers and the drapery festoons. It had cost Ridge nearly two moons' ferry proceeds to have it freighted across the Cherokee hills. Of course, Ridge couldn't read the letter, but he didn't want to disappoint the boy. A chief was supposed to know everything, so Ridge opened it and stared at the strange characters on the page. "Why do the whites write everything down on paper?" he asked Sehoya, who sat busy at her loom. "I can't understand a word of it."

"I'm happy to oblige," the boy said, and Ridge handed the letter back to him, watching the strange dance of the boy's pupils. ' "My dear brother Ridge: Perhaps Nancy has mentioned this during her visit home from school, but in case she hasn't I send the following progress report. Both of your children and your nephew, whom we've named Buck, thrive at our school. John and Buck have proved especially keen. Already they are both well versed in Mr. Webster's *Elements of Useful Knowledge, The American Accountant,* and *The Economy of Human Life,* as well as the arts of arithmetic, geography, and history.' "

"What are those things he's just mentioned?" Ridge said.

"Why, they're books, Chief Ridge."

Ridge clapped his hands in jubilation. "Is Gambold saying that my son and nephew have read a book?"

"No. He's saying they've read several."

Ridge couldn't believe it. For some time the *adawehis* had claimed that the source of all Ani-yonega power lay in their books, especially in their Bible. Could it be true that John and Kilakeena had already learned to decipher the mysterious black scratches? If so, the secrets of the whites were about to unfold for the Cherokee under Sehoya's roof.

"Well, of course they have," Ridge said, smiling at Sehoya. "Isn't that why we sent them there?"

"Would you shut up and let him finish?" Sehoya said.

" 'Just as you promised,' " the boy read on, " 'all of these children possess quick, agile minds and are much taken with their religious studies. Nancy is quite dear to our hearts. Buck is a warm, gentle child, always eager to please and quite innocent, and my wife and I are much taken with him. Our hope is that John will soon join his cousin in this pious state, for although articulate and quite promising as a scholar, young John seems reserved and calculating, given to pride and haughtiness, traits at odds with the Christian way. The boy is circumspect to a fault, even to the point of expressing skepticism for the Gospel story, which all Christians must accept on faith. Nevertheless his heart is good and his feet are on the right path. Visit us as you wish. Father Gambold.' "

McCoy folded the letter, smoothed it out on his thigh, and carefully placed it back in the envelope. White people sent talking leaves hidden in husks like peas in a pod. Curious. What did it matter if others heard this news? Ridge intended to tell everyone. He set the envelope on the mantel and lit his soapstone pipe with an ember from the fire.

"Are you hungry?" Ridge asked.

"Not at all. My parents will worry if I stay gone long."

"On your way, then, little brother. And thank you for coming all this way."

Ridge escorted the boy to the threshold, watched him pass safely into the night, and then bolted the door shut. He returned to the sofa and sat cross-legged before the fire, the letter between his fingers.

"The boy has pride," Sehoya said, "and they treat it as if it were some disease. What do they expect from the son of a chief?"

Sehoya's gaze never left her work at the loom. It was soothing to Ridge to listen to the rhythm of her efforts. "John's learned to read. Bring him home to us, Ridge," she said. "I miss him so."

"Please," Ridge said. "We've talked of this."

Sehoya answered that with a snort. His wife didn't need words to set him in his place.

"And from what I've heard of this story they tell — the Gospels — the boy is right to wonder," he said. "Only a fool would accept it as true. It's clearly a myth, the stuff of witches, I say, and I've told the man Gambold as much."

"Their faith is strong."

"Their education is stronger. And John stays until he masters it."

Sehoya shot him a look that would wilt weeds.

"With your blessing, of course," Ridge said.

Trouble.

Ridge reached through waves of cotton mist to return from so far away. Something was wrong. He heard a distant rumble growing louder, until at last it reached him with a deafening roar. When he opened his eyes, he found himself riding a bed that was teetering across the room. Glasses, plates, and jars clinked while windows rattled violently until they cracked and crashed to the floor in shards. The entire house trembled on its foundation until he felt the southwest corner slip from its cedar piers. One whole quarter of Sehoya's house slumped to the earth like a candle too close to the fire.

His first thought was of his children. Nancy was home from school, and the youngest, Walter, slept in a room down the long hall. Ridge tried to rise from his bed, but was thrown out of it instead. His knees wobbled so that he was unable to walk across the shifting, splintering puncheon floors. Pine rafters as thick as a bull's neck snapped like twigs, allowing their burdens to crash down around him. Afraid Sehoya would be crushed beneath the crumbling structure, Ridge dragged her from the room and carried her out the front door. Then he came back for Nancy and the simple-minded Walter, who always looked so lost, so pitiful.

Ridge had walked ten paces — cursing the white construction and the carpenters of this fool's enterprise that was collapsing in on itself — before he understood that the entire earth was trembling.

He'd heard the rumors. He'd seen the signs. Snakes of all kinds had emerged from their dens in the dead of winter. You couldn't walk from the house to the smoke shed without stepping over a dozen confused, listless serpents. Hunters reported swarms of squirrels escaping the Nation's western lands. At dawn, they'd seen twin columns of lightning, as straight and thick as the oldest oak trunk, flash from the earth to the heavens, leaving behind them a foul odor and the most curious haze hanging in the air. Passenger pigeons plagued the Ohio River valley like locusts. Nonmigratory songbirds completely abandoned the whole of the Nation. For days the eerie, solemn stillness had descended upon the Ani-yunwi-ya like a deep snow. The *adawehis* sensed doom.

Now, under clear skies and an infant moon

— the ninth he'd seen since the appearance of Tecumseh's twin-tailed comet that still tore across the black fathoms overhead — ancient trees crashed violently to the ground and large stones dislodged and thundered downhill, destroying everything in their path. The ground fissured beneath Ridge's feet, some of the cracks hungry enough to swallow a mule. Elsewhere, the earth rippled like an old man's face and vented yellow vapors so noxious they rivaled the stench of week-old dead. Ridge sought shelter for his terrified family in an open field, where at least no house or tree could fall on them. He wrapped Sehoya and their two children in a blanket he had ripped from their bed, watched their home undulate like a sapling in a storm, and waited balefully for the dawn.

Daybreak delivered no assurance. The sun was no longer powerful enough to shine through the dust and pungent smoke that shrouded the earth. Ridge tried to remain stoic for his wife and children, but his heart was distraught. Ever since he was a boy, the most gifted *adawehis* all agreed that the earth was dying. Was today the beginning of the world's death throes? Were the stone cords that supported Turtle Island crumbling at last? Sehoya comforted Walter while Ridge held Nancy still against his breast. Normally he would've rocked her, but with the ground trembling the stillness calmed her better.

Before the day was done, runners brought news to him and all other chiefs they could find. Throughout the Nation structures that had stood as long as Ridge could remember lay in heaps. Even the stout council houses were destroyed. Once-clear springs belched foul, scalding water. Terrified ducks landed on the shoulders of men. Prey and predator were seen standing together in open fields, all enmity between them forgotten as if the night had brought a new natural order. The Cherokee sang their death songs as they wept inconsolably around fire pits that cradled only cold, gray ashes. No one thought to cook anything. No one ate. The wind gave way only to human wailing.

In the west, the news was worse. The Father of Waters had risen and fallen like a storm tide. For a while it even flowed backward. Lake bottoms rose above the land around them. Fields and forests gave way to pits of quicksand and sinkholes and bubbling springs hot enough to boil fish. Survivors waded up to their chests in black water for miles, chin to chin with desperate snakes and varmints. Entire settlements had been wiped from the face of an angry earth. Five American towns had been swallowed whole. Water, sand, and steam spewed from the depths as high as the tallest cottonwoods. Sulfurous fumes rose in clouds, fouling the air and poisoning the animals. Lightning shot from the earth to the sky with thunderous booms like cannons. The ground was so hot that it could peel the sole from a man's foot. Great gars, carp, and catfish — some longer than war canoes — beached themselves on the banks as if it were pointless to carry on against the currents. The destruction ran far enough north and south along the great river that it would take a horseman one moon to travel to country untouched by the quakes.

Ridge had never seen such fear and misery on the faces of his stricken people. He calmed them as best he could, but when the trembling continued, the witches held their ears. Even they could not agree on the cause. Some said Uktena, the great serpent, was moving deep within the bowels of the earth. Others said the people were being punished because their chiefs had ceded so much land to the whites. The Great Provider was angry because so many of the ancient traditions had been disregarded, and the quaking of the earth was his final warning to all Cherokee that they must return to the old ways. Everywhere people reported sightings of strange spirits, avenging ghosts, and menacing apparitions. Almost all felt that one way or another, the end of all life was upon them. And Ridge was beside himself about what to do.

Through his public assurances and personal misgivings, Ridge heard Tecumseh's warning in his ears. Was it possible that the Shawnee's drunken brother truly spoke for the Great Provider, that he was truly His voice on this earth? How could Tecumseh have known such devastation would occur? The thought crossed his mind that his and Big Warrior's treatment of Tecumseh had brought his wrath down on their kind. To be held accountable for such emotional destruction and despair was worse for Ridge than the damage done by the earthquakes. Should he have listened to Tecumseh instead of threatening him? Was it possible that this Shawnee possessed the power to drive the whites into the sea?

Ridge trusted only one educated Ani-yonega — Father Gambold. As soon as he'd calmed his horse enough to mount it, he left his family with Oo-watie and galloped almost all of the way to Spring Place. The first thing he did was locate John Ridge. He clasped the boy so tightly to his chest that John swore he could not breathe. When he was certain his son was safe, he sought out the black-robed Moravian.

"Is it the end?" he asked in Cherokee.

"Of course not, Ridge Walker," the missionary said. Ridge noted the beginnings of a grin in the corners of his mouth. "You've nothing to fear. It's an earthquake, a shifting of the earth's energy, a mere settling of conflicting powers that long ago pushed the continents up from the sea."

"Is it a natural force, then?"

"Absolutely. Part of God's plan. Earthquakes are indeed frightening things, very destructive, as we've seen. But they occur all over the world, and have done so since the beginning of time. There'll be many more eruptions and trembling, but slowly things will return to normal."

"Do you know this because you've experienced such a thing or because you've got books?"

"I'm afraid I learned from the books."

"Oh," Ridge said. "And you feel that's as good as seeing it for yourself?"

"I'd say it's much better."

"And knowing all that's happened, you have no concern?"

"I'm concerned for the injured, the damage to our villages. The hardships of our people as they rebuild what they've lost."

"All of that can be undone," Ridge said, finding his balance. "It was the appearance of the earth breaking apart, its pieces being hurled into the void like pebbles into the depths of the oceans, that formed the larger problem, to my mind."

Father Gambold laughed. "It has happened before," he said. "It will happen again."

"Ah," Ridge sighed, drawing a deep breath. "I was greatly troubled by this."

"It's merely God's way of encouraging the Cherokee to follow him."

Ridge didn't like the sound of that. You could never have a decent conversation with these people without being pressured to adopt their religion. Ridge hurried here in terror to beg for help, and again Gambold manipulated the opportunity to pursue his personal agenda.

"Are earthquakes a natural occurrence or not?" Ridge asked.

"Yes, quite so."

"Then don't frighten us with some talk of punishment. What have we done to deserve such destruction?"

"Nothing more than live in ignorance."

"And that's changing, is it not?"

"Oh, yes," Father Gambold said. "We're winning souls for the Lord each day."

"Tecumseh's won more, I can assure you. Not only among the Cherokee, but with the Choctaw, Chickasaw, and especially the Creeks." Ridge thought a moment. "I've heard things about your God, Jesus. That he could perform miracles, and even once calmed a storm. Do you believe it?"

"With all my heart."

"Can a man — a powerful, spiritual man — will an earthquake and make it so?"

"A man cannot," Gambold said. "Only God commands the earth and the heavens."

"What if that same man professes to speak to God — the same God that is father to us all? What if he claims to be a part of God's purpose? Do you feel that God would shake the earth to punish His doubters?"

"He doesn't work like that."

Again Ridge sighed. "I didn't think so," he said. "It was chance then?"

"Exactly."

"Tecumseh could not be luckier," Ridge said. He gathered his reins and mounted the horse. "Look after our children, Gambold. I can still the Cherokee hearts. It's the Creeks who will suffer."

John Ridge bolted free from the protective skirts of Father Gambold, raced for his father, and clamped onto his leg just as he'd done the day Ridge delivered him to the school. Ridge lifted him up and sat him across his saddle. He hugged the boy, taking in the sweet smell of his curly black hair. Ridge missed him every bit as much as Sehoya did.

"You people spoil your children so," Father Gambold said. "You've probably never lifted a hand to that boy."

"And I never will," Ridge said. "It's not our way." Then he whispered into his son's ear, "Don't be afraid, Skah-tle-loh-skee. How would that look to these people who complain about your pride? Go on with your studies. Turtle Island is not yet doomed."

CHAPTER SEVENTEEN

The first person Ridge sought out once he'd arrived at the Oostanaula council house was his oldest and least impressionable friend, White Path. Running the war trace together had further strengthened their boyhood bond and Ridge could think of no other Cherokee whose opinion he trusted more when he needed to understand the traditional mind. Ridge was keenly aware of the demoralizing effects of the New Madrid earthquakes on his own neighbors. As one of Pathkiller's thirteen grand councilors chosen to manage the Cherokee's national affairs, Ridge was charged with restoring their confidence. He had hoped that White Path could provide him with a better grasp of how the outland full-bloods were reacting before this witch whom half the tribe had come to hear had a chance to compound the problem.

"Before the tremors faded, awful rumors began in my village," White Path said as he dug his fingers into a gourd full of beef-and-potato stew. The Cherokee ate together before their council began just after sundown. "Terrified that Turtle Island was ripping apart," he said, "the people desperately sought answers. The conjurers in my region called for a great medicine festival so that we could all seek together."

After the quakes, Ridge had attended many such ceremonies in the vain attempt to calm his people. The women danced with pebble-filled tortoiseshells strapped to their ankles, singing songs that vowed death to civilization and a return to the ignorance that had chained the Cherokee to savagery. Old, scarred warriors vowed to shun all modern conveniences out of respect for the glory of times past.

"It's the same everywhere," Ridge said. "The earthquakes laid waste to the Cherokee's judgment along with their homes. Everyone thinks we're being punished."

"Aren't we?" White Path said.

Ridge threw up his hands. "What have we done to deserve destruction?" he said. "Live just a little like white men? The quakes claimed white and red lives alike for as far as they reached. I don't believe for an instant that the Provider singled out the Cherokee for punishment."

"Would it be all right with you, Chief Ridge, if a Cherokee had a different opinion from your own?"

"In your case no, Chief White Path," Ridge said. "When a chief wallows in ignorance, he leaves his people ripe for sorcery. Next, we'll have fires burning around us as far as we can see. The earthquakes were just a bruise compared to the disaster wrought by another war with the Americans."

"Listen well, Ridge," White Path said, leveling his glance. "My people are worried. You and your mixed-blood farmer friends move too fast for us who love the old ways."

"Civilization doesn't have to mean the opposite of our traditions," Ridge said, gesturing emphatically with his arms. White Path stopped chewing to study his frantic demeanor. Ridge understood that much more emotion had entered the conversation than he would've liked. He drew a calming breath. "Why do people always see things as black or white?" he said. "Surely you know that I love the old ways, too."

"I sometimes wonder," White Path said. "As your friend, I have to tell you that some people say you live too much for profit."

"Which I share with my neighbors and those I represent at this council and any others who ask. What does it matter if my money comes from white hands when I give so much away to the Cherokee?"

White Path considered this as Ridge caught a whiff of his beef stew. He looked up at the sky in wonder, mouth agape. When White

Path did the same, Ridge snatched his friend's gourd. "Is this any good?" he asked, tossing a cube of steaming beef into his mouth. "I haven't eaten all day."

"What was that you said about sharing?" White Path said, his expression rather hang-dog. Ridge moaned in satisfaction to taunt him. When White Path finally chuckled, Ridge handed him back the gourd.

"Anyway, that's enough of your gossip," Ridge said. By now, warriors were sparking flints in the dried grass beneath the waiting council fires. "I'd like to hear the facts. Who is this conjurer who's made all this fuss?"

White Path explained that this mixed-blood prophet who called himself Charley had come down from the isolated peaks of the Great Smokies. Few Cherokee had ever seen him before. No one knew either his kin or clan. While meditating, Charley claimed to have witnessed a disturbing vision of great import to the Nation, or so he explained to the council when he insisted they hear him. The people flocked in from all regions to hear what he had to say.

"What does he look like?" Ridge said.

"Admittedly, quite strange," White Path said.

"In what way?"

"Something like that." White Path pointed to a twig of an old man in ragged buckskins and a dingy turban, with wide loops of tarnished silver hanging from his droopy ears as he cut a swath through the crowd with two identical black wolves by his side. Astonished Cherokee parted to make room as Charley floated to the heart of the council grounds. Normally Ridge would have dismissed the hermit as a lunatic at first sight had it not been for the wolves. The Cherokee feared them as powerful, avenging spirits. He'd never seen them tamed, but there they stood like lapdogs by Charley's side as he took his place near the council fire. Ridge elbowed White Path and together they moved within range of Charley's voice.

"I have a message for the Cherokee," Charley said, addressing not only the council but the awestruck villagers as well. "I encountered gigantic Indians on the backs of black horses, riding the heavens above where the clouds had parted. One of these ghost riders, who beat a drum as loud as thunder, told me that the Great Provider is angry that the Cherokee have taken up the white man's ways. The grain mills, looms, clothes of cotton, feather beds, eating tables, books, and house cats are all things contrary to the natural way. For this reason, the Great Provider has taken away the buffalo, the elk, and the whitetail. And worse yet, why he caused the earth to break apart, why the old women have dark, troubling dreams, and why your children cry at night. The seer, Charley, tells you only what was told to him."

Ridge rolled his eyes at the notion, partly because Gambold, an educated man, had explained the earthquakes to his satisfaction, and partly because he had heard the words of Tecumseh himself, the same from which Charley borrowed now. Regardless of how this conjurer spun his version, Ridge predicted that he'd soon urge the Cherokee to join Tecumseh's brewing war.

He sat silently and listened, watching the expressions of his people as Charley wove his tale, wondering if they would be wise enough to discard it as nonsense, or whether the myth would take root like a weed, as Tecumseh's message had among the young, thoughtless Red Stick Creeks.

"Return to the ways of our fathers!" Charley pleaded. "Kill your cats, your stupid cattle, and mud-wallowing hogs. Dress as becomes Indians and warriors. Set aside all fashions and practices of the whites, for anyone can see they are different from us. The Cherokee were made of red clay; they of white, shifting sand. Make not your mark upon talking leaves, nor pay heed to their meaning, but speak to one another through the mouth the Provider gave you. Plant Indian corn and Indian crops. Burn your mills, for their constant grinding wears down the bones of the Mother of this nation, and for this reason she has abandoned you. Walk away from your houses and let time take them. Adorn your bodies as we did in ancient times. Hold feasts and dances, and listen to the Provider's blessings that enter your dreams like a cool breeze. Do all this and the whites will go away. When they're gone, the game will return."

Charley turned back to stare down the chiefs behind him. "Deny not the Great Provider's plan for the Cherokee." His stern gaze fell last on Ridge, the least impressionable of the chiefs and the one exhibiting the most blatant disdain. "For any who dare will be struck dead before him. So spoke the vision that came to me."

Before Charley's words died in the wind, Ridge was on his feet. "This talk will lead us to war with the Americans!" he shouted. "This man will be in the hills when their wrath falls upon your heads. He won't hear the screams of your wives and children. I, the Man Who Walks the Mountaintops, defy him. If what he says is true, let death come upon me!"

He spread his arms and turned his face to the heavens. He heard nothing save the gasps of the crowd and the crackling of the council fires. Those near him yielded space, White Path among the first. Ridge waited. Nothing. When he felt he had made his point, he turned to the prophet, expecting to see him broken, as Ridge had done to the venal chiefs years before. But before Ridge could even see Charley clearly, young warriors rushed from the crowd, their weapons poised and ready.

Ridge was knocked to his knees with the first blows. He tasted both blood and metal. He kicked at the warriors' knees, knocking down two and pummeling them with his fists, but there were far too many. They dragged him through the mud and beat him in the face and head until he was nearly senseless. They would've killed him had it not been for White Path, who cleared them out with his ceremonial war club before they could crush his skull.

"This is not the way," White Path said. "I will not see a chief mobbed for what he says in council."

The offending warriors hesitated, but Ridge didn't see any change of heart in their lean expressions. He shoved himself up from the sticky soil and gathered himself. He spit out the blood and wrung the mud from his hands, glaring at his attackers through burning eyes. He unleashed the anger that had once made him a warrior and Ridge let it take him.

"You young men want war," he said, snatching the war club from White Path's grip. "Let your first battle begin with me."

Bellowing his war cry, Ridge pounced on them with a ferocity he thought had left his body ten winters before. He rammed the first attacker in the stomach, doubling him up on the ground. He saw the flash of a blade darting for his ribs. He swung the club downward in one crisp motion against the man's arm. He heard the snap of the warrior's bone and then only his screams after that. Ridge jutted the handle into a skinny man's nose, watching the blood explode over his face. Ridge dropped to his knee and with a wide swing of the club he hamstrung two others who stalked him from the rear. They both hit the ground with a dull thud, and when they did, Ridge buried the flat of the war club on top of their chests. They both heaved to their sides and lay still.

White Path jumped in beside him and they fought back-to-back. Ridge's friend had only his fists for weapons, but he knocked out another of Ridge's assailants cold. None of White Path's own people dared to attack him and bowed out of the brawl. But others they did not know still came at them with knives and tomahawks. Together, Ridge and White Path tore at them like wild dogs.

"Come on," White Path said, wiping the blood from his mouth. "You boys cry about lost traditions and you behave as shamefully as this at the council ground? Come and take us if you can."

For Ridge, time slowed as if he were dreaming. He focused on one warrior at a time and then went at him, swinging the club over his head to clear his enemies out of immediate range and deny them anything but defensive movements. When his target went down, Ridge kicked him hard in the stomach. If he tried to get up again, Ridge kicked him in the teeth, all while continually whirling the club blade-first over his head. Big White Path moved slowly along with Ridge, covering his friend's back and pummeling any warrior who came close enough. If they swung at him with a tomahawk, he stepped forward into the blow, grabbed their arm as it passed him, elbowed them stiffly in the gut, and flipped them over his shoulder at Ridge's feet, where his friend knocked them senseless with the club. Powerless to stop the violence, the chiefs, elders, and clan mothers stood by in agony, watching it run its course. Ridge picked out yet another enemy, yelling his war cry so loudly the hair on the back of his neck bristled. When that one went down, he picked out another.

One by one Ridge's enemies fell before him and White Path, and either crawled away bleeding or were saved by their wives and mothers, who begged Ridge for their lives until at last there was no one left standing to challenge them. When it was finished and nearly twenty warriors lay on the ground, Ridge, washed in sweat and blood, his heart pounding, and his chest strong with victory and proud air, faced the astonished crowd.

"Yuh!" he cried loudly enough to make Charley's wolves yelp. "Listen! I am *Kahnung-da-tla-geh* — the Man Who Walks the Mountain tops! I see both paths clearly. One offers hope; the other certain doom. The Ridge will lay down his life before he'll watch false prophets lead the Cherokee to their destruction."

Charley, undaunted, stood his ground. His wolves growled and bared white, shiny teeth. A thread of drool strung from their fangs to the red mud. "I will bring a hailstorm on this nation three days hence that will claim all who follow this man!" Charley railed. "As the earth cracked beneath your feet, so shall the skies open up and rain destruction upon all those who travel apart from the Great Provider. Let those who truly believe return to the mountains from whence we came for their salvation. Let those who stand by the Ridge Walker perish with him."

Charley, his stare locked on Ridge, fell silent. While his wolves snarled and snapped at Ridge, Charley walked out of the council. At the edge of the fire's light he stopped and clapped his hands once and the wolves abandoned Ridge to accompany him into the brush. The night and the wilds reclaimed them, and all was still again.

Ridge watched them go. He had broken the man, but the wolves left him uncertain. One of White Path's followers laid a bucket of springwater at his feet and handed Ridge a cloth to wipe the blood from his face.

"These council meetings are getting better all the time," White Path said, flashing a grin that nearly connected both ears.

"I can't say I enjoy them like I used to," Ridge said, pressing his palm against his swelling eye. Most likely Sehoya would get a dodder poultice after him when he got home. At least, she would after she mocked him for getting in a scuffle with young hotheads.

By then, White Path was laughing. He wrapped his big arms around Ridge's shoulder, and Ridge laughed, too.

"If you'd have fought like that with Dragging Canoe," Ridge said, "we wouldn't be in this mess. Instead, as I recall, you were always behind me."

"The Americans had bullets," White Path said. "I'd rather you caught one than me."

White Path looked around at the injured and angry faces of their kin, and then at last upon the disgusted stares of the chiefs and elders. His laughter died.

"Our people are unhappy to see the Cherokee's blood on their own council ground."

"Better to find a few sprinkles here," Ridge said, "than to see the hills covered. That's what will happen if we don't stand up to Tecumseh and whatever witches he spawns."

"I'm not ashamed," White Path said. "I did what my heart told me was right."

251

Ridge reached over and grabbed him by the back of his neck and turned his head toward him. "Let me tell you something, old man. What you did was courageous. We hurt a few people. We offended quite a few. But as far as I'm concerned, we saved thousands, especially when Charley's squall doesn't come." He tugged a little tighter. "The friends whom the Ridge loves best are the ones he knows will fight for him. I will never forget what you did for me tonight."

"Don't worry about that," White Path said. "I'll never let you." He smiled a little and then Ridge let him go. White Path peered up at the skies while Ridge washed off the blood and dirt. "Storm coming," he said.

"We'll see," Ridge said.

Ridge lay in his bean field beside Sehoya, gnawing on a blade of grass. The picnic was her idea. All three of their children were with them, as were Oo-watie and his wife and members of their extended family and clan. Dawn broke quietly on this, the appointed day of the Cherokee's doom. Heavy gray clouds hung low in the breathless sky. Ridge had to admit that there was something ominous about their appearance, but he didn't dare let his concern show on his face. He smiled at his wife, wrestled with John and Walter while Sehoya brushed Nancy's hair, and waited for the sun to climb across the

Sky Vault.

By noon the sky had cleared. Dry, warm winds kicked up in the heat of the day, chasing clouds north where they would shroud the peaks of the Smokies. Ridge grinned, settling underneath heavens as clear and blue as mountain springs.

"My brother," he said to Oo-watie, who was still nibbling on some of Sehoya's anies' ta, boiled corn mush that Sehoya had cooled, sliced, and fried in fresh butter with just a splash of bacon grease. "Care to wager on the chance of hail today?"

"I've made some mistakes in my life," Watie said. "But I don't think I'll make that one."

"That's a shame," Ridge said. "Because if I could've fleeced you for twenty dollars today, I could've bought that brood chestnut mare from Cavendish tomorrow. I'd fatten her all summer to breed her this fall, and in the spring I'd have a wonderful colt to sell — or maybe keep for one of my children to ride. But in any case, I can plan on doing something in the spring because we clearly are not going to die today."

He kissed Sehoya, who stuffed another wahes' di in his mouth. Ramps were his favorite, especially the way Sehoya prepared them.

"Did you collect the ramps yourself?" Ridge asked her.

"Of course," she said. "I'm the only one who knows the proper way."

"Which is what?" Nancy asked, always curious.

"Like my grandmother taught me. Leave the first three you find out of respect for the spirits and collect only the fourth."

"Or better yet," Ridge said, "send a slave —"

Sehoya shot him a menacing glance. "I've told you a thousand times that we don't have slaves. We have servants."

"Very well, my dove," Ridge said. "Send one of the people that I bought to perform labors and save your heart the trouble. You've got no business up in those mountains alone."

"My business is my business," Sehoya said.

"I've got enemies," he said.

"If they come after me you won't have them long."

She ran her finger across Ridge's black eye to remind him that his stubbornness often brought him pain. He pulled back from her touch, but he had to smile.

"Cook what you want then, woman," he said. "Just don't wander out in the mountains unprotected. I'd be lost if something happened to you."

Sehoya patted his hand to assure him that she understood. Ridge rolled Walter's hoop between the furrows and Walter and Stand, Oo-watie's youngest boy, got after it with their sticks. Ridge tossed the extra shaft to John, who stood up from the blanket to join the chase also. He took just a few painful steps and then fell with a cry. Ridge jumped up to go help him, but Sehoya grabbed his arm.

"Let him do for himself," she said. "Today's no different for him from the rest."

John lay in the dirt, sobbing. Ridge's body tightened as he restrained his impulse to help his child. John sat up and flung a handful of dirt into the air. When he looked back at his father, Ridge managed to smile. Then John climbed up to his feet, snatched his stick, and limped off after the others. Ridge relaxed when he heard John's laughter.

"He has your heart," she said, stroking Ridge's hair.

He nodded and then forced his mind to think of more pleasant things than his son's daily struggles. "My stomach feels like it's stuffed with walnuts," he said to Oo-watie as he stretched. He checked the position of the sun. "Let's go to water."

He trotted out to catch John and Walter, letting John avoid him much longer than his younger brother. His crippled son squealed in delight as Ridge chased him. Ridge soon caught them both and packed each boy under an arm as he led his entire family to the river. Oo-watie carried his boys. Sehoya brought their rifles and leaned them against a snag.

Ridge was the first to wade in. He put Walter up on his shoulders. Watie did the same with Stand. Kilakeena rested his head in Sehoya's lap and stuck his nose in a book. It pleased him to watch Sehoya stroke his nephew's hair as he read. Ridge locked his arm around Oo-watie and headed out to the eddies. The surface was warm, but when he sank to the depths he found the water fresh and cool. Ridge stayed under, allowing the currents to wash around him until his lungs nearly burst. And then he yelled, precisely as he had on the night he became a warrior and the river had washed the blood from his body. Only this time it was not from pain, but from joy.

The day had proved the absurdity of Charley's vision. Soon the embarrassed Cherokee would come down from the mountains to find their friends alive and their homes intact. Ridge would greet them graciously in the hope that they would never again question his leadership. He hoped that he had regained their trust. He would use their renewed faith in him to save their lives. He thought of this as fathers and sons tussled in the stream.

Every now and then he'd look upriver toward Sehoya and the women sunning themselves on river rocks. She'd look back at him, sweep the hair out of her face as if she were some seductive maiden, and smile. At first Ridge thought Sehoya would find herself pregnant again if she kept that up. Then that sense of grace and reflection that comes with middle age washed over him and he thought, *How could my life be any better?*

If there was a dark cloud on that brilliant day, Ridge felt certain it loomed over the Creek Nation. Tecumseh's vision was alive and well among the young Red Stick warriors. Whenever they spoke, Big Warrior adamantly maintained that all was right among his people, but Ridge knew better. Guns would soon be fired and the blood would flow, and that great faceless American giant would stomp among their Creek brothers until they were crushed like dead grass underfoot. Ridge knew it just as he'd known Charley was a pitiful fool. But Tecumseh was no Charley, and the young Creek warriors weren't sitting up on some mountain waiting for the deluge. Against the admonishments of Big Warrior and the elder chiefs, the Red Sticks were preparing themselves spiritually and materially for a war they would lose, and Ridge knew there was nothing he could do but watch it run its course.

Something snatched him from his more distant worries. He heard commotion inconsistent with the peace of twilight — hoofbeats of many driven horses accompanied by the voices of whooping men beyond the rise. No Cherokee pushed horses like that unless they were running from danger, and if that were the case, they would neither stay together nor make so much noise. Ridge responded to his first instinct and waded ashore to pick up his rifle. Before he'd reached the bank, he saw the thin cloud of dust drifting out over the river.

Then he saw them. White riders — more like children — beating the flanks of their horses, herding the twenty or so of the other head they'd stolen from some Cherokee ahead of them. Ridge shouldered his weapon and cocked the hammer, daring them to come any closer. Oo-watie reached the bank, grabbed his rifle, and took aim. John limped up beside his father with a tomahawk in his hand. Stand palmed a rock.

The thieves cut hard ahead of them and splashed into the river, whipping their horses with their hats. When the last of them climbed up on the opposite bank, one of the riders paused, reared up his horse, and bowed before Ridge with his hat in his hand. Then he tore into the thickets to rejoin the rest in their race for the Georgia line.

"You put one fire out," Oo-watie said, "and another flares up."

"One enemy at a time," Ridge said. "First we must fend off Tecumseh and maybe solidify our bond to the American Father at the same time. Then we'll see about them."

CHAPTER EIGHTEEN

The General

Why shouldn't you question me? Confronted with the horror of a war of extermination — the ugly details of our destiny — how could you not ask why the killing must be so? I have some experience in elocution. Permit me a moment of your time to explain.

What's happening here — all of it — is the will of my people. I can acknowledge that their resolve might have faltered had they viewed this dreadful carnage as intimately as I do now. But mine never did. I've waited a long time for a confrontation like this, where one final victory would crush any remaining hope among the Indians that we could be defeated, our dreams thwarted, our ambitions checked by any of the tribal nations, civilized or savage. I hastened here sick, wounded, emaciated, a fresh pistol ball flattened against the bone of my left arm, yet I resolved to make an example of the Creeks or perish in the attempt. As God is my witness, I came to see my purpose done.

I loathe the British. My family forfeited everything for the Revolution to expel that repugnant breed from our shores. I had seen but fourteen years when I lost my brother and mother to the ravages of war, so my own cost was dear. A British officer once ordered me to clean the mud from his boots. When I refused, he thrashed me with his sword, gashing my left hand and forehead to the bone. To this day I carry the scars.

Some may swear that Tecumseh and his one-eyed brother sparked the uprising of the Creeks. But it was the British, known to manipulate the heathens as a matter of foreign policy, who gathered the kindling and stoked the flames.

There's nothing new in any of my views of the Indian nations. Removal of the tribes to the west has long been considered inevitable and far more merciful than allowing them to sink into oblivion through swindling, poverty, and grain spirits. The trend in the United States is for the young, rough-and-ready folk to move west to make their way in the world. I am myself a product of this migration. Our people will hunger for the tribes' hunting grounds until there are only two options available to the red men: accept the sovereignty of the states in which they live, embrace civilization, and commit themselves headlong to becoming industrious citizens of our nation; or remove to the wilderness, where they can retain their ancient customs, which are wholly incompatible with our way of life.

That's it in a hickory nut, my friend. As a veteran of the Revolution, I dedicated my life to a glorious dream — giving birth to the only true republic in the world. Now that I've seen a hint of our potential, does it not stand to reason that I would likewise do most anything to nurture and defend it? Long ago, I came to grips with the grim realities of the frontier, one of which is that Christians and heathens cannot share the same land. God ignores the savage. History has left them behind. The future compels us to run them over or sweep them out of our way.

You disagree? You're not alone. Your kind are all around me and I don't pay them much mind, either. It's always best that heirs to a great fortune not look too closely at how the money was made. Make no mistake. The faint hearts represent a balking minority in a nation where the majority rules. I, on the other hand, am undaunted. It remains incumbent upon me to do my duty regardless of the opinions of these fireside patriots. These fawning sycophants and cowardly poltroons can turn their heads away if they must, but regardless of what they do they can't deflect me from our God-directed destiny. No man or nation can.

The southeast is too important to the Union for its safety to be jeopardized. We cannot leave independent, potentially hostile Indian nations behind us as we forge our way west. For this reason, I have long viewed treaties with the savages as an absurdity, not to be reconciled to the principles of our government. Like it or not, the Indians are subjects of the United States, and they must bow to its sovereignty and adhere to its laws.

You do not know these people. I would kill a hundred red men to avenge one murder of an American and lose not one minute's sleep. The Indians are a wild, violent, vindictive race, hopelessly rooted in their savage traditions, and I have little hope that they can ever live in harmony among our people. The Creeks proved my point at Fort Sims, and I vowed to hunt them to extinction and lay claim to their land, which rightfully belongs to us after we drove the British back to their island in '83.

The issue is primarily one of security. Our frontier borders leave us vulnerable. We are continually threatened by European powers — particularly the British and the Spanish — whose agents prey upon the anger and resentment of the red men and urge them to vent it toward our people. I've seen the grim result many times, the savagery of Indian depredations against our settlers. I saw it this August past at Fort Sims when a thousand Red Stick warriors under William Weatherford butchered four hundred men, women, and children. The skulls of babes were bashed against the stockade walls. Women were scalped alive and left to bleed to death. If pregnant, they were eviscerated alive, the unborn babies plucked from the womb and impaled on spears before their mothers' very eyes. Almost all of the victims were bludgeoned and hacked to pieces. Some were strangled with their own intestines. Ten days had passed before reinforcements arrived to bury the dead. We found buzzards and wild dogs picking rotten flesh from their bones.

Look upon such a horrific abomination, America, and urge me to find compassion for a race that wages war like this! What place on God's earth could be a refuge for this manner of ignorance, wickedness, and evil? Why should such inhuman behavior be afforded humanity? I tell you, the scourge of Indian infestation will end only when the last of the savages slumbers beneath freshly plowed fields. The process begins here, at the Horseshoe of the Tallapoosa, where I stand among smoking ruins and bloody slaughter to utter these few bleak words.

I see I have your attention now. On to specifics, then. I believe you're ready to hear the rest.

This mission was never easy. I had under

my command the Thirty-ninth U.S. Infantry, a couple thousand Tennessee volunteer militia, five hundred Cherokees, and a hundred friendly Creeks. The Indian allies were a blessing. They knew the way through the river bottoms and marshes and how to forage for sustenance while we traveled with a handful of supplies. The rest of my company gave me nothing but consternation. Constantly threatened with desertions and mutiny, I pointed both of my cannons at my own recruits, who did not waver in their treachery until my gunners sparked their torches. And make no mistake about it, had one man taken a step more, I would have touched flame to fuse. My will burned hotter than theirs. From that day forward they called me Old Hickory. I'm proud of the name. But the Cherokees refer to me as Sharp Knife, and I like that better.

I maintained the strictest discipline on this campaign. I drilled my militia. I kept them occupied clearing new roads and maintaining those that already existed. I tolerated no whiskey and no dissent. And I had a man — a boy, really — eighteen-year-old John Wood, executed before a firing squad.

Many came to me to plead for the boy's life. He had abandoned his post to eat his breakfast on a cold, rainy February morning. His officer had given him permission to do so. But when another discovered him in his tent and ordered him back to his post, Wood threatened to shoot him. Under other circumstances, I would have been the first to pardon him. But this was war, we were in hostile territory, and I had no choice but to make an example of this boy for any others so rebelliously inclined. I gave the order myself, stood before him as the charges were read, saw his wild eyes as the riflemen took aim against him. I watched John Wood die, and I didn't hear so much as a whimper after that, not even the mornings we woke to a breakfast of boiled acorns. As sick as I was with the dysentery and swamp fever, I ate them myself. General Jackson issued an order, and it was obeyed to the letter.

On the day I buried the unfortunate John Wood, I marched my army south to the banks of the Coosa River, then east toward Emuckfaw until we finally reached Tohopeka, the Horseshoe, a hundred-acre bend in the Tallapoosa River. In this place, my spies told me, waited over one thousand hostile Red Stick warriors.

I was stunned by the Creeks' fortifications. It was impossible to conceive a position more eligible for defense than the one they had chosen, a place well formed by nature and rendered more secure by art. They had run a tidy eight-foot-high breastwork of earth, stone, timber, and trunks clear across the 350-yard neck of the bend, its center curved inward with portholes throughout to expose any frontal assault with cross fire. Had I been charged with defending this place, I would have fortified it exactly as the Creeks had done.

Thus, the battle lines were drawn.

Prior to engagement, I sent my old friend and confidant, General Coffee, across the Tallapoosa with his cavalry and the Cherokee contingent to cut off all escape. Once I knew they were securely in place, I rolled up my six- and three-pounders and gave the order to fire at precisely ten-thirty. This was yesterday morning, March 27, in the Christian year of 1814.

For two hours, my cannons were trained on a single spot in the Creek defenses. The Red Sticks peppered the gun crews as often as they could, but my Tennessee volunteers answered with their long rifles. That said, my bombardment didn't make a dent in the breastworks. And I couldn't order my men against the wall to be slaughtered while it stood whole.

The Cherokee in the rear had grown restless. The chief known as the Ridge, a tree trunk of a man whom I myself commissioned weeks into the campaign as a major for his unmistakable qualities of initiative, leadership, and courage, sent his brother and two other warriors paddling across the Tallapoosa for the Creek canoes moored on the opposite bank. A few vigilant Creeks fired upon these brave men, but Major Ridge had organized his command into rifle companies, and he protected them well. The swimmers returned with canoes, stocked them with a few warriors, and paddled back across for more, always under intense Red Stick fire. I don't know how the Cherokee avoided slaughter, but I can testify to their courage. Major Ridge was one of the first to float across the river and engage the enemy hand to hand.

Enough Cherokee were soon across the Tallapoosa, and after slaying the Creek vanguard, they attacked the wigwams, flushing the frightened Creeks toward the breastworks. When the Cherokees set fire to the huts, I saw the smoke and knew the time had come for a frontal assault.

No sooner had I shouted the order to attack than the men of the Thirty-ninth took up their own voices. They hurled themselves at the breastworks in the teeth of withering Creek fire. I saw a number of musket balls plastered against their bayonets, badges, and buttons. I witnessed Major Lemuel Montgomery, the first to scale the barricade, receive a ball to the head and fall dead in a bloody arc. Ensign Sam Houston scrambled to Montgomery's place, only to catch a Red Stick arrow tipped with British steel in the thigh. Terribly gored, Houston leaped over the breast works anyway, and dozens of brave men followed him.

Their fortifications breached, the Creeks fled for the bottom briers of the Horseshoe. Some tried to cross the river, but Major Ridge and his Cherokee flanked them, cutting them to pieces with trained rifle fire. The Cherokee dove after the Creeks who had already reached the river. I saw six men fall to Ridge's tomahawk. The few Creeks who were lucky enough to reach the opposite bank ran dead into Coffee's men, who had freshly loaded rifles and plenty of targets. I've never been witness to a more desperate contest. The killing went on for hours.

Soon enough the Red Sticks realized there was no escape. Warrior, wife, and child all huddled in a brush embankment for a final stand. My resolve faded at first sight of the noncombatants in harm's way. I did not have it in me to order these courageous people to be shot down like dogs. I sent an interpreter to offer the Creeks clemency if they would only surrender.

I suspected there would be reluctance, especially after what happened last November in the Hillabee towns. The chiefs of those Creek villages had sent an emissary to me to seek terms of surrender, and I accepted. But I could not get word to General Cocke in time, and in his ignorance he attacked and massacred them. I was held responsible for this tragedy, and the consensus among the hostiles was that Sharp Knife's tongue could not be trusted. I know this came into play when I tried to save the Red Sticks at the Horseshoe from their fate. They mocked my messenger, who pleaded with them anyway, until at last they ran a ball through his chest. There was nothing I could do for them after that.

My volunteers set fire to their embankment and then calmly walked back some distance to find a good rest for their rifles. One by one, the Creeks fled the flames, only to be shot dead. Hour after hour, I heard the screams of women and children, some of whom were burned so badly they begged for some leather stocking's bullet to end their pain. Human grease pooled, crackling near glowing coals. Black smoke choked the river bottoms. I held my pipe to my nose to mask the stench. When darkness fell, the riflemen waited for the Creeks, whose frantic forms were perfectly silhouetted by the fire, to make a dash for the woods.

The carnage was dreadful. It went on until the last of the Creeks lay silent and all we could hear were the hungry flames. Major Ridge and his Cherokee made victory possible, yet they wanted no part of the final slaughter. I distinctly remember seeing him uncock his rifle and walk away from the firing line. His warriors soon followed his example. My soldiers were left to their sport.

The wailing of the Creeks will forever torment me. I tell myself, as I've admitted to you, that this struggle was the will of my people. We were also retaliating for the massacre of the innocents at Fort Sims. In truth, these notions fail to console me, not after I've looked upon the cost of our nation's destiny with my own eyes. Never has the moral burden of rightful conquest fallen so heavily upon me. The worst of it was that my own people were as keen as any savage to murder in this brutal manner. I'm sickened by the thought.

Inspecting the dead, I came across a handsome, dark-eyed, raven-haired Creek boy, his cheeks smudged black with soot and streaked with tears. He couldn't have been more than four years old. The few Creek women who remained alive were oblivious to the child's misery. There was a distant stare, the look of great loss, in their vacant eyes, but I couldn't understand why they wouldn't console the child.

"Will one of you women not comfort him?" I asked through my interpreter. We had destroyed so many lives, I immediately vowed to redeem this one. I don't know how this happened, except to say that when a soldier goes into battle against an armed enemy, he never expects to confront such a pitiful situation. The boy's plight touched me. That's all I can say.

The Creek women sat in silence, unmoved.

I loudly repeated my request until at last one of them fixed me with an icy glare.

"You've killed his parents, Sharp Knife," she grunted at me. "Kill him, too."

"I'll do nothing of the sort," I said. I gathered the child against my breast with my one good arm and sat him on my cot. I dissolved a little brown sugar into fresh water and dripped it down his throat. The child didn't warm to me much, and who could blame him? But I took to him in three beats of my heart. What else could I do but send him home to my beloved wife, Rachel, instructing her not to treat him as some slave or servant, but as she would one of our own.

I'll raise that child and love him, give him everything I have at my disposal. And when he's a man and old enough to comprehend the complex circumstances by which he was brought to live beneath my roof, I will beg his forgiveness. And he will have to love me with the whole of his heart to give it earnestly, for there's no getting past the fact that I, Andrew Jackson, destroyed his people.

And what crime did the most militant of the Red Sticks commit? They were willing to fight and die for their way of life against a greater people equally determined. The Creek War is not an issue of right versus wrong, but rather two rights tragically locked head-to-head in a bitter contest that only one will survive.

I grow weary. I'm sick in body and spirit. I miss my home. I long to be near my beloved wife. I had to look that child in the face and try to convince him that I was still capable of the most basic human compassion. I admit to you that I am not the man I was when this campaign began. Yet I will carry forth. I will see the business through regardless of what it costs me. There's nothing more to discuss.

But mark me on this final point: We must never forget that there was a grand purpose behind all of the violence. Remember that destiny is a burden and our glory has a price. There is still the dream that we call America, and I reach for it through the smoke of this battlefield. The planting of such terrible seeds will reap a gracious bounty. Opportunity, prosperity, and security will rise above the fresh graves of those who suffered and died at Tohopeka. The service of the Horseshoe was my duty, and I ask for nothing save your understanding in return.

I did this for you.

CHAPTER NINETEEN

Ridge and Tsan Usdi stepped heavily among the smoldering ruins of Tohopeka, watching Sharp Knife's soldiers clip the nose off slain Red Sticks just to make sure they didn't count any one corpse twice. The morning sunlight flashed off busy blades, their skill lending the dead the macabre illusion of haughtiness or arrogance. In life, Ridge knew, the Red Sticks had been the wolves of war, choosing death rather than bend to the whites. Though Ridge had lent his hand to their destruction, he could not help but admire their courage. Just a few winters ago he had been prepared to meet his fate in this exact manner. How could he forget that now as he stared at the grimacing black corpses, the proud, unyielding dead?

It had been Ridge's wish that the Cherokee choose sides in the Creek Civil War. Big Warrior had appealed to him with gifts of a tobacco sheath laced with a string of wampum, to be smoked in the presence of the

Cherokee council. Ridge had delivered the ceremonial tobacco along with the Creek chief's words.

"The Red Sticks have placed the Cherokee between two fires," Ridge began without a trace of emotion as he addressed the chiefs and elders and beloved women. "The whites consider the Red Sticks as merely Indians, the very same to them as the Choctaw, Chickasaw, Seminole, and even Cherokee. The Ani-yunwi-ya see many faces; the Ani-yonegas see only one. If we refuse to take up arms with the Americans against the Red Sticks, as our brother Big Warrior begs us to do, we lose the opportunity to make a friend out of our most dangerous enemy. The fire that began in the Creek Nation will almost certainly spread to our villages. The deprivations of only a few misguided Cherokee hotheads could lead the white soldiers back to our homes. Once we defend them as we must, the result will be an all-out war between us and the Americans."

Ridge had paused to let old Pathkiller and the others absorb his reasoning. "On the other hand," Ridge continued, "should Big Warrior fall, and the prophets return the Creeks to savagery, our young men will be inspired to follow the same path. Those of us with gray hair on our heads will be forced to lift our tomahawks against our own angry sons just as Big Warrior must do now. Then it will be our turn, as much as it humiliates us to do so, to look to the Americans for aid. Once the whites go to war against an Indian nation, the killing always becomes indiscriminate. In the confusion, many innocent Cherokee will die."

Pathkiller massaged his temples while he considered Ridge's analysis. The color bled out of his face. His hands collapsed by his side. "The very idea of Cherokee killing Creek rests heavy with me, Ridge Walker," he said.

"As it does with me," Ridge said. "But my uncles and beloved women must understand that no matter which way the Cherokee turn, many Indians will die. It's the opinion of the Man Who Walks the Mountaintops that the fewest will fall under the knife if the Cherokee rise up with Big Warrior and destroy the Red Sticks. In doing so, we contain the inevitable fire on Creek soil."

As Ridge had expected, there was only a brief deliberation among the chiefs and elders and beloved women. They thanked him for his wise words, but they could not bring themselves to order Cherokee against Creek, regardless of the measure's practicality and political expedience.

"Both of our nations," Pathkiller said, "share the grief of the alliance with the British in the American Revolution and during the ten winters of war that followed it. All enduring tribes are precious to us who are old enough to remember what we used to be before fifty winters of fire and death. The disturbance in the Creek Nation is a family matter to be settled among them as the Provider wills. Tell Big Warrior our thoughts are with him, but our young men must stay home."

Ridge bit his lip and signified his understanding with a reverent nod of his head. "Would my uncles object if the Ridge asked for volunteers?" he said. "Big Warrior is my friend, and when a friend begs the Ridge for help, he cannot turn his back."

"Your heart is true, Ridge Walker," Pathkiller said. "Do as it bids you. We will not stand in your way."

"Let any of those so inclined gather your weapons and follow the war trace with me," Ridge said. He swept out of the council house, leaving whispers and dull murmuring in response to his grand gesture, devastated to hear only one set of footsteps in his wake. How could the gift of persuasion have abandoned him at such a crucial moment? He kicked at the dirt.

"Ridge," a voice called. "Can I speak to you?"

Feeling like a hollow log, Ridge turned to regard the form of Tsan Usdi, the young, mixed-blood merchant. Tsan Usdi was only one-eighth Indian, grandson of the Scotch trader John McDonald, who had been loved by the Cherokee. McDonald's only daughter had married another Scotsman, Daniel Ross. Tsan Usdi was their third child.

The young trader was the product of white tutors brought in by his father, as well as Reverend Blackburn's mission school at Chickamauga. He'd even attended a white academy in Tennessee. Once back home in the Nation, the ambitious merchant opened up his own firm with the son of the Americans' Cherokee agent.

Tsan Usdi quickly established himself as an honest and capable businessman, but for some reason Ridge noted that the young man was frequently drawn to the Nation's affairs. Assistant principal chief Hicks was quite taken with Tsan Usdi's abilities, and served as his advocate and mentor. Tsan Usdi had also come to Ridge to speak of his ideas, just as he was obviously about to do now.

"I'd be happy to visit with you," Ridge said. "It seems I'm short of followers today."

"The council doesn't understand what you're saying," Tsan Usdi said. "I do."

Ridge smiled. "Well, that's one." Tsan Usdi's Cherokee was wretched. Ridge struggled to comprehend his clunky phrases.

"I want to ride with you against the Red Sticks."

"I'm very grateful," Ridge said. He hadn't expected such courage from a clerk. "But I'm afraid Big Warrior will be disappointed when only you and I show up to war against Weatherford."

"Let me go back and talk to the council, Ridge," Tsan Usdi said. "You can understand their reluctance, but they've got to consider the longer view. I'm very close to Colonel Miegs. One nod from Pathkiller and I'll ask Miegs to approach General Jackson about a Cherokee alliance with the Americans. Your vision is accurate. A little patience, my uncle, and it can all happen as you planned."

"All right," Ridge said. A fire burned in this mixed-blood. "I'm grateful for anything you can do. But take a linkster with you when you speak to the chiefs, won't you? Things are confusing enough as they are."

The sun had not set on another day before the chiefs rescinded their position of neutrality. The little merchant had proved quite the diplomat after all. The Cherokee declared war on the Red Sticks and offered their warriors to their agent, Colonel Miegs. Miegs sent word to Jackson, and Ridge and Tsan Usdi rode beside Sharp Knife on the hunt for the southern Creeks.

Never once had Ridge questioned the logic of this unlikely alliance; he accepted the complexity of the times, and he'd long ago hedged his silver on the Americans to dominate the land between the warm Spanish Sea and the frozen wastes of the north. Where they walked, they ruled.

Yet as he stepped with Tsan Usdi among the scorched, noseless dead and the smoking ruins of Tohopeka, a cold dread hung over him. He'd known some of these warriors who lay mangled in these woods. He had loved and admired the Creeks, and only this morning he'd wiped their blood from his knife and tomahawk. Standing with the stench in his nose, Ridge found it hard to justify his part in their destruction as he watched the frontiersmen, their coarse, homespun hunting shirts dyed with butternut juice, now stained with Creek blood, scalping the dead.

These buzzards collected body parts for souvenirs. Some stripped the flesh from dead Creeks, from the ankle, up the calf and thigh, across the back, over the shoulder, and then down again all the way to the top of the feet — horse reins for spiritless men, who spent the morning eating Creek potatoes stewed in human grease. "Who," Ridge asked Tsan Usdi, "are the savages here?"

"These are not the ones we intended to reach with our alliance with the Americans," Tsan Usdi said. "By fighting with Sharp Knife, we built faith with the civilized, cultured people in the cities. Only they can protect us from these animals who've been let loose in the wilderness. Don't let the worst of the whites distract you from courting their best. I'm convinced it is the latter who rule."

Tsan Usdi's words consoled Ridge enough to consider the longer view. But the immediate image of Tohopeka still unnerved him. Five hundred and fifty-seven noses sat in a pudgy, bloody burlap sack. Five hundred and fifty-seven Creeks lay stacked like cordwood to rot in the sun. The Tallapoosa had carried away maybe four hundred more to bloat in piles of driftwood for the carp and catfish to pick apart. There were maybe a hundred survivors alone in the woods, and by daybreak Indian trackers were already on the blood trails they left on the dead leaves. Few Red Sticks would reach the Seminole swamps to fight again another day.

Ridge exhaled loudly, hoping to vent the remorse from his chest. His soul walked two steps behind him. "For any Cherokee who would urge war against the Americans," he said to Tsan Usdi, "let the waste of the Horseshoe be their answer. You will rise among us, my friend. Everyone says so. And when you and I stand together to plot our people's course, we must remember that war is no longer an option."

"Such slaughter will never touch us, Ridge," Tsan Usdi said. "The Americans will never splinter the Cherokee one against the other."

"I fear they already have," Ridge said. "To reach toward the whites is to pull away from the full-bloods. The crack widens as the seasons pass."

"It's a matter of appearance," Tsan Usdi said. "A wise chief shouts the value of tradition while he quietly opens schools. Progressive Cherokee like you and I know we have to civilize ourselves to survive. But we need not flaunt that fact before the full-bloods. Let the Americans see what they must, while we allow the full-bloods to see what they want to see."

Ridge stopped and looked at Tsan Usdi. "Suddenly you strike me as a very dangerous young man."

Tsan Usdi blushed at Ridge's rebuke. "I only love my people," Tsan Usdi said. He waved his hand over the carnage. "I would do anything to keep this from happening to them."

Ridge was reassured by Tsan Usdi's earnest manner. He patted his shoulder to let him know that he was far from offended.

"Perhaps I speak too frankly," Tsan Usdi said, "but I feel a kinship with you and your views. Like you, I see both sides of our dilemma. It's up to the mixed-bloods to find the common ground between old and new. If we're clever about it and our hearts remain pure, we can save the Cherokee in spite of themselves."

"I understand," Ridge said. "You're blessed with a practical mind where I am ruled too much by my emotions. I have a white ancestor, but I consider myself a full-blood. It's in my nature to lock horns with ignorance and let all the Cherokee see me do it in the light of day. The struggle will earn me many enemies, but it will also win me many friends."

"You've won one on this campaign," Tsan Usdi said.

"Ho, Major Ridge!" Ridge swung in the direction of Jackson's voice. The general trotted up on a magnificent horse. Ridge had never met a white man who commanded authority like Jackson. He had shouted orders even as he dangled from a sapling with his breeches around his knees. When his men had argued with him, Jackson dug several graves and then asked them if they wanted to argue some more. Ridge didn't understand the wiry soldier with eyes like blue ice, but he saw much to admire and even more to fear. Ridge respected Jackson, and now after the Cherokee had bled with him he hoped Jackson respected the Cherokee. That was what this awkward alliance had been about from the beginning.

Some of the fire had burned out of the general's eyes. His voice was hoarse with fatigue. His hands trembled. "I wanted to see you before you got off."

Ridge shook his hand, and then made sure Jackson gripped Tsan Usdi's, as well.

"You were splendid in this engagement, Major Ridge," Sharp Knife said. Ridge turned

282

to Tsan Usdi to translate. "The Cherokee turned the tide in this battle. I'll say as much in my report to Colonel Miegs."

"It was an honor to be of service to our friends," Ridge said. Like Jackson, his enthusiasm was tempered. He found it difficult to be diplomatic watching Jackson's militia mutilate the dead.

"The honor was all mine," Sharp Knife said, stroking the neck of his mount. The general had a way with horses.

"We trust," Tsan Usdi interjected, "that our contribution to this victory will be remembered in your report to Washington, as well. The Cherokee have our troubles, too. Our cause would benefit greatly if the war department looked upon us with favor after the sacrifices we made here."

"You're Cherokee, are you?" Sharp Knife said, looking down his nose at the diminutive mixed-breed.

"A portion by blood," Tsan Usdi replied. "All by clan and heart."

"Strange world," Jackson said, tapping his corncob pipe on his pommel to knock out the ashes.

"You'll hear from this one," Ridge said. "The Cherokee expect great things from him."

"Is that so? I'll expect I'll be hearing from you both, from what I saw here. What's your name, young man?"

"I'm John Ross," Tsan Usdi said.

"I expect I'll remember that," Jackson said. "My government thanks you both for your service. Please send my regards to Chief Pathkiller and Chief Hicks. Tell them that their Cherokee warriors shed their blood for a worthy cause. Sharp Knife was proud to run the war trace with such noble men. Safe travel, brother Cherokee."

Ridge rode beside Tsan Usdi on the long journey home. They sat up talking late at night beside dying fires. They pitched their blankets together under the spitting rain. Ridge didn't mind when John Ross pressed him for his views on Cherokee affairs. He candidly discussed not only his regrets and failures, but also his ambitions and hopes for the Cherokee as they walked a new and dangerous path.

On the last night of their travels, Ridge told Ross the history of their people as Waesa had once told him so Ross could better understand the minds of the full-blood majority.

"The full-bloods are the best of who we are," Ridge said with a yawn. He rubbed his aching muscles and dabbed a little ointment on his healing cuts and bruises. He couldn't shake off his injuries as quickly as he once had. "They must be protected. Never make a move without fully considering their welfare."

Ross listened carefully as all bright young men should. "There's a full-blood woman who's quite special to me," he said, piling green pine boughs to make beds for the night.

"Marry her," Ridge said. "She'll make you a fine wife and you'll advance your position among us in the meantime. Chief Hicks wants to see you rise, and so do I."

"I could marry only for love."

"Yes," Ridge said. "But I see three loves in your life: this woman, your people, and your politics. Choose a wife wisely, and you can marry them all."

"I don't think with your ambition," Ross said.

"Yes, you do," Ridge said. "You just don't know it yet."

"I can see you're tired," Ross said. "But there's one more thing I'd like you to consider before we rest for the night."

"I hope it's short," Ridge said.

"There are weapons hidden in the old treaties," he said. "By advocating education, the Ridge has set young Cherokee on the path to find them. The next thrust should be to learn how to use the Americans' promises against them."

Ridge propped himself up on one elbow. "How do you mean?"

"You and I both agree that the Cherokee can't win their peace by war," he said. "We must move the battle into the American courtrooms, because if the whites value anything, they value their law. First, young, educated Cherokee must learn how the American legal system works. Then we'll use it to make them honor the words written on the treaties. One step follows another."

Ridge batted his eyes as he remembered Waesa's prophecy of so long ago. *The final challenge,* the old conjurer had said, *is to endure. And you'll never achieve it with a gun or a tomahawk.* Ridge was so excited by the unseen possibilities of education that he could barely sleep. He finally saw a destination at the end of this hard path he'd been walking, a way to fight his people's battles without blood. He had much to think about alone in the high places, once he'd seen about his family.

In the morning, the young merchant brought him his breakfast and fed oats to his horse. Before Ridge mounted for the day's ride, Ross checked his saddle girth and primed his rifle with fresh powder. Ridge studied him with warm eyes.

"I have a son who reads books," Ridge told him. "I hope that when he grows up that he carries himself like you."

John Ross's face beamed in the early morning sunlight. "I hope that when I have children of my own, I become the father that you are to him."

CHAPTER TWENTY

Cold rain fell like some forgotten god's tears during the whole of the flower moon. Ridge returned from the swamps of the Creek War to find his own country mired in a sinking bog. A rottenness hung in the air, as if the whole world were reduced to waste and decay. If the breeze blew at all, it drifted in from the south dragging thick, dark clouds the color of Jackson's cannonballs, and just as heavy with relentless rain. Normally Tsi law'nee, April, was a month of rebirth and renewal. Under the burden of gray cloud banks as solid as shale, Ridge felt only the deepest, inconsolable gloom.

When Ridge returned home, there was more misery to lump onto his misgivings. While the Cherokee had served as the vanguard of Jackson's army, picking a path through the bottoms and feeding his troops with its hidden bounty, the militia in the rear had ravaged the Cherokee's homes. Horses, cattle, and hogs had been requisitioned.

Corn, beans, pumpkins, and maple syrup stolen. Smokehouses and fish racks raided. Fences, corn cribs, barns, and outbuildings were demolished. Some of the white soldiers had ripped the very clothes from Cherokee backs.

Ridge was stunned. His head pounded in anger as if he'd been struck by a stone. No Red Stick had endangered the Nation, not even after the council declared war. He had killed dozens of Creeks in Jackson's name, and now he bore witness to what his white allies had done under that same pronouncement. Upon first sight of the devastation and the hungry Cherokee left in its wake, he tumbled from his horse and crawled on his knees to the side of the trail and wailed until the bile choked his throat. He stormed back to his horse and yanked his rifle from its scabbard and splintered its stock against an oak. He threw the bent barrel as far as he could into the weeds. His bold gamble to ally with the Americans had failed even before he'd killed the first Red Stick. What more could he do to protect his people from the treachery of this faithless race?

He slogged up the mountain bluff that overlooked Degayelun-ha Gap, the Printed Place, where ancient human and animal tracks were pressed into the rock face back when the world was still soft. For two sleeps, Ridge sat cross-legged without food or water, letting the rain fall on his bare head, searching for the answer. He struggled with serious doubts about teaching young Cherokee to adopt a culture that was inherently corrupt. The only thing more disastrous than fighting with these chickensnake Anglos was fighting against them. Ridge had broken Black Fox and Tahlonteskee for advocating emigration when he should have moved mountains to advance their cause. His pride had blinded him to the harsh reality that he should have seen from the start. Now that Jackson's militia had stuck a dagger in his back, his humiliation was complete. He had to stand before Pathkiller and confess that everything he'd advocated for the last ten winters had been a terrible mistake. He no longer saw a way to live in peace with the Americans.

Then he remembered the words of John Ross, a young, educated mixed-blood wise beyond his years who understood the American mind better than any other Cherokee. *Don't let the worst of the whites distract you from courting their best.*

The sentence echoed in his head during a sleepless night until it grew loud enough to drown out his misgivings. Clearly there were only two paths open to the Cherokee — to leave their land, which was unthinkable; or to keep it and push headlong toward education in spite of Jackson's betrayal. The Cherokee must reach over the hills where the frontiersmen squatted and take the hand of the sons of Washington and Jefferson in the great cities of the Atlantic seaboard. Ross had convinced him that this was where American law lived. If Ross was correct about the weapons hidden in the treaties, then the Cherokee had to go on the hunt to discover them.

Ridge saw the way opening to him. His early ambition had fallen short, but the overall vision remained accurate. The Cherokee should not abandon education, but aggressively escalate its pursuit. His people were desperately in need of educated minds that belonged only to them. Still trembling with anger, he came down from the mountain. He trotted his horse most of the way home, as if he alone had to maintain what little momentum the Cherokee had left.

When Ridge finally arrived at Sehoya's home, he had agitated so long that he barely had enough strength left to walk. He handed his reins to his slave, Jumper, instructing him to care well for this animal, the one he'd ridden in war. He shook off the rain and the chill, and with his pistols in his hands he stepped toward the door of his home, wondering if his fields would ever be dry enough to plant. Then his eyes caught the circular wreath of black feathers, Sehoya's symbol that someone close to their hearts had slipped from this world. All cares of wars and weather vanished as it occurred to him that a neighbor might have placed the wreath here.

He rushed through the threshold and repeatedly hollered for Sehoya. She soon appeared, carrying a kettle of springwater and bunches of herbs, her face languid with worry and long hours. She moved heavily across the room. She must have gained ten pounds in his absence. At the sight of her, he clutched his chest in relief.

One whiff of the pungent odor and Ridge knew his wife was brewing medicine for someone who was deathly ill. She stayed busy with her potions, his return from the wars not worth more than a glance.

"Who ails?" he asked with all the tenderness he could muster.

"We all do, Ridge Walker," she said in a voice tinged with anger and exhaustion. "When you left, the rains came, and with them, the fever. I lost my mother a week ago."

"I'm so sorry, Sehoya." He wondered why trouble had its season, like the hot, still days of summer when the sun baked the earth for days on end. "We'll mourn her in the ancient way."

"I've got no time for that now. Skah-tle-loh-skee battles a fever."

Before his son's name had left her mouth, Ridge dropped his pistols and knife on the floor and raced for his son's room, trailing mud and rain water behind him. The wall sconce's candlelight found the boy sleeping.

Ridge knelt at the foot of his feather bed, listening to the slight rattle in the boy's chest. He pulled the covers back to check if the scrofula had returned, encountering a poultice of mint, wild ginger, sassafras, and who knew what else. He probed every limb, every muscle, at last pressing his cheek to the boy's forehead. No fever. A cool sweat. No trembling. Ridge knew then the worst was over.

John opened his eyes and tried to focus — his pupils like black pebbles lying in the bed of a mountain stream. Ridge watched the blood rush to his son's chalky cheeks.

" 'Doda!" the boy said.

"I am here, little man," Ridge said in a whisper. "Are you well?"

"Much better, Ridge Walker," John said with a raspy voice. "I bet I'll be able to return to school next week."

Ridge rubbed his burning eyes and looked out the window. The clouds had broken. "If you can ride, you can go today. It's your choice."

"We were reading the work of the Greek poet Homer. You'd love the stories, Ridge Walker. It's about great warriors who battled for ten winters. I'd hate to miss it."

"Dress warmly then, and we'll go."

Sehoya delivered a steaming cup of her concoction. "What's this?" she said. Ridge continued to fumble with John's buttons. "Back in your bed, boy."

"He's ready to return to school, Sehoya," Ridge said in a deadpan voice.

"I don't need more worries, husband," Sehoya said, pleading. "His fever broke only yesterday. We almost lost him. What business does he have out in the rain? What if he takes a turn for the worse?"

"The worst is if he remains in ignorance," he answered, his emotions rising through his exhaustion. "I've just turned my back on the results of that. The boy says he's well enough to travel. And he goes back to Spring Place."

Sehoya propped her hands on her hips and set her jaw to let Ridge know he was in for a row. She backed him out of John's room, down the stairs, and next to the hearth before he risked the first word.

"You have no idea how important it is that the boy return to school," he said.

"What good is his education if you kill him?"

"You know I'd never do anything to hurt that boy. He says he's fine. He must go back."

Sehoya slapped her hand down on her table. "Of course he says he's fine!" she snapped. "When has he ever admitted to you — warrior and scalp-carrying outa-cit-e — that he was ill? That he wasn't up to what was expected of him? He'd kill himself to impress you! And what's worse, you'd let him!"

"Sehoya, I —

"He goes back to school when I say he can!" she yelled, the veins on her forehead bulging with anger. "Do you hear me! This isn't some council of drunken chiefs or a tavern full of young fools in search of your favor. This is my home and I run it as I please! You take my son out in this weather and I swear, Ridge Walker, I'll run a ball through your back. If you manage to live, you'll find yourself half a blanket hanging on that hickory yonder and your clothes in a heap out in the rain. I'll get myself a sensible man, and you can take up with some empty-headed woman and we'll both be happier!"

"Sehoya —"

"What do you have to say that concerns me? There are two more children in this house. You would leave without a word to either one. My mother's body waits for her grave, I've cared for three sick children and five sick servants, white soldiers pointed rifles in my face while they ravaged our farm and took what they pleased, and you return home with more orders for me and plans for my children as if I'm not capable of running my affairs."

Ridge accepted the hopelessness of his situation. He was supposed to influence his nation and he couldn't even persuade his wife. He was too tired to battle her now. He'd hole up in the barn and lick his wounds, old and new. He took an oil lamp and a blanket and walked toward the door.

"You think more of the Nation than you do your own family," she said, following him as he sank beneath the door frame. Somehow the rain felt colder.

"You don't understand," Ridge said.

"I understand what is and isn't going to happen in this house," she said. "The rest is for you to sort out somewhere else."

The door slammed on his back.

Ridge awoke and picked yet another shaft of straw from his matted hair. His skin crawled from where the fodder had scratched him. He might as well have slept on a pile of arrowheads. He sat up rubbing his groaning shoulder, noticing that it was daybreak or maybe midmorning. Hard to tell in all the gloom. His stomach grumbled as he caught a compelling whiff of Sehoya's breakfast, the aroma so strong it was as if she were cooking it in the barn. He didn't know where to go to get a meal, what Cherokee home would welcome him after his Creek policies had gone so wrong. Ridge had no idea that leadership could be such a lonely affair.

He pivoted at the waist and damn near swallowed his tongue to find Sehoya sitting there in silence. Steam rose from one of her pewter pots.

"The man who came through my door last night was not my husband," she said, tapping her finger on the cookware's lid. "Can you explain to me what's driven you out of your mind?"

"You'll have to feed me first," he said. He wiped the sleep from his eyes while she considered the bargain. Then she spooned steaming potatoes and corn mush onto her best china and handed it to him.

"How are your children?" he asked her, inhaling the first bite.

"Very well," she said, watching his expression as he engulfed her stew. "It agrees?"

"Always."

"Down to business then," she said. "Tell me what's happened that upset you so. I need to understand."

For most of the morning he lay beside her and explained every facet of his dilemma in detail. When it was done, when he was weary of talking, he reached out and held her hand between his.

"And that's why I was frantic for Skah-tle-loh-skee to return to school," he said. "The whites will never accept us as equals until we master their ways. Once they see themselves in us, the laws that govern them will protect the Cherokee. As things stand now, the whites of the cities are as ignorant of our troubles as we are of theirs. Sending our brightest sons and daughters among them will win their hearts. Their leaders will have to listen to their cries for us even if they want to ignore ours. To please his own people, the Great Father must honor the treaties. Despite these terrible setbacks, education remains my greatest hope."

He sat up and rolled back on his heels, wondering if he had reached her. He couldn't tell one way or the other by her expression.

Sehoya snatched the fork and scooped a healthy bite of corn mush for herself. "I was thinking that if Skah-tle-loh-skee continues to improve, he could return to school as early as tomorrow or the next day."

"Well," he said in between shoveling bites into his mouth, "you know me. I'm not one to rush." He saw how worry had drawn shadows around her eyes. Her burdens were every bit as great as his. "I think we should mourn your mother as a family as soon as the children are well enough. And when that's done, you should catch up on your rest. The servants can see to things for a while. If you agree, of course. Because if you don't, I'd appreciate enough notice to get me out of pistol range."

"You make jokes when you're hurting, Ridge Walker," she said. "I've learned that about you."

He laid his head down on her lap, closing his eyes as her fingers raked through his hair. "I'm sorry about last night," he said. "I was so distraught after everything that happened that I couldn't think straight."

"I can see how deeply you're troubled," she said. "You're forgiven."

"Truly?"

"I know you love our children," she said. "And I know you can love one more."

His jaw dropped. "What's this?"

"I'm with your fourth child," Sehoya said. "A girl, I'm told. I think I'll call her Sally."

Ridge escorted John to his place in the classroom. The boy immediately took out his books, chalk, and blank slate, glanced over to his cousin Kilakeena's text, and flipped to the correct page. The missionaries, always keen to change Cherokee names, called Ridge's nephew Elias Boudinot. Ridge didn't care for their arrogance until he learned that Oo-watie's boy's namesake was the most revered among the teacher priests.

To see the boys' bright eyes devour the written word was like watching a flame engulf a cinder. The mechanics of it were a hypnotic mystery, but no one could dispute its benefits. And what was happening in their heads as they flipped through the pages? Did they hear wise men talking? See great and beautiful things? What was it like to *read*?

Ridge stepped to the rear of the classroom, crossed his arms, and listened to the Cherokee children — his children — speak a language he could not understand. This delighted him. Yet one by one, the children's stares left their talking leaves to fix on him. He was a chief of a nation that valued respect, and they'd probably been told of his deeds with Sharp Knife among the Creeks.

"Come and speak to them, then, Ridge Walker," Father Gambold said. "It's useless to go on with our instructions while you're here."

Ridge nodded and walked to the head of the class. "I am Kah-nung-da-tla-geh, the Man Who Walks the Mountaintops," he said. "I see the path ahead clearly. You who sit in this place, learning the new ways, walk it for all of us. You children are the hope of this nation. Education is to you what the war path was to your grandfathers. Embrace it with an ambitious heart."

He took a book from Father Gambold's desk and held it before them.

"The Cherokee fight with these now," he said with conviction. "There'll come a time when we put away our rifles and tomahawks, and rely only on our minds to live. That is why you — the brightest among the seven clans of our people — sit in these wooden chairs."

He pulled the nearest empty seat to him and worked his stout buttocks between its arms. The chair groaned as it took his weight. The children giggled in delight.

"I know it's hard for you to be away from your families and loved ones," he said. "But remember what your chief says to you this day: that what you learn under this roof bears far more importance than young people can comprehend. I charge you to listen well to these good white people. Apply yourselves with all you possess. Study hard. The Cherokee love you, have great hopes for you, and will soon depend on you for what you know."

Ridge briefly bowed his head before he squeezed himself out of the chair and replaced the book on Gambold's desk. He looked upon his son with pride, and walked quietly toward the door. The Moravian followed him outside.

"I wish I had your way with these children, Ridge," Gambold said.

"I wish I had yours," Ridge said, thrusting his moccasin into the stirrup. "They are all, in their own way, good children."

"Are they learning as well as we hoped?"

"Far better," Gambold said. "I'm satisfied with the majority of my students' progress, but I fear that John and your nephew have outgrown my instruction. Perhaps it's time to consider other arrangements."

"I'll look into it," Ridge said. "I want to thank you for what you've done for my son. He has a hungry mind, and I know you've fed it well."

"John has a gift. While he doesn't possess your physical strength, he is strong in many ways like his father. He's the brightest of them all. His intelligence comes from you."

"And his mother. And know that if I were his age, I would sit among you and learn your language and hear your words."

"One is never too old to hear the word of God, Chief Ridge."

"Maybe so," Ridge said. "But one can be too tainted, I expect. I was born into the blood of the old ways. I've killed many in battle, as was expected of me. But I also assassinated a member of my own clan, a wicked Indian named Doublehead. I'm often haunted by this deed, and hearing my son speak of your God and His path of enlightenment, I sometimes wonder if He will punish me."

"I wouldn't expect so, Ridge. God sees the goodness in your heart."

"Nevertheless, I resolved never to do such an evil thing again, unless the council orders me to rid the world of a bad man, as was the case with Doublehead. I brought my oldest surviving son to this place to learn how to walk your path. But I know this way is forever closed to me, for I am worthless in your world, and I can accept it."

"You are far from worthless, Chief Ridge. And ours is a forgiving God."

"I've heard this," Ridge said. "It's what I like most about Him."

"Pray to Him from your heart. Admit to

Him your transgressions. Beg Him for His mercy."

"Everything I have done, Christian, was from my heart," he said. "My transgressions, as you call them, were expected of me in a dark and dying world you can't understand. I sometimes feel the weight of guilt, it's true. But I'm a chief of a frightened people. The Cherokee look up to me, so I'm not at liberty to beg either man or spirit. I had my reasons for all the bad things I've done. I trust that my God will forgive me, and for me, that's enough."

Ridge nodded to affirm that what he'd said would be his last words on the subject and squeezed his heels against the flanks of the horse. He rode on, thinking of the faces of the schoolchildren. Soon those faded, replaced instead by the look of death on the faces of the Red Stick children at Tohopeka. Shot, stabbed, or burned alive — dead, wasted children. Some he'd seen playing while on his diplomatic missions among their tribe. There had been hope and joy in their faces, just as there was today at Spring Place. Ridge could not stem the tide of tears rolling down his cheeks. He was one of the few who understood how close death had come to the Cherokee. The fire that claimed so many had passed close enough that he felt its hot breath on his neck.

Ridge forced all thoughts out of his head

except the first step toward finding a suitable school for his son and nephew. He and Sehoya had made the decision to send John and Kilakeena to the American cities long before he learned that they had outgrown Father Gambold's school. The matter was now more immediate, and no place was too far or too expensive to get the Cherokee what they must have.

■ ■ ■ ■

Book Three:
A Nation Rises

1821-1832

■ ■ ■ ■

CHAPTER TWENTY-ONE

The Headmaster

I must confess that I, the Very Reverend Herman Daggett, principal of the American Board of Commissioners of Foreign Missions at the Cornwall Green Academy of Massachusetts, had reservations about these new Cherokee students. They were bright-faced, intelligent-looking boys, some of whom, especially Elias Boudinot and John Ridge, could pass for white. It was pleasing to see how well red blood mixed with white in these living experiments. Breeding with Anglos had no doubt tempered the wildness in their aboriginal natures, rendering them suitable for higher pursuits, even the opportunity to enter Our Father's kingdom. Much has changed in this year of 1821.

The cousins Ridge and Boudinot came highly recommended by Brothers Elias Cornelius and Daniel Butrick, our missionaries to the Cherokee Nation. Reverend Cornelius was once a pupil of mine, a man of abounding faith and integrity, and I accepted without question his evaluation of the new students. Yet had my former student been present when I first laid eyes on the Cherokee, I would have asked him a thing or two.

Please understand that I'm proud of what we are accomplishing here. We have with us Hawaiians, Hindus, Malays, Bengalese, Chinese, Choctaws, Marquesans, and an Abanaki, all making vast educational and spiritual progress. Idleness being the devil's tool, the students are occupied throughout the day. We rise precisely at six A.M. for prayer, read a chapter of the New Testament, and allow one of our older pupils to lead the others in their devotions.

After breakfast, the children attend to their chores, either in the gardens or the fields. There is also the stock to care for and the buildings to maintain. In the summer, we send the students to Colt's Foot Mountain to cut our cordwood. The good people of Cornwall donated the buildings, the grounds, and the fields that adjoin them. They lend us their oxen, plows, and tools to till the ground, and a steady hand when we need it, as well. Most of the labor, however, falls on the shoulders of our students to teach them determination and self-sufficiency through the discipline of hard work and piety.

Once the morning chores and prayers are

behind them, the students spend the bulk of their days in the classroom. They receive instruction in rhetoric, biology, anatomy, geography, English grammar, surveying, common and ecclesiastical history, the classic literature of the Greeks and Romans, and natural philosophy, as readily as each student can devour it. In the end, it becomes an issue of hunger. After dinner, the students are left to their devotions and prayer. They may read to themselves for a time if they wish. Whale-oil lamps are snuffed sharply at eight o'clock. No exceptions, praise be to God.

How these Cherokee boys would fit into this scheme I did not know. I perceived a haughtiness about them, too much confidence, flightiness, a passion I would relate to their being full of contaminating animal spirits. John Ridge, their apparent leader, had spent the bulk of his expense money on a pocket watch in Salem, which sent him shamelessly to Dr. Dempsey for a loan. In this one act alone, I perceived vanity and selfishness. In the others, I observed a total lack of seriousness and piety. I feared they viewed the academy as somewhat of a lark. My goal, from the beginning, was to redeem these souls from savagery.

As one might expect, I met difficulties toward this end. Old and new students did not mix well. The established scholars were immediately aggrieved and came to me expressing their fears that the school would not prosper with the Cherokees enrolled. I commanded them to bite their tongues, to think of what Christ himself would do and conduct themselves accordingly. Time, I assured them, would tell.

But secretly I was also worried. You have to understand that the Cherokee in no way believe in Original Sin. Truly they don't! They see no evil in nature, and being born children of the forests, they consider themselves as natural as any plant or animal in it. Add to this basic ignorance the fact that their parents make no effort to discipline them and that they correct through some hedonistic example rather than the Christian concept of guilt, and we find nothing in place to check their animal appetites.

Their ignorance stains them, as well. John Ridge, for instance, adamantly refused communion. Young Elias willingly consented, but his cousin snatched the wafer from his hand. I attended to this particular rebellion myself. I went to the boy and said, "John, why would you forgo the sacraments?"

"To eat the flesh or blood of any man is taboo among my people," he said petulantly. "Animals who eat the flesh of their own kind are abominations in nature."

My first impulse was to fetch a switch and put his convictions to the test. But, alas, I am a temperate man. I assured him that the practice was absolutely symbolic, done precisely as our Lord Jesus himself instructed.

"My people place blood and flesh in opposite categories," he said. "They go together no better in the natural order than fire and ice. Mix opposites, and the world is thrown into chaos."

Jumping Jehoshaphat! Have you ever heard such nonsense? Is there any wonder why the heathens rage? I drew my patience, I thank the Redeemer, from a deep, still well. I calmly replied, "John, you've come a great distance to learn a new way."

"That's certainly true," he said. "But no one said I must abandon one to study the other. My father has sent me here to merge two worlds."

Oh, how I wrung my hands! Job endured his trials, so I set my mind to conquer my own.

Even once I'd brought his deficiencies to his attention, however, John Ridge remained unrepentant. He refused, for example, to profess that Christ was his savior, claiming instead that there were so many similarities between our religion and that of his ancestors that he saw no reason to abandon the latter. Young Ridge assembled his tribesmen once a week to meet, speak, and pray in their own language. This one's will was strong, and I feared for his soft-spoken, deeply reflective cousin, Elias Boudinot, who was under his spell.

After they were at the academy for only a few weeks, I observed a remarkable improvement. Both Ridge and Boudinot excelled in their studies. They mastered composition and even wrote poetry. In May of each year, it is our practice to introduce our students to the citizens of Cornwall. I chose John Ridge to speak first, which he did in English with stunning articulation.

I wish one could express the surprise and delight of the townspeople upon hearing the young Cherokee's eloquence as he argued the problems of removing his people to the wilds of Arkansas. Such a display of talent and intelligence won the school many friends and benefactors, and so the academy prospered with the Cherokee in attendance — a pleasant surprise. We even received a hundred ducats from Baron de Champagne of Switzerland. When Elias Boudinot wrote to thank him, the baron was so moved by the grace of his letter that he sent fifteen hundred florins more. Not to be outdone, John Ridge corresponded directly with President Monroe. I kept a copy of this letter and would like to share parts of it with you:

I rejoice that my dear nation now begins to peep into the privileges of civilization — that this great and generous government is favorable to them, and that ere long, Congress will give them the hand of strong friendship — that they will encircle them in the arms of love, and adopt them into the fond embraces of the Union.

I ask you, brethren, is this the mind of a heathen? It was always easy for me to forgive his pride and arrogance whenever he spouted magnificence such as this. He was, after all, the son of a chief, the descendant of a distinguished warrior clan. If the foal be from the thoroughbred, is it the trainer's place to chain it to a tree and stop it from running?

Someday John Ridge will have a son, and I pray his trust in me is such that he'll send the boy to me as his father did before him. I will take this boy another step closer to God and so on until they are as righteous as we. With the wisdom of my fifty-one years, I now understand that we Americans ask the Cherokees to propel themselves in one generation to this lofty level that took our own kind one hundred to obtain. I've learned that it may be my fate to plant seeds for others to harvest. In my faith I find patience. In the eyes of savages, I see God.

And I've come to admire John Ridge's spirit so that I could not bring myself to break it. Let me say also, lest I be misunderstood, that I learned to love the boy with all my heart. To this last reluctant and patient virtue, the boy responded best. I, the man who came within a hairbreadth of beating him into submission with a switch, am proud of what we accomplished.

My one continuing, deep disappointment, however, was my failure to convert John Ridge to our religion. I believed I could wear down his resistance, when in fact he exhausted mine. "Both of our cultures believe in one God," he told me. "Why can it not be the same one?"

What was I to say to that? Besides, his heart was so good, his manners so refined, his mind so acute, his bearing so polished that after a time, his reluctance to accept the Christian faith did not trouble me as much as it once had. The boy had a simple, abundant relationship with his creator which I felt entertained a *hope* in Christ, and I chose at last to settle for that.

There is one last blight to mention. Illness stalks this boy, now eighteen years of age. I fear conditions under our gambrel roof are too cramped and stale to cure him of this fearsome scrofulous condition. The Massachusetts winters have been especially hard. The boy is terribly pale, paper-thin, and often racked by debilitating fevers. He stoically limped about the commons attending his classes, kept up with his studies as best he could, until he could no longer muster the strength to rise out of his bed. When the

Cherokees met to pray in their own language, I'm told they prayed for the life of John Ridge.

The ministrations of our local physician did little to disturb the course of his disease, nor did the treatment of the specialist we consulted in New Haven. When I felt it was likely that the boy would never lay eyes on his native country again, I sent word to his father that he should come in all haste. I pray to God he arrives in time to bid this remarkable soul farewell.

CHAPTER TWENTY-TWO

Above all, he smelled the sea.

"Bid him keep the lash to the horses," Ridge said to his linkster, Albert Sims. "I'll see they get extra rations of oats and a good coat of liniment this evening at the livery of his choice. Tell him I'll slip an extra gold eagle in his pocket for his trouble as well."

Ridge held Reverend Daggett's letter in his hand as Albert passed his wishes on to the hired hackman. He couldn't read a word of it, and he'd fiddled with the paper so much it now had the consistency of one of Sehoya's lace dinner napkins. For weeks now this lone talking leaf had been the only link between him and the son who might not live long enough to lay eyes again on his father.

Ridge hurtled toward Cornwall. The image of arriving in time to find John still and lifeless haunted him as mile after mile rolled by. Worse was imagining him cold in some lonely white man's grave. At night, his worries for his son drowned out all thoughts of sleep. He rehearsed the ancient chants and prayers he intended to whisper into John's ear in preparation for his final journey. Nothing was more important than that. Damn the money. Damn the distance. He wanted to hear the coachman crack the whip one more time.

Yet for all his love and deep concern for John — and his desire to comfort him in his last days — he couldn't deny that this private journey had public repercussions. The newspaper editorials read to him by literate Cherokee indicated that these northern whites had finally kindled a sincere sympathy for the beleaguered Indian nations. Ridge intended to fan those coals a little, knowing that the Americans must always see the Cherokee at their best if they would ever come to view them as equals. He had not forgotten, rolling past the Middlesex farms of manicured pastures and straight-rowed fields, that powerful warrior tribes that had once battled the whites for this part of the earth had now slipped into the clutches of oblivion. The Cherokee fought now with words and ideas. And today, with an image of who they were and what they could be.

For the last leg of his journey, Ridge hired the finest carriage available, an Abott, Downing Company Concord with padded leather seats as soft as cribbed cotton, scroll-worked panels, and doors hand-painted in a scenic relief like those he'd seen in the parlors of the finer Ani-yonega homes in Charleston and Baltimore. Reinsman and footman adorned with matching cloaks and four fine white horses with ribbons woven in their braided tails were all included for a reasonable price.

Ridge thrust his arms through the sleeves of his Creek War uniform, trimmed in gold braid, hand-brushed free of all road dust and stale bread crumbs from his compulsive nibbling. Ridge was proudest of the major's insignia he had earned from Sharp Knife himself. In his vest pocket, carefully wrapped in tanned buckskin as soft as a child's cheek, he carried Cherokee herbs and teas. The conjurers' brews had seen the boy through before. He slipped his bare feet into white-topped Hessian boots. He could abide most of the white man's clothing, at least the practical aspects of it, but he couldn't bear those scratchy woolen socks. Thus attired, he'd stepped proudly into his carriage. Whenever he noticed that the coach had slowed, he looked at Albert and said, "Beg him to make haste, please."

He was about to repeat the whole routine when Sims pushed the curtain back. What Ridge saw left him breathless.

"Colt's Foot Mountain," Sims declared. And sure enough, at the end of nearly three-quarters of a moon's journey, Colt's Foot Mountain loomed before him. At its base, cradled in a valley strewn with spruce, hemlock, and cedar, and checkerboarded with farmers' fields, lay the town of Cornwall.

As the coachman rolled through the brick streets and row houses of the village, Ridge marked well the throng of human activity at the city's core. From the signs he'd seen in the Carolinas, Virginia, and Washington City, Ridge discerned the symbols for barbers, blacksmiths, bootblacks, tinkers, wheel-wrights, coopers, and cordwainers — all specialized feathers on a strange and power-ful bird. Peddlers hawked their wares of fish, charcoal, strange-smelling stews, pecks of red apples and pink peaches, and ears of freshly grilled corn.

"Smoking hot! Piping hot! Oh, what beau-ties I have got!" Sims translated the words coming from the dirty mouths of street children, so many of them in these American cities. In the race to come so far so fast, the whites had abandoned their young to their cold brick streets. Was comfort and conve-nience worth this price? How did such a cal-lous culture continue to thrive?

When Ridge stood in the shadow of the great seaboard cities he was struck by the same thought: The stone structures and brick streets were built in reaction to the whites' terrible fear of nature. Strip away one hun-dred winters and the land around Cornwall would be as pristine and beautiful as any Blue

Mountain cove. The immigrants had paved it under for their wagon wheels and leather shoes delicate enough to be ruined by a heavy dew.

"The Foreign Mission school, sir," the hackman announced in a raspy voice. Sims translated the coachman's statement into Cherokee as Ridge took stock of the damp chill in the air. No wonder John ailed.

At last, they arrived at the doors of the mission school. The tidy structure featured trimmed windows, a bell tower, a redbrick chimney, and finely milled clapboard siding, lending the place the appearance of the country barns they had passed in the last week. The building was austere, a terrible place for a sick and lonely boy to await his end. There was nothing remarkable about the large shack except the stoutness of its construction, squatted as it was on thick piers of oak. If its quarters were cold in these brutal northern winters, they were also clean and well kept. Ridge observed that the surrounding grounds were well-groomed, fruit trees pruned, cordwood neatly stacked, fall fields freshly tilled, awaiting the heavy hand of winter. The leaves of the lone maple tree at the front of the school had already started to turn. The atmosphere of pride comforted Ridge a little. But most of what he saw in this New England hamlet bespoke organization, skill, and determination, much like one observed in a colony of red ants. These northern whites seemed an industrious breed.

Once the coach rolled to a stop, Ridge's thoughts returned to his son. Had he made this long journey in vain? He made inquiries through Albert of the first white man he saw, a thin, humpbacked drudge clawing beneath the hedges with a rusty rake. The man left silently, only to return with others, teachers or missionaries, Ridge assumed. Ridge stood with a patient dignity, shoulders back, head erect, watching the teachers watch him.

Soon the headmaster stepped forth in his dark, hopelessly wrinkled frock and stiff white collar. A black tie in the shape of a cave bat hung loosely around his neck. From John's detailed letters, Ridge recognized him as the Reverend Herman Daggett. A good man by his son's accounts, but frail and sickly-looking, with a quiet, cool demeanor.

"Major Ridge, I presume," the reverend said, poking out his coarse hand. Ridge gripped it while he struggled with his English.

"How do you do?" he said.

"It's so good to finally get to meet you. I've heard so much."

"We've heard more of you," Ridge said. "Please know that the Cherokee are truly grateful, not only for educating the brightest stars in our sky but also for how well you've cared for my son."

Ridge hugged him as any earnestly appreciative man would do. Daggett seemed surprised, standing as stiff and rigid as a tree trunk.

"How is John Ridge?" he said.

"I'm delighted to report that he's much improved," Daggett said.

Ridge looked hard at Sims for the translation. "The boy lives yet," Sims said in Cherokee. "He still coughs a bit, but the worst is behind us." Ridge closed his eyes and clasped his hands to his chest in relief.

Daggett rattled on about something else that Sims began to translate before Daggett stopped talking. From what Ridge could gather, John was being kept alone in special quarters in the commons. The wife of the school steward, John Northrup, was caring for the boy's every need. Hearing the news, Ridge sighed in relief.

"Would you care for refreshments after your long journey?" Daggett said. "I'll take you to see John just after lunch." Ridge listened as Albert rapidly translated the English words. Albert was keen for his vittles.

"I've traveled far," Ridge said. "I'm deeply concerned for my son. I could neither eat nor rest until I've seen him."

"Of course," the old man said. "How thoughtless of me. Come. Please."

They followed Daggett through the halls and up the stairs until he paused before a wooden door. The principal rapped his knuckle against the higher panel. Ridge was confused when a girl's voice answered.

"Please come in," she said.

Ridge reached past Daggett and pushed the door open to the complaint of squeaking hinges. The window's light found John sitting up in his feather bed, slurping chicken soup spooned to him by a bright-faced, yellow-haired, blue-eyed white girl who could not have seen more than fifteen winters.

Ridge had expected to find the dark shadow of death smudged across his son's face, but John's color was robust, his eyes were clear and bright, and he smiled warmly. His light copper coloring contrasted nicely against the white cotton nightshirt. If ever Ridge had felt the impulse to thump this boy in the head, it was now. How worried he had been. Sehoya would be beside herself until she heard the news. Here sat the nearly departed, being spoon-fed in a feather bed by a young Ani-yonega with hair the color of strained honey. Ridge should be so ill.

" 'Doda!" John exclaimed. He nudged the spoon away. The girl dabbed his lips with a napkin. Then, pausing, he looked almost ashamed. "You shouldn't have come so far. I've just written to say that I'm much better."

"Whether well or ill, I would have crossed oceans to see you," Ridge said, sinking to one knee beside the bed. "Think not of the hardships of my journey but of the joy I feel at its end."

John reached for him. They embraced just enough so that Ridge could get a feel for his son's strength. Then he laid the back of his hand against his son's cheek to test for fever. He felt joyously cool.

"I'm glad you're here, 'Doda," John said. "I've been lonely for you, Etsi, and our home." Ridge was pleased to hear his son remember his mother.

"When your time's done here, we'll welcome you back."

"Until then," John said, his face brightening, "there's much to accomplish. I want the people of Cornwall to meet a Cherokee chief."

"When you feel better, then. There's no hurry."

"I feel fine. And with your blessing, I'll arrange introductions today."

"Do it, then," Ridge said, smiling. The boy had not forgotten his purpose. Ridge heard footsteps in the hallway, and then Elias Boudinot rushed through the door.

"My uncle!" he said. "I heard that you were here." Ridge hugged his nephew tightly.

"That's from Oo-watie," he said. "We're all very proud to hear how you've excelled here."

"It's my duty," Elias said. He looked at John. "And how are you today, cousin?"

"Well," John said in English. "We're about

to go out and meet some people. Will you come?"

"Of course," Elias said, also in English.

Ridge fished four gold quarter eagles from his pocket and dropped them into his linkster's hands. "Perhaps our friend, Mr. Daggett, can recommend lodgings for you."

"Will you not require my services?" Sims asked.

"These boys speak for the Ridge," he said.

It was so good to see the blood rush into John's cheeks, the way the pupils danced in his head. He was as fit as ever. Ridge felt the dread wilt out of his body like a mushroom caught in the sun.

Ridge wiped the beads of sweat from John's brow. Nearby steeped the herbs the conjurer had sent for this very occurrence.

"Go and see the people," John said. "I'll be fine."

"I've seen all the people I care to," Ridge said. "And you don't look fine to me." Ridge fetched the cloth from the water bucket and wrung it enough to dampen his son's pillow. "I had meant to spend this last evening alone with you anyway," he said.

Ridge figured John's ambitious social itinerary must have summoned the return of his fevers. As the days had worn on, Ridge had noticed that his son's limp had become steadily more pronounced. He grimaced with each unsteady step. His appetite waned. His face drained of its ripe color until it had the texture of fine dust. When the sun fell, the boy's chills returned. But John never complained, spending the last moments of each evening before bed scribbling invitations for the following day. The boy's pride never once wavered.

Half a moon, a fortnight, had passed swiftly. Each day John, Elias, and Ridge met with the people of Cornwall. Every evening they were invited into their cold homes to dine. How confidently his son and nephew moved about these rigid people. Ridge met Cornwall's mayor, officials, and constables, the city's doctors, judges, and clergymen, and even Lyman Beecher, revered for his wisdom, who had recently retired to his farm. The tedious man spoke of nothing besides clearing his land, plowing and farming his land, and most disconcerting, his wish to acquire more land than he could possibly need and bend it to his will. There were so many of Cornwall who intrigued and fascinated him, though Ridge was troubled that the wisest among these people was infected with the same disease that ran rampant among the most base ruffians and leatherstockings running corn liquor in the Smokies and Blue Mountains. Ridge kept his distance from this man Beecher, "the sage of Litchfield," John called him, with his obsession for land.

Among the rest of the New Englanders, Ridge exuded warmth, good will, and genuine interest, although he remained reserved and dignified, for he did not understand them as John and Elias did. Their customs and mannerisms were so foreign that he knew it would be easy to make a terrible mistake and defeat his larger purpose. Both boys whispered advice in his ear at their dinner tables on how to place the cloth in his lap before each meal, when to bow his head for their devotions, which silver utensil to use for each course of their dinners, the proper time to wear his beaver hat and when to tip its black brim to pale ladies. Ridge had skill as a diplomat. He had learned all of the strange customs of the Creeks before those of the white people. He got the hang of these odd occasions soon enough. At least their ceremonies didn't begin with consumption of the black drink and another half hour of spilling the contents of his stomach.

Through his son and nephew, Ridge made friends in the north, knowing that before long he would call upon them as allies of the Cherokee. He would ask them to say to their chief in Washington that the Cherokee were no different from them, save for the tint of their skins. Had not John Ridge and Elias Boudinot, "princes of the forest," born in ignorance, come naked to their schools and excelled there? Through his young kin, Ridge was building acceptance and consensus just as he'd envisioned that morning when he watched a conjurer bathe a sick child in the river.

At this late hour, Elias had excused himself to his books while Ridge stayed up with John. "I'll stay another week or so," Ridge said, "until you recover enough to make the journey home."

John bit his lip. His expression paled. "I'm not yet ready to go, 'Doda," he said. "I beg you for one winter more."

Ridge heaped two more blankets over his son's body to stave off the night's chill while they waited for the girl to bring him his dinner. "For what purpose?" Ridge nearly growled the Cherokee words, but the reason was due more to fatigue than irritation. John had surprised him with his request.

"To learn."

"Ah! Enough learning," Ridge said. "Time to *do.*"

There was a soft knock on the door. John propped himself up on his pillows, ran his fingers through his hair, and blew into his hand before answering. The yellow-haired girl — Sally Northrup — entered with a tray of beef stew, half a loaf of fresh bread, and a peeled apple cut into quarters.

"Pardon me, Chief Ridge," she said softly. "It's time for your son to eat."

John quickly brushed his father aside to

make room for the girl. She tucked another white cloth under his chin and spooned the stew into his mouth.

"One winter more," he said quietly, "and it's done."

"I'm not sure you'll survive up here another winter," Ridge said frankly. "I can't afford to come scrambling up here every three or four moons. Come home with me to your family. The southern climate will cure you. It's too cold here."

"All I require is rest, 'Doda. Please don't worry."

Don't worry, he says. Did the boy not realize how much responsibility the Nation had heaped upon Ridge's shoulders? How much pressure would be relieved by having his son home to help ease the burden of leadership? Ridge needed someone he could trust to translate all the talking leaves that blew his way, more than a half dozen a week and thrice that when the fall council approached. He needed his son by his side.

He rose, the plank beneath his feet creaking under the strain of his mass. He knew he should insist. Sehoya was sick with worry about her son. John certainly understood what was expected of him. And his conduct over the past few days indicated that the boy was truly born for public service. Why would he want to stay another year at the clapboard academy? And how much longer could he bear the northern chill? Would another year of book learning be worth the risk of losing the Cherokee's most educated warrior?

Perhaps John's health was far worse than he would admit. Ridge hadn't considered that his son's request was a ruse. Of course the boy would prefer to be home with friends and family. He just wasn't strong enough to travel. Maybe it was best to leave him here, where he received excellent care, rather than force him home over an arduous journey with the winter snows on their heels. Late spring would be better, say in Anasku'tee, the Planting Moon, May, before the oppression of the summer heat. This would give him the extra year he was asking for.

"As you wish," Ridge said. "We plan to leave at dawn. I'll come by to see you before I go."

Ridge watched the girl feed him, her tender touch as she dabbed the napkin to his chapped lips, the way she giggled when she bumped his nose with the spoon. John's gaze never left hers.

"Surely not," he said quietly to himself as he let the door swing closed behind him.

CHAPTER TWENTY-THREE

"Oh, so he was too sick to come home, was he!" Sehoya shrieked.

"Hush, now," Ridge said. He rarely assumed the risk of scolding his wife but her ranting proved a distraction. "Can we hear the end of his letter before we go mad?"

"Why read more?" she said. "Don't you know what's coming?"

Ridge prodded Sims to carry on. When he finished, Sehoya snatched the leaves from his hand, wadded it into a ball, and tossed it to the hearth's flames. Ridge looked at his translator, who in turn nodded to signify that he had read and understood the contents exactly as they appeared in the now smoldering communiqué. Then he directed his efforts to peeling the stamp from the envelope.

"Surely not," Ridge said, his face withering to match his mood.

"I knew the boy was stone-headed," Sehoya said, snatching the envelope from Sim's hands and tossing it beside the ashes of its contents. "What else could he be with you as his father? But I never took him for a fool."

"Your reply to his last request was not strong enough," Ridge said.

"It most certainly was!" she snapped. "Brother Butrick wrote the words exactly as I screamed them. John was told that a white woman was apt to feel above our people. I reminded him of his purpose, and also that he would prove more useful to the Cherokee if he were to choose a wife from among the chiefs' daughters. He could have his pick." Sehoya hung her head. "You heard yourself how he answers. This white girl has stolen his heart. He'll have no other. What am I to do?"

"What is there but to say yes, Sehoya?"

"And what of the pain I feel when I say it, Ridge Walker?"

"What pain, Mother? Accept his decision."

"Shall I accept the dilution of my blood?" she said, the lines deepening around her tight mouth. "That my grandchildren won't belong to a clan? As a boy, John hated that he had just a little white blood. Now he'll bring half-breeds into the world. All of us will walk a hard road. Would you have me sit idle and accept all of that?"

"Every one of those things can be overcome," Ridge said. "The girl will be accepted among our people."

"Yes, but will John be accepted among hers?"

"Of course he will," Ridge said. "I've seen for myself how well they think of him."

"Not when he has a white woman for a wife, you haven't," she said.

"I know their hearts, Sehoya. They're different from the southerners."

"You mean you've seen their drawing room faces and heard the polite wag of their tongues," Sehoya said. "Their hearts they keep to themselves in a dark closet. Since you seem suddenly ignorant of the basic facts, let me assure you that whites are whites wherever they are. There's trouble in the wind, Ridge Walker. See if it doesn't find my son while he's far from us."

Sehoya tossed another log on the fire and stomped toward the door. She stopped cold, turned, and leveled a glance at him that would scorch a moth. "What exactly were you doing up there with him? Did you see none of this going on?"

"I suppose I saw it," Ridge admitted. "I just didn't understand it."

"What does that mean? The more time you spend around white people, the more you double-talk just like them. I can't even get a straight answer out of my husband's mouth. Why should I expect any better from my oldest son?"

"Sehoya —"

She slammed the bedroom door behind her. The barn beckoned. He gathered a folded blanket and a full coal-oil lamp, glad that only this morning he'd ordered the slaves to put out fresh hay. In some ways he was still a lucky man. Just not in the ways he'd like.

CHAPTER TWENTY-FOUR

Ridge craned his neck toward the Federal Road, listening for the dull thud of horse hooves or the rhythmic jingle of brass tack. He motioned for John Ross and White Path to still their tongues for a moment.

"Do you hear anything, Mother?" he asked Sehoya.

"No, of course not," she said. "Hush now and let the Very Reverend Brother Butrick read it again. I'd like Quatie to hear."

"Reverend Butrick will do," the pale missionary said. "Or Brother Butrick, if you prefer. Or just Butrick, maybe, to save us all some time." He exhaled in exasperation and rubbed his hands together.

Ridge had heard enough, but Sehoya, perched on the edge of her rocker beside John Ross's quiet wife, still hung on every word. As full-blooded wives of mixed-blood Cherokee chiefs, Sehoya and Quatie had much in common. Butrick popped his copy of the December 1822 edition of the *Niles Weekly*

Register as one would do to smooth the wrinkles out of wet buckskin. And then he commenced to read the article for the seventh time.

Various newspaper accounts of John Ridge's speeches had reached the Nation over the past few weeks. John had traveled south with James Fields, Thomas Basel, Darcheechee, and a Delaware by the name of Adin C. Gibbs. His first cousin, Kilakeena, christened by the missionaries as Elias Boudinot, greeted them in Charleston. The Reverend Reynolds Bascom paraded the educated Cherokees before the more learned elements of the genteel southern city, where the curious crowds gathered to see what had come of the heathens after four years at the northern universities.

Writers reported that entire audiences were stunned by John's knowledge, eloquence, charisma, and spirit. His moving oratory mocked any who scoffed at the notion that the Indian nations could rise above savagery. He railed against the prevailing idea that uncivilized people were happiest in a lesser state.

"Read that part about extermination," Sehoya pleaded.

"Oh, yes," Butrick said with a casual moan. "It's my favorite, as well. And I've had ample opportunity to choose."

I have made this contrast to show the fallacy of such theories, and to give you a general view of the wretched state of the Heathen, particularly of the aborigines of this country, who are gradually retiring from the stage of action to sleep with their fathers. It is on the exertions of the benevolent that their safety depends, and only the hand of charity can pluck them from final extermination.

"Will that do, Madam Ridge?" Butrick said, folding the paper on his knee.

"Would you mind reading that part about the response to his speech?" Sehoya said. "I'd like Rebecca Goingsnake to hear this," she explained to Quatie. "She used to go on about how badly John stuttered." Quatie politely smiled and patted Sehoya's hand.

The people of the southern cities answered John's appeal with money, books, and wagonloads of good wishes, flowing like a river into the nation for the missionaries to use in shaping young Cherokee minds. John Ridge could reach the whites as no Cherokee ever had.

But another aspect of the articles appealed to Ridge. Butrick put the paper aside, slurping the last of his tea from Sehoya's navy blue-on-white china cup and saucer. Ridge would never understand why she prized these things. The china was as thin as an eggshell, and fractured just as easily. Butrick set his cup down, smoothed the thighs of his black trousers, and began to rise. "I'd better step out to see that all is prepared for our welcome," he said.

Ridge clamped his hand down on the missionary's bony shoulder. "I hate to impose, but could you read those words where people say what they think rather than what they do?"

"The editorial, you mean?"

"I think so."

"Why not?" Butrick said, snatching the paper off the floor. "One should examine editorials several times. Three or four readings are simply not enough. By the way, have either one of you considered learning to read?" He looked down his nose. "You seem to be keen for the written word."

Ridge watched his eyes dart across the pages. He loved watching people read.

"Or obsessed, rather," Butrick added. "Here we are."

He is not a professor of religion, nor have we any reason to think that his character and temper have ever been regulated and softened by the influence of that Spirit upon his heart without which the native corruption will show forth, in spite of all the influence of philosophy or literature.

Ridge relished the editorial's pronouncement. As a young man, John Ridge had never relinquished the "lack of piety" that had plagued his teachers. For ten winters, his body and mind had belonged to the whites. The boy had been challenged — commanded, rather — to absorb their language, their ways, their books, their manners, their history, their politics. But he had never accepted their religion, which was shoved daily down his throat, though his reluctance probably brought their canes to his backside. For Ridge, that simple fact relieved his greatest worry, second only to his son's health. He saw the editorial as further proof that John Ridge would return a Cherokee.

"I'm certain I could read it three or four times more before the vapors claim me, if you like," Butrick said.

Ridge waved him off. He could now hear the sound of horses and cheering crowds outside, and knew that at last his son was home. He herded Ross and White Path out the door ahead of him, pausing beneath the threshold to wait with his arms across his chest. Sehoya adjusted the wreath of white flowers that signified that all was well within her home and stood beside him, holding hands with Quatie.

John dismounted, taking the hand of any who offered, and they all did — he was already a hero among the mixed-bloods. The neighboring full-bloods stood back, reserving judgment. They wanted to know more about what had become of him after so many winters in the white man's world.

"He's grown taller in the last three years," Sehoya said. "His color's good. His cheeks look like ripe peaches. He's filled out a little, too."

"He's filled out a lot," Ridge said, eyeing the crutches strapped to his saddle. Once the boy was free of his admirers, father and son locked eyes. John limped toward him, and they embraced. Ridge could feel how his son's chest muscles had swelled and hardened in response to the prolonged use of the crutches. Everything about this boy screamed of burgeoning personal power. This occasion was the first time Ridge knew in his heart that his son would one day lead the Nation. He introduced him to John Ross. White Path hugged him like a long-lost son.

"Are we done with education then, Skah-tle-loh-skee?" Ridge asked.

"We are. I belong to my people now."

"And the woman?" Ridge whispered into his son's ear.

He caught the spark of anger in his son's dark eyes. "If after two years I can walk without crutches," John said, "I'll return to Cornwall and claim her. On this, I have her parents' word."

"Will they honor it?"

"It doesn't matter if they do or they don't. If I keep my part of the bargain, I'll have Sally for my wife, if she'll have me."

"Fair enough." Ridge stepped aside so Sehoya could see her boy. She gasped as she opened her arms. Sehoya trembled as her son squeezed her. John tore loose while Sehoya wiped the joyous tears from her cheeks. Limping out to his horse, he ripped the crutches free from his saddle thongs and hoisted them over his head.

"Now that Skah-tle-loh-skee sleeps in the bosom of his own country among his own people," he said, "he has no need of these!" He splintered them against a millstone before a delighted audience. Even the full-bloods cheered him. He performed the steps of the Green Corn Dance as he made his way back to his mother's adoring arms.

"It was a boy who left my house," Sehoya said, drawing John's head to her shoulder. "It's a warrior who returns."

John Ross quietly collected his wife and they skirted arm in arm from the middle of the celebration to its edge. He looked out of place in his business suit, chuckling with full-bloods dressed in buckskins, hunting shirts, and turbans with silver rings dangling from their noses. Even the mountain people who had come out of curiosity to see John Ridge soon gravitated around the young mixed-blood chief. They sought him out to hold his hand or caress the back of his head, always smiling. Ridge had many, many loyal full-blood friends, and even those who didn't know him personally were always respectful. But he himself was seldom exposed to the reverence he observed in their attitude toward John Ross. Ross did not know these people, yet they made it a point to know him.

How had Ross made up so much ground so quickly? Taking Quatie for his wife accounted for a portion of Ross's social success. But the young man had other magnetic qualities that perhaps Ridge had underestimated. Ridge battled the mixed-blood stigma; Ross had effortlessly overcome it. Clearly John Ross no longer required Ridge's endorsement to step forth among the Cherokee. Watching how easily he moved among the full-bloods assured Ridge that Ross would rise on his own virtues.

"They love him," White Path said, who read Ridge's envious expression as well as deer tracks in the woods.

"That's good," Ridge said. "He loves them."

"Come, Ridge," White Path said, wrapping his arm around him and escorting him into Sehoya's home. "No politics today. We're celebrating the return of this son of yours. He'll be the one to watch for a while."

Ridge turned one last time to regard John Ross. The mixed-blood chief smiled warmly at him, and Ridge returned it as graciously as he could. It was wrong to feel jealousy when Ridge had received so many blessings, especially now with John Ridge home in the Nation. But he felt it just the same — a sense of being only slightly off-kilter, as one experiences before the onset of a fever. Ridge shook it off and rejoined the celebration.

John's face colored as he flashed a sheet of paper before his father's eyes. "Look what your cousin Sequoyah has accomplished!" he said. Elias Boudinot and his friend, Darcheechee, floated beside John, both about to burst with enthusiasm, completely inconsistent with the quiet that had blanketed the earth late in the Snow Moon of 1822.

"Sequoyah?" Ridge said. "Not much of anything, I expect. Everyone knows he's mad as a spring goose. And who wouldn't be, sitting in a dingy shack all day, scribbling on bark with pokeberry juice, incessantly smoking that pipe."

"He's a genius, Ridge Walker." John pointed at an array of symbols, most similar to the talking leaves of the whites, as far as Ridge could tell. They were as meaningless to him as the designs on the bottom of a turtle shell. Interesting to look at for a moment, but there were always better things nearby. "Each of these symbols represents a sound in our language," John explained. "You string the sounds together like beads on a necklace and they form a word in our language. You learn the symbols and you can write in Cherokee."

"Nonsense," Ridge said. "When I was young, a great conjurer taught me that the Provider gave a book to the red boy and a bow and arrow to the white boy. The white boy came and stole the book, leaving only the bow and arrow to the red boy. Ever since, the Cherokee were not meant to have their own books, and the whites, of course, have learned some very bad habits from them."

His son doubled over with laughter. "Do you really believe that?"

"Which part? About us not having books or the whites having some bad habits? In either case, yes, I think they're both true."

"It's a myth. A story. This," he said, holding up the talking leaf, "is reality." After a moment's hesitation, he took Ridge by the hand and dragged him into another room. "Tell me something."

"What?"

"Tell me something. Anything."

"I'm hungry, and Sehoya put too much salt in the rabbit stew."

John plopped down at the table and scribbled the strange symbols on paper with a goose quill. He snatched the paper from the desk, blew the ink dry, and towed his father back into the main room. He handed the paper to Darcheechee. "What does this say?"

Ridge watched Darcheechee's eyes follow

his son's symbols from left to right. "I'm hungry, and Sehoya put too much salt in the rabbit stew." John stared at his father, his eyebrows arched on his forehead.

"Did he tell you what I said?" he asked Darcheechee.

"He didn't have to, Chief Ridge. I read it here."

Ridge snatched the paper from Darcheechee's hand. "Don't you mock me, boy! Who told you what I said?"

The youth held up the talking leaf. "This did," he said.

Ridge clapped his hands in astonishment. His whole body felt hot. He opened the door and his wife nearly fell into him. "Do you hear, Sehoya!" he said, steadying her frame.

"There was nothing wrong with the stew," she said.

"Of course there wasn't," Ridge said. "We have what they have! And we'll use it the same way." His mind's eye conjured up the image of a chief saying something one day and the whole Nation reading it the next. Best of all, no English speaker could understand it. Written language would be the Cherokee's most powerful weapon since educated men walked among them. Once again the conjurers were wrong, and Ridge would make sure that the full-bloods knew it. "How long will it take us to learn this language?" he asked.

"A few weeks, at most," John said. "I could teach it to you in a couple of days."

He turned to his wife. "Come, Sehoya, and learn how to write in Cherokee."

"My time might be better spent learning to cook," she said.

Ridge danced over to the kettle, dipped in a bowl, and slurped some of the steaming broth. "Ah, just the way I like it," he said, choking down the brine. The broth would've fared better with fewer ramps as well.

"Will you not learn also, 'Doda?" John asked.

"I don't think so.

"Why not? You don't have to learn English to read and write Cherokee. This belongs to us!"

"Make no mistake, John," Ridge said. "I'm very proud of Sequoyah's accomplishment, especially for how it will awe the whites. But I belong to another time, when a man's greatest gift was an ability to move people with his tongue. The greats of my day could ignite the whole Nation to war, or reduce it to tears just by their spoken words. Oratory is a thing alive, powerful enough to move mountains. Nothing else compares."

John appeared stupefied, but Sehoya only grinned, which reassured Ridge that at least his wife accepted his willful ignorance. Among the warrior societies, oratory was prized above all male qualities save cunning and courage. Words were spoken, not read.

His son had also forgotten the prophecy: *The Ani-yonegas will teach you to read, but that is only a means to deceive you.* Ridge couldn't afford to be fooled. And how could his son know that conjurers had warned Ridge long ago that if he spent his days staring at talking leaves he would never again be able to see as far? The Man Who Walks the Mountaintops would never trade vision for the ability to read, especially now that John was back by his side. He'd groomed his son to be his reader and writer, a new beneficial tool, like the plow was in his youth, or a new weapon, like the rifle in the time of his grandfather, Ada-gal'kala. The Ridge would spend his days with his mind free of deception, peering into the distance so he could guide his people along an increasingly twisted path.

Sehoya reached for the paper and said, "I'll learn, son. But it's no use trying to reason with him."

"I really don't understand," John said.

"It's not that hard," she said. "He's a savage."

"And proud of it," Ridge added.

Sehoya pulled up a chair and patted the cushion. "I'll learn. And then I'll read to him. That's as far as he goes."

CHAPTER TWENTY-FIVE

"I have a plain question," Ridge said abruptly to William Chamberlin as soon as the missionary stuck his nose through the crack in the door. "And I expect a plain answer." It was difficult to control his outrage as he spit out the bitter words. His gut churned as if he'd eaten a half dozen green apples, but Brother Chamberlin seemed to understand that Ridge's anger was not directed at him.

"Of course, Chief Ridge," Chamberlin said, opening the door to offer Ridge his home. "Ask whatever you'd like."

"Two winters have passed with letters flying back like leaves in a windstorm between my son and the white girl he loves. Although John still walks with a minor limp, he returned to Cornwall without crutches to claim Sally Northrup's hand. The girl's parents honored their daughter's wish as agreed and set the wedding date for January. The distance and my duties in the Nation prevented Sehoya and me from attending, yet I'm told the ceremony took place at the Northrups' home."

The missionary studied him blankly. "What problem is there in all of this?"

"I'll tell you."

Ridge complained about how the same ministers and community leaders who had welcomed the Ridges into their homes now railed about John's marriage from their pulpits and podiums. Newspaper editors, once praising the Foreign Mission's noble experiment, condemned this despicable result. The people of Cornwall mobbed Ridge's son and his young wife, even threatening them with the hangman's noose.

"It was perfectly acceptable for an Indian to live among them," Ridge said. "He can wear their awkward fashions, stomach their overcooked meals, contort his tongue to speak their disgusting language, send his children far from their mothers to attend their schools and churches and adopt their lifestyle. But for this same Indian to stroll into a civilized community and carry away one of its finest daughters is viewed as nothing less than a crime by these hypocrites. Though the fruit be ripe in Cornwall, the tree that bears it is rotten to the roots."

Chamberlin chewed on all of this while Ridge considered his nephew, Elias Boudinot, who was steering down the same dangerous road. Elias had fallen in love with Harriet Gold, a niece of the physician who had cared so long for John Ridge. The girl's parents opposed the marriage, yet she mustered the courage to defy them. Her minister threatened her with an ultimatum: Give up the Indian or the affair would be made public. She refused. When the townspeople mobbed her home, Harriet was secreted away. She saw her figure burned in effigy above a vat of tar. It was said her brother, Stephen, set the fire himself.

"And so I've come," Ridge said, "for straight talk about the source of their contempt."

Brother Chamberlin met Ridge's simmering indignation with calm, precise words.

"We're friends, Chief Ridge," he said. "Expect a sincere answer to whatever question you pose."

Ridge was disarmed by the missionary's sympathetic reaction, but he remained suspicious of his intent. Had the Cornwall clergy also not acted sincere in his presence? So many responses from white men were equivocations. Ridge was weary of weeding through their words.

"You've seen the newspaper accounts of my son's marriage, have you not?" Ridge asked, pressing.

"I have."

"You are aware that the agents of the Foreign Mission school have publicly condemned mixed marriages?"

"I'm sorry to say that I am."

"Tell me this! Where in the Scriptures — or anywhere else in the books referred to and held dear by these people — do they find one word spoken truly by the Great Provider to justify their reactions to the marriages between Indian men and white women?"

"I'm not certain they worship the Great Provider, Chief Ridge."

"Of course they do!" Ridge snapped. "Regardless of what they name it, what Cherokee call the Provider is one force and one spirit. Any fool would know this."

"Forgive my ignorance, Ridge Walker. You are once again correct."

"So," Ridge fumed. "Where in the Book does it say it's wrong for my son to marry a white girl?"

"I know of nothing in the Scriptures, Chief Ridge," the missionary said calmly. Ridge considered this tone of voice a practiced art whereby passion was separated from wisdom as if danger lay in their combination. Not so among the Cherokee. To be wise — to be right in any decision — was not a thing to be dispassionate about. Truth was something one *felt* from its source, like warmth from a fire. Ridge sensed nothing of the sort from the black-suited, emotionally flat missionary.

"The common people in the north respond out of fear," Chamberlin continued. "I regret the Foreign Mission's position as much as any man of reason and faith, but they've been threatened with extinction, and you must understand that they've bowed to public pressure to preserve a greater good. Consider the complexity of their position if you can."

"It is beyond me," Ridge said. "For over a hundred winters, white men have taken Indian women for their wives, and I've never heard one word spoken against it. My son and nephew fall in love — *true* love — with white women, and their lives are threatened."

"Time is on our side, Chief Ridge. I'm in favor of mixed marriages, and so is President Monroe. You still have quiet, enlightened, and very powerful friends in the north who speak well of John and young Boudinot."

"Yet there is so much shouting," Ridge said, "who can hear them? If it's true that the Great Father Monroe must yield to the majority, it's clear enough to my eyes that regardless of what he favors, he can *do* nothing for us."

"It's a simple matter of overcoming human ignorance."

"I'm no longer willing to overcome mine. I believed in my heart that if we lived like the more cultured whites, we would be accepted among them. Now after great pain and sacrifice, my eyes at last are opened. I see our path much more clearly, and I've presented my view to the council."

"What would that be?" Chamberlin said, his curiosity obviously piqued.

"If the Americans won't have us as equals among them, let us live forever apart. Tell the missionaries, the newspaper editors, the government agents who move among us like copperheads — anyone who will listen — that the Cherokee won't cede another foot of land."

Chamberlin stared long, his expression dimming. "If I may speak frankly, Chief Ridge, the idea in Washington is that once the Cherokee are well advanced in their farming and civilized pursuits, they won't require so much land. The most promising course for your tribe is to diversify your population and vie for statehood. Along these lines, the government will want to sell some of the Nation to homesteaders, where we'll live close enough to one another to put our prejudices aside."

"Let the whites put their contempt of my people aside first," Ridge said. "Let our sons marry their daughters without threats and hatred, and then we can talk again. As things stand, we feel that Indian haters make poor neighbors."

"Take caution, Ridge," Chamberlin said. "General Jackson and the Georgians may take issue with an absolute position. It's best that we continue to talk about our differences."

"All they want to talk about is taking our land," Ridge said. "And both of them can be damned to your hell for all the Cherokee care."

"I've never seen you in such an uproar."

"I've never seen my son so disgraced," he said. "I've never heard such lies. And I don't think I feel like discussing the matter further."

The interview was over. Ridge mounted his horse and jerked its head around. "Tell them, Chamberlin. No more cessions. No more treaties. We'll give up nothing more until they treat us as human beings."

He cracked his crop against the horse's hip and galloped away, slowing to a trot only once he'd reached the soothing silence of the woods where no man lived.

CHAPTER TWENTY-SIX

When the seasons turned to the annual diplomatic mission to Washington City, Ridge was not in the mood to compromise. He and John Ross and the other delegates checked into Tennison's House, where they traded their hunting clothes for cravats, boiled white shirts that smelled of lye water, and freshly brushed black suits. Ridge politely refused an invitation to the White House to receive the obligatory meaningless medals. Young Cherokee scholars had unearthed a serious discrepancy between the terms of the old treaties and promises the Great Father made to the Georgians. Ridge was stung to learn that Thomas Jefferson, second only to Washington in the hearts of the Cherokee, had betrayed them with a stroke of his pen. As a result, Georgia had laid claim to roughly a quarter of the Cherokee Nation promised forever to his people, and Ridge intended on some straight talk as to what the Americans planned to do about it.

The usual linksters were not retained. For the first time in Ridge's memory, Cherokee chiefs would speak for the Cherokee. Ridge served as the spirit of the delegation and as the eyes and ears of Pathkiller himself. John Ross, fluent in English, would evaluate all written or spoken American responses directly from their source. John Ridge, fluent in both languages, would make his father understand not only what was being said but also exactly what it meant. For Ridge, such a powerful delegation was the fruition of the dream he'd held on to for twenty-five winters. Thus prepared, the Cherokee marched to the War Department to dispatch the first volley.

Secretary of War John C. Calhoun's assistant returned the disputed document to its file. Ridge conceded to himself that twenty-two winters before, Cherokee chiefs either deceased or long ago deposed for their corruptions had possibly agreed with the Georgia Compact that had brought that state into the American Union. Nevertheless, the talking leaves now in Calhoun's hand in no way represented a treaty between the Cherokee Nation and the United States. They constituted, rather, a discussion of claims between the federal government and the State of Georgia, and were of no consequence whatsoever to his people. The Cherokee clearly owned the disputed land in Georgia by virtue of the treaties of Holston and Hopewell, and it wasn't within Jefferson's power to surrender it to Georgia without their consent. Such was Ridge's position, as agreed upon by John Ross and the other Cherokee diplomats present.

"Do you understand the provisions of the compact as agreed, gentlemen?" Calhoun asked.

"We understand the text as written, sir — the meaning of its words," Ridge answered through his son. "We take issue, however, with the term agreed as it applies to the Cherokee Nation. The State of Georgia drew its own line across our country, that which was promised by the Great Father Washington to remain ours forever. How can two men agree to take land from a third without his consent and then expect him to abide by it?" John Ridge whispered in his father's ear. Ridge nodded, and his son spoke the words. "What legal precedent can you cite to justify such a request?"

Ridge recognized Calhoun as one stern, powerful white man. It looked as though the launderer of his crisp white shirts had smeared a little of the stiffening agent on the man's face and gray hair. His nose was like a war hatchet, his eyes hard like musket balls, and both features appeared to be aimed at the Cherokee.

"Georgia entered the Union in the exact manner of all other states before her," Calhoun said. John translated. A few words out of his son's mouth and these white leaders sat frozen in awe. Ridge enjoyed watching them squirm.

"The citizens of Georgia submitted their terms," Calhoun continued. "The federal government approved them. The boundaries drawn as I've shown you are part and parcel of the compact of 1802."

"The Cherokee have rightful treaty to much of these same lands, sir," John Ridge said. "Why were we not consulted?"

"The compact was agreed to twenty-two years ago, sir," Calhoun said. "Long before my tenure in this office. I can only assume that the prevailing thought at the time was that the Cherokee living within Georgia's limits would willingly emigrate beyond these borders long before now."

"And now that we haven't," Ridge asked through his son, "what is to be done?"

Calhoun cleared his throat. "That, sir, is the precise question the representatives of Georgia are asking this administration to address as we speak."

"With all due respect, sir," John Ridge said, "should we not take the matter immediately before President Monroe? We would like to make him aware of our resolve not to cede more land. Perhaps the president can persuade Congress to make adjustments to the Georgia Compact, as least where these boundaries encompass land that never belonged to either the federal government or the State of Georgia. We are prepared, sir, to support our position in this matter. We carry in our hands original copies of all treaties and agreements entered into between the Cherokee Nation and your government. It is our intent to put this matter to rest once and for all."

When Ross heard John Ridge's reply to Secretary Calhoun, he nodded in solemn approval. Twenty-two-year-old John had spoken well for their nation.

Calhoun massaged his forehead, pinching the bridge of his formidable nose. "You speak well for yourselves, gentlemen," he said. "I almost wish you didn't. If you were the savages people say you are, it would render my burden lighter. But as you have proven yourselves to be learned men, perfectly suited to understand the complexities of our federal system and the rights of states guaranteed under our union, I intend to speak frankly."

Ridge's son quickly translated the secretary's words. Ridge lifted his chin, as if preparing his head to absorb the weight of a coming blow.

"The federal government — that is, the Great Father — has already accepted the boundaries that now incorporate the State of Georgia. Like it or not, land that traditionally belongs to the Cherokee falls within Georgia's limits. You are within Georgia's domain and subject to their laws. The Great Father does not have the power to redraw the line as he sees fit, and it is therefore impossible within the framework of our system for you to remain indefinitely as a separate entity within the boundaries of this state." He paused to take a deep breath. "Your choice is simple. Either you plan to become integrated within the social and political fabric of Georgia, or you emigrate, as so many of you have done already, beyond the waters of the Mississippi."

Calhoun paused to allow John Ridge to catch up with his words. As Ridge heard them his anger burned, yet he could not allow his face to express it. His gaze met Ross's, and without another word they agreed it was time to plead their case before Monroe.

"This, sirs, is firm advice," Calhoun added. "Consider it well."

Ridge nodded politely, thanking the secretary for his time. Then he whisked all of the Cherokee into the muddy streets of Washington City, herding them onward toward Tennison's House. Ridge and John Ross cackled like two roosters caged in the same coop, with John making sure they both understood each other, as John Ross still did not speak Cherokee all that well. On the walk home, the two friends decided they'd formulate a written response to Calhoun's advice.

John Ridge and Chief Ross agonized over every written word in the final draft. When it was done, John read their response in Cherokee to his father:

Sir: We beg leave to remind you that the Cherokee are not foreigners but original inhabitants of the United States; that the states by which they are now surrounded have been created out of land which was once theirs; that they cannot recognize the sovereignty of any state within the limits of their territory. An exchange of land twice as large west of the Mississippi as the one now occupied by the Cherokees east of that river, or all the money now in your treasury, would be no inducement for the nation to exchange or sell their country.

"There," Ridge said to his friends as he blew the ink dry on the page. "Tell Calhoun that the matter has been considered. We'll see what Monroe has to say soon enough."

Ridge tucked his legs under the table, a white napkin stiff as a roofing shake draped from his neck, wondering which dishes the Georgia congressman would spoon onto his china plate. The most curious aspect to Washington City was that adversaries could sit down at the same table, as they were this evening at Tennison's House, and make polite conversation, seemingly oblivious to the bad blood between them. Such civility between enemies was a white man's convention that Ridge found difficult to abide, seeing that this man not only represented a faction that wished to expel the Cherokee from their ancient homeland, but had also insulted them publicly on the floor of the House of Representatives.

Had the dinner been at another place, in another time, Ridge would have jerked the hair from the man's head until he'd stretched his neck enough to hack it free with a flint-bladed tomahawk. For that was what this hypocrite deserved for referring to the most civilized Indian delegation the Americans had ever seen as "savages subsisting upon roots, wild herbs, and disgusting reptiles."

The Georgian smiled graciously at the Cherokee, like an opossum that had been discovered after it had rummaged through your grain. He wore a blue velvet frock coat, gray breeches buttoned at the knee, and a boiled white shirt so brilliant it reflected the candlelight. Ridge watched the heat of the room slowly uncoil the man's earlocks. The Negro servant sliced juicy white meat off the breast of a broiled chicken. The smell of hickory coals and unfamiliar spices filled the air. An order for black-eyed peas came next, followed by a slice of bread carved from a warm loaf. Ridge waited, watching.

The Georgian helped himself to steamed carrots, boiled potatoes bathed in butter and green, leafy herbs, and, last and best of all, a heaping portion of sweet potatoes coated with honey and cinnamon. Ridge winked at his son, who returned the gesture to John Ross, and on down the line until at last kindly assistant principal chief John Lowrey, who answered only to aging Pathkiller, examined the Georgian's course.

Lowrey looked quite the part of the gentleman, except for the dangling loops in his ears, which normally supported silver medallions the size of a woman's fist. He had abandoned his customary turban, silver gorget, and nose ring and wore only his presidential medal in the American fashion outside the lapels of his frock coat.

"Excuse me, sir," Lowrey said to the Negro, "would you be kind enough to pass me some of those *roots*?"

"Roots, sir?" the waiter asked.

"Ah, yes," Lowrey said. "The same roots the gentlemen from Georgia is having. Give us all a generous portion of those tasty *roots.*"

Ross snickered. John Ridge concealed his grin behind his napkin. Lowery kept shouting for roots, roots, roots. Ridge's cheeks warmed as he struggled to maintain his deadpan expression. "We Indians are *very* fond of roots," he explained to the Congressman. "They're new to you, of course, but we've enjoyed them for generations." John Ridge translated his words dutifully, pausing only once to snicker. But once he'd faltered, the rest of the Cherokee howled.

"Will you be having chicken, sir?" the Negro servant asked Ridge.

"Only if there's no snake or lizard to be had," he said in Cherokee. John gathered himself well enough to translate, and then he lost all control.

The Cherokee erupted, loud enough to make the china ring, as did many of the other politicians and businessmen at the table. One of the Negroes used the opportunity to sample the wine. Beads of sweat broke out on the Georgian's forehead. His earlocks had straightened like straw, giving him every appearance of a finely dressed scarecrow. He rose abruptly from the table, turned on his heel, and marched for the door. He paused, returned to the table, where he stashed a few slices of bread into his napkin, and left without a word.

Ridge snapped off the tip of a carrot in his teeth and watched him go. He looked at the waiter. "I wasn't kidding about the snake or lizard," he said. The door slammed on riotous laughter.

"I'm surprised to see you again in this office," Secretary Calhoun said with impatient eyes.

"We have other matters to discuss," Ridge replied through his son.

"I've told you before that I cannot keep the Georgians from breathing down your necks," Calhoun said in the harshest tone Ridge had ever heard him use.

"They make hot talk," Ridge answered diplomatically. "I suppose it was intended for the people at home."

"You have been successful in your appeal to President Monroe," Calhoun said. "He was not as fortunate before the House. The Georgians cannot simply take your land within their limits, but you must be aware that Congress has appropriated funds to send another commission to negotiate with the Cherokee for the disputed tract. The government will not dismiss Governor McMinn as your agent. Your Light Horse Guard will not be paid by federal funds, but you have been given the authority to tax white traders operating principally within the Cherokee Nation. This is the best that can be done for you at present."

Ridge did not have to look upon the faces of the other delegates to see the hollowness of failure in their eyes. He believed Monroe and the others in the government who had spoken in their favor. But they were clearly outnumbered, as John Ridge had witnessed when he monitored heated discussions on the House floor. Ridge knew his delegation had only succeeded in buying time.

There were other disappointments. Ridge could not find a suitable school for his youngest daughter, Sally. Colonel McKenney at the Indian Office made it quite clear that there were no funds for the education of Indian females. The Quaker-funded school run by Mrs. Corbett also turned Sally away. The headmistress's benefactors had caught wind of John's writings, especially his outrage against the Georgians. Such a militant attitude, the Quakers reckoned, would not suit their school. Even the Moravians had failed to find Sally a place in their facility for girls at Salem. Their unstated reason: John Ridge had been invited to learn at Cornwall, repaying the Moravians' generosity by carrying off a white woman for his wife. They were still scampering, tails tucked, to stamp out these flames, and refused to add more kindling.

Ridge still fumed from these humiliations, not to mention the open hostility of the representatives of Georgia and their vow to dispossess the Cherokee in what was supposed to be a bastion of equality and justice among men. Too many white people wanted Cherokee land. And now even soft-spoken Calhoun had been short with him. The time had come to speak of promises broken.

"When can the Cherokee expect to draw

the one-thousand-dollar annuity owed to us by the Tellico Treaty of 1804?" Ridge said.

"Tellico Treaty?" Calhoun answered. "I know of no such accord."

Ridge turned to John and nodded his head. His son unfurled the original parchment, signed and sealed, and laid it before Calhoun. "The Cherokee refer to this accord, better known as the Tellico Treaty," Ridge said. He then withdrew, giving Calhoun time to review the document.

"Baxter! Washbourne!" Calhoun yelled. Two young gentlemen appeared at once. "Search the War Department files and locate the government's copy of this document." They started for the door. "Make haste!" Calhoun added.

Ridge heard hurried heels on the marble floors, doors squeaking open and slamming shut. People shouting, papers flying. Calhoun sat drumming his fingers on his desk. And then the sound of heels on the floor grew closer, until Baxter, his face as pale as goose down, handed an aged document to Calhoun.

"I believe this is what you're looking for," he said apologetically.

The secretary of war blew the dust from the government copy and matched it against the one handed him by John Ridge. He ran his finger across faded signatures, slammed his palm down on his desk, and exhaled in exasperation.

"Payment will begin at once," he said quietly.

"With interest," Ridge said, having been prompted by the Scotch-bred merchant John Ross.

Calhoun glared at his assistants, who quickly turned up their palms. "Oh, yes," the secretary said. "A fine thing, education, isn't it? You shall have your interest."

John Ross winked at Ridge once they'd stepped out of Calhoun's office. Ridge wondered why. The delegation of his dreams had been successful only in this one token victory. The Americans would dump a few thousand dollars in their hands, while the best farmland in the nation, home to Ridge and John Ross and all their extended family and closest friends, remained at serious risk. What good was the money if they lost their land?

"Cheer up, Ridge," Ross said. "We've accomplished more than you know. Today the Cherokee have altered the face of Indian policy. We've just taught the Americans that the game has changed."

"What in the name of the Provider should we do now?" Ridge said.

"Nothing," Ross said. "We've proven by their own law that our claim is superior to that of Georgia. Jefferson made a promise to Georgia that Monroe can't honor and still sleep at night. As long as the Cherokee remain on our land, we own it."

"Treaty commissioners will move among the chiefs before the leaves fall," Ridge said.

"Let them come," Ross said. "In the meantime, the Cherokee will centralize our affairs and drive all dissenting chiefs from our council. The Americans won't find a Doublehead or Black Fox among us to accept their bribes. The Cherokee will politely refuse Calhoun's commissioners in one loud, clear voice."

"And the Georgians?"

"We sit back quietly and allow them to make the next move," Ross said without the least hesitation. He'd thought all of this through and had discussed none of it with Ridge. "The more desperate they become, the better. We have right on our side, and after today the Americans know it. If the Georgians persist in their unjust claim, they'll make enemies of the northerners while the Cherokee continue to reach out to them as friends. I like to let my adversaries cut their own throats while I sit home and play with my children."

"Surely there's something more we can do," Ridge said.

"There is," Ross said, resting his hand on John Ridge's shoulder. "I think I'll plant my fields and tend my orchards and let my people see me do it. You taught me that." He looked confidently at John Ridge. "And you, my apt young friend, should invest a little of your father's money in some law books."

His son engaged Ross in a discussion in English. Ridge walked three steps behind them, listening to the emotion behind their quick words and watching the animated gestures of hurried hands. Excluded from their conversation, there was nothing for him to do but follow them like a kid goat in search of its mother's nipples. Truly, the game had changed.

Once outside, Ridge breathed the fresh air deeply. He looked beyond the buildings and houses to the distant hazy hills. The pause provided him perspective. He'd been so proud to help breed these fresh, strong Cherokee horses. Now, at his first opportunity to watch them run free in the open field, he wondered if he still had the stamina to keep up with them, let alone guide their course.

To Ridge, the art of war required only blood, skill, cunning, and courage. For the new generation of chiefs he had himself inspired, the coming battle would be fought with minds trained in unnatural arts that spoke a language he could not understand.

This was what he had expected. This was what he and Sehoya had sacrificed and prepared for. It remained beyond him to imagine a time when he would not be at the heart of Cherokee affairs. Yet in that one instant of peering above the buildings he caught a glimpse of the future, and he saw the youngest men ever to rule the Cherokee choosing the path ahead. What more could Pathkiller, John Lowrey, White Path, and the Man Who Walked the Mountaintops do besides hope that wisdom walked hand in hand with education?

CHAPTER TWENTY-SEVEN

The Young Diplomat
Civilization has shed the beams of gladness among this people. Religion's lamp is seen to illuminate the darkness of ignorance. The Indians know their value, and with fond delight, anticipate a time when liberality will place them on a footing with other nations whose merits have not been sacrificed by prejudice on oblivion's altar.

I wrote that. My mother was so proud of me when it appeared in the *Boston Recorder.* I believe every word of it, too.

The Cherokee had plans for me when I returned from Cornwall. I accompanied every delegation to Washington. I was elected the youngest member to the thirty-two-strong National Committee in 1824. To enlighten those who had been denied the benefits of education, I launched the Moral and Literacy Society of the Cherokee Nation. I repeatedly toured the northern seaboard on the lecture circuit soliciting contributions and goodwill.

With some of the proceeds, my cousin, Elias Boudinot, and I sponsored a museum. Relics of peace and war flowed in from all over the Nation. The chiefs were so pleased with my activities that they planned to build a two-story brick national academy so that we would not have to depend upon American generosity to educate our children.

Sally and I built a home near my mother's and almost immediately we blessed Sehoya with little blond-haired grandchildren. Even Ridge rolled around on the floor with them, giggling as they tugged at his hair. I had forgotten how much my parents adored children. Sehoya showed up at our house with her arms full of toys. Ridge led a pony behind him. My father was supposed to be sharing his farming expertise with me as I cleared new fields, but he'd slip away to go swimming with the children instead. I'd never seen him or Sehoya happier. They were useless for any serious matters.

Everything was going so well for me. I accepted every new responsibility the council heaped on my shoulders. I worked hard for my people. And then, in the spring of 1827, I made my first mistake.

I took the money.

It did not concern me in the least that my advocacy for the Creeks provoked the ire of Office of Indian Affairs head Colonel McKenney. The American government's interest and that of the Indian nations had always widely diverged. Their opposition to my legitimate efforts was inevitable.

But when Little Prince himself, aged and ailing as he was, looked upon me with eyes of distrust, I realized that David Vann and I should have represented our Creek brothers without fee. Then maybe they would have seen that my efforts were pure of heart. But I was young and ambitious, a little full of myself perhaps, and I had a young white wife to care for in the manner to which she was long accustomed. I also desired to establish an estate and enterprises that would serve as a demonstration of the Cherokee's ability to live on par with the most sophisticated of the whites. I needed to acquire what my professors in Cornwall termed "the means of production." All of this required money.

The Georgians, once again, were the authors of the acrimony. The Creek chief General McIntosh, perhaps in frustration, anger, or, as many assumed, for his own greed, ceded the whole of Creek lands in Georgia and Alabama, and darkest of all, agreed to remove the entire Creek Nation beyond the Mississippi. This in spite of the fact that it was well known he had been induced by bribes and lucrative incentives, the very same he suggested John Ross accept for advancing a similar scheme among the Cherokee. Ross promptly exposed him, but the Creeks did much worse.

McIntosh was broken, as all corrupt chiefs were, and he paid dearly for his irresponsibility. Two hundred Creek warriors appeared at dawn at his home on the Chattahoochee and burned it to the ground. The lives of his family were spared. His was not.

His body was mutilated and buried naked in the same soil he had sold for personal gain.

McIntosh's treaty was a base corruption, and everyone knew it. But the government of the United States, through its Office of Indian Trade agent, Colonel McKenney, intended to enforce this illegal and nefarious accord. I, Skah-tle-loh-skee, known to the whites as John Ridge, waded into the midst of all this confusion, fraud, and ill will as translator and adviser to the Creeks in their coming battle with the federal government. It was my opinion then as it is now that I was more than qualified for this appointment. I was, in fact, the best possible candidate, and my father, longtime envoy to the Creeks, provided me with an unqualified recommendation.

Rumors had already begun to circulate in my own nation about my character and conduct. I was a wife beater, a whoremonger, a drunk, a twisted soul whose licentiousness was exceeded only by arrogance and greed. From whence came this malice, I know not. Though utterly baseless, I confess these scandalous rumors wounded my pride. Many powerful men in the Nation — Cherokee and Anglo missionary alike — publicly professed my innocence in all of this. But a shadow had been cast upon my character, and I would learn too late that it had followed me to the Creek Nation.

I anticipated that Washington would object to my advocacy. The surprise came when the Cherokee council made it known that they, too, were troubled by my involvement in our neighbors' affairs. I was forced to retire my elected seat in that body in order to serve the Creeks. I felt such a sacrifice was the lesser of two evils, because even the dullest of Cherokee had to understand that if the Creeks were vanquished in their appeal to save their country, the Cherokee would be the next to fall. We, as Indians, had to put an end to all this land grabbing. We had to fight to set a clear precedent.

The problem was that leadership within the five civilized tribes was by nature and tradition fractured. We could not move as one, as it seemed the Americans and Europeans did, and government agents could always bribe some lesser, obscure "chief" to give them what they wanted. My father, John Ross, and many others recognized that our nation had to organize and solidify its leadership to ensure that the Americans could no longer find a Doublehead or McIntosh to sign away the rights of thousands for some trinkets, cheap whiskey, and ready cash. The Cherokee had taken solid steps toward centralizing authority. Regardless of what anyone within or without the Indian nations said to the contrary, my purpose from the beginning was to encourage the Creeks to follow a similar course.

But first we had to undo McIntosh's sham. David Vann and I were brought into the Creeks' diplomatic fold just before negotiations were to begin in Washington. The Big Warrior, their champion, was dead. Opothle Yoholo, Tuskenaha, and Little Prince struggled to fill this void. I was invited to sit among the Creeks and their counselors, and I dipped the gourd into the thick, black arsee, drinking until I vomited. Thus purified, I listened as the wisest of the Creeks plotted their course. I spoke, as the Ridge Walker advised, only when spoken to.

The Creek delegation left for Washington and Jesse Brown's Indian Queen Hotel. The remnants of McIntosh's faction took lodgings across town at Tennison's, and, to place things in the Indian perspective, the Creeks spoke to the Great Father with two tongues.

It was obvious to me that those loyal to the spirit of Big Warrior were faced with a painful compromise. James Barbour, secretary of war, made it quite clear that it was the government's opinion that the McIntosh treaty, abrogated in some degree by subsequent agreement with General Gaines, would hold. Opothle Yoholo stalled for time to consider this appalling position. The honor fell to me to pen the reply of those I considered to be the true representatives of the Creek Nation.

I took great pleasure in informing the Americans that although the Creeks were willing to negotiate with their agents, there would be no "exchange of lands." They would instead sell their holdings east of the Chattahoochee only, and this for a substantial sum. The Creek Nation intended to keep what remained, and removal from this last parcel was not an option.

"We," I wrote, referring to the Creeks, "may as well be annihilated at once as to cede any portion of the land west of that river." The Creeks, remembering well what had become of the Red Sticks, would not resist removal by use of arms, but they would not cooperate with federal authorities either. The Creek position was simple: Should the United States assert their treaty with McIntosh and banish the whole of the Creek Nation, they would have to do so at the point of a bayonet. Such passive resistance was my idea. My time in Cornwall convinced me that the American public would be outraged to learn that their soldiers had slaughtered unarmed Creek women and children. Nevertheless, the measure was a desperate gamble. We were in agony as we awaited Secretary Barbour's reply.

To our surprise, our terms seemed acceptable, probably because so many of the northern representatives in Congress recognized McIntosh's treaty as a shameful affair and wanted no part of it. Barbour agreed, in principle, to purchase the tracts the Creeks were willing to sell, and leave the rest. What remained to be negotiated were the specifics. On this, regrettably, we again met obstacles and painful choices.

Opothle Yoholo saw our compromise as a miserable failure, and was so despaired that he attempted to take his own life. I did my best to soothe his wounded pride, while I explored what could be done to salvage as much of the Creek Nation as possible. I received private correspondence from Colonel McKenney expressing the government's desire for a more western branch of the Chattahoochee as the boundary. To this measure, the Creeks grimly acquiesced. Thus, for the amount of $217,600 in cash and a perpetual annuity of $20,000, the Creeks ceded almost all of their lands within the limits of Georgia. I learned later that the McIntosh faction received monies and support to remove beyond the Mississippi, which was of their own decision and was none of our affair. Our business in Washington was done.

The trouble started when I submitted a list of people the Creek chiefs had designated to receive a portion of the treaty money. Opothle Yoholo, for instance, along with every chief on the delegation, was to receive $5,000. Little Prince and Tuskenaha and all within their sphere were to be awarded $10,000. I asked for $15,000 apiece for myself and David Vann, and $10,000 for my father, amounts acceptable to Opothle Yoholo.

"We are obliged to pay the treaty money to the Creek Nation," McKenney advised me, his stark blue eyes scanning my letter. "The distribution of it is their own affair." I noticed he paused when he came to the Cherokee names on the list. He lifted his hawklike beak, cocked his head so sharply that his clump of white hair teetered a bit on his scalp. He looked upon me with the gravest suspicion. "Does every member of the delegation understand the distribution proposed by this document?"

"No," I answered. "But Opothle Yoholo and Charles Cornells know, and that's enough."

And it should have been. They were trusted in their office, authorized to negotiate as they saw fit. The money paid to Vann and myself, and the honorarium to my father, had been a token of Yoholo's general satisfaction with my personal services. Despite his despair over ceding lands, we had successfully nullified the McIntosh treaty and preserved much of the Creek Nation.

McKenney informed me that the apportionment would be read to the entire Creek council so that everyone would know where the money went. I insisted that our compensation, as McKenney himself had stated, was a matter for the Creeks to resolve.

I knew the Creek chiefs, especially Opothle Yoholo. All possessed the deepest concern for the welfare of their people. The Creeks were in desperate need of agents they could trust, preferably of Indian blood, fluent in English, and comfortable enough among the whites to faithfully translate the talking leaves. I was this person, and I served them as best as I could, in the end rescuing several thousand acres of Creek land. My compensation was merely their way of expressing their gratitude.

McKenney didn't view things this way, nor did other southern representatives in Congress. David and I were blatantly accused of fraud and corruption. Our enemies assumed that we, as Cherokees, had manipulated the Creeks' difficulties for our financial advancement alone. I was incensed by this accusation but also quite alarmed, for I knew the Creeks to be a passionate people, and I remembered well what had become of McIntosh, who had been guilty of the same crimes of which David Vann and I now stood accused. I didn't sleep well. I listened to sounds at night, wondering if an owl hoot heralded my doom.

But I had given my word to Opothle Yoholo that I would stand beside him when he read the terms of the treaty to the Creeks. I honored it. There was, to be true, some amount of clamor, but in the end the treaty was upheld by the council, as was the apportionment of the money involved. I was, at long last, relieved.

Then it came time to draw the lines on the map. The western boundary of Georgia had never actually been surveyed. When at last it was, the Creeks found themselves still in possession of a sizable tract of some 192,000 acres. When McKenney came knocking again, I advised Opothle Yoholo, who by this time had been elevated to the position of prime minister of the Creek Nation, to refuse him.

"The Americans struck their bargain," I told him. "Let them live with it."

McKenney insisted on pressing the matter further. I was invited to attend this presentation. My arrival delayed things some three days, which fueled McKenney's animosity toward me. He was always cordial when I was viewed as an agent of compromise, but I saw another face when I acted as his foil. I took delight in his reassessment. The mistake belonged to him and the Georgians, the land in question to the Creeks; it pleased me to see Opothle Yoholo rub McKenney's nose in it.

McKenney's address to the Creek Nation

was condescending and absurd, a mixture of how white men think Indians speak among each other and disgusting flattery, language better suited perhaps for the Osage and Sioux, not the Creeks, who had lived and interbred with white men for over a hundred years. McKenney's irrelevance would have been laughable had there not been so much power behind his silly words.

And then at last he came to the pith:

"There was a small strip of land which the treaty of Washington did not embrace," he said, "and as the Georgians wanted it, and as the delegation promised, if the treaty lines did not reach it, that they would throw it in."

Throw it in, he said! "Oh, yes," I joked to my Creek friends, "I specifically remember agreeing to that!"

McKenney added that all this was a wonderful development for the Creeks in that it meant much more money for them. I resented his officious implication. *Give it all some thought, my barefooted children. Why, I can put silver in your hands this very day.*

When he at last fell silent, Opothle Yoholo stood. "No," he said, and he didn't see the point in saying anything further.

Then I saw that scowl of McKenney's turn toward me — the very same I'd seen the day he came to my name when I'd given him the distribution list. The temper of his words to the council took a darker hue.

"Look closely at the affairs of your diplomats," McKenney said. "There is mischief afoot between them. They'll sell that strip of land the Creeks promised us. Oh, yes, they will. But they'll keep the proceeds to themselves."

My mouth went dry. My hands felt like ice. It was true that the prime minister and I had discussed the possibility of my appointment as treasurer of Creek funds, a duty I would have fulfilled as faithfully as I had performed everything else. I had some experience in these matters, whereas the Creek leadership had none. But I heard the murmur of the gathered warriors. I watched their eyes narrow.

"Tell him he talks too much," Opothle Yoholo instructed his interpreter. But I could see that he was clearly shaken. In one fleeting instance, after a white man's groundless accusation, no less, he'd lost the trust of his people. As he tumbled, so did I. Images of McIntosh's horrible death again flickered in my mind.

"I'll take my talk to Little Prince," McKenney threatened. And he stomped off with all his aides and uniformed lackeys to do just that.

I don't know what he told the aging chief, but I know what became of it. McKenney did say that no letter I had written, or even had a voice in drafting, would be considered by the federal government. What authority did this man possess to say such a thing? And yet this pronouncement doomed my efforts to benefit the Creeks. McKenney departed as if painfully aggrieved by my involvement in the negotiations, leaving the Creeks in turmoil. Little Prince sent his runners after him, catching him at Fort Mitchell.

Little Prince and the other chiefs, the disgraced Opothle Yoholo excluded, treated with McKenney the following day. That evil done, he instructed McKenney to forward this message to the Cherokee council: "If your young men come among my people again, I will kill them!"

I was undone in the Creek Nation, and the shadow that loomed over me among my own people darkened, especially since the council had asked me not to come. I knew then that I had powerful enemies in Washington as well. I was guilty of no fraud or personal corruption. What made me a criminal in the Americans' eyes was my spirit and determination, my ability to use what they had taught me against them. To once again break Creek resolve, they had to break John Ridge.

I remained close to Opothle Yoholo, but I was never again truly welcomed by the Creek leadership. What choice did I have but to turn my energies to the struggles awaiting my own people? The aftermath of my term as a Creek diplomat were some of my darkest days. I was beside myself with inconsolable grief. When at last my depression waned, my anger waxed. I paid a heavy price to learn that no tactic was too base or deceitful when an educated Indian stood between the Americans and Indian land.

I informed my parents of all that had happened and all that I had learned. They listened quietly, and then I saw the sadness swell in their dour expressions.

"John Ross is organizing a new government with written laws and a constitution like the Americans have," my father said.

My mother did not look pleased with this development. She knew as we all did that Ross's vision of government was modeled after the American system. As such, women had no say.

"Turn your eyes toward home," Ridge said, "and help guide Ross's hand." I could see, however, that he was troubled by what had happened in the Creek Nation. Ridge knew American policy would include pitting the more progressive mixed-bloods against the rigidly traditional elements of our tribe, and finally, should this fail, my family against our friends and neighbors. The Americans had learned that they could drive a wedge in a small fissure and the whole log would split, and everyone knows it's easier to saw the limbs off a tree rather than pull it out by the roots.

This political leap toward a written constitution would no doubt deepen the fullbloods' disillusionment with our changing world. After my debacle in the Creek Nation, I think Ridge Walker feared that I could very easily become the focus of their growing discontent. My father had endured a lifetime of setbacks and frustrations, but this was the first time he had ever looked upon me with eyes of disappointment.

I knew that I would never be free of the Creek scandal.

I should not have accepted the money. That is my only regret.

CHAPTER TWENTY-EIGHT

Seasoned wood from seven different trees burned in the council fire stoked by rebel chiefs in this unseasonably hot June of 1827. Hard-eyed headmen and warriors arrived at Ridge's invitation to throw more wood on the bonfire and stand with their arms crossed before the flames. They were led by a full-blood who spoke no English, owned no slaves, and refused to worship the white man's god. Over the last few months, this chief had broken off all communication with the Cherokee leadership and formed a council of his own. He called for all-night dances on the heels of all-day ball plays. He sponsored a festival to celebrate the true religion, joined by swarms of full-blood chiefs, conjurers, and warriors who wished to continue the true path.

For Ridge, the rebel council had resurrected Tecumseh's spirit, a dangerous ghost dance that bespoke a proud but doomed way of life. Yet Ridge, who spoke little English, considered himself a full-blood, and also refused to worship the white man's god, entirely understood and sympathized.

Against John Ross's advice, Ridge invited the charismatic malcontent and his confederates to New Town, recently renamed New Echota after the Cherokee's ancient refuge in the days before the Europeans arrived. Ridge had hoped that on the eve of the constitutional convention, two old recently estranged friends could search for a compromise. "White Path's rebellion," Ross had predicted, "was a noise that will end in noise only." But Ridge adhered to the old style of leadership where chiefs ruled by consensus and where debate and dissent were encouraged in open councils before the sacred fire.

Ridge understood that White Path's followers were no minority. More than three-quarters of the Cherokee were isolated, independent, self-sufficient, illiterate, and blissfully ignorant of how complex and unstable their world had become. For these traditionalists, the affluent mixed-bloods who organized their constitutional convention were too ambitious, too loud, too condescending, too contaminated by white culture to lead the way.

Ridge sat quietly, watching, listening, going at dawn and at dusk to the rivers to pray, waiting for White Path to speak his mind. On the third day of his council, Ridge crouched beside the rebel fire munching shu le, a grilled bread made from last fall's crop of yellow acorns of red oaks. Ridge knew its preparation was an arduous process. The acorns were dried, hulled, sifted, and pestle pounded in an oak mortar to meal. For one night, the mixture was kept in a cloth-covered basket continually leached with springwater to dissipate its bitter taste. Then the meal was dried and mixed with bear grease and grilled. Shu le was rare in Sehoya's cook shed. But it was a Cherokee staple, as ancient as the great oaks that spawned it, and a reminder that the Provider in His wisdom had always sustained Ridge's people. The aroma rekindled memories of the days Ridge had spent in his family's lodge beside his mother in simpler times. He savored each bite until he heard moccasin steps on soft ground and the jingle of loose silver bracelets on swinging arms.

"I am here," White Path said in the old style.

"So you are," Ridge answered after he swallowed. He peeled the cloth from his basket to show White Path that he had plenty of shu le cakes to spare. "Have you eaten, old friend?"

"I have." White Path squatted beside him and lit his pipe with an ash ember. "How do you like my fire?"

"It burns hot," Ridge said, shoving himself back from the flames.

"It will get hotter," White Path said.

The old chief eyed the level acres of New Echota. Streets sixty feet wide cut a square bare-earth grid across surveyed lots. One-acre homesteads had been auctioned off to the highest bidder to fund the construction of the new council house in the new capital's heart. Ridge saw prosperity, ambition, and hope in all the improvements, but he knew White Path saw something else. "I don't feel comfortable here, Ridge Walker," he said.

"Why not?" Ridge said. "We're building it for you."

"Are you?" White Path said. "In that case, stop what you're doing and let the trees grow back. Your structure looks more like a Christian church than a council house to me. Your straight roads lead to a place I don't want to go."

Ridge stood and took his hand. "You have concerns. Let's discuss them."

"Ah, you wish to *enlighten* me, Chief Ridge?" White Path said.

"Call it what you like," Ridge said, resuming his seat. "I'm just here to talk."

White Path squatted beside Ridge and held out his palms to the fire. "Have you heard of the prophecy?"

"I've heard of many."

"This one will interest you," White Path said. "A woman near Turnip-town gave birth to triplets. Odd enough, but each of them arrived with a full set of teeth. Before the third was born, the first spoke to its mother in Cherokee."

"What in Selu's name did it say?"

"The child called on her to account for her godless way of life. He warned her that the coming generation would scorn those who abandoned the ancient religion."

"Sounds like the colic to me," Ridge said. "I bet the mother's nipples are raw as a corncob breast-feeding three sets of little squirrel's teeth."

"It's no joke, Ridge Walker. The people are unsettled."

"They should be," Ridge said. He reached for White Path's tobacco pouch and filled his pipe. "Would you welcome my opinion?"

"I can't think of a single recent occasion when I've welcomed your opinion, but I'm sure you'll voice it anyway."

"If you wish to remain in these hills and valleys," Ridge said, "stand with the mixed-bloods against those who threaten to expel us. Many of us who've dealt with the Americans for twenty winters or more have come to believe that we need an organized government and written laws to prove that the Cherokee are no longer savages."

"Are you ashamed to be a savage, Ridge Walker?" White Path said. "I'm not. Not if being a savage means holding on to a religion and a way of life I hold dear."

"I'm not ashamed to be Ani-yunwi-ya, if

that's what you mean," Ridge said. "But I'm ashamed to remain in ignorance, especially if it leads to our destruction. Our intent is to give where we must in order to hold on to as much as we can. I can't be more specific than that."

"Oh, yes, you can," White Path said. "The new laws are quite specific. No more clan revenge. A man can't take more than one wife. A mother is no longer head of her house. Her husband owns her property and owns sway over her children. Women can't vote in your elections, and even the clan mother's voice is silenced in council. People will cast down their eyes if a woman leaves an unhappy marriage. Gaming is frowned upon and conjury is disgraced. We are obliged to observe the Christian Sabbath and worship the Christian god. If I say that I respect only the Great Provider, whom we both know made all things, I could be excluded from public office. There is talk of a poll tax that favors the mixed-bloods who live for profit. Treaty money is siphoned off to translate the Christian Bible into Sequoyah's language and to build these structures to house mixed-bloods who are too good to speak to me. I've heard of plans to build churches and libraries, even a school to teach Cherokees to become Christian ministers while conjurers are forced to teach apprentices deep in the woods." White Path tossed another log on the fire. "And so my question to your unspecific intent is, are we being true to our ancestors by turning our backs on their way, or are we busy mimicking the whites who treat us as an abomination because our skins are dark?"

"Where's the surprise, White Path?" Ridge asked. "These laws have been approved in council over the last ten winters."

"By whom?" White Path said. "Certainly not me! The council began a few winters ago with only a dozen or so written laws, which I couldn't read anyway. Now we have a hundred. Pathkiller and Charles Hicks are not yet cold in their graves and John Ross, who can't even speak to me in our language, proclaims a hundred more."

"These are more suggestions than laws, White Path. Most have never been enforced."

"They are snares in wait to trap me, my family, my clan, and the people I've sworn to protect as headman of Ellijay," White Path said, coloring. "I defy these laws by living as my grandfather did. Must I wait for a lash to fall across my back before I learn that your half-breed council no longer wishes to be lenient with their *suggestions*?" The old chief angrily tapped out the charred contents of his pipe on a stone. "The Ridge Walker has the gift of seeing far into the distance. White Path, your friend since child hood, has always known this. But the time has come to look under your nose. Your people won't stand to be trampled. And I'm not the only chief who feels this way. Speak to Terrapin Head, Kelachulee, Big Tiger, Anchatoueh, Frying Pan, Cabbin Smith, Atosotokee, George Miller, Rising Fawn, and Katchee."

"Hard words," Ridge said. He focused on the pulsating coals. "Do I stand accused of Doublehead's crimes?"

"No," White Path said. "You're confused if you feel my anger is aimed only at you. Your only fault is that you're too easily swayed. As to the others, I object to their arrogance. Doublehead died because he sold our land without our permission. The mixed-bloods are guilty of plotting to sell our souls."

"They are trying to save our nation."

"By destroying it? How far will they go to live like the Americans? What will be left for us who have no skill at imitation?"

Ridge reached into his basket for another cake. "What do you propose?"

"The other chiefs and I turned our backs on their council," White Path said. "We formed our own, the right response when the chiefs disagree. We'll live apart from the mixed-bloods and govern ourselves. Sequoyah's written language is welcome, but the Cherokee Bible is not. We won't have a missionary among us. We'll dance as we please, observe the old festivals, our young men will bloody their bodies in ball plays that last all day. If we're sick, we'll chant with a conjurer. If an enemy spites us, we'll conspire with a witch. At dawn we'll go to water and pray to the one true God."

Ridge tilted his head back and sighed. "Fifteen winters ago I heard the same talk among the Creeks. You know what's become of them. Other Cherokee have spoken those words. Beats the Drum and Tahlonteskee wanted to live their own way; and they do — beyond the Father of Rivers in the west. That path is open to you."

"It's a path I'll never follow," White Path said. "I'll never leave these hills and valleys."

Ridge made a fist. "Then bind yourself to us in the fight to keep it. Don't turn your nose up at our infant efforts. Follow it inside that house," he said, pointing to the council structure, "and sniff out where we've erred. I understand your misgivings. You and I, White Path, were born into the same world. The difference between us is that I've traveled beyond it. Not because I wanted to, but because the journey was thrust upon me. I have looked into the distance and I see what *is*. I know better than you how dangerous the whites are to our people. And I couldn't help but recognize that some of our traditions will doom us. The hard truth is that the Cherokee can't govern as we have and endure."

"Why?" White Path asked. "Is the old way wrong?"

"No," Ridge said. He quieted his voice. "It

is the world that is wrong. The question that remains is what can the Cherokee do about it?"

"I don't like how the mixed-bloods have answered that question."

"Fair enough," Ridge said. "But I swear on the graves of my ancestors that I believe their hearts are in the right place. We're fortunate to have those among us who speak and read English, who understand the white culture as well as they understand their own. They have a foot in both worlds, just as you and I straddle both old and new. Like you, I don't understand why so many laws are necessary. Like you, I'm not a Christian. But I trust my friend and brother John Ross to do what is best for us even if I don't understand his methods. I trust John Lowrey, Going Snake, Alexander McCoy, and the others. I trust my nephew, Elias. And most of all, I trust my son."

White Path pursed his lips and breathed deeply. "Knowing how I feel about this matter, what would you have me do?"

"Help us pick our path," Ridge said. "If a child beginning to walk attempts to run, he soon falls and cries. The wise parent doesn't fault him for his efforts, but encourages him to try again. Have your followers run for the election. Beseech your people to vote for them. Make certain the full-bloods sit on the benches in that awkward house and let the half-breeds hear their voices. Help me bridge the gap between those who would swallow the white world whole, and those who would have nothing to do with it. Encourage the mixed-bloods to move more slowly. Help me search for balance. Show us how to temper the shouting into one clear voice."

The old chief sat silent, poking at the coals with a twig. "How you muddy the water, Ridge Walker," he said.

"I'd hoped to have the opposite effect."

"I'll think on what you said." He leveled his finger at Ridge. "I promise nothing, mind you, but to think about it."

"That's enough for now," Ridge said. "Search your heart, my old friend, and the answer will come. And please, White Path, let there be no anger burning between your lodge and mine. As young men, we ran the war trace together. There's blood between us, and all the politics that mire the Nation these days is not strong enough to tear us apart."

"We knew what to do back then, didn't we, Ridge Walker?"

"We thought we did. And we were wrong."

White Path laughed. "Do you remember, Ridge, when we were with John Watts hunting the stragglers of General Martin's soldiers, and that witch — I forget his name — commanded us to eat buzzard's flesh so that the Americans' bullets wouldn't touch us?"

"Uuuhhh," Ridge groaned. "You had to

mention that while I'm enjoying my breakfast. If I had that to do over again, I think I'd prefer the bullets."

"I think you're right. But as stringy and rancid as that buzzard flesh was, you have to admit that it worked. We're still here, still fighting."

"I'd like to think that's due to other reasons," Ridge said.

"Let's give the witch some credit. He knew his trade."

"It's hard to believe we were ever that young."

"Ah, we had the fever back then, Ridge. We were hungry for honor."

"I wasn't very hungry after I ate a chunk of that nasty buzzard. That witch was some talker. Or I was some fool."

"You're right on both accounts," White Path said.

"I never saw that skinny conjurer again. I've often wondered what became of him."

"He sleeps with his ancestors," White Path said.

"Well, it was probably his diet that killed him, I can tell you that much."

They rose together and clasped each other by the forearms. Ridge sensed the strength remaining in the old warrior's grip. In his day, White Path walked the earth a fierce outa-cit-e. Ridge watched the grin wither from his face.

"Sad times, eh, Ridge?"

"They may get worse."

"Please," White Path said. "No more predictions." He motioned toward the basket of grilled cakes. "Is the offer still good?"

"Of course," Ridge said. He looked at the smoldering rebel council fire. "It needs more wood."

"Let it burn out," White Path said. "It doesn't warm me anymore."

CHAPTER TWENTY-NINE

"Why do you hesitate?" John demanded. Ridge witnessed firsthand that lack of piety in his son's pained expression that had vexed countless missionaries. What was the reason for John's harsh tone? This issue between them was simple.

In 1827, Charles Hicks ascended to principal chief during the gloom that descended upon the Nation after old Pathkiller's death. Yet only two weeks later, the honor fell to Ridge to speak over Hicks's walnut coffin, delivered to rest the year before in Unu la ta nee', the cold moon, January. The two old chiefs were ignorant of civilized ways, but at least they unified and reassured the Cherokee people. With them gone, the Georgians smelled weakness like the bobcat smelled blood. And so did the Great Father. Before the end of the summer, John Quincy Adams sent three commissioners to treat again for Cherokee removal beyond the limits of Georgia.

Ridge, speaker of the council, rallied with his friend, John Ross, who rose to become president of the National Committee. Together he and Ridge worked to thwart all efforts to dispossess their people. They thought and moved as one as they drafted written responses to Adams's commissioners, often using — much to Ridge's delight — the words of Pathkiller himself. The Cherokee would not sell a single foot of Pathkiller's "last little," promised to them for as long as the rivers ran.

And then there was the matter of White Path's dissension. The full-blood rebellion subsided without violence, but Ridge knew that doubt and suspicion still simmered in traditional hearts, waiting to boil over with the least provocation.

There was trouble within, and trouble without.

The year 1827, however, did not bring only vexations. For two winters, Elias Boudinot had circulated among the northern cities to solicit funds for a Cherokee printing press. By all accounts, his nephew had stunned his audiences, bringing home cash and his new white bride, Harriet Gold of Cornwall.

Early in 1828, the press rolled north up the Georgia Road to arrive at New Echota. Ridge had seen the contraption himself, a small Royal Union, as his nephew would tell him — a description, Ridge assumed, of its make and model. Constructed of cast iron, the machine required a team of four mules and a dozen sweaty Cherokee to move it, but Ridge's nephew oversaw every detail personally, supervising the two white printers who had come to operate it, editing the English and Cherokee copy that would run side by side.

In the hungry moon of February, Ridge held the first Cherokee-printed talking leaves in his hands. Boudinot, under the influence of his friend and collaborator, the blue-eyed, twig-limbed, pale-skinned missionary Samuel Worcester, christened the paper *Tsalagi Tsu-le-hi-sa-nu-hi,* or the *Cherokee Phoenix.* Ridge was at a loss to understand what some mythical European bird had to do with the Ani-yunwi-ya, but he liked the Cherokee translation that stood by its side: "I will rise."

Meanwhile, a committee had drafted and approved the Cherokee Constitution on July 26, 1827. Using the American document so admired by educated Cherokee as a template, the framers formed the Tsalagi Tinilawigi, a bicameral body composed of the council and the National Committee, with members being elected by the people to serve a limited term.

Boudinot had wisely printed the whole of the new Cherokee Constitution in the Cherokee tongue to put to rest fears of those of White Path's persuasion. Ridge wanted the full-bloods to be pleased with the nation's newest efforts, and once they'd read about them in their own language, he felt they were.

Even Ridge was awed by the press's power. The Cherokee Constitution was applauded in the north, where Ridge was relieved to learn they still had many friends. In England, people took note of the Cherokee's progress and will. Even Washington mouths gaped in wonder, for they also found nothing in this accomplishment to scorn or ridicule. The Georgians alone found fault, which Ridge had anticipated. They were alarmed to see how organized the Cherokee had become with their laws, which their own governor declared he would supersede with his own if the federal government would not remove these stubborn people. The Cherokee title to land within the Commonwealth of Georgia, to use his own words, was "only temporary."

If all this wasn't enough to convince the whites that the Cherokee deserved a place in their world, Ridge was at a loss to think of what would. Everything was more or less working. Then, in 1828, after the deaths of Pathkiller and Charles Hicks, came the task of selecting a new principal chief. And with it the argument with his son.

"I'm telling you it must be now, 'Doda," John repeated. The endearing term seemed inconsistent with his son's tone, almost vaguely manipulative. "Reach for it, and they will give it to you."

Ridge sank onto his rocker and puffed on his pipe. "Understand me, John. I still hear Pathkiller's words in my ears assuring me that I would one day walk in his place. For so many winters, I assumed it would come true."

"And it can. William Hicks bent his ear too closely to the Georgians' agent."

"He's done nothing."

"It doesn't matter if he has or hasn't. He's lost the people's trust."

"That's a shame. William's a good man, the equal of his brother."

"Both of whom are lesser than you," John said, drawing up a chair to sit in front of him. Ridge could not avoid the piercing stare of those coal-black eyes.

"Listen to me, John," Ridge pleaded. "Leadership of the Cherokee continues to be a battle between old and new, but the Americans remain the larger threat. To deal with them the principal chief of the Cherokee must speak the English tongue fluently, be able to see and understand the danger of the talking leaves."

"I can do this for you. You know I can."

Ridge's glance dropped. "As you did for the Creeks, John?"

His son flared. "To hear that from your lips stings me. You know I did my best for the Creeks."

"I do," Ridge said. "But what of the others

in the Nation? What do they think? You've been falsely accused, I know, but accused nonetheless. I would need you by my side to conduct the Nation's affairs, and thus your cloud would hang over us both."

John hung his head. "I'm sorry, 'Doda."

"For what? For the times we live in?" He gripped his son's jaw and lifted his head toward him. "You're young, bright, and ambitious, exactly as I was in my day. These attributes intimidate some of our people, but they're no crime, and to lead a nation is to inspire contempt among those who envy your gifts. I sent you among the whites to become what you are. When the people learn what I already know, the Great Spirit willing, they will elect you, Skah-tle-loh-skee, son of the Man Who Walks the Mountaintops, to principal chief. Your time will come. But mine has passed me by."

"Nonsense. The people trust and admire no other man above you."

"Then they'll believe me when I tell them that I should not be their principal chief. It's best that I —"

John pressed his fingers against his father's lips. "Don't say it."

Ridge smiled. "That I rest my hopes with you. But until your skills are seasoned, Tsan Usdi must lead us."

"That dwarf is only one-eighth Cherokee," John scoffed. "What message does this send?"

"The best one," Ridge said. "What John Ross lacks in size he makes up in energy and integrity. He fought as a warrior beside me in the Creek War. He walks tall among the full-bloods. His wife is a full-blood. And though his own blood is mostly white, few doubt that the heart that pumps it belongs to the Cherokee. This man and I have stood together for many winters, both in war and peace. He has the heart of a lion and an iron will. I've seen how he operates among the whites. Ross is capable of battling them with their own weapons. I wouldn't want him as an enemy, but I'm proud to accept him as my principal chief. I gladly step aside and let him pass."

John ran his fingers through his hair. "He barely speaks our language."

"He can say we won't cede another foot of land to Jackson or the Georgians, and those are the only Cherokee words he needs to know."

"You're making a mistake."

"I've made many before."

"There are others who could advise you. I'll move away, distance myself from you."

Ridge slowly shook his head. "The people, knowing me, knowing how I feel about you, would never believe it. Nor should they, because it's not in my heart to have my son apart from me. The Ridge steps aside in the light of day and lets his friend pass."

Ridge stood, smoothed the wrinkles from

his trousers, and walked over to Sehoya's hearth. "It's decided," he said calmly. "I urge you to serve John Ross as well as you would have served me. He needs you. Your people need you. Honor me by giving them everything you have."

"I —"

"Speak of it no more," Ridge said, and he walked out of the room toward his sleeping wife and the warm bed they shared, hoping he would dream of something else besides becoming principal chief of the Cherokee.

CHAPTER THIRTY

Ridge drew a deep breath. He looked upon
the demure faces of the Cherokee gathered at
Turkey Town in the Hungry Moon of 1829.
No doubt they had heard the rumors about
John Ross's diplomatic mission to Washington. He laced his fingers, allowing his hands
to fall across his waist, the classic posture for
Cherokee oration. Since the news was not
good, Ridge felt his demeanor and delivery
should do everything possible to reassure his
people.

One moon after John Ross ascended to the
highest position in the Cherokee Nation,
Andrew Jackson was elevated to the highest
office in his. For the first time in American
history, a westerner and a Tennessee frontiers-
man occupied the White House, the first
military leader since Washington. Knowing
Jackson's record on Indian affairs, Ridge
anticipated trouble. Yet he hoped that Sharp
Knife would remember the allegiance of the
Cherokee during the Creek Civil War, that he

would consider their aggressive strides toward civilization, that he would make an exception for an exceptional people.

John Ross had since learned different. Despite the president's inaugural pledge that he would observe a just and liberal policy toward the Indians, and give humane and considerate attention to their rights and wants, John Eaton, Jackson's secretary of war, turned a deaf ear to any mention of Cherokee assimilation. The word Ross heard over and over was removal. Three decades of Cherokee advancement had stunned the world, but had done nothing to impress Sharp Knife's prejudiced mind.

The time had now come to advise the people what their leadership would do about it.

"The sentiments we will express will be simple and plain," Ridge began. He heard the scratching of his son's goose quill on stiff paper. The idea was to record his words for the *Cherokee Phoenix* so that everyone in the western world would know what had been said on this overcast day.

"The Americans' grounds for complaint," Ridge said, "have always been that we, as hunters, possessed too much land. Now the wild game is gone, as is much of the land we once hunted, surrendered to the Americans to satisfy their hunger. We have been reduced to this last little, have abandoned the hunt to raise stock and crops, and to feed our children in the exact manner advanced by their agents and councilors. Now they come to us again to inform us that the Cherokee have too much land. What, I ask you, is the language of their objection this time?

"It is this, my friends. In one generation, the situation is now reversed. Where once the Americans saw us as ignorant savages, they now see us as civilized. Like they, we have a constituted government. Like they, many of us have become Christians. Like they, we have agile, educated minds. We have our own written language. And we now have the means to print it on the talking leaves. We have learned all that the Americans have asked of us. So why are we once again threatened with expulsion?"

Ridge brushed his hair back against the bitter February wind. The flames of seven blazing bonfires churned in the winter gusts. At first, the people huddled around them, but they now pressed toward the council house podium, as if they were warmed more by Ridge's words.

"We have traveled too far, too fast," he said. "This is our crime. It is too much for us now to be honest, and virtuous, and industrious, because then we are capable of aspiring to the rank of Christians and politicians, which renders our attachment to our soil stronger. Therefore we are more difficult to defraud."

Ridge unlaced his fingers to plead with his hands. "The Americans have never faced our kind before. The Cherokee are a thorn in their heel. They don't want us among them. They don't want us in their way. They don't want to remember that the Great Fathers Washington, Jefferson, Madison, and Monroe were all most congenial to our attachment to our land, offering us instead the knowledge of the means necessary to live upon it exactly as they do. The Cherokee believed the Great Fathers of the past when they told us that all men are created equal."

John Ross clapped, as did the elders behind him, until at last Ridge heard approval sweep through his people. Ridge held up his hand.

"Now comes Jackson," he continued, "who carries in his heart a different and darker view. He closes his ears to the promises made by his predecessors and turns a blind eye to the treaties they signed. He tells us, 'Turn west, Cherokee, beyond the Mississippi, where game abounds and the soil is rich.'

"His offer begs the question: If this country is so desirable, why has it remained so long a wilderness and in waste? Why is it uninhabited by respectable white people? What good land is there that white people don't want?"

He paused a moment, and then started again. "We've heard correct reports of this western country and we've formed an ill opinion. But even if Arkansas were known to be a land of plenty, flush with fertile soil and crystal steams of water thick with silver fish, the Cherokee's answer would remain the same: We will not go! We will not go!"

Cherokee traditionally remained silent until a speaker was finished, but Ridge was pleased that the people could not restrain themselves on this occasion. He paused to let them hear their neighbors' shouts of support and approval. When the roar subsided, he pressed on.

"Let us commit ourselves to spending the rest of our lives on the soil that gave us birth," he said, "the same soil in which our ancestors and noble dead have long slumbered. We turn our backs to the setting sun to watch it rise at dawn the following day. If it becomes the Great Provider's will that the Cherokee should be sacrificed, let it be the Americans who draw first blood. Stand proud in your own country. Conduct your personal affairs above all reproach. Lift not one hair on a white man's head. But if he comes and whispers into your ear, 'Come, trade your land here for better in the west'? Let him hear one, loud, unified response: The Cherokee *will not go*!"

Before Ridge's last words were absorbed by the hills and thickets, the crowd erupted. Jackson's unfortunate election had suppressed their spirits, but had failed to break them. Hearing them so jubilant, so defiant,

413

Ridge knew there remained many warriors among them still. John Ridge, his quill bobbing as he recorded the words, smiled. Ridge turned to the other chiefs present, who in turn, nodded their turbans firmly toward him.

"What I would give for your voice," John Ross said, grasping his hand. His eyes were warm.

"You already have it, my friend."

There was one white scowl among all those joyous faces. Colonel Montgomery, their agent since the death of Return Miegs, stood alone with his arms across his chest, drawing fiercely from his pipe.

"He doesn't appear happy," Ross said.

"Let him go and do what he will," Ridge said. "Montgomery is bound by his laws, and he knows, as we do, that they favor the Cherokee."

The colonel tossed another log on the nearest fire and drew his black cape around his neck. Ridge watched him walk downwind from the council fire, coughing from his own smoke:

Ross leaned forward and whispered in his ear. "Will you go for a ride with me after sunset? I think there's something you need to see."

"I'd be honored," Ridge said.

"I don't believe you will," Ross said. He pointed in the direction in which the agent had left the council grounds. "All we have to do is follow Montgomery's tracks."

Ridge sat mounted in the shadows as night fell, stroking his horse to keep it quiet. A lantern light flickered in the colonial window of a fine house owned by Alexander McCoy, secretary of the Cherokee council.

"I don't like the idea of sneaking around like a wood rat, spying on my friends," Ridge said. "Why not just go down there and knock on his door?"

"I'm afraid he shows one face to us and another to the Americans," John Ross said.

"I don't believe he'd ever betray us," Ridge said. "He was the one who exposed McIntosh's bribery offer to the council. Nobody understands better the price McIntosh paid for betrayal. McCoy would never take the chance."

"Stranger things have happened," Ross said. "And money brought Doublehead to his doom. We've got to know for certain the extent of McCoy's dealings."

"I'd need solid proof to expose Alexander."

"I said the same thing. But yonder stands Colonel Montgomery's horse tethered to McCoy's rail. What business with McCoy would bring Jackson's agent out so far under the cover of night?"

Ridge bit his lip. "The kind he can't conduct in the daytime."

He tugged the reins to still the beast, backing it into the brush when Montgomery emerged from McCoy's fine house, mounted, and rode off. There could be no doubt that something spurious was afoot between them. Ridge hung his head in disappointment.

"It's a dark day for us, Tsan Usdi," he said. "Our friend schemes. We'll have to set him aside."

"And soon," Ross agreed. "Will John Ridge accept my nomination as secretary of the council in McCoy's place?"

"With all the ability at his disposal." Ridge shook his head in disgust. "My blood chills to think that some of the greatest among us would connive with Jackson."

"It's McCoy's own affair if he chooses to immigrate," Ross said. "He thinks it's useless to resist, and he's obviously accepted their bribes. The problem is that he's not alone."

Ridge tilted back his head and sighed. "Let the others go, but McCoy walked tall among us."

"Apparently he's walking away now," Ross said. "I lose all respect for any man who buckles before Jackson. What matters now is how much land he's agreed to sell. His personal holdings or ours?"

"Knowing McCoy, I normally wouldn't wonder," Ridge said. "But why meet at night in secret?"

"If he cedes more than his own estate, Mc-Coy will pay dearly. I'll see to that. He has no authority to sell tribal land to Jackson on his own."

"What does Sharp Knife care about authority?" Ridge said. "He finds himself a willing chief and he makes his bargain. After that, the soldiers come with a paper in their hands. It's too late to discuss the matter of proper authority then."

"Agreed," Ross said. "They'll do all they can to splinter us one from the other."

"They've already tried to set me against you with their gossip."

"Don't listen to it." He thrust his arm toward Ridge. "Take my hand, my friend." Ridge held him in his grip and they locked stares. "I know your heart as well as I know my own. I would not have been elected principal chief if you hadn't stepped aside. We're of one mind and one purpose. Together, always."

"We have so many troubles," Ridge said. "Don't let my loyalty to the Cherokee be among yours. Know that the Ridge would lay down his life for his people."

"I've never once doubted it," Ross said. "That's why I chose you to witness McCoy's activities."

"I've seen enough." Ross let go of his hand and Ridge clucked his tongue and gave the reins a little tug.

"What are you doing?" Ross said.

"I'm going to ride down there and face Mc-Coy."

Ross grabbed Ridge's horse by the bit. "That's not good enough. We'll confront Mc-Coy soon enough, but his scheme must be exposed in public with all the shame and humiliation we can heap on him. We punish one man publicly in the harshest way possible, and at the same time we warn a thousand others."

"He's a trusted friend, and thanks to you I have good reason to believe he's betrayed me and my people. The manly thing to do is ride down there and force him to account for his treason or show proof that he's been falsely accused. I'll listen to what he has to say. But if he lies to me, he'll meet Doublehead's fate." He reached for his pistol and cocked it. "I swear it."

Ross yanked Ridge's bit harder than before. "No, my friend. We have laws in place that deal with men like McCoy. And even if we didn't, what you have in mind will not have the impact we need. You know how to kill a man. But I know how to destroy one." Ross continued to stare at him as he let loose of his bit. "You taught me how to be a chief. Now let me teach you how to cripple dissent."

"More politics," Ridge said. "We need a permanent solution. The thing to do is revive the ancient code. As much as I detested the

418

Blood Law, there's little doubt it dealt with those of McCoy's inclination."

"Propose it in council," Ross said. "I'll support you, and so will the full-blood majority. We'll eliminate the problem and solidify the Cherokee at the same time." His eyes narrowed as he peered down the hill at McCoy's darkening home. "But leave him to me."

Alexander McCoy crawled away from the council podium after John Ross finished with him. At first, Ridge was eager to see justice done. But watching one of his friends so completely humiliated in front of his family and friends bought Ridge little satisfaction. Ross never once raised his voice. He simply presented McCoy with the opportunity to stick his head through a very public noose and let the full-bloods yank it tightly around his neck when he provided a false answer. In the time it took to saddle a horse, a man Ridge knew had served the Cherokee faithfully for most of his adult life had been ruined.

"There's no use resisting the Americans," McCoy said as a parting shot. "I thought if I sold my holdings for good money and left for the west, others would follow my example."

"That's an opinion you should have expressed before this body before you took it upon yourself to bargain in secret with Montgomery," Ross said. "Regardless, your constituents have spoken on this issue, ex-secretary McCoy. You disgrace yourself further by offering excuses after the fact."

In all the clamor that erupted during McCoy's departure, Ross whispered in Ridge's ear, "I hope he had the foresight to grease his wagon wheels," he said as the full-bloods stared at McCoy's back with narrow eyes. "He should make for Arkansas, and soon." He checked his pocket watch. "Now on to that business we discussed before."

"It's already done," Ridge said. "Resume the meeting and let it happen."

After McCoy's departure, The Tsalagi Tinilawigi's mood at the fall council at New Echota in 1829 became as somber as any Ridge could recall. He had discussed the problem of independent land cessions with council and committee members, offering his thoughts on the matter. But he had prevailed upon Choonungkee to place the bill before the council. Ridge closed his eyes as the full-blood read the words:

Whereas a Blood Law has been in existence for many years, but not committed to writing, that if any citizen or citizens of this nation should treat and dispose of any lands belonging to this nation without special permission from the national authorities, he or they shall suffer death.

Be it further resolved, that any person or persons, who shall violate the provisions of this act, and shall refuse, by resistance, to appear at the place designated for trial, or abscond, are hereby declared to be outlaws; and any person or persons, citizens of this nation, may kill him or them so offending, in any manner most convenient, within the limits of this nation, and shall not be held accountable for same.

When he opened his eyes, his gaze met Ross's. He knew Ross wanted him to rise and speak in favor of it. Ridge raised his hand to request the floor, but Womankiller, another full-blood with eighty winters on his head, was acknowledged first.

He spoke in the old way, recollecting why Ridge had urged that the Blood Law be set aside in the first place. Things were different now, he said, and the Americans were already searching for another McCoy. Only the Blood Law was strong enough to discourage them. "Save my home and yours," Womankiller said. "Bring back the ancient code."

Womankiller collapsed into his seat to passionate murmurs. Ross called for a vote, and the measure passed easily. Those known to have registered with the emigration agent skulked out of the council house, no doubt motivated to finalize their arrangements, pack their wagons, and head west before the law went into effect.

The remaining council and committee members lined up to sign the bill. Ridge scratched his mark where his son indicated.

"New teeth in an old dog, eh?" Ross said.

"Rest assured that someone will soon be bitten," Ridge said. He managed a smile, but there was no consolation for him that it had come to this, the reenactment of the law he himself had set aside as an ambitious young chief kicking at the shins of his elders. Ridge had no doubt that the new law, as proposed, would soon bring a Cherokee to the gallows for some crime other than murder. He wondered if he would have the stomach to enforce it against a friend or colleague convicted by hardliners as an enemy of his own kind. A written law was a cold, dangerous thing, and just because men created the code did not mean they could control it. Under the right set of circumstances, the Blood Law could run loose among them like a pack of wild dogs and rip out the throats of good or evil Cherokee with equal enthusiasm.

Was this rule by consensus? Or was it another step closer to the mixed-blood tyranny that White Path feared? What other traditions must be trampled to keep the Alexander McCoys from breaking rank? And though this Blood Law they enacted dealt with the problem in the Nation, Ridge knew the greater threat lay without. What laws could the Cherokee pass to keep Sharp Knife at bay?

In his annual address before the joint houses of Congress, Jackson made clear his intention to enact laws that would remove the civilized tribes beyond the Mississippi. It was all the Georgians needed to hear to reassert their claim on Cherokee lands within their borders. Their enemies acted as if the Cherokee Nation had ceased to exist the day Jackson spoke the words. What, Ridge wanted to ask his principal chief, would the Blood Law do about that?

What about the discovery of gold in the hills that cradled the Chesta-tee River, the $2,000 of ore stolen each day from a Cherokee government desperate for funds? The hundreds of prospectors mad to reduce the southeastern Cherokee hills to rubble, the thousand of squatters on Cherokee soil who had preceded them? What could be done about whiskey runners drowning the spirits of lost young men, or the "Pony Clubs," squads of Georgian wretches who raided isolated farms, burning houses, stealing stock, terrorizing Cherokee into accepting the emigration agent's terms? Did Womankiller have any thoughts on this? Did anyone?

No, Ridge felt no satisfaction from making his scratch on that flimsy piece of paper. There was no security in the Nation, little chance for peace. If he properly gauged the expressions on the chiefs' faces, they were not much relieved, either. They knew the Cherokee could kill two dozen chiefs for treating separately with the American agents, and still the common Indians among them would still worry if they'd see the sun rise over their land another day. The fate of their nation lay in Jackson's hands, and Sharp Knife had no qualms about making his intentions known. He vowed to sign his name to another law and thousands would lose their homes or die defending them.

What was the answer? What should the Cherokee do? When would the Man Who Walks the Mountaintops at last see clearly both sides of his people's future? And when he did, would he have the courage to act?

CHAPTER THIRTY-ONE

Ridge tugged at the horned buffalo headdress until it rested just above his brow. Thirty winters had passed since he'd worn it. The musty war bonnet felt like a stone lashed on top of his head. He had fresh charges in his rifle and pistols, a honed edge on his bone-handled knife. With him rode thirty hand-picked warriors, all dressed in leggings, hunting shirts, dangling silver earrings, feathers in their hair, faces painted red for war and black for death. The raiders had come near the line drawn between Alabama and Georgia to burn Cherokee-built houses. Now that the Americans had pushed them to violence, Ridge had no compunction whatsoever about risking first blood.

Georgia's legislature had been busy last fall. They annexed Cherokee land and carved it into five Georgia counties. They nullified all Cherokee laws in the district and forbade the Cherokee council to meet. By their decree, all contracts between red men and white were null and void unless two whites had witnessed them. Now, in the winter of 1830, no Indian could testify against a white man in Georgia courts, no Cherokee could mine the gold that lay beneath their hills, and, most incredible of all, any Cherokee who attempted to talk his neighbor out of western emigration would be subject to arrest and imprisonment.

Ridge was outraged. White charlatans began to circulate forged notes attributed to him and other influential Cherokee. Courts pressed them for payment in cases in which Ridge could not testify on his own behalf. Even Georgia juries could not rule in favor of such wretches, but Ridge's indignation stemmed from having to answer such ludicrous claims in the first place. The Pony Clubs were increasingly brazen. The rumors of gold attracted the lowest rogues among the whites, who were no longer satisfied to merely rob Cherokee farmers of their crops and livestock. They settled where it pleased them and dug the dull blades of their plows into Cherokee earth.

Those in the houses below him now were cut from this kind of dingy cloth, settling into homes abandoned by demoralized Cherokee who saw no other remedy than to turn their feet west. Ridge could not abide the intruders, and neither could General Coffee, who had come to investigate the situation on his government's behalf. Coffee was Jackson's friend, of Jackson's persuasion, but even he could not find any justice in Georgia's claim.

John Ridge translated as his father discussed the matter privately with General Coffee in John Ross's Coosa River home — an abode, like Ridge's, that the Pony Clubs threatened to reduce to ashes if they couldn't steal it outright. Ridge poured his heart out to his old Creek War comrade, desperate to know his mind, and Jackson's. Coffee was reluctant to step between the Cherokee and their agent, Colonel Montgomery, but at least he said he believed that the duty to police the Nation ultimately rested with the principal chief.

Ross weighed the dilemma and then handed the assignment to Ridge, who dusted off his old war regalia and found himself thirty trusted warriors.

"Extend toward the squatters all possible lenience and humanity," Ross told him.

"Let me understand you," Ridge had answered. "You wish for me to treat these outlaws better than they've ever treated us?"

"I'm afraid you must."

"Are they criminals or not, Tsan Usdi?" Ridge said. "Let's make an example of them. If they resist, they die."

Ross shook his head in disappointment. "I'm not sure you're the man for this job."

"I am definitely the man," Ridge said, his anger bursting out of him. "But sometimes I wonder if you're the man for yours." He'd stormed out of Ross's home set on assembling his war party, leaving John behind to smooth things over.

He regretted his harsh words for his principal chief now, as he pulled up the reins on his horse and turned toward his warriors. John Ross was an understanding, forgiving man. Ridge hoped that he would see his outburst as a symptom of his smoldering frustration.

"Remember your instructions," he said to his warriors, his breath frosting in the winter air. "This must go well."

He pointed the barrel of his rifle at the settlement, put his heels to the horse's flank, and screamed in a voice he had not used in nearly twenty years. His warriors followed, bellowing their war cries louder than he, so that together with the beat of horse hooves on the frozen ground, the crashing of brush, and the tumbling of loose rocks, they bore down on the squatters like a storm.

The whites scrambled out of their shacks in their undergarments, rifles in hand. Ridge saw their eyes widen at the sight of the painted, angry warriors. They dropped their rifles and dove back inside.

"Out!" yelled Thomas Blackcat, the most fluent in the English tongue among them. "Take your things and go now and you won't be harmed."

"On what authority?" said one from out a darkened window.

Blackcat translated the squatter's response and Ridge answered by pointing a rifle bore in his face.

"His," Blackcat said. "Chief Ridge says you ain't welcome on Cherokee land."

Most started to pack their wagons and hitch their teams under the leer of warriors. Ridge answered the few game enough to argue by tossing a torch on the roofs. They were too busy salvaging their goods and furniture after that to protest. Ridge rode from one house to another until eighteen homes were alive with fire. When he came across a keg of whiskey, Ridge put a bullet through it, and watched the liquor melt the snow where it drained.

"Touch not a drop," Ridge admonished his warriors, who seemed chagrined by his efforts. "Above all reproach."

One by one, the squatters bundled their children and turned their wagons south. When the last had rolled out of Beaver Dam, Ridge's warriors followed, the clanking of hastily loaded goods and squeaking wheels breached by the taunts of renewed, spirited warriors. His riders kept their distance and slowed their pace until Ridge couldn't hear the whites any more. Then, removing his headdress to scratch his scalp, he turned his war party east, across the icing river, for home.

It felt good to run the war trace again.

Elias Boudinot delivered the Georgia newspaper to Ridge's home, which was now surrounded by dozens of Cherokee warriors, as
were the homes of Ross and other threatened
leaders. Georgia's men retaliated almost as
soon as Ridge returned home. Four of his
warriors had defied him, rescuing a cask of
whiskey from the cinders and drinking it until
they could no longer see. Georgia militia
scooped them off the roads the next day. One
died from blows to the head on the way to
jail and two others sobered enough to escape.
But the last remained in chains behind bars
as proof that the Cherokee were responsible
for the "raid" on their own soil. Whiskey and
trouble were close cousins.

Boudinot thrust the newspaper in Ridge's
face.

"You'll have to read it to me," Ridge said.
"I'm too —"

"Yes, yes," John scoffed. "We know. You're
an ignorant scion of the woods and waters."
He looked at his mother. "Why will he not
learn Sequoyah's alphabet?"

"Hush," Sehoya said. "Have some respect
when you speak to my husband." John sank
into a distant chair.

" 'War in Georgia,' " Boudinot said, running his finger across the bold, black print.
"I'm afraid you've given them the excuse they

needed."

Ridge's nephew was much more reserved in his emotions than his son. Elias could present an opposing opinion without offense. He was as gifted in his own way as John Ridge was in his. Ridge was proud of his kin, but he didn't particularly enjoy arguing with him.

"What does Ross say?" Ridge asked, rubbing his temples. Sehoya sat beside him and draped her arm across his shoulders.

"What else can he say?" she said. "We have the right to protect our property. Thanks to my husband, the whites know we mean business." Ridge appreciated his wife's support. He didn't feel it from any other source.

"Ross says that you did as exactly as you both agreed," Boudinot said, "but that it was wrong to provoke the Georgians." Ridge's nephew knelt beside him. "If we kill one of them, Ridge Walker, they will kill us all. Forbearance is the only way. I wanted you to know beforehand that I've written an editorial for the *Phoenix* that says as much."

"I've never before led a successful war party that spilled no blood," Ridge said. Sehoya, sensing his frustration, stroked his hair. "We had to make an example. I did so without any loss of life and still my own relatives second-guess me."

Ridge's bile was reserved for the Georgians rather than his son and nephew. But there was pain in facing their judgmental expressions. He'd done what he thought was right and they didn't approve.

"Forbearance," he said. "Where's the end of that?"

"Listen," John said, holding a finger in front of Ridge's face. "Do you agree that Elias and I have seen more of the white world than you?"

"Of course I do. You mother and I are the ones who sent you there."

"Then listen to us when we tell you that there are better ways to fight them."

"Better, maybe. More satisfying, certainly not! These aren't missionaries and teachers who are stealing our land from us. They're the rot of the American bushel and it pleased me to watch them run."

"There's a way that will please you more," Elias said.

He looked at Sehoya. "You see? They've been scheming again."

"Will you listen to what he's telling you?" John said.

"He will when you curb your tongue," Sehoya said. "We didn't raise you to take this tone with us. This is an attitude you brought home with you from Cornwall."

John sighed in exasperation.

"I've already heard his suggestion," Ridge said. "Forbearance. Well, you boys forebear all you want to. I don't have the stomach for

432

it. I'm too old to stand by and let them take all that they want and do nothing in return." Boudinot bowed his head. "For the life of me, I see no alternative but to meet blood with blood."

John crossed his leg over his knee and put down his cup of Sehoya's steaming hot sassafras tea. He fixed his father with a sharp, piercing stare.

"I do," he said. "I know exactly what our next step must be. John Ross agrees with me. You hear me out, Ridge Walker, and see if you don't agree, too."

As he listened to John's words, his frustration faded until at last he rose from his seat and erupted into his war cry. John looked at Elias and they both laughed. And they whooped also.

At first, Sehoya's mouth hung open, and then, seeing her family so invigorated, she raised her chin. "I think your father agrees," she said to her son and nephew.

"Make it so, my kinsmen!" Ridge said, making the steps of the Scalp Dance on his way to slap them both on the back in joy. "I've searched a lifetime for a way to battle back the whites. I dedicated my son's and nephew's lives to this one cause, praying to the Provider that one day they'd see the path open to them. Now that it has, there's nothing left to do but go forth like warriors and *make it so*!"

CHAPTER THIRTY-TWO

The Nation Builder

In a sense, I'm alone here. I belong at the Hermitage, next to the warmth of my kith and kin. I'm needed at home. But my people were troubled. Their leaders had meandered from the spirit of the Revolution and I saw disunion as a possible result. The people came to me, Andrew Jackson, to set things right. Their confidence in me overcame my reluctance to campaign for the presidency. After being swept into office, I knew what had to be done.

Indian removal was in motion long before my tenure. My intent was to hurry the ugly, inevitable business along and get beyond it. I said so in my inaugural address back in '29. On May 28, 1830, I appended my signature to the Indian Removal Act, and then it was time for the federal authority to get down to business with the five civilized tribes. The state of Georgia, by the way, already had.

There was much gnashing of teeth and pulling of hair, but one way or another we convinced four of the five civilized nations to cross the Mississippi. What did the Cherokee do? They hired lawyers — Wirt and Associates in Baltimore and Underwood and Harris in Georgia — to assert their claim.

I knew and detested all of these attorneys, in particular former Attorney General William Wirt. He took this case solely to fleece the Indians for his fees. The federal government owed the Cherokees an annuity of $6,000, which almost certainly funded the litigation against us. I didn't see where this agreement specifically stipulated that the sum be paid in bulk to the Cherokee treasury. We decided to distribute the funds on a per capita basis — around 44 cents a head, which this administration rounded off to four bits.

This was but one of several setbacks to the Cherokees during this period, and they met them all with fortitude and resolve. There were rich men in the nation and wealthier benefactors in the north. The tribe raised the money while sending their lawyers on the warpath. It used to be the other way around, but that was the Cherokee.

Essentially, the thrust of their litigation was to render unconstitutional the Georgian jurisdiction over their southern territory. The fact is, both parties had a legal claim — the Cherokees through the Treaty of Hopewell and various other documents, and the Georgians by way of Jefferson's compact of 1802. One tract of rich soil, fertile plantations — not to mention gold reserves — promised to two different parties. The controversy boiled down to which pledge the federal authority intended to honor.

The only thing the poltroon and scoundrel Wirt required in order to get the horse race under way was a suitable case.

Of course, he hunted one up directly. Wirt applied to the Supreme Court for a writ of error in the case of convicted murderer Corn Tassel. To my knowledge, the cagey barrister didn't dispute the facts of Georgia's conviction of this man; it was a matter of whether they had jurisdiction over the Cherokee in what used to be the Cherokee Nation. Justice Marshall found for Corn Tassel, but Georgia didn't flinch in the least. They stuck the old warrior's head through a noose in short order. Case moot.

Next, the Cherokee again, through the sluggard Wirt, sued Georgia for an injunction against their laws. This case squirmed onto the court's docket back in March of last year, if memory serves. Marshall read the bench's decision in July, which surprised even me. The Cherokees couldn't sue before his body because they were not a "foreign, independent state," but "a dependent, domestic nation . . . in a state of pupilage." The injunction was denied, but for some strange reason both parties claimed victory.

Major Ridge's boy, John, came to see me shortly after this affair. He was taller than his father but thin where Major Ridge was ferociously stout. But John Ridge was as shrewd as his father was courageous. The Cherokees placed a heavy load on this boy's shoulders, and I assumed they'd chosen him because he was up to the task. Accordingly, I was deliberate with my choice of words.

"I'm particularly glad to see you at this time," I said after we made introductions. Young Ridge was socially refined and dignified. Every bit the gentlemen, this red fellow. "The court has sustained my views in regard to your nation. I fear your lawyers have fleeced you, and will make promises even after this." I coughed into my fist. I had a fever, a little rattle in my chest. But I felt well enough to make my position vividly clear to one of the smartest Indians I've ever encountered. "I've been a lawyer myself long enough to know how attorneys will talk to obtain their clients' money." I shot him a wink.

"The money was spent in support of our national rights," John Ridge said. "We don't believe you'd blame the Cherokee for our efforts to maintain our rights before the proper tribunals."

"Oh, no," I assured him, though I remained enough of a lawyer to covet the fee they had paid Wirt and the other grub worms. "I am a friend of the Cherokees. They fought with me in the war and freely shed their blood with the blood of my soldiers defending the United States. How could I be otherwise than a friend?"

John Ridge seemed impatient with this sort of language. "Sir, are the Cherokee not entitled to their abstract rights of justice?"

Abstract rights of justice. Simply inconceivable to me that this young Cherokee could take this tack. His sophistication made me think a little about how far they'd come, but more about where I was resolved they'd go. I simply changed the subject. "Many things have changed since 1783 — the year we defeated your allies, the British."

I cocked an eye at the boy ambassador lest this statement send the conversation off in a sour direction. I just wanted to remind him that the Cherokee had made the wrong choices before. My point made, I pressed on. "I remember the Catawbas in my younger years. Powerful, fierce, majestic warriors. Enemies of the Cherokee. They once took Cherokee warriors prisoner, threw them alive into the fire, and when their intestines were cooked, the Catawbas ate them. I saw that with my own eyes."

John Ridge's stared silently, obviously wondering what this recollection had to do with current events.

"Now the Catawbas are poor and miserable, vastly reduced in their numbers, wretches in a state of squalor and alcoholic despair." I raised a finger in the air and wagged it back and forth. "Such will be the condition of the Cherokee if they remain surrounded by the whites."

It registered, I think, but not deeply enough. That would come later during my second interview with John Ridge. This one was cut short when my aides announced a representative of Georgia had also come to call. The Cherokee would sooner lie down with a rattlesnake than share the same room with a Georgian. They shot up from their seats to scurry out the side door, but I took my time to make sure that they understood my message. I took each of their hands in turn, professed my friendship to their nation, which was in earnest, I assure you, for John Ridge was the walking embodiment of Cherokee resilience, industry, and resolve. Bright as a new brass button, to boot; a remarkable individual by any measure.

"You can live on your lands in Georgia if you choose," I said, the implication of course being that this had also been the flawed choice of the Catawbas, "but I cannot interfere with the laws of that state to protect you." Enough said, or so I thought.

Then, earlier this year, the Supreme Court decided on Wirt's third and final effort in behalf of the Cherokee: *Worcester v. Georgia.* Let's just serve up all that mess on one plate while we're at it.

Everyone knew the missionaries bolstered the Indians' resolve against immigration. Georgia, enhancing its already aggressive position, applied certain laws to the white missionaries, as well, like requiring them to sign an oath of loyalty to Georgia if they wanted to remain on Georgia soil. The obvious intent was to drive them from the nation. For most clerics the measures were successful, but the Presbyterians and Congregationalists, stubborn Scotch weevils all, dug in their heels.

They wiggled out of their first imprisonment by claiming their duties as postmasters rendered them federal agents. Georgia governor Gilmer wrote me for my position in this matter. I responded by relieving the missionaries of their postal offices, and off to jail they went, this time convicted to four years of hard labor for their transgressions. This sentence was far too harsh in my view, bound to dredge up additional sympathy in the north. But if nothing else it impressed upon the Cherokee that the Georgians intended to play rough. And as the federal executive, it was not my business to interfere with the internal affairs of any one state.

Until the Cherokee's attorneys appealed the case to the Supreme Court.

And Chief Justice John Marshall found for the Cherokee.

I can't recall the exact wording of the old buffoon's opinion. It went something like this:

The Cherokee Nation is a distinct community, occupying its own territory in which the laws of Georgia can have no force and in which the citizens of Georgia have no right to enter but with the assent of the Cherokee. The act of the State of Georgia is . . . null and void, not to mention repugnant to the constitution, laws, and treaties of the United States.

Merciful God! What a quandary.

I can't imagine how the Cherokee must have celebrated. Marshall's decision reinforced their hopes to preserve their lands, and along with it, their way of life. They had placed their faith in our system, and it had sustained them — which is why I consider Justice Marshall the most culpable villain in this entire travesty.

"John Marshall has made his decision," I was supposed to have commented. "Let's see if he can enforce it." I never said any such thing — but I sure thought it. In fact, I knew the Supreme Court's decision had fallen stillborn, for how could the court coerce Georgia to yield? Where were the soldiers behind the briefs and paper opinions?

Why, you ask, did I turn my back on the judicial branch? I'll tell you: I had to consider the grander view.

Worcester v. Georgia was but one of the many snarling heads rearing within the States' Rights' hydra. Had I severed this one, another three would've taken its place. The game was a losing proposition, and I refused to play it. What choice did Marshall have but to sit on his pedantic hands and scowl?

Once word got out about my position, it didn't take John Ridge long to cut a swath to the White House. I dropped everything to meet with him, for this time I wanted him to understand *exactly* what choices this administration saw ahead for the Cherokee. I could see the boy was in anguish, face flushed, hands agitated, dark eyes animated.

"Sir, could this be true?" he said in a huff.

"Is what true?" I asked. "And I'll thank you to mind your place, young Cherokee."

He handed me a well-worn copy of the *National Journal,* tapping the article we'd all seen and cast aside as backbiting tripe given currency by my enemies in the press. " 'The prerogatives of nullifying laws and political decisions by denying their conformity of the court,' " Ridge read, " 'makes the president supreme — the final arbiter — the very Celestial Majesty.' "

Such editorials were the beginning of the "King Andrew" talk. I paid them no mind.

Anyone who knew me well understood that I wanted nothing to do with politics after my beloved wife died. I longed to return to my Tennessee home and spend my final days beside her sad grave. But the trials of my Union anchored me here, in Washington City, where there's too much commotion to mourn. I vowed as my patriotic duty to see my country through this States' Rights crisis.

"I'm aware of the assumptions presumed by the article, Mr. Ridge," I said. "What is your business with me?"

"Sir, based on your curious position, the State of Georgia intends to ignore the Supreme Court's decision. Will you not exert the power of the United States to put them down?"

"I will not, sir!" I said crisply, like a green hickory twig snapping in two. John Ridge recoiled from the timbre of my voice. "Federal law gives me no power to do so."

"Forgive me, sir, but you have publicly threatened to send federal troops to South Carolina to enforce federal tariffs. Georgia has put into practice what South Carolina has merely asserted as a theory. Do you not yourself see a contradiction?"

I should have known that sooner or later, John Ridge would get around to this. Everyone else did. I suppose I owe you an explanation. You understand my position on Indian removal. In the central and southern United

States, it has long been a foregone conclusion. I'd like to remind you that those in the north who resisted these measures are the very same people who no longer faced a significant Indian population as their neighbors. Their compassion for the red man, I believe, stems from guilt, for their fathers and grandfathers were every bit as ruthless as we must be now when it came to dealing with Indian affairs. At least I've also proposed generous terms for removal. Consider what became of the Mohawks, the Mohicans, the Iroquois, and the Manhattans. The entire episode is to every degree as ugly and shameful as the Salem witch trials, and our northern friends would love nothing more than to rid their consciousness of it by taking a convenient, moral stand on other people's problems.

South Carolina threatens to ignore federal laws precisely as Georgia has done. Young Ridge was right. I have reacted differently to both. Why?

To preserve my Union! Slavery continues to loom over us, but nullification is the first real threat to federal authority. South Carolina would like nothing more than to welcome other states as allies, especially when I threatened to send federal troops to execute the tariff with express orders to hang any so-called nullifier (especially that insufferable

blackguard John C. Calhoun) from the nearest oak.

Regional factionalism is the reality of our
day and the sole binding adhesive remains
the federal authority. And while I'll crush the
nullifiers like so many crickets, I won't lift a
finger to stand in Georgia's way to oust the
Cherokees from lands the Georgians were
given back in 1802! If I did, Georgia would
be welcomed by South Carolina, as would
Alabama, Mississippi, and, quite possibly,
even my own state of Tennessee — all of
which are thumbing their noses at me as we
speak. That's civil war. And I won't have it in
my country.

The cost now, as I've concluded long ago,
is the sacrifice of the Cherokee Nation.

I'll placate the other southern states by allowing them to legislate the Indians out of
existence, by unconstitutional measures or
not, for who are these red people, anyway?
They are not now, and never will be, Americans. My plan is to isolate South Carolina.
She will be alone in her rebellion, which, by
God eternal, I will crush! And that is the only
precedent I wish to set.

The Constitution forms a *government,* not
a league. To say that any state may at pleasure
secede from the Union is to say that the
United States is not a nation. Secession by
armed force, in my view, is treason. And those
who oppose federal authority will incur the

dreadful consequences of treason's guilt. And while the northern politicians will make poetic display in Congress on behalf of the beleaguered Indian tribes, they will drop their cause like fresh cow manure when they see that this position leads to the unraveling of the Union, and ultimately to war with their southern brethren.

To tuck their tails after all this commotion will pain the northerners greatly. They will be embarrassed, quite possibly ashamed. But they will not risk their country to save the Indians. That I can assure you. And so I've acted all along in confidence, stomping back and forth along this razor's edge, knowing in the end that my view would prevail.

The Cherokees could not see their place in the larger scheme. As for me, I knew my place in mine. That is why John Marshall's opinion was a token effort, a fool's enterprise that did nothing more than give hope to the hopeless, prolonging their misery and suffering. I had to make this young, brilliant, charismatic Cherokee understand this, and then convince the leadership who sent him that to live as Cherokees, the Cherokees must remove across the Mississippi. Otherwise they are doomed to the Catawbas' fate.

"Sir, I see no contradiction whatsoever," I said after a long pause during which our stares intensely locked. Ridge didn't flinch, nor did I. "This administration cannot interfere with the laws of Georgia. North Carolina and Tennessee will soon follow suit, I assure you, until every single acre of Cherokee land belongs either to the federal or state government, or in the private hands of white citizens. All of this has been explained to you."

"But —"

I held up my hand. "You, my friend, have argued persuasively for your people. You have won many white hearts. Yet even your staunchest admirers realize that you and your cousin are the exceptions to your race, not the rule."

Young Ridge closed his eyes and gathered himself. "Does your own document not say, sir, that all men are created equal?"

"Oh, yes," I said. "But the devil's in what it doesn't say."

"And what *doesn't* it say?" he asked, and by now I had forgiven his arrogance because I truly admired his spirit. I remembered a time when an English officer ordered me to wipe the mud from his boots. Ridge and I drew our courage from the same well.

I leaned forward, speaking almost in a whisper. "It doesn't say red men are the equal of white."

He gasped, just as I see you're doing, and that's all right. But in the fifty years that had passed since the framers penned our Constitution and the Bill of Rights, tolerance of the races had run its course. The Great Experiment became too much of a burden, too much of a struggle, the American people less naive. The field narrowed considerably in just one generation. This Cherokee lawyer was educated, refined, gracious, but even he must have foreseen the shock he created in Cornwall, that liberal bastion of goodwill toward all, when he took a white woman for his bride. He struck a nerve among the most fervent Indian sympathizers in this country. His bride's neighbors threatened to lynch him in Concord. In Atlanta, they would have.

I watched John Ridge connect these events — for I knew what was going through my mind was now going through his. The time had come to drive the nail a little deeper.

"I have told you, your father before you, and the Pathkiller before him, that as much as it breaks my heart to say these words, I can find no relief for the Cherokee. As your friend, as one who truly cares for you, I charge you to go home and tell your people that their only hope is abandoning their country and removing to the west."

Young Ridge drew in a deep breath, and exhaled loudly. All anger in his face dissipated with his wind. His complexion paled. His eyes darkened and closed, and his chin dropped to his chest.

"I can see you are in despair," I said quietly, in the beseeching tone a father adopts with a rebellious son who at last is broken in spirit.

"Good. That is the appropriate emotion. You can receive favorable terms from this administration to remove. If, on the other hand, you choose to stay, you will face total annihilation. I'm loath to see that. But you've got to understand that there is *no place* for you in my country. There will be no Cherokee state — and certainly no Cherokee Nation — within the borders of the southeastern United States."

"But, sir, the treaties —"

"Talking leaves," I said abruptly, for there was a twitch in the boy yet. "Is this not what you people call them? They last for one season and then they wither and die to blow with the wind." I paused to let the weight of that statement press upon him, and then added, "The winter, my friend, falls hard upon the Cherokee."

John Ridge stood there like a ghost who had lost the ability to frighten. I sat with my hand against my cheek, swinging slowly side to side in my swivel chair like a pendulum in a loosely wound clock. This time, I was certain, he understood the situation as well as I.

I stood and offered John Ridge my hand. He would not take it. I watched his gaze climb from my cold fingers until he met my stare. It was the first time I saw the wildness in him, a glimpse of the savage heart, the place deep within that civilization would never reach. And I must confess that in my advanced age, I was in awe of it. Ridge's eyes threatened me as his deeds and words could never do. I knew then that he truly belonged where I was urging him to go. The Indians need another hundred years and far more white blood coursing through their veins before they're advanced enough to become Americans. It won't happen in my time. I'm not certain that it will occur in yours.

I didn't flinch before Ridge's belligerent posture. When my alarmed aides stepped up I motioned for them to stand where they were. In the end, the boy's rage would serve me well.

"I've told you what is," I said. "It's for the Cherokee to decide what will be." Then I turned on my heels, blew out the taxpayers' candles, and walked out of the room.

I don't know if I'll ever see John Ridge again. But I know I'll never forget him. And rest assured this entire situation haunts me, for as I've maintained all along, I *am* a friend to the Cherokee. I wish there had been some other way to settle the Cherokee question, some mythical middle ground between degradation and banishment. I assure you there was none. Before God almighty, I swear there was none.

You judge me harshly. That's all right. At least now you comprehend the complexity of our time, and only children see the world as either black or white. I'll leave you with a question: What did you want? One nation under God, stretching from the Atlantic to the Pacific, or a chessboard of squabbling feudal states? Have we not seen enough of the latter throughout this sad globe? We are the only *true* republic in the modern world. Brave men died for a dream and a destiny, and it was not within me to waver in my ambition to fulfill them both.

To build one great, modern nation we must destroy a thousand lesser, antiquated others. So be it. Our Union is sacred and manifest! All other considerations crumble before it. Cry for the Cherokee if it comforts you. They are certainly innocent, but they are also squatting in our way. You must understand that we cannot do justice to ourselves and the red man at the same time. The issue is as simple — and as horrific — as that.

Now you know.

CHAPTER THIRTY-THREE

Even in the hills, the Cherokee were dancing.
In the afternoon, after spirited ball plays, they
feasted on the first of the ripe, river-cooled
melons and fresh-picked dewberries. Children prowled the woods for cicadas emerging
from their dusty hulls. Lightly grilled before
their wings dried and their bodies hardened
into armor of green or black, the insects were
a favorite seasonal delicacy. People emerged
from their farms to visit their neighbors. At
night, Ridge heard their voices float in song
on the cool breeze, pleased to see that the
Ani-yunwi-ya had rediscovered their joy of
life. He felt the urge stirring as well, frolick-
ing a bit with Sehoya before she poked him
with her knitting needles.

"Act your age, you old fool," she said, and
sat back down shaking her head. But her eyes
danced along with Ridge's body. Ridge
caught the glint of his wife's smile as he
taught their youngest, Sally, the stomp dance
steps of his youth. Ridge felt renewed. The

Supreme Court's decision assured the Cherokee's future. With their blessing, Ridge's thirty-year burden dissipated like a late-season snow. His country was free.

Before the sun set on that day in Anasku'tee, the planting moon of 1832, when the crop seeds were entrusted to Mother Earth to provide for the coming winter, heavy clouds drifted in from the east and sank below the crest of the hills. The air turned warm and oppressive, the sky the color of a new English skillet. Into this sudden gloom rode John Ross and the Washington delegation. The celebrants cheered their arrival, but the diplomats passed them by with sullen expressions and holed up alone at the principal chief's Head of Coosa estate. The Cherokee's festival came to an abrupt end. The whole country fell as silent as the grave.

For three sleeps, Ridge and Sehoya agonized for news. Their son did not come to them. Nor did any other delegate. It seemed strange that John Ross and the other negotiators would behave so mysteriously. Had Ridge been directly involved, he would have immediately ridden night and day to consult with the chiefs of the eight districts, and then, regardless of the news, he would have called a council to inform everyone about what had gone wrong.

When Ridge heard his dogs bark he shot up from his chair with Sehoya following closely on his heel. Oo-watie drifted behind them like a ghost. The form of a heavyset, slow-riding warrior emerged from Ridge's ferry crossing. Ridge stood with his arm around Sehoya, waiting for White Path to close the distance.

"White Path is here," Ridge's friend said.

"So he is," Ridge said. "But does he know anything?"

"Very little, as always," White Path said after he'd hugged Sehoya and gripped Watie's hand. He drew some cold water from the well and drank his fill from the bucket.

"What could John Ross be thinking?" Ridge said. "His secrecy will spawn only more uncertainty and distrust."

"That's the problem of placing power in the hands of a few," White Path said. "I believe I mentioned the danger of that at New Echota five winters ago. You talked me into supporting the new government, and now it appears that the new government is not talking to you."

"It irks me that Ross would leave me in the dark like some high-country witch," Ridge said. "I may be ignorant, but I'm still the voice of my people. I was a fool to step aside for John Ross. My reward for self-sacrifice is to be tossed aside like a cornhusk."

"My guess is that John Ross wants to argue with only one Ridge at a time," White Path said.

"What do you mean?" Sehoya said, crossing her arms over her chest.

"One of my people saw the delegates on their way to Ross's home. They said nothing to us waiting at home, but they said plenty to one another."

"Did they hear anything or not?" Sehoya asked.

"They didn't have to. They saw angry words between Ross and John Ridge. Ross waved off your son, but twice young Ridge rode up again, imploring him. Obviously they don't agree on some important point."

Ridge gripped Sehoya's hand. He'd often wondered if John's temper would weather the pressures of diplomacy. It was entirely possible that John's rebellious nature had offended the pious principal chief. In a squabble between them, Ross believed that Ridge would take his son's side. That was why Ross refused to send for him.

"Come inside and wait with us for news," Ridge told White Path. He pointed to the dozens of Cherokee who camped under the shade of his apple and peach trees, occasionally plucking ripe fruit from their limbs. "I'd like to hear what you're doing with yourself these days. I could use a little amusement."

"I can't entertain you with my foolishness today," White Path said. "My people are waiting around my house for news, just like yours. I won't abandon them to their worries." He

455

mounted his horse. "You'll send word to me when you hear something, won't you?"

"Of course we will," Sehoya said, taking his hand.

"Safe journey," Watie said.

White Path rode back down to the ferry. Ridge nodded to his slave to let him cross without fee. He went inside with Sehoya and his brother to discuss what little they had learned.

"So," he said to his wife behind a slamming door. "Ross suddenly treats me like an outsider because he's at odds with my son. I can overcome that when we get a chance to talk. But what's John's excuse for shunning me? It'd better be good or else I'll get a cattail stalk after his skinny hindquarters."

"You've never raised a hand to that boy," she said.

"John errs if he thinks it's too late to start."

"Maybe you no longer have the patience for politics," Sehoya said, smiling.

"I have plenty and then some," he said. "But I'm starting to have my doubts about having enough to stay in this marriage. Can you not see what a state I'm in, woman?"

She touched her finger to his lips. "First find out what the problem is," she said. "Then you can let it drive you insane." She handed him his pipe.

"We've spent a small fortune educating that boy," Ridge said. "Could he not at least use the most elementary of his skills and send us a note?" He threw open the door and pointed at the people who had descended upon Sehoya's house, hungry for information. "It humiliates me that their chief knows nothing more than they." He glared at his brother. "Do you ever have anything important to say?"

"Always," Watie said. "But unlike you, I don't move my mouth until it's time to say it."

"I should've let wild dogs carry you off after Agan'stat' and Etsi passed on," Ridge said. "No one would've known."

"I wish you'd done it," Watie said. "It'd have saved me the embarrassment of being related to such a ranting jackass."

Watie looked at Sehoya. "This from a chief," he said.

"No more jokes," Sehoya said in a warning tone.

Ridge pounded his fists on her table. "I want to know what's going on in my Nation!"

Sehoya and his brother left him alone after that.

Another sleep passed without word from John Ridge. Ross's first official statement called only for a day of fasting and prayer. Stunned, the people filtered back into the river valleys and hills from whence they had come. The camps and ball fields were abandoned. The bonfires of communal joy and celebration were left in cold ashes. The Nation froze over like a river in winter.

An hour after sundown on the fifth agonizing day of his vigil, Ridge heard two horses approaching his home in a slow gait. He tensed, listening carefully to what the sounds told him. Pony Clubs were out on the roads again after dark, accosting Cherokee. The dogs cocked their ears but didn't bark, which told Ridge that it was John. Ridge stepped outside his door and looked west, toward the flowing dark Oostanaula and its ferry crossing, and watched two forms rise from the riverbank and emerge out of woodland shadows. Elias Boudinot rode alongside his cousin.

Ridge had old Jumper catch the reins of their horses, while another slave splashed last year's corn in the trough of smoothly worn oak. John failed at a smile for his father. Boudinot, always reserved and contemplative, did not even try. When at last Ridge gripped their hands in greeting, John's head fell against his shoulder.

Ridge, his frustration gone, hesitated a moment in surprise. It had been a few winters since his proud son sought comfort against his breast. But soon enough he stroked the dark coils of John's head. "Come and see your mother," Ridge said softly into his ear, "and then you can tell me what troubles you."

His son stiffened and stood erect. He

turned his head away to wipe a tear. "What I have to say to you, she should hear, as well," John said. He looked at the Cherokee skulking around his father's estate for information. "Inside now, Chief Ridge. The news is grave."

Ridge sat motionless as John's words fell hard on him, each a stone piled upon his chest. The weight of his son's account left him too weak to breathe. The rhythmic squeal of Sehoya's loom fell silent.

"I didn't believe Sharp Knife was capable of such a thing," Ridge said. "I always thought if anything he would honor his country's laws."

"He's a chickensnake, Father," John said angrily. "He honors only what suits his whim. Our staunchest supporters in Washington are stunned by his position, and even they say our only choice is to remove."

Ridge's gaze fell to the oak slats of Sehoya's varnished floor. He slowly shook his head. "It's early yet," he said. "We should do nothing but wait."

"Early!" John said much more abruptly than Ridge believed appropriate. "I fear that it's far too late! Five hundred and fifty Georgia surveyors are loose in our country with their instruments, chains, and axes. They're carving up our land to dole out in a lottery as we speak! The crops our people plant will be harvested by worthless whites while we sit

watching in the rain. The Georgians will steal the land from us, and I heard from Jackson's own mouth that he won't lift a finger to stop them."

Ridge searched for the longer view. "Like it or not, John," he said calmly to defuse his son's antagonistic tone, "the deciding issue falls not upon the Cherokee, but upon the missionaries. Worcester and Butrick have won their case. I was told that if the Georgians won't release them, the courts must, even if it takes federal troops to make it happen."

John pursed his lips and shook his head. "I have it on good information that the missionaries will accept a pardon long before the deadlock comes to violence."

Ridge couldn't believe it. The clerics, knowing their defiance of the Georgian laws formed the crux of the Cherokee's hopes, had already spent two years in jail. Ridge admired their will, as did all the Cherokee, who had looked after their families. He couldn't understand why they couldn't wait a few months longer to make all their suffering worthwhile. He looked to Boudinot, closest friend to the imprisoned missionary, Worcester. "Would he do such a thing?"

"He will before he sees his country reduced to civil war, Uncle. As will our northern supporters in Congress. They see a pardon as the only dignified way out of this mess. Others are already whispering in Worcester's ears.

He'll see accepting a pardon as the lesser of two evils. And so will Butrick. Much pressure will fall on their shoulders to accept." Boudinot folded his hands. "And when they do, the matter is quietly settled."

Ridge slammed his fist down on the arm of his chair. "Why do the Americans consistently wiggle around their laws like cottonmouths in the swamp grass? Do they know how to look a man in the face and speak the truth?"

"Jackson does," John said. "He looked me in the eye and told me the Cherokee were doomed in the east. Now it's my unpleasant duty to come home to my mother's house and repeat it."

"So now we know," Ridge said. "Well enough." He looked at his son and nephew. "What do you suggest we do about it?"

John's gaze met Boudinot's. Ridge's nephew arched his eyebrows and his son drew a deep breath.

"Jackson says the terms for removal will never be better," John said.

"I'm aware of what Jackson says," Ridge said, his impatience returning. "My question is what do we do? Surely you've discussed this while you were holed up with John Ross, hiding from your people."

Again the cousins' eyes met. Why did they look as if they were conspiring? Ridge couldn't understand why his son failed to get to the point.

"All right," he said, clapping his hands together. "Let's start from the beginning. What do the lawyers say?"

"They say it's over," John dutifully replied. "There's nowhere else to appeal. Jackson's gutted the authority of the Supreme Court. It's never happened before."

"What does this mean?"

"It means we've got no choice but to submit to the laws of Georgia."

"That's disaster in the making. We'll lose everything."

"Unless we sell," John said. His tone was uncharacteristically sheepish.

"What?" Ridge said, cocking his head. "What was that you said?"

"I'm saying — and the lawyers and our politician friends are saying — that we should negotiate with Jackson and get out with as much as we can."

Ridge, smoldering, bit his lip. "That's absurd! We send you to Washington to fight for your people and you come home with this idea? Is this the best you can do?" Out of the corner of his eye, he saw Sehoya glaring at him. She stomped the loom's pedals to the floor and yanked the board to her chest.

"Can you discuss the matter with my son without humiliating him?" she said. Ridge recognized yet another warning. He held up his hand.

John dropped to his knees before him.

Ridge looked at the wood grain between his feet.

"Ridge," he pleaded, "it's over. Jackson will let the Georgians have their way with us. He assures me that the other states will follow suit. If there's anything we can both agree on it's that state rule will destroy us. It's our duty to go before the council and insist on removal. There's no other choice."

Ridge wrung his hands in anger and then slowly looked up at his son. "Let me understand you," he said in exasperation. "You would have me, a chief who has dedicated his life to preserving his nation — the man who enacted the Blood Law that made it a crime to do what you propose and once *killed* his own clansman to enforce it — go before his people and tell them that I was wrong? That having seen the light, I now advise that we must surrender our country? Is that what you're saying?"

"Do you think it was easy for me to come and tell you this?" John said.

"I think it was far too easy," Ridge snapped. "You blow with the wind."

"Again," Sehoya said, "you resort to personal attacks, Ridge. There's no point in being so ugly."

"I'm sorry," he said. "I didn't expect this."

"Nor did I," John said. "But here it is in front of us. The Creeks have capitulated to remove west, as have the Choctaw, Chickasaw, and Seminole. The Cherokee stand alone against the Americans, Father. They'll crush us."

"They have the treaties to trample first. Sharp Knife's our enemy. Where's the surprise in that? But he's only one man, and one man can't topple the Cherokee. Jackson has many enemies among his own people. Honest Americans can't possibly bear the shame of his deceit."

"They can if honoring the treaties means civil war," Boudinot said.

"Washington's name is on those papers! Will they dishonor his memory by destroying us?"

"Rest assured they will," John said, "if they will profit in the process." He put his hand against Ridge's cheek. "We can't survive here anymore. If we want to save our nation, we have to go."

Ridge knocked his hand away. "I won't hear talk like that in this house!" John withdrew to the fireplace and hung his head. Ridge hounded him, squaring off shoulder to shoulder.

"Who are you?" he asked his son. "What part of you is Ridge, and what part of you is the white world I sent you to conquer? What's left of my oldest son, my Cherokee champion? Who put these words in your mouth?"

Sehoya kicked her loom aside and ripped the apron from her waist. "Stop it, Ridge! I won't have you treat him like that!"

"I say only what I know is true," John said, eyes glistening from the beginning of tears.

"Maybe," Ridge said. "But who — red or white — controls your mind? I sent you to schools when I should've sent you to the woods with a blow-gun. I should've let the war chiefs rake the scars of honor on your body. I should've let you be what nature intended. Then I would know who you are."

"That's enough!" Sehoya said with fire in her eyes. "As a boy you sent him against my wishes to learn the ways of the whites. He's done all that was expected of him and more. He is what you said you wanted him to be. And now he tells you what he thinks and you reward him with insults!"

Ridge looked vacantly out the window. "I want to know," he said, "when my son speaks to himself in his own head, does he say 'John,' or 'Skah-tle-loh-skee'?"

John stood blankly, refusing to answer.

"It's important to me to know," Ridge repeated. "What do you call yourself?"

"You keep your mouth shut, Ridge," Sehoya said, "until you can speak without injuring my son! Don't you turn your back on me when I'm speaking to you! And don't even think about turning away from Skah-tle-loh-skee!" She pinched his chin and ratcheted his head around. "Look at him! Look at your son! Do you have any idea what it took for him to come and tell you this? Is there any wonder why he stayed away all these days before he came here? He's got courage to face you. I'm proud of the man he's become. But I'm ashamed of you!"

Ridge didn't know what to do once Sehoya let go of his chin. He reached for the pitcher to pour himself another cup of tea. Sehoya snatched it away from him and shattered it against the bricks of the fire place.

"Are you as ignorant as the rest, Ridge Walker? Your son spoke with Sharp Knife himself. Why do you shun him when he tells you what Jackson said? Would you make a boy of my son for speaking the truth?"

"Whose truth?" Ridge said. "I once fell under Jackson's sway. I killed many Creek for him. He wouldn't think twice about bending John's mind to kill Cherokee! Of course, we won't live to see it. John speaks one word of removal among our people and they'll bring your house down around us — and his!" He pointed at Boudinot. "And yours, as well!"

Ridge's head throbbed with rage. He repeatedly spread his fingers and clenched them into a fist. Sehoya held him at bay with her eyes.

"Can you calm yourself?" she asked. "Otherwise I want you out of this house."

"I'll try," he said. "I'm greatly disturbed."

"We're all disturbed," she said. "Let's take a few breaths and then put our heads to-

466

gether. You're not some hothead, and John and Elias aren't fools. This is terrible news. But we must all cool off and decide what we should do as a family."

Ridge pressed his fingers to both temples. "There's much to sort out," he said. He walked over to John and set his hand on his shoulder. "I'm sure you can understand my anger. I didn't mean to take it out on you."

"Why did you do it, 'Doda?" John asked.

"Why did I do what? And don't ' 'Doda' me. We're political adversaries at this point in our discussion."

"Ridge," Sehoya warned again. She shook her head.

"Why did you agree to fight the Creeks?"

"Why else but to save my people?" Ridge said. "That has been the sole reason I've done anything. There were two paths before us: Perish with the Red Sticks or ally with Jackson and live. It was an ugly business. At the time, I thought it was worth it to destroy the Red Sticks' homes to save ours. But I was wrong. Look where we are! Listen to what I'm hearing! Jackson's turned on us now and his first shot is fired by my own son."

"Stop your raving, old man," Sehoya said. "You know you did the right thing."

"Did I?" Ridge said. "I no longer think so. Better to have fought to the death with Tecumseh and the Red Sticks than to sit here helpless in this white man's house and watch my country whittled away by liars and cheats. Had I known that Jackson would betray us, I would've run him through with a Creek lance and been done with him."

"Father," John said, "another hard choice is before us. That's all we came here to tell you. The Cherokee did everything we could. We exceeded all the Americans' expectations. We beat them in their own courts. Jackson let us play the game only because he hoped we'd lose it. Now that we've won, things will only get uglier." His hands trembled as he reached for his water. "You and I both know what will happen once we fall under state rule. The only question that remains is do we accept it and stay here and face whatever comes, or remove to Arkansas and be free of it?"

"That's no choice."

John swallowed hard. "That is exactly the choice. Can we survive state rule?"

"No, I don't think so," Ridge said. "The whites will make beggars of us."

"You see, we agree after all," John said. "State jurisdiction will lead to the ruin of the Cherokee. Should we put our land above our people?"

"I never saw the two apart," Ridge said vacantly. "We belong to this place. If we leave it, we'll never be what we were."

John stood and dug his hands in his pockets. "If we don't," he said, "we'll be destroyed, one life at a time." He pointed out the window. "Look around us, Father. Do you not see the despair on our people's faces?"

"They took heart when the news came from Washington."

"As did I," John said. "False hopes, I'm afraid. The time has come to choose the lesser of two evils, Ridge Walker. We did not ask for these troubles. The whites built lie upon lie until they've walled us out of our own country. Let's move beyond the sound of their voices and begin again."

"You don't know what you ask," Ridge said. "The Cherokee will never go."

"They will when they understand that there won't be anything left of the Cherokee if they don't."

"Who could ever make them see that?"

John pressed his palms against his father's cheeks and stared into his eyes. "You, Chief Ridge," John said. "Only you."

"I can't if I don't believe it myself," Ridge said, breaking away. John dropped his head. Boudinot poked at the fire. Sehoya snorted.

"What man," he asked his wife, "spends an entire lifetime in pursuit of one thing and then in the course of an hour turns around to pursue the direct opposite?"

She wrapped her arm around her son. "The one with courage," she said.

"Understand me — both of you," Ridge said to his son and nephew. "I've heard what you said. No doubt John Ross is deliberating at this moment. And now so must I. My thought is go among them and hear their words with my own ears."

"Among who, Uncle?" Boudinot asked.

"The removal agents. The missionaries' lawyers. The secretary of war. Jackson himself, if I must. I've got to see their faces for myself, and then I'll know. Once that's done, we'll talk again. That's the best I can do for now."

"For now it's enough that you will consider it," John said.

He pointed his finger first at his son and then at Boudinot. "And while this thing is being done, speak not a word of removal to anyone. If this becomes our course, we'll promote it as chiefs must — in the open air of council for all to hear. In the meantime, maintain your affairs above all reproach. Tend to your families and your farms in silence." He opened the door. "Be gone now and leave me to my deliberations."

Once the two had left, Sehoya was unbearably silent. Ridge couldn't stand the squeak of her loom, especially since she was only working the contraption to annoy him. "What else would you have me do?" he shouted.

"I would have you love and respect your son regardless of his opinions."

"Neither is in question," he said.

"They're not?" Sehoya said. "He carries a terrible burden and you won't help him with

470

it. Instead, you treat him as if all of this is his fault."

"That's ridiculous! What do you know of politics?"

"I know that my son — the same sickly boy who went to school in the rain to please his idiot father — just got his heart ripped out. You shame yourself."

"Ah, that's enough for tonight." Ridge snorted, rising from his chair. He took a step toward the stairs that led to his bed. Sehoya slammed the entry hall door in his path. Ridge craned his neck to look down at her.

"I also know that there's no place in this house for you until you make amends."

"As you wish," he said. "I'll be out of here by dawn anyway." He stashed two blankets under his arm and lit a lantern.

"Who do you think you'll fool on this journey, Ridge Walker?" she said. "You already know John's right. The people will read the despair in your face. Just as I do now."

"They won't see my face," he said, shutting the door behind him.

For nearly a moon Ridge rode about the country, alone when he went to inquire of Cherokee about immigration to the west, with a trusted linkster when he knew he was to interrogate whites. He spoke to the immigration agents about the specifics of their terms. His journey took him to Washington

471

to speak to the secretary of war, Lewis Cass, about Jackson's position on removal and the mood in Congress. Last, he sought out Elisha Chester, attorney for the missionary Worcester, known to be an agent of Jackson. There was no man the Cherokee despised more. Would there be a pardon? Ridge asked. Soon enough, Chester predicted. The missionaries had written to the American board for advice on their situation, and Chester knew what the board would recommend in the face of an American civil war.

As for Jackson, Ridge had heard his thoughts from the lips of his own son. As Ridge began to stitch the information together he could no longer doubt that powerful forces were at work against the Cherokee. Nor could he deny John's opinion that their supporters' passion for their cause had cooled. Ridge saw the sorrow in their eyes as soon as they took his hand. He sensed their shame as they parted.

The Man Who Walks the Mountaintops spent much time alone in the hills, listening to the clear streams gurgle beneath him. Chester was a snake, but Ridge believed he spoke the truth when it suited him. The Supreme Court case would come to naught with the missionaries pardoned. Georgia, with Jackson's blessing, would have her way. It was a matter of time before Alabama enforced her laws on the portion of the

Cherokee Nation that lay within their limits. Tennessee was being pressured to follow the same course. According to all information available to him, state jurisdiction was inevitable, and Ridge knew well that no Indian nation had ever survived it.

Secretary Cass patiently explained the process. Were the Cherokee to stay, each head of family would be deeded 160 acres. Once that was done, the "excess" would be surrendered to the state and opened to white settlement. With the farmers would come the knights of green velvet, the grog shop owners, the land speculators, and the scoundrels. The Cherokee would drink, and when they drank they would become quarrelsome. Many would run afoul of the white laws, and the whites would use the opportunity to strip the ignorant of what little they had left. Ridge had little doubt that the Cherokee would sink to a level of shiftlessness and beggary just as the Catawbas had done.

And what of the other nations he'd known as a boy? What had become of the Susquehannock, Mattapony, Pamunkey, Nottoway, Chickahominy, Monacan, Saponis, Tutelos, Ocaneechis, and Massawomeck? For the life of him, Ridge didn't know where to find a single member of these proud and ancient tribes, but he knew the common link between all of their disappearances: One way or another they'd bent their knee to state rule and that was the last he'd heard of them.

Would Cherokee advancement protect his people? Ridge didn't think so. The hard truth was that civilization was a mixed-blood illusion. Four out of five Cherokee didn't know how to read or write. The full-bloods didn't understand the government that ruled them, let alone take part in it. Common Cherokee didn't own grand manses and estates and slaves to work them like the mixed-blood elite. The full-bloods wanted most of all to live in the old ways and be left alone, a simple luxury that would be denied them under state rule.

The communal lands — the hunting grounds and graveyards, the mountains and rivers — would be desecrated. Their government would be obliterated. Their villages ripped apart and overrun. The voices of their chiefs and headmen muffled by the bustling din of white life. Each Cherokee family would find themselves isolated in a world they did not understand. The Nation would disintegrate like a rotten stump. At dawn, with the cool running waters of the Conasauga swirling around him, he saw their future clearly.

He thought of the prophecy, already old when Waesa first told it to him as a boy. *The Ani-yonega will teach you his language and to read and write. These are but the means to destroy you, and to eject you from your habita-*

tions. He will point you to the west, but you will find no resting place there. But once your feet turn west, they are never to turn around again.

He rode north to the Hiwassee River, his boyhood home, and then east toward the Blue Mountains, to the ridges and valleys cut into an infant Turtle Island made only of mud by the tips of the Great Buzzard's wings. Where the spirits still whispered and the old religion still reigned. Full-bloods watched him pass in their turbans, hunting shirts, sashes, and buckskin leggings, soapstone pipes stuck between their lips. What would become of these people? he wondered. The Americans had never touched them. Jackson would as soon ask the pines and sacred junipers to move west as the mountain Cherokee. These uncontaminated Ani-yunwi-ya would never leave these coves and balds alive.

He rode on. Every place had a name, and every name had deep meaning. He came to Akwe Ti Yi, a pool between shoals on the Tuckasegee River, where legend claimed a dangerous water monster lived. Farther up-river, he came to Datle Yasta I, Where They Fell Down, the site where two large uktenas, horned serpents, had been locked in mortal combat, rising up in battle and crashing back to the surface, never to be seen again. Before dusk, he arrived at Gakati Yi, the Place of Setting Free, where Cherokee war parties had let a few of their captives go because they caught the favor of the clan mothers. The rest had met a captive's fate.

He rode on, camping at Atsi La Wa I, Fire's Relative, where the ancients had witnessed a fireball crash to the earth, destroying everything for two leagues around it. At dawn, he forded the Cheowa at Da Nawa Sa Tsunyi, War Crossing, where long before his time a party of Cherokee, hounded by Iroquois warriors, had crossed the river to safety. Nearby stood Yawa I, where a mysterious man, said to be a giant but of human form, haunted the hills. People heard the sound of thunder around him though there were no storm clouds in the sky. He always shouted "Ya wa! Ya wa!" though no one knew what it meant. The Cherokee were frightened to go near the place, though the hunting was said to be spectacular.

According to custom he set a stone atop the stack at Degal Gun Yi, Where They Are Piled Up, the site of an ancient battle on the south bank of the Cheowa River. Brave Cherokee warriors had lost their lives in this quiet place, and generations of their descendants left more rocks on the stack to pay tribute to their courage, a reminder that the people had not forgotten. He went to Skwan-Digu Gun Yi, Where the Spaniard Is in the Water, where angry Cherokee had ambushed one of the armored intruders and thrown him screaming his Christian curses into the Soco to drown. Ridge looked on in silence and remembered.

He skirted the mountain ridges around Valley Town and scaled Grandfather Mountain, one of the highest of the Blue Wall. There he wound his way through the sprawl of ash trees and pink-blossomed rhododendrons, plants the Cherokee admired for their shared traits. Both plants and people could wedge their roots between fissures in the mountain rocks and thrive. Ridge hiked the rocky crest, where he could see far into the distance in all directions. He spent three suns and three crisp sleeps bare to the wind with no food, fire, or water, meditating on what the Cherokee should do. He prayed for wisdom. And when wisdom came before dawn on the fourth sleep and he understood which of the two evils the Cherokee must choose, he prayed for strength. Ridge came down from the Grandfather, leaving the legends behind him, and rode home to ask Sehoya what she wanted to do.

The people stared at him as he passed by, but Ridge was so lost in thought and agony that he offered little in the way of talk. He let their warm hands slip from his grasp and rode on in silence. No one ever asked why he wore the black mask across his face. They looked at his eyes and wondered. He rode on.

He went first to Sehoya and their home on the Oostanaula.

"I've been a fool," he said.

"That you have," she said, draping her arms around him. "But as fools go you're the dearest."

He pulled back so that she could see his eyes. "We have no choice but to leave. The Americans will crush us if we don't."

"This is no longer news, husband," Sehoya said. "I'm already packing. But I want my son to hear our decision from his father's lips."

Ridge rode with Sehoya to John's home at Running Waters — two stories of white-washed pine siding, stout oak doors, six glass-paned windows, proud balcony, and gabled roof, all surrounded by a white picket fence, all blessed by the laughter of his grandchildren. For Ridge, the structure symbolized his son's pride, tangible proof that the Cherokee could live exactly as the whites.

John stood back with his arms crossed and his feet planted when he saw him, waiting to hear what he had to say. Ridge reached for him, and embraced him as he had not since the boy's time in Cornwall. Ridge rested his head on his son's shoulders. It was John's turn to hesitate.

"The path ahead is hard," Ridge whispered in his ear. He felt his son begin to squeeze him until their embrace made it difficult for

Ridge to breathe.

"Wherever you lead, 'Doda," John said, "I will follow."

Ridge smiled along with Sehoya. "That's good," he said. "Because I'm about to lead you into battle against John Ross."

"He'll listen to reason, just as you have."

"He will, in time," he said, thinking about how Ross had kept his distance from the Ridge clan, just as he had isolated all others who had strayed from his views. John Ross's pattern was undeniable by one who knew him so well. "But between now and then, we're in for one hell of a storm."

"That's enough for tonight," Sehoya said. "You'll wake the children."

Ridge took her hand and started for the door.

"I think of myself as Skah-tle-loh-skee," John said.

"What?" Ridge asked, turning back to his son.

"When I speak to myself, I use my Cherokee name. I am the warrior Skah-tle-loh-Skee, proud son of a great chief. I wanted you to know that."

"I knew," Ridge said, choking back his tears. "I always knew."

■ ■ ■ ■

BOOK FOUR:
BLOOD, SOIL,
AND WATER

■ ■ ■ ■

CHAPTER THIRTY-FOUR

Emotions simmered as the Cherokee crowded into the valley between two sets of hills that cradled the Red Clay council grounds. Ridge had begged the council to convene at the capital of New Echota so that the people could see the survey markings and the ax blazes on the trees and know that the Georgia lottery was in progress. The council, at John Ross's urging, had voted to meet beyond the reach of the Georgia Guard at Red Clay. For Ridge, it was the first of many disappointments.

Ross's position made no sense to Ridge. The principal chief understood their dire circumstances as well as he. Ridge had carefully cultivated John Ross, trying often to gain his ear and calmly discuss the facts as Ridge grasped them. Ross was gracious, but he bowed out of all conversations by insisting that the proper place to discuss politics would be at Red Clay.

Very well, Ridge thought. *We'll do it in public.*

When Ridge and his family and followers arrived at council ground to solidify a consensus, he found instead a copy of the letter written by a Georgia congressman posted on a tree for all to read:

The Cherokee delegation at Washington have at last consented to recommend to their people to make a treaty with the government of the United States upon the general basis that they shall acquire a patent for lands over the Mississippi.

Ridge calculated that the mass of Cherokee — at least those who could read — assumed from the letter that they had not gathered at Red Clay to discuss events in Washington, but rather were assembled to be warned that a once-trusted faction within their leadership conspired against them.

Ridge scratched his head. Ross seemed disposed to allow their people to believe that the dubious, unauthorized, and nonexistent treaty was about to be shoved down their throats. Ridge and his family arrived to the murmurs of treason and his confusion quickly gave way to bile. Seeing the Cherokee's disgusted reaction to the posted letter reminded Ridge of how Ross had broken McCoy and the Creek Chief McIntosh. Now he understood that the principal chief's game had begun.

"Welcome, Ridge," Ross said. "No mask today?"

Ridge laughed off the ridicule, but inside he bristled at his friend's abrupt tone. He thought less about bridging the gap between them and more about setting Ross in his place. "It served its purpose while I searched for an answer."

"I didn't require a mask to search for mine," he said.

"Yet you hid your face just the same," Ridge said. "The fact is neither one of us fooled the people. They know there's trouble in the air."

"That's what we're here to talk about."

Ridge ripped the Georgian's letter from the tree. "You pour mud in the water when the Cherokee are better served if the stream is clear." He wadded up the document and tossed it aside. "I'm prepared to tell the people what I know is true. Are you?"

"Oh, yes," Ross said. "I'll make my position quite clear."

"We had hoped for an open discussion of the facts," Boudinot interjected.

"The people will be told what they need to know," Ross said.

"That's fine," Boudinot said. "But I'd like to offer a more detailed account in the *Phoenix* about what transpired in Washington."

"The time has come for unity of sentiment and action for the good of all," John Ross said sharply, revealing the hardest edge that

Ridge had ever witnessed in the soft-spoken chief. "There'll be no discussion of removal in the Nation's paper."

Boudinot looked blankly at his uncle. "I'll resign," Boudinot said, "before I'll be dictated to in regards to editorial content. What is the *Phoenix* for if not to enlighten our people? You yourself once said that the paper was to be as free as the breeze that glides upon the surface. Have you altered your position?"

"There'll be no talk of removal in the *Phoenix*," Ross repeated. Then he fixed his stare upon Ridge. "And it was not I who altered his position."

"Sir," Boudinot said, "I cannot satisfy my own views and that of those in authority. I demand an open discussion of the full situation to facilitate, if possible, some definite and satisfactory conclusion while there's still time."

"With regret," Ross said, "your principal chief accepts your resignation, effective immediately."

Ridge reached for his nephew's arm to remind him that it was useless to butt heads with John Ross. Instead, Ridge's thoughts turned to breaking Ross's circle as he and his son had already discussed. "Let it go, Elias. It's time for national elections. The next principal chief will be more sympathetic with your views."

"There'll be no elections this year," Ross

said. "In view of the instability in the Nation over the Georgia matter, the council has decided to indefinitely maintain those already elected."

"What is this?" Ridge protested. White Path's warning came immediately to mind. "We have no voice? No elections?"

"It wasn't only me, Ridge," Ross said. This was the first time Ridge sensed any regret in Ross's voice. Prior to that, Ridge had heard only confidence. But Ridge knew that Ross wasn't really worried about how he would react to the news. His worry was reserved for the full-bloods who had grown to love their constituted laws. "The council agreed on this decision. I am bound, however reluctantly, to abide by their collective will."

"You've chosen to deny my son the chance to run against you," Ridge said, hearing his anger in his voice. "Your council is now a puppet that speaks with your tongue. Regardless, you overstep your bounds. I don't believe that in reaction to American oppression, the principal chief has the authority to oppress the Cherokee. Our people have a right to know what Jackson intends for us. I don't understand why you're doing this."

"My intent is what it's always been — to do what's necessary to save our land. What, my old friend, is yours?"

"I'll make that clear when I stand before the people, Tsan Usdi," Ridge said. "You'll let them hear me, won't you? Or has your council restricted that right, as well?"

"Do as you see fit, Ridge," Ross said. He looked coldly at John and Elias, but still managed a courteous nod. "I assure you I will." He buttoned his coat. "Now, if you'll excuse me, I have a council meeting to conduct."

Ridge steadied his family. "Easy," he said, patting John's breast pocket. "We have other news for him."

John Ross, through his customary linkster, welcomed the gathered crowd before he would allow Elisha Chester to speak.

"Sir," the principal chief said to Chester, "would you please present your credentials to this body before you address our people?"

"For what purpose?" the white lawyer said. "They know who I am."

"They know you were counsel for the missionaries, sir," Ross said. "Now you approach our people as an agent of the United States government. Your position, sir, strikes me as rather uncouth. We ask you to make it clear to all of us who you represent and why you're here."

Chester removed an envelope from the breast pocket of his frock coat and unfolded a letter, which he raised before the crowd. "In May of 1832, I was commissioned by Lewis Cass, secretary of war for the United States of America, as special agent to the Cherokee. The proposal I'm about to deliver is sanctioned by him."

Ross perused the letter and turned back to his people. "There you have it, my friends," he announced with squinting eyes. "The man who spoke for our beloved missionaries yesterday speaks for Jackson today. I suggest you listen carefully." Then he relinquished the floor.

"Your Great Father," Chester began, "the president of the United States, has recently been informed that a change of heart has probably taken place in the sentiments you have hitherto entertained on the subject of removal, and that propositions will be favorable."

The crowd rumbled. Dark eyes glared at the Washington delegates, falling at last upon Ridge.

"Shut your ears, I entreat you, to bad counsels," Chester continued. He raised his voice in response to the crowd's growing clamor. "Whatever may be told you, it's impossible for you to remain here. If you persist in the effort, the time of regret will come, I am afraid, after the most injury to yourself."

John rolled his eyes at his father at Chester's supplicant tone. Why, Ridge wondered, does the lion send a weasel to speak for him? The Cherokee hated Chester above all other whites. There could not have been a worse choice. Only John Ross smugly approved because Chester's selection played well into his hands.

Chester read through the seventeen provisions of Jackson's latest treaty despite the crowd's escalating din. He claimed that the Cherokee would be given land in the west forever without the boundaries of any state or territory.

"Forever?" Ross said, interrupting him. "For the Americans, I think that means five years at most."

"May I?" Chester said, his voice gruff.

Ross answered by rotating his hand around his wrist. "Please," he said. Chester pressed on. The People could expect complete self-government with the right to appoint their own agent in Washington to oversee their affairs. The Cherokee would be compensated for their losses and improvements. The expenses of removal would be paid by the government, while the process would be under the jurisdiction of the Cherokee. The United States would provide subsistence for one year after removal, with an annuity after that. Perhaps a few could remain, provided that they would accept citizenship and a limited headright of acreage. No sooner had Chester's voice died in the hills than the treaty was soundly rejected.

"We are astonished," Ross said, "that the president has heard that there's been a change of heart among us. As you can see yourself, he is in error."

Ross nodded to Cass that the Cherokee appreciated his time and efforts and rose to speak again. "There is better news," he said with a forced smile. "I have in my hand a letter from Elbert Herring, commissioner of Indian Affairs. It reads, *'I have pledged a military force to be sent to the assailed parts of your country for the purpose of expelling and peeping out intruders.'* This is a reversal of Jackson's indifference to our plight. The first sign in some time that our original treaty rights will prevail."

John Ridge stood. "Much has been made of the principal chief's letter, yet I tell you all that I heard different words out of Jackson's own mouth. Feeling that perhaps Mr. Herring had erred in some manner, I decided to correspond directly with Secretary Cass. In his response, Cass makes it quite clear that Mr. Herring's offer to expel intruders pertains only in states that have not yet extended their laws over the Cherokee, which means there will be no relief in Georgia. Mr. Ross deludes you if he leads you to believe otherwise." He sat down beside his father as the murmurs rose around them. Ridge patted him on the thigh to steady him.

"We see here the danger of two tongues talking for one head," John Ross said. "Mr. Ridge takes it upon himself to negotiate with

491

the War Department and succeeds only in influencing the secretary to modify a policy that would have benefited the Cherokee."

John shot up. "Nonsense," he said. "What part of this did I *negotiate* or *modify*? I simply asked Mr. Cass to clarify his position where it pertains to our nation. He has done so quite plainly, and yet you still manipulate the loose text of an earlier letter in the interest of generating false hopes. You grasp at straws, sir, and it's our hands that will come up empty."

John reached into his breast pocket and pulled out a second letter. "I have here a petition signed by twenty-five members of this council. We respectfully request that the principal chief explain his reasoning for pursuing his present course, which, in our view, assures the Cherokee everything they want to hear except a solution to our problems. Spell it out carefully, Mr. Ross — in your preferred language. Let your translator tell the Cherokee what you have in mind."

As soon as his son dropped back into his seat, Ridge snatched him by the sleeve and leaned close to his ear. "Take the spite out of your voice. That's the principal chief you're ridiculing in front of his people. John Ross, like us, is doing what he feels is best. His heart is good but also proud. Make an enemy of him, and he will make us an enemy of the Cherokee."

"He's a politician. He'll say what serves him best."

"If you want respect, my son, you must first give it to others. And passion has no place in council."

John nodded and reluctantly sat silent while Ross discreetly conferred with his friends.

"If you will allow your principal chief until the October meeting to answer the petition, when all of the People are gathered here and can understand, I will speak my mind freely. Let my friends the Ridges do likewise, and let us all promise to be governed afterward by our joined decision."

John whispered in his father's ear, "We should press him where he stands. The man is agile in open country."

"No," Ridge shot back. "He has other, more unsettling news. He's about to rob them of their elections. Let this gamble fester along with everything else until October." He put his hand on his son's shoulder and stood to speak.

"The petitioners see no reason why the principal chief should not be given the time he requires," he said. His voice was strong and clear to let John Ross know that he couldn't easily make a McCoy out of Ridge. "We assume, however, that in order to advise this body properly, he will agree to send forth an advance party to Arkansas to observe conditions there and report their findings to the Nation."

"So be it," Ross said, chagrined. He pulled the brim of his hat low over his brow to shade his face from the sun.

"Very well," Ridge said. "The petitioners believe wisdom will prevail in October. Now, is the principal chief aware that surveyors are busy in my home district laying out plots of our homes and farms to be auctioned off in Georgia's lottery?"

"Rest assured he is aware of the unlawful proceedings," Ross said. "Countermeasures are being discussed."

"Countermeasures?" Ridge said dryly. "Do you mean other than seeking justice in the American courts? If our delegates learned anything in Washington, it's that the white man's laws do not apply to us."

"I do mean other measures," Ross said.

"Such as?" Ridge said.

"We are in deliberations, Chief Ridge." He fumbled for the right words to continue. "To speak of them now would be premature."

Ridge was delighted that Ross could not provide the full-bloods with a single detail of how the Cherokee could thwart Jackson. He observed the questioning looks on their faces. Even John Ross did not have the answers.

"Very well," Ridge said. "We'll wait until October for the specifics. Perhaps the Georgians can be persuaded to postpone their lottery, as well."

John smiled. "You are the master, Ridge Walker," he whispered into his father's ear.

Ridge put his hand out to silence his son as he moved in for the kill. "Should we not conclude, then," he said, "with the business of the national elections?"

Ross squirmed at the podium. Stares that had been reserved for the Ridges turned his way. He daubed the sweat from his forehead with an already damp handkerchief before he answered.

"The representatives of several districts have advised your council that it would be unwise to provoke the state of Georgia by holding our elections this year. By reluctant agreement, your principal chief and council members will remain in office for another term with vacancies to be filled by appointment."

Ridge sensed the anger swelling in the astonished crowd. Ross's path would be no easier than Ridge's own. Suddenly Ridge was encouraged by the possibilities.

"For what period of time will the principal chief suspend our sacred constitution?" John asked.

"The principal chief did not personally suspend the constitution," Ross answered with a slight tug of his collar. "The entire council voted to do so."

"I have no doubt," John Ridge said. "But I wonder if the principal chief will tell us who initially proposed the measure?"

Ross swallowed hard. "I did."

"For what period of time, did you say?"

"Indefinitely."

"Pray tell our people," John said, "the difference between Georgia's oppression and yours?"

Ross ignored him. "I'm truly sorry to inform you of this measure," he said, stuffing the handkerchief in his breast pocket. "It was adopted with the sincerest hesitation with the best interests at heart."

"For whom?" someone asked, and Ross's stare fixed coldly on Ridge.

"For us all."

Ridge drew a deep breath and stood again. He raised his arms, pleading with the malcontents to be quiet. John Ross had carried out his threats, and he'd seen the faces of the people in reaction. Ross did not hold them as he thought he did. Ridge knew that the Cherokee Constitution, barely four years old, was precious to all Cherokee as a symbol of their enlightened abilities. At least, this was how it had been sold to White Path and the other full-blood malcontents. Even a principal chief as popular as John Ross would sooner stick his head in the fire than discard the constitution on a whim. To do so was a gamble that Ridge knew would favor him. Ross was as shaken as his people were angry, and Ridge had words for them all.

"The Man Who Walks the Mountaintops begs forbearance for our principal chief," he said in smooth, even tones as if he were singing. "Patience, my friends. The decision to suspend the elections was made for good reason — at least, that's what we're told. Let us abide by it in peace, at least until the October council. In a few months, we'll be called upon to decide whether to submit always to the evils and difficulties increasing around us each day, or look for a new home that promises freedom and national prosperity. That is the hard choice before us. And when that choice is made, the Ridge hopes we'll find the wisdom to bury animosity between us, to stay or go in the Cherokee character of true friends and brothers."

He looked toward the makeshift podium to see if he'd won John Ross's ear as he was winning the others. Ross wasn't there.

"Not too long ago," Ridge continued, "when we saw a future before us, the Cherokee were one. Take heart, my friends. For whatever comes, one we will be again."

Ridge felt hands upon him. He met his friends in embrace. In every ear, he whispered two words: *Patience, courage.* For his enemies, he had only a reserved though faintly confident smile. He plowed ahead for the podium to seek out John Ross. He wanted to speak with him as a friend instead of an adversary, to assure him that although they disagreed there remained blood between them all the way back to the Creek War.

Ridge regretted his militant reaction to these first public shots fired at him and his family. Ross had also erred by unsettling the full-bloods for no other reason than to silence Ridge. Both men were now scrambling to influence their people, and Ridge saw an opportunity opening in the confusion. If he acted swiftly, he could stitch up the fresh tear between Ridge and his principal chief before the entire fabric was ruined. All he had to do was talk to Ross now, when the principal chief had to wonder if he could really control the Cherokee Republic. Ridge tore through throngs of mingling Cherokee, but he could not find the black-suited mixed-blood among all the dark and troubled faces.

Then he heard hooves pounding on the hard clay. John Ross snapped the reins against his mount's shoulders, leaving behind him a group of his most loyal supporters. Ridge stepped forward. And when he did, their ranks closed. Ridge bowed his head. His best chance to repair the damage had just slipped away.

Sehoya, John, Elias, Watie, and the rest of his family worked their way toward him. Behind them walked a fuming White Path. Ridge welcomed them all with protective arms.

"Can you explain to me what that council

meeting was all about?" White Path said.

"Not yet," Ridge said. "And you won't hear it discussed in the *Phoenix* either. This summer my family and I will come to your Green Corn Dance. We'll explain our views on our problems at that time."

"Come with plain talk, my friend," White Path said. "Otherwise you waste our time."

"Say the same to John Ross when he comes among you also," Ridge said. "Ask him to tell you exactly what Jackson told him and what he plans to do about it. That is what we all need to know."

"None of us full-bloods understand what's happening between you and John Ross. We only know that we don't like it."

"I'm a full-blood," Sehoya said. "I don't like it either. But you know my husband will tell you the truth. And when he does, you must listen."

White Path clasped his hands together and ground one against the other as he sighed in exasperation. "Why did I not burn down New Echota when I had the chance? Now the Cherokee are ruled by a handful of men who won't talk to us."

"I'll talk to you," Ridge said. "This summer. And I wouldn't worry about leaving New Echota standing. The Georgians will burn it down for you."

He escorted his family from the council ground, loading them all into his carriage.

He looked at John and Elias. "Organize your personal affairs immediately," he said. "We'll all be out all summer long winning hearts."

He mounted the lead black horse in a team of four. He balanced himself to ride without a saddle, sat erect as a chief should, and prodded the beast with his heels. At the present time, Ridge saw his and John Ross's chances for swaying their people as roughly even. As persuasive speakers, however, Ross could not touch him. The wagon lurched forward, leaving Red Clay behind.

CHAPTER THIRTY-FIVE

They stood in the rain, waiting, allowing the fresh drops to wash the blood from their faces and chests. Reason and understanding had been banished along with the sun. Ridge stood quietly among his people, sick of the acrimony and weary of the weather, wondering why even the heavens had turned against the Cherokee.

The tension of the June council had escalated throughout the summer moons. There was neither quiet discussion in the *Phoenix* nor earnest debate among disputing tribal leaders. There was only the open wound left raw and seeping.

Ridge, along with his son and his nephew, spent most of the end of the fruit moon and most of the moon that followed talking face-to-face with their people, speaking wherever they could be heard, campaigning. A few listened in grim silence over the course of August and September. Most turned away, however, to cling desperately to the counsel of their principal chief, who was also out among them, reassuring them that regardless of what the Ridges and other malcontents preached, the land could — and would — be saved.

The widening rift between Ridge and Ross contaminated feasts, dances, and ball plays. Earnest discussion turned into passionate argument. Once the angry voices escalated into shouting, out came the knives and clubs. Half of the people waiting to hear John Ross speak at the fall National Council had blackened eyes, bloody noses, or an occasional stab wound in the back or chest. As always, whiskey had something to do with the violence, but frustration lay at its core.

It tore at Ridge's heart to see how the Cherokee spirit and determination, proven powerless against the American onslaught, had at last turned against its own kind. He had Jackson and the Americans to thank for that. The only issue that remained was if their leadership could put their differences aside and unite them.

The rains fell in sheets, muddying the Red Clay council grounds. Swollen rivers delayed the arrival of the principal chief. Once he had arrived, Ridge saw a confident glint in his eye that had been absent the summer past. Was it hope or delusion? Ross refused to speak under shelter, choosing instead to deliver his speech in the same rain that fell on his people.

Chester was there again, adamant on repeating the treaty provisions that had been rejected only four months before. His reception was even cooler than in June. Neither Ross nor any other Cherokee — Ridge included — wanted anything to do with this double-dealer. That business concluded, the Cherokee pushed closer to hear of their chief's crucial decision.

"I promised you an explanation of my position in May," Ross said through his linkster. His eyes searched for John Ridge. Once he found him, Ross politely nodded. "I'll keep my word. It's true that our resolutions forwarded to Secretary Cass have received no satisfactory answer. There is no guarantee from the United States that Cherokee rights will be protected in Georgia. This is grim news. But there is better on the horizon." John Ridge raked his toe in the mud, shaking his head in contempt. "Alabama's courts, on the other hand, have declared similar laws unconstitutional. Our land in that state will not be a matter of dispute as it has been in Georgia."

"Matter of dispute," John said to his father. "Before the month is out, the Georgia Guard and their lottery winners will evict us. The man dips bitter words in honey."

"Ssshhh," Ridge hissed. "Learn to listen more than you talk."

"Furthermore," Ross said, "President Jackson is up for reelection in his nation. Sharp Knife has many enemies. May we see them prevail."

The crowd cheered.

Ross threw up his hands, asking for quiet. "But regardless of who should occupy the White House for the next four years, they will be faced with our own delegation — sworn patriots all — who will insist that the United States honor their earlier promises to this Nation before we agree to make new ones. We stand on the word of their founders. Let them honor it before they ask more of the Cherokee."

Ridge heard war cries and turkey gobbles. The full-bloods were weighing in. Ross drew strength from their vigor. Ridge had never seen the reserved principal chief speak so charismatically. Though Ridge couldn't stomach what Ross said, he admired how he well he delivered it.

"We still have powerful friends in Washington," Ross said. "It's true that some of them have suggested that we consider removal to the west. We have done so. I've heard from many of you over these past months. I believe my heart understands the majority sentiment of the people I've sworn to represent. The Cherokee people have chosen their way. Their will is my compass. And let me assure you all that your principal chief stands *against* removal *at all costs*!"

This time the crowd erupted.

"Do you love your land?" Ross asked. The crowd roared in affirmation. "Then allow your principal chief to go on fighting for it! Right is on our side! American law is on our side! Most of the American people know that Jackson has wronged us and they will not return him to office! With your prayers and blessings, I assure you we will prevail in Washington!"

The people's response grew louder each time Ross paused. He held up his hands again and looked solidly at Ridge.

"To those of you who continue to speak in favor of removal," he said, "I ask you to listen to the power of your people's voice. You asked them a question and they have answered you. If you want to go west, do as you please with our blessing. But if you remain here among us, for the sake of unity you must yield to the majority view."

Ridge's gut burned. "What did you expect, Father?" John asked.

"It's not over yet," Ridge said. "You go and tell them what you told me. In front of John Ross, the chiefs, and the council, under the light of day. Speak the language of your heart and don't be afraid. They'll still listen to the truth."

John Ridge asked for the floor. Ross confidently bowed to him. John climbed the platform and stood in the rain just as John Ross had, speaking in the beautiful language of his people.

"Have no doubt that Jackson will be reelected," he said. "It's an accepted fact among our powerful friends in Washington — men John Ross himself has spoken to and then ignores. What service does he do us to say differently today? Everyone knows that in spite of the Supreme Court's decision, the American government has refused to put down Georgia's claim on our land. Forces are at work to persuade the missionaries still rotting in prison to accept a pardon. When they do, all hopes for an appeal and subsequent enforcement of the Supreme Court's authority over the states will die. Before the October moon has waned, the wheel of the Georgia lottery will turn just as Elisha Chester has explained the process to us, doling out Cherokee land to whites unfit to be our neighbors. We'll soon be dispossessed of our homes — mine among the first — in that country. This is what your principal chief should've told you."

It was so quiet Ridge could hear the rain fall. John caught his breath, draped his hands across his waist, and continued. "While it's certainly true that the Cherokee have powerful allies in Washington who have been with us from the beginning, all of them without exception have counseled that time has run out. Two years ago, the American Congress passed the Indian Removal Act by only one vote. For Jackson, that was enough. Our removal is not only the Americans' wish, it is recorded as American law. The Creek, the Chickasaw, the Seminole, and the Choctaw have all yielded before this injustice rather than see their nations destroyed by it. The Cherokee stand alone. And Jackson is coming."

John held up a drenched copy of the Cherokee newspaper. "This is what you should have read in the *Phoenix*," he said, "so that you would know the truth. Then our purpose here today standing in the rain at Red Clay — because we would be arrested by the Georgia Guard had we convened in New Echota — would be to put our heads together and decide what's best for the Cherokee Nation. Instead, your principal chief has censored your newspaper, silenced all public debate, canceled your elections, suspended your constitution. And, worst of all, closed his ears to the voices shouting at us in the east!" John paused at the perfect place to let all of this sink in. "Consider where your principal chief concentrates his considerable talents. Is he solving the problem or is he busy hiding it from you?"

Ridge stood erect, nose tilted skyward, coat buttons taut. John Ridge possessed his father's tongue. Ridge nodded in approval, urging him on.

"My people," he said, "the question before you is not, Do you love your land? We all do. The real question is, Do we keep the land only to lose it along with everything sacred to us, or give it up and save ourselves? I tell you Jackson is coming! Where will the Cherokee be when he does? Safely away with our western brothers beyond the reach of his lies, or under the heel of his soldiers' boots?"

He turned to Ross, whose linkster whispered the translation into his ear. Ross's eyes narrowed.

"Does the principal chief know our legends?" John said in English. "Is he familiar with our oral history?"

Ross waved him off with a flick of his wrist.

"If not, I'm sorry to put you on the spot," John said. "I forget sometimes that you are seven-eighths white and reared differently from all of us common folk."

Ridge's face fell into his hand. John Ridge could never keep from being John Ridge. He looked up sternly at his son, blinked, and shook his head.

John glanced at his father, heeded his warning, and spoke again in Cherokee. "Had the principal chief enjoyed the opportunity to sit among the old *adawehis,* as my mother insisted that I do, he would understand that our myths tell us that we did not originate in this place. We migrated from the frozen north

— sometimes because of blood feuds, sometimes for lack of game, sometimes to escape a harsh climate, or maybe because we had as a people grown too large for the land to support us. But always because we faced a difficult choice: to perish where we stood, or to take heart and travel to some place unknown and unseen with the hopes that we would thrive there. Many times we were threatened by forces greater than ourselves, and yet we have always survived." He turned back to John Ross. "Ask the old ones. They remember."

He faced the crowd. "And now you must all remember, too. The Cherokee made this land a home for our people. The land did not make the Cherokee. We've always gone where we *had* to go and always we've prospered. And now, through lies, treachery, and betrayal, we are faced with the very same decision our ancestors made time and time again before a white man had ever walked a crooked step on Turtle Island. What is best for the Cherokee? Should we stay or should we go?"

"What you say is true," said a voice in the crowd, "but our ancestors always refused to go west, to the land of disease and death."

"Cherokee have lived there for thirty winters, my friend," John said. "Do they not tell us that they're content? What other direction is there for the Cherokee to go? How far west must we travel before hope ends and doom begins? Take heart, as our proud ancestors did, and go in search of a new home where we can be free. There's still hope in the west. Here, my friends, we have none."

Ridge looked out at the astonished faces. It pleased him that his son had based his position on the sturdy roots of tradition and myth.

John turned to Ross and the seated members of both houses. "I move we honestly reconsider Mr. Chester's proposal and bring the matter to a vote. I move also that we elect a delegation to send to Washington to hammer out final negotiations."

"There's a motion on the floor," Ross said, usurping the podium with confidence. "Do we have a second?" There was. "The agent's terms of removal are all fresh in our memory. I see no reason to discuss them further. All in favor of Mr. Chester's proposals say aye."

"Aye," said Ridge, Stand Watie, Elias Boudinot, John Ridge, Oo-watie, and dozens of others, mostly mixed-bloods Ridge had persuaded over the course of the summer.

"Opposed?" Ross asked.

The nos boomed like thunder. Ross dropped his gavel on the soaked podium. "It should come as no surprise to all but our last speaker that this motion fails. Now to the matter of the Washington delegation. I nominate Joseph Vann, Richard Taylor, and John Baldridge to represent this nation, with the stated purpose of vigorously pursuing our treaty rights and rejecting all concepts of so-called removal."

"Seconded," Vann said, "providing that John Ross accept the nomination of chief counselor."

The measure was voted upon and adopted, and Ross adjourned the fall council with a Christian prayer. Dejected, John drifted back to his kinsmen, but the fight had not gone out of the Ridge. He stomped through the mud to find his friend, John Ross. And when he did, Ross greeted him graciously, taking his hand.

"Do you lead the people, Tsan Usdi?" Ridge asked him. "Or do the people lead you?"

"My old friend," Ross said, "how it pains me to hear my political mentor speak against me."

"I'm not against anyone. I'm for my people."

"If that's true, come with me to Washington and help us persuade Sharp Knife to honor his promises."

"I've heard his promises. And there's no doubt in my mind that he will definitely honor them."

"I fear you've been misguided, Ridge Walker," Ross said. "It's particularly difficult to reject bad counsel when it comes from someone close. My own brother, Andrew, has turned against me to scheme with your son."

511

"What scheme?" Ridge said, his gut twisting to see a mind that he knew so well close off to him. Once-warm eyes looked at him as if they were covered by a sheet of ice. "We have a difference of opinion on an important issue. All we've ever asked is that you consider our position."

"I've considered it day and night," Ross said.

"How can you say that you've considered my view when you've never talked to me about it?"

Ross looked down at his shoes. "I'm truly grieved that I can't have you stand next to me when we face Jackson."

Ridge sought the words he needed to turn things around. He lifted his hands and spread his fingers as if he were about to strangle his principal chief. The words did not come, and his hands collapsed to his side. "Do what you will in Washington," he said, unable to avoid the ring of failure in his voice. "But please don't close your mind to the thought of moving west. I can't reach you, but I still hope that wisdom will prevail among us. You want to walk apart from me because we don't agree. That's all right. I didn't come by my views easily. In fact, I fought the truth as you do now. But you'll see it soon enough. When you do, you and I will lead our people together to the west, where they will be free of the whites. I live to see that day, my friend."

"You and I won't live long enough to see that day, Ridge," Ross said.

"I may surprise you yet," Ridge said with a wink. He knew if he kept trying, he could break through Ross's shell.

"Rest assured that you have already surprised me," Ross said, yielding two steps to keep his distance. "Go if you want to, Ridge Walker. I wouldn't blame you. But I've sworn to protect the rights of my people, and they have a right to stay in these hills. I've seen and heard all that John Ridge knows. Between you and me, I know it's possible we may lose this land. But I can't abandon my people in the fight to keep it, not while I draw breath in my lungs."

"And while I draw air in mine," Ridge said, "I can't abandon them, either." Ross saw Ridge's change of heart as a capitulation, a character flaw. Ridge wanted him to understand that it was quite the opposite. "I won't leave them behind to waste away."

"So, in a way, we're of one mind, wouldn't you say?" Ross said with a cock of his head. He could taunt Ridge this way with victory close behind him.

"No, my friend," Ridge replied, again stepping closer, pointing nose to nose. "You value land above the people. I value the people above the land. There's a steep, wide valley between us."

"Sooner or later," Ross said, "one of us

must make the leap, no?"

"Or fall in the attempt," Ridge said. "The question is, how many of our people will fall with us?"

Ross dug his hands in his pockets and rotated to point his shoulder at Ridge's chest. "I'm glad we had a chance to speak, Ridge," he said. "Understand that there's no anger between us. We're both doing what we must."

"And my son?"

"He's a boil on my chin," Ross said tersely. "But I was young and passionate once. I remember when I and another young chief stood up against our elders and unified this nation." At last, the conversation had warmed. Ridge welcomed the change. "Those were good days, Ridge Walker," Ross said. "We knew what had to be done, and we acted on it."

"John Ridge is what we once were."

"The difference is we were right and he's dead wrong."

Ridge pursed his lips, hearing a politician judge his son's earnest convictions. Ross fished his watch out of his pocket and checked the time. Ridge looked up at the sun to do the same. Time had run out for them both today.

"He can say what he likes, Ridge," Ross said. "I'm not a violent man; you know that. As long as he keeps his place and submits to constituted authority, he'll have no trouble from me."

"That's just it," Ridge said. "We no longer have a constituted authority."

"I can't go down that road again with you, Ridge. I've got other people to see. Safe travel."

Ridge watched him walk through the rain to shake hands with his supporters. Hundreds of common Cherokee waited to greet him or just to touch the cloth of his drenched coat. How they loved and trusted him. There had been a time when the people equally revered the Ridge. After he'd spent his summer opening his heart to them, he drew only their derision. What had gone wrong? How had he alienated himself from his own kind?

Ridge's doubt crept up on him again as he walked alone in the rain. Ross stood firm where Ridge wavered. The people smelled his uncertainty like a dog smelled fear. Could he fault them for clinging to John Ross? He could not help but wonder if his son and cousin had convinced him to follow the right course. Intelligence was one thing, wisdom another. Was he certain that removal was the only way? Could Ross truly ride out the crisis and save the land? Ridge wasn't sure about anything anymore.

He felt like a man diminished. His joints ached on cold mornings. His war wounds nagged him. He was constantly battling a cold or a cough. Regardless of his exhaustion, he no longer slept well. He was up four times a night dribbling into the chamber pot. He couldn't remember things Sehoya had told him a few moments before. A few steps in the woods on a warm afternoon, and he was struggling for breath. Each day, he felt older and weaker than the day before, and he was no longer certain of how long he could keep up the fight he was losing to John Ross.

Clouds hung like specters in the valleys as Ridge walked his horse toward home. He said little to his son, his nephews, and the others who rode alongside him. He would've preferred to travel alone, but his family wouldn't have it. Already there was talk that some of the young hotheads in the Nation would try to take his life. How had it come to this?

The rain continued to fall as Ridge picked his way south from Red Clay to intercept the federal turnpike. The horses slipped and stumbled in the mud. Just before reaching the ford at Cooychutte Creek, Ridge rode upon an oak, ancient when he was a boy. He'd hunted squirrels in that tree with his blowgun. He'd napped in its shade listening to the breeze whisper through its mast. Since he'd passed the tree last, lightning had struck it and split its trunk in two. Both sides lay mangled directly apart from each other. Both would die. He dug his spurs into the horse's side and jumped over the split. He slowed the horse and rode on without looking back.

CHAPTER THIRTY-SIX

Sehoya

Have I been so quiet through all this that you
don't know my mind? Are you curious about
my response to leaving our ancestral home?
I'm sure you're aware that the bloodline runs
through my body, that my children belong
only to my clan, that house and hearth belong
to me. But what did this mean in my marriage to a civilized, mixed-blood Cherokee
chief? What was my part in his politics? Where
was my place in the new Cherokee Republic?

In all councils in our memory up until
Pathkiller's day, the clan mothers, the beloved
women, had the final say in all issues regard-
ing our tribe. When it came to my home and
family, so did I. While Ridge went to the
mountains, I considered my family's choices.
When he returned, Ridge asked for my blessing to emigrate west. I willingly gave it. Then,
and only then, was the decision made.

It's true that I've come to appreciate the

conveniences of civilized living. I love the comforts of the modern home we built. I have become skilled with the loom, but I prefer the feel of store-bought cloth, the look of finely dyed patterns. I own one of the first cast-iron stoves in the Nation. I no longer have to stoop over a fire all day. I cook our meals in a matched set of brass pots that were made in England, and I serve them on the most beautiful china. We eat with silver forks in our hands. I feel assured shopping in Ani-yonega stores with money in my purse, despite the whites looking down their noses at me. I don't think twice about using whatever Ani-yonega devices I think will make my life easier, but I've never been blinded by them. I own the things; they don't own me.

I'm glad that I sent my children to the mission schools. John's education served his father, but it served me just as well. My son explained what the Americans have in store for us and I don't like it any more than Ridge. Or John Ross. Or even White Path. The whites are taking our land and that disturbs me terribly. But they are taking something else, and that disturbs me more.

The Americans expected our leaders to treat our women as they treated theirs. The whites are ruled by men. Their women are powerless, possessions to be kept like blooded horses or fine dogs, to be flaunted in public and neglected in private. They live quietly in their houses like dolls. Our chiefs, knowing we deserved better, knowing that we had earned our place — knowing that we were born to be a part of guiding the Cherokee — are ashamed to relegate us to live in their shadows. But they wanted to please the whites to prove that the Cherokee were their equal, so they did it anyway.

On paper our leaders now say that Cherokee women are less than men. They passed laws that say women can't vote in our elections. We aren't allowed to hold office. We no longer own our homes. Our husbands hold sway over our children. The chiefs did this, they say, so that we could keep our land. But for Cherokee women, this price is too high.

What does this land mean if I have to surrender my pride to keep it? Like my husband, I feel that our culture is more important than these hills. I want my only surviving daughter to respect me. I want her to believe that women can accomplish something in the world. I want to walk tall for my granddaughters so they will know that Cherokee women have power, too. So when my husband asked for my blessing to emigrate, I gave it without hesitation.

I wanted to go where I could be the Cherokee woman my mother had been.

My husband displayed a brave face in public after his humiliation at the Red Clay council in the fall of 1832. But I've noticed how the light in his eyes has dimmed these past two years. I think his heart began to grow empty.

Our life together had always been difficult. But in the past, the Ridge Walker could rise above his worries to visit with his friends and play with our grandchildren. For all his worldly cares, he maintained a passion for life. It was the quality I loved most about him. Regardless of the tragedies that marked his early years, his political disappointments, the deaths of our young children — especially the loss of our eldest daughter Nancy, who died suddenly last year in childbirth — Ridge was by nature a happy man. I fear that has changed. My husband has become a shadow in his own home.

Not too long after the Red Clay council, I found myself standing beside Ridge in a long line of our people. They were mixed-bloods, mostly, for my son, John, had long been a hero among them. I suppose they saw him as a model of the civilized Indian, but I think they also admired him because he had met the whites on equal ground and bested them. My son was one of the few Indians who was not intimidated by the Americans. John moved easily in a world that most Cherokee could only imagine, and no one of my generation — myself included — knew what to make of him. He was our paper warrior and I was proud to be his etsi, his mama.

Once Ridge publicly supported John's position on removal, these lines grew longer, if only a body or two at a time. As a chief, my husband was waved to the front.

"I'm in no hurry, my young brothers," he told them. "I can wait my turn." So we stood there with my brother-in-law, Oo-watie, who these days went by his Christian name of David, his sons, my nephews, Stand, and sweet Elias Boudinot. We made small talk while we waited, although my husband said little. We were, after all, attending to a grim and unpleasant business.

Our names were called at last, and we entered the office. There were three bookish white men — they always appeared pale and sickly to me — waiting at a round pine table, the agent and his two clerks. Our son John sat with them, shuffling through stacks of talking leaves that only he could understand. I was offered a chair next to him. Ridge, as was his custom, preferred to stand.

I marveled at the way my son's intense, dark eyes absorbed the words on the page. He explained the meaning of the American terms in our own language. John was fluent in Creek and English, among other strange languages he described as dead, but he spoke Cherokee beautifully, with his father's passion. The eloquence and tone of his voice, however, were all his. I listened quietly as John explained the details of our agreement.

What we were allowed to take with us, what we would receive for the things we must leave behind. The agents fixed a dollar amount for our home, barns, sheds, smokehouse, corn cribs, and everything else.

Ridge was somewhat shocked at the figure allotted for our ferry. It was worth thrice that, he said, and John translated Ridge's protest to the agent, who nodded his head, scratched out the figures with his quill and ink, and put down new ones. I felt better having a lawyer in the family. We knew the terms would be generous, mostly because both the governments of Georgia and the United States were encouraged by the prospect of a Cherokee chief of the Ridge's stature standing in this room. Most Cherokee would sooner lop off a foot than set it inside this place.

I knew we had received other courtesies. Our estate had been pulled from the lottery. Others had not been so lucky, including John Ross, who had returned home from one of his Washington trips to find that an American who described himself as a "fortunate drawer" had taken possession of his property at Head of Coosa not too far from us. His wife, my dear friend Quatie, had been relinquished with all of her children into two cramped rooms of her home. The fact that she was terribly ill made no difference to the fortunate drawer. He demanded the home, the buildings, the ferry, all the livestock —

including Ross's prized flock of starbirds, his peacocks — and even took possession of the horse Ross had ridden home. Our principal chief had little choice but to borrow a wagon and haul his family across the Tennessee line to a log cabin near Red Clay.

Many others were similarly dispossessed of their homes and fields, flocking to our northern country to squat where they could. White families replaced red and set about the business of working their fields and livestock as if it were part of God's plan. I can't describe our people's shock and misery, and I felt guilty that we had been spared their fate because of my husband's change of heart on removal.

"Should we not go with them?" I asked Ridge. "It's wrong that the Georgians treat us differently."

"Our fate is the same as the others," Ridge said. "And when our time comes, we are going much farther than Tennessee."

"It doesn't seem right."

"Set your mind to the notion that nothing will ever seem right again," he said. "Ross was warned that the lottery was in motion. So were the rest. Now the people know we told them the truth. As hard as it is, they have to understand that John Ross can't protect them. And neither can I."

When at last John had translated the documents for us, Ridge asked where he should make his mark. John tapped the page with a slender finger, and Ridge penned an X, shook hands with the agents, and hugged our son. I could tell that my husband was anxious to leave that place, though John chose to stay behind and translate for the others. We stepped outside, where our people were waiting.

"What I've just done should convey my optimism for Mr. Ross's visit to Washington," he told them. "Listen to my son carefully. Ask plenty of questions. Understand every term of the agreement; look hard at every sum offered. Make the best arrangement you can. It's my view that the Americans will become less generous with time."

He took a moment to take each hand of the few who still believed in him and bade them farewell. I turned to look back at the office, noticing the American words on the sign.

"What does that say?" I asked Elias, who was escorting us to our carriage.

"It says Emigration Agent — Department of Indian Affairs."

"Oh," I said. "Of course."

My husband opened the door, wrapping me in a blanket to shake off the chill. He seldom liked to ride inside of the carriage when he wasn't around white people. He'd tie his horse behind it and mount the lead horse on the team, a habit, I suppose, from his warpath days, when the strongest led the way. The servants sat beside me, sharing my blanket. As we were leaving we encountered a group of Cherokee. They gathered around my husband, holding his hand, grasping his ankle, touching the cloth of his coat.

"You must go to Washington," they said. "Let Jackson know that you are not the only one."

"I was not appointed by our leaders," he said. "It's no longer my place."

"You are our leader, Ridge Walker," they said. "We trust you to do what's best. So many of our friends and relatives cling to Ross. You must go to Washington and persuade him that we must all remove together."

Ridge lowered his head and closed his eyes. I could tell he was considering what he should do. At last, he lifted his head and pressed his lips into a smile.

"Let me think on it," he said, and flipped the reins. The team stepped forward on the soft ground. In the distance I saw Ross's men. They were always there, sitting quietly where the woods ended and the fields began, cloaked in dark blankets up to their eyes, lurking. They said and did nothing, but they threatened us with their presence.

I don't believe John Ross had any inkling that his supporters stalked us. Ross was not the kind of man to rely on violence to get his point across. These men harassed us on their own. Ridge paid them no mind, just as he did whenever he saw them at the fringe of the wood near our house. At first, he would walk out to speak to them, to ask them their purpose. But before he'd taken more than a few steps toward them, they vanished into the depths of the woods. These watchers always frightened me. But they served only to anger my husband and strengthen his resolve.

Of course, John and Elias did go to Washington. John was still a member of the National Council. No one talked to him, but he was still a member. I suppose as a token of compromise, John Ross had asked him to sit as chairman of the select committee to draft a report of what the deputation intended to accomplish. John wrote that this group was a "delegation in whose wisdom and integrity we can confide to carry the subject of a treaty before the legislative branch of the general government, and if possible to draw from it a favorable resolution for the relief of our afflicted Nation." Ross scratched out the words *a treaty* and replaced them with *our difficulties.* This report appeared as Ross wanted in the November 23, 1833, issue of our *Phoenix.* I used that edition for kindling.

Naturally, John had every intention of seeking treaty terms for our removal, but Ross had held out his hand to him, and for the sake of unity and owing to the fact that Ross had once been one of his father's closest friends, he went along with the watered-down language. My husband continued to hope that Ross would see that the Cherokee had no chance of remaining in the east. He urged our son to be patient and make every effort to keep peace with our principal chief. I love my son dearly, but patience was never one of his virtues.

When Ross asked for every member of the council to sign a power of attorney, John was no longer in a compromising mood. He felt Ross would use the document to mislead the Americans into believing that the delegation possessed the powers to treat, when in fact that right belonged only to the council. Ross acknowledged that this was true, but the power of attorney was, in his opinion, necessary for earnest talks with Jackson. In the end, every member of both Cherokee houses signed it, save John Ridge.

The bickering thus began before the delegation ever set foot outside the Nation. They went on to Washington. Things soon grew worse.

First came the omens. In the middle of Na Da'Na'Egwa, the big trading moon of November, the stars began to tumble out of the sky. I was awakened in the dead of the night to hundreds of meteors slashing violently through the darkness. By daybreak, the shower had intensified such that the entire horizon was engulfed in flames the color of blood. I had seen nothing so terrifying since the New Madrid earthquakes in Tecumseh's time.

I saw true fear on Ridge's face for the first time during the meteor showers. He stepped out trembling into the fields around our house, threw back his head and stretched out his arms, and recited the conjurer's incantations of our youth.

"Have the atsil-tluntu'si, the fire-panthers, severed the stone cords?" he screamed to the heavens, referring to our myth that the world is an island suspended by four rock pillars. "Are we to sink back into the depths of nothingness from whence we came?"

"Ridge!" I yelled. "Stop that racket and come inside for your breakfast."

"Would you sit at our table and eat from our English china when the end of the world is at hand?"

"I would if I had a husband who had a brain in his head," I said, hoping to distract him from his despair. But I wasn't at all convinced that the end time was not upon us. To see the heavens ablaze unnerved me, as it did every Cherokee I knew who laid eyes on it.

"Go and see the missionaries if it will console you," I said, thinking that I would go, too.

"What can men do," he answered, "when

the stars crash from the heavens?"

There was nothing to do but leave him to his screaming until it was over or the veins burst in his head. I was sure it would be one or the other.

The shouting ceased when the sun rose. Daylight banished the shooting stars and their trails of fire from the heavens. When I checked on Ridge again, he was sitting cross-legged out there alone, watching the sky. He stayed that way for hours. Around noon he climbed to his feet and strolled back to the house as if nothing had happened.

"Is there nothing to eat in this house?" he asked. I should've dusted off his old war club and rapped him on the head.

"What? Will the last day find you eating at an Ani-yonega table?"

"I'm the first to admit that I overreacted," he said. "It was a sign, nothing more."

"A sign of what?" I asked him, almost afraid of his answer. Ridge was a slave to his superstitions.

"For me to go to Washington and convince John Ross that we don't have much time left. He must have seen this awful display."

"What makes you think he'll pay any attention to a meteor shower? Unlike you, he's an educated, reasonable man."

"Why, Sehoya," he said, "what do you find about me that's unreasonable?" I scoffed, and it delighted him. I saw some of the old glow in his eyes. I found much comfort in the renewal of his spirit, even if it stemmed from ignorance and superstition.

"You have to admit, Sehoya," he said, "things looked bad there for a while."

"If you want to persuade anyone of anything, Chief Ridge, I'd suggest you forget about the meteor shower and thank God that I'm the only one who heard you make such a fool of yourself." I buttered another slice of bean bread and flipped it onto his empty plate. Nothing works up an appetite like terror. "How soon will you go?"

"As soon as I see the sun rise another day. I'd just like to make certain."

"Uh," I groaned. I knew then that my husband would always be what he was. No matter how far he reached, no matter how strongly he propelled our people to grasp new ways and new I worlds, he could never convince himself to let go of our culture and traditions. He wore clothes in the American fashion, lived in an American-style house, and had a head for American business, raising cotton and indigo to sell to their factories in the north. But deep in the marrow of his sturdy bones, he would always be Cherokee.

And though I was a Christian impatient with conjury and even questioning heathen myth, I don't think there was a day when I loved Ridge more, not even that time some forty-five winters distant, when an orphan knocked on my parents' door wearing worn moccasins, a stained hand-me-down calico hunting shirt, and a boy's grin, and asked their blessing to tie his blanket with mine. From that day on I would have followed him anywhere, and if the Cherokee had known the warmth of his heart as I did — understood how deeply he loved them — they would have gone west without question.

Ridge went on to Washington, leaving much gossip behind him. In the end, there were no fewer than three Cherokee delegations meeting with President Jackson: Ross and his "Nationalists," my husband and his supporters, and another led by John West, John Walker, Jr., and John Ross's brother Andrew, who seemed determined to sign a treaty at all costs. Chief Ross had thorns in his side much closer to him than the Ridge family.

I heard the whole story from my husband's mouth. Jackson made it clear that he would talk about nothing but removal with John Ross. Such being the case, Ross saw little choice but to open the door to tentative discussions. He inquired, assuming the Cherokee would cede a portion of their lands, whether the federal government would offer them protection on what remained. Jackson said no. What if the Cherokee accepted United States citizenship? No. Ross then pursued a course that would allow the Cherokee to remain in the east, accept state jurisdiction, and, at some point, merge their culture with that of the whites. How could Jackson dispute this intention?

But my husband could.

"If this is your solution," Ridge told him, "say as much before the people. Let them clearly understand what you intend for them, and see how tightly you hold them then."

"If Jackson can't promise us protection in the east," Ross argued, "how can he guarantee our safety in the west? Even if we remove to Arkansas, our problems will follow us. I assure you the Americans will come knocking again. Best to stand our ground on principle and legal rights and settle the issue once and for all."

"You and I once dreamed of a nation, John Ross. Don't abandon that hope now."

"If we can't be a nation here," Ross said, "we can't be a nation anywhere. Not within the boundaries of the United States."

"They'll rip us apart," Ridge said.

"Haven't they done that already?" Ross said, and that was the end of their private discussions.

Ross went back and forth with Jackson and his War Department, all to no avail. He entertained notions of removing beyond the American borders to Mexico or the Oregon country, but my husband assured me these measures were pursued out of Ross's desperation.

The solar eclipse of December 1834 not only sent the people reeling again, but also the beasts of the woods and fields. Whitetails stood out in the open as if the Cherokee could explain to them what had happened to the sun. Screaming horses tore loose from their tethers. Dogs howled inconsolably or skulked beneath their masters' feet for assurance. No Cherokee could give it. For an eclipse on the heels of the most fantastic meteor shower they'd ever seen was too much, too soon. The missionaries wore out their black brogan shoes hustling from one house to the next, consoling distraught Cherokee. Witches did a brisk business, too.

The delegations pressed on. Of course, Jackson treated Andrew Ross's adherents more kindly than the others because they were saying the words Jackson wanted to hear. Andrew Ross was prepared to sign a treaty immediately, but even Jackson advised him to return with more prestigious chiefs so that the agreement had a chance to be ratified. Young Ross convinced my husband to return with him, but as soon as Ridge and Elias Boudinot understood the terms of the agreement, they immediately saw it as Jackson's document. They wanted nothing to do with it. My husband stood in the middle of extremes, with no common ground.

Andrew Ross and young John Walker signed this treaty, ceding all of the Cherokee land in the east. Even the American senate could not take it seriously. When news of his affairs reached the nation, the Cherokee erupted with rage.

After two years of shouting at each other, Ridge and Chief Ross both returned home empty-handed. Ridge, weary of the whole affair, kept to himself. At night, he sat out alone and watched the stars, wondering if they would crash to the earth again, leaving us all to sink into the depths of the eternal ocean.

Word was that John Ross planned to make quick use of his brother's treaty to tarnish the names of all those in opposition to his cause. As the most prestigious Cherokee chief to advocate removal, Ridge became Ross's most formidable adversary, and as such, his primary target. The principal chief threatened to publicly read Andrew Ross and John Walker's agreement to the people at the summer council at Red Clay, the implication being that those who favored removal also favored these ridiculous terms. Of course, Ridge Walker had washed his hands of this disgrace while he was in Washington, but when he arrived home he was stunned to discover that he bore the blame.

To see his people turn against him so violently crushed him. That day, I saw the dimming lights in his eyes snuffed out completely. Most days he couldn't summon the strength to get out of bed. And when he finally did, he refused to leave the house. He wouldn't go to water for his devotions. He hid from his friends. He wouldn't eat anything. His health was failing. His spirit was dying. And I, Sehoya, the person who loved him most in this world, prayed to two different gods to tell me how to help him. Both religions failed me.

This morning a runner brought news to my husband that the council had called him to defend himself for his conduct in Washington. Once again, his name was connected with Andrew Ross and John Walker's treaty. I took him the letter and read it to him in his bed. He rolled over and snatched it from my hand as if he could read it. Then he wadded it up and threw it on the coals to smolder.

He threw back the covers and hopped around the room trying to get his legs through his trousers. "Have the slaves —"

"The servants?" I corrected him. It wasn't right to own an other human being.

"Yes, yes," he snapped. "Have the goddamned servants saddle my horse. The council will hear my defense, and more."

I knew then that the fight had not yet gone out of him. "That's the man who fathered my children," I said.

"Send a note back with the runner, Sehoya," he said, slipping his bare feet into his boots. He hated socks. "Let the council know that a chief is coming." He paused and stared at me. Then he squeezed my cheeks between his hands and pecked me on the lips. "You do understand that I paid money for the Negroes, don't you?"

I started to answer him when he corrected himself. "Well, some I won as spoils of war and some, I'm ashamed to say, were just stolen." He winked. "I was young once."

"It doesn't matter to me if you paid money for them or not," I said. "We do not own them, husband. They're a part of our family because the whites robbed them of their own. To treat them like lesser people only justifies the way the whites treat us. Our Christian duty is to help them until they adjust to the world, just as the missionaries helped us."

"You're quite right, darling," he said. "Until that time, would you mind, if one of them adjusted my saddle upon my fastest horse? I've got a terrible argument waiting for me in Red Clay."

CHAPTER THIRTY-SEVEN

Having read his brother's treaty to his people, John Ross brushed the pages aside. Ridge knew there was an omission on Ross's part — the subject of his own negotiations to submit to state authority or emigrate beyond American borders in Mexico and Oregon. But that was John Ross. The mass of people on hand to bear witness raged and ranted, but Ridge smoldered beneath his frock coat and cotton ruffles at the principal chief's duplicity.

Tom Foreman, a sheriff in the Nation, was the first to gain access to the floor. "Had I known Ridge said one thing during the day and did another under cover of darkness," he said, "I'd never have voted for him. He walks among us in good boots and fine clothing. His land is fertile. He has fifty slaves to work it while he rests in the shade. Why is he not content with his own riches? Why must he seek to suck more from the veins of our country?"

Angry murmurs swept across the crowd like an ill wind. Ridge listened, stifling his indignation. When he heard one warrior say, "Let's kill him!" he instinctively reached for his pistol. But before any could move against him, his son scrambled to the podium.

"Where is Ridge's signature on this treaty? Show it to me!" John Ridge's finger shot out to the crowd. "Show it to them!"

Everything went still while the clerk studied the document. "Ridge's mark does not appear," he said as if it disappointed him.

John glared at the angry warriors. "Ridge's mark does not appear on this sham because he had nothing to do with it! Why do you threaten his life? Is it a crime now for a man to speak his mind?"

John glanced angrily at Ross and then turned again to the People. "How did the Ridge betray you? He sees the Cherokee on the precipice of ruin, ready to tumble down, and he told you so. Did he speak the truth or not when he warned you that the Georgians would take your land?"

The crowd grew silent.

"Let every man here look to our circumstances and judge for himself," he continued. "Is a man to be denounced for his opinions? If a man saw a storm cloud charged with rain, hail, and lightning, is he to be scorned for warning his neighbors? Would you take his life?"

John paused to measure the Ani-yunwi-ya's mood. Ridge moved slowly through the restless crowd. A few Cherokee touched him out of respect, but most stood their ground with their arms by their sides, glaring at him as he passed by in silence. When he came to a belligerent warrior who squared off with him, Ridge bowed his head and tried to slide around him without a word. The warrior cursed him and Ridge said nothing. Then he tore the pockets of Ridge's coat, and Ridge, standing with open arms, let him vent his anger until another Cherokee grabbed the warrior's hand and motioned for Ridge to walk on. As he neared the podium, his son stepped aside.

"May the Ridge speak?" he asked the secretary while he smoothed his torn coat.

"You are recognized," he said.

Ridge struggled for breath after the short climb to the podium. He closed his eyes to compose himself, and then slowly he reopened them to see faces he no longer recognized. "The sun of my existence sinks low," he began. "I have only a short time to live. I'm still a chief among you, but I no longer hope for honors in my declining years."

He inhaled deeply while he sought out the man who impugned him. When he found the sheriff, he fixed him with his stare.

"It may be that Tom Foreman has better

expectations for himself," Ridge said. "He hopes that by slandering me he may establish fame among you. If he succeeds, I have little doubt that it will be short-lived."

He lifted his gaze to the middle of the crowd, where he could not discern a single face. What he had to say was for a dying Nation.

"The destruction of the Cherokee is at hand!" he shouted. "You have no government! You have no laws! The seats of your judges have been overturned! The tongue of the *Phoenix* has been stilled. It was once a forum for many wise opinions." He looked over his shoulder at John Ross. "It is now the voice of one man."

He turned back to the crowd, his hands draped across his waist. "In my time, the councils were long," he said. "Every man and every clan mother spoke the language of their hearts, and we listened respectfully without interruption. Once everyone had given their opinions, the wisest and most experienced among us — the ones we *elected* to lead us — deliberated until they could see clearly the path before us. And then they chose. It was our way until just a few winters ago. Today, after I have conducted my affairs in the open air of this council, after I have given you an opinion based on everything I've seen and heard — often from the mouths of our persecutors themselves — I am threatened with murder. What is left of my warrior's heart beckons me to pull out my weapons and strike back. But in my soul I know only sadness. I ask myself, What has happened to my beloved people? Where are the Cherokee of my youth? I don't see them before me. I don't hear them anymore."

He glanced over his shoulder to regard John Ross and his council, hoping to see a trace of shame in their faces. It wasn't there. Ross sat calmly with his hands in his lap, allowing Ridge to speak only because he hoped that Ridge would hang himself with his own words. Ridge looked upon the angry faces of his people. Their ears were closed. Their hearts were frozen.

"I see how you gawk at me," he said, hope leaking out of him with every breath. "I hear your laughter. When harsh words are uttered by men who know better, I feel nothing but the deepest sorrow. I stand on the graves of my ancestors and beg them to forgive me for not leading you as well as I was led. As for you, the living, I mourn your calamity. Do what you will to me. I'm too old and heartbroken to raise my hand in anger against those who slander me. Follow them into oblivion if you choose." Ridge sank back from the podium and collapsed into a chair next to his son. Elijah Hicks, new editor of the *Phoenix,* swept in behind him. Ridge's lip curled at his appearance. He knew what to expect from John Ross's brother-in-law and political lackey.

"I have in my hand a petition," Hicks said, "signed by one hundred and forty-four Cherokee in six districts, requesting that the Ridges be impeached for maintaining opinions contrary to the majority view, and advancing a policy to terminate the existence of the Cherokee community in the land of their fathers. I open the floor to discussion."

Ridge shot up. "What discussion? Who would dare speak one word against the principal chief's tyranny in the face of such a petition? Madness! Why discuss anything anymore? Set us aside and be done with it!"

Now it was John's turn to control his father. "The battle is not over," he said in his father's ear.

"But the war is already lost," Ridge said.

"Those in favor of the petition," Elijah Hicks said, "vote aye."

"Aye," Ridge said. So many others shouted that he could not hear the sound of his own voice. Ridge shot up from his seat and walked to where John Ross was sitting. It didn't matter to Ridge if Ross's allies overheard him tell his principal chief that a great leader didn't drive his herd from the rear. Ross leaned back in his chair, legs straight, his hands deep in his pockets, waiting confidently for Ridge to say whatever he pleased. A rider galloped in on a lathered horse, leaped off, and ran breathlessly before the council.

"John Walker, Jr., has been murdered on the roads from Red Clay! A copy of his treaty smeared in his own blood lay at his feet."

"Aaahhh," Ross groaned. Ridge could see that the principal chief seemed earnestly disturbed. "Not good," Ross said. "Not good at all."

"At least you won't require a petition to silence him," Ridge said, unaffected by Ross's performance. "Your brother signed that treaty. Will you have him killed, as well?"

"I had no knowledge of this offense, Ridge," Ross said. It was the first occasion Ridge had seen the principal chief react in anger.

"You made an enemy out of anyone who disagrees with you," Ridge said. "Maybe you didn't order this thing, but you put the knife in the killer's hand and pointed at Walker."

"I resent the very implication," Ross said. Ridge enjoyed seeing the spark of anger and uncertainty in his chief's eye. His actions had started this fire, and now even Ross worried whether he could control it. "Walker dug his own grave," Ross said. "His conduct rendered him subject to arrest and sent to trial by laws you and I enacted some ten years ago. Some misguided Cherokee has robbed him of due process, of course, but everyone knows he was guilty of treason, and you know well the penalty for that."

"To turn a blind eye to murder is to encourage it."

"As you've no doubt observed," Ross said, scrambling for composure, "the mood of our people is ugly. Walker was unwise to provoke them. Nevertheless his unfortunate demise should serve as an example to others similarly inclined."

"I had nothing to do with Walker's treaty, as you damn well know," Ridge said, seething. "His murder is merely an example of how poorly you influence our people, and how badly they are in need of true leadership."

Ross bristled. "Do you have any idea how it pains me to hear you say things like that? To this day, despite all that's happened between us, I would have you stand beside me and be our voice." He straightened his jacket while he sent two men out to check on Walker's body. He motioned for the rest to leave him and Ridge alone. "I'll speak in earnest in the hope that you and I can repair our differences and see our people through."

"What can I do but listen?" Ridge said. "Your council just cut out my tongue."

Ross held up his palms, pleading with Ridge to abandon his tack. "Time is on our side in Washington," he said. "My thought is to stall every effort against us long enough to outlive Jackson's administration. With another president comes another chance for justice."

"You still don't understand," Ridge said. He hoped Ross could sense the frustration in his voice as he said it. "It's not only Jackson who wants our land. It's his people. Regardless of what your friends in Washington tell you, whoever follows him will pursue the same course."

"We don't know that."

"Have no doubt that we will be expelled from this country," Ridge said. "You cannot stop it from happening. But you can negotiate the best terms possible, and I'm of the view that the most generous will come from Jackson's mouth. To wait is to prolong your people's suffering."

Ross sighed. "Oh, Ridge." He moaned, slowly shaking his head. "I'm so sorry that we can't agree." His demeanor turned more formal. "For the sake of tribal unity, will you give us the chance to ride things out with Jackson without interference? Please tell me that you will."

"You've had five winters' worth of chances," Ridge said. "You've not yielded one step toward reason. All you know how to do is stall as if all this will go away. Only Walker's ill-conceived response is worse. Both reactions promise nothing but extinction for our people. I'm not prepared to be idle — to be stripped of my voice and authority by a faction led by popular opinion — and sit beside the fire with old men and watch the

Cherokee die. The Ridge," he said formally to match Ross's tone, "must speak to Jackson."

"I can't protect you if you do, Ridge. Not if you go against the people and their constituted authorities."

"The Cherokee have no constituted authorities," Ridge said, his still-broad chest heaving. "You saw to that. But by our traditions the Ridge is still a chief, and many of his people still look to him for leadership. Your methods leave him little choice but to negotiate personally with Jackson. He will do as his heart bids him to save his people, regardless of the cost."

"The cost will be dear, my friend," Ross said. Ridge heard pity in his voice and it insulted him. "You don't know what you do."

"Not completely," Ridge said. "But I'm convinced I know better than you. And I'm not afraid to act against popular opinion."

"The people will call upon you to answer for your actions," Ross said. There was no mistake that this was a warning. Ridge was determined to defy it.

"I answer only to my ancestors," Ridge said. "They know that the heart of a chief still beats in my chest. I often wonder, Tsan Usdi, what beats in yours?"

Ridge left him there to return to his waiting family. John held out the reins of his horse. Ridge stuck his toe through the stirrup and swung his leg over the horse. Ross was gathering his people. He looked shaken, perhaps because another young, promising Cherokee had been murdered by his own kind. Ridge wheeled his horse to look back.

"Raise not your hand against your brothers," he heard Ross say to those who stood in two lines to shake his hand before they departed. "Be patient and go in peace. Your council is working together to save your country."

"We are away from here," Ridge told his son. "And by another road than the one Walker took."

He said nothing to his family on the long ride home. His eyes constantly watched the edge of the woods ahead to warn him of a murderer crouching in wait to cut his throat or a witch hoping to spit on him to infect him with a curse. He should have been rehearsing what he'd say to Jackson when they next met, but instead he heard the same thing over and over in his head. *I'm done with John Ross.*

CHAPTER THIRTY-EIGHT

The talking was over.

Ridge stayed outside his nephew's prim, pale blue home, smoking his pipe in the bitter winter wind on this Tuesday night, December 29, 1835. His nephew's house was smaller than Ridge's. Four cramped rooms for his family and books. Kitchen and root cellar detached from the main house. A shallow rock-walled well stood between them. It was a modest structure, befitting the modest man who built it, a stone's throw from the council and courthouses constructed back when the Cherokee had hope.

The New Echota council house was a grog shop now, owned by a white Georgian who thought nothing of serving whiskey to Cherokee children if they held silver coins in their copper hands. For the heart of the Cherokee government to have been reduced to a tavern bore witness to how completely the Americans had humiliated the Cherokee. So be it.

In a few minutes, Ridge could go inside,

scratch his mark on the talking leaves, and change all that. At least, that was what his head told him. His heart, however, told him something else.

Throughout the last winter, the most bitter in his memory, a cold so intense that water had frozen in kettles near the hearth, the arguments continued among the Cherokee. Ridge no longer wavered, which meant he had nothing to say to John Ross. It was John Ridge who found himself between them.

In person, Ross was warm and personable, always offering the younger Ridge the hand of compromise and goodwill. But there were more rumors in the Nation than lies on white men's tongues, and Ridge suspected most of them began with Ross. For the Man Who Walks the Mountaintops to advocate a treaty, some whispered, was to forfeit his life.

The threats were not idle. Hammer was beaten to death, the first after Walker to die. Wise, humble Crow was murdered at the very dance where he had been chosen to keep order. Before the celebrants parted, Crow was asked to speak a benediction, long the custom in the hills. He addressed the sad state of affairs afflicting his nation and said he had come to believe that the Ridges had truly chosen the lesser of two evils. He ended by urging those present to support the Ridge treaty. The dancers answered with sixteen knife wounds. Before the summer had ended,

Murphy and Duck were likewise hacked to death. Their crime? They had stitched their hopes with those of the Ridge.

By the fall, John astonished his father by pronouncing that the Ross and Ridge factions had put their differences aside. Despite Ridge's bitter feud with Ross, he hoped the surprising turn of events was true. He had always maintained a faith that the principal chief would accept the inevitable and plot the Cherokee's course by Ridge's side. The U.S. Senate offered Ross five million dollars for their lands in the East. Ross boldly demanded twenty million. These sums created a substantial gulf to leap before reaching an agreement — among other challenges, since Ross shrewdly kept the substance of his negotiations secret from the Cherokee majority. Ross ran a grave risk by failing to convince the Cherokee to sell their land to the Americans before negotiating the price. Ridge had sunk to new depths in the full-bloods' contempt. Ross had to know that he could be the next to fall.

Ridge wondered why such a calculating man would take a chance on alienating his full-blood supporters. Ross's terribly inflated counteroffer was also suspect, akin to his earlier whimsical queries to foreign officials about emigrating to Mexico or Oregon. All of these desperate developments were so inconsistent with Ross's plodding character that Ridge didn't really know what to make of them. Ross had the intelligence to assess that the Americans had already stolen the Cherokee's land. What he had always lacked was the courage to say as much to the full-bloods.

John Ridge, on the other hand, bared the truth to the bone, and he claimed that Ross was finally ready to deal. Ridge accepted his son's analysis with great relief. Aside from the price, Ridge assumed that the rest of the treaty's terms were acceptable to the principal chief. Ridge once again stepped quietly out of Ross's way. John and his cousin, Stand Watie, accompanied Ross to Washington at his request for final negotiations with the secretary of war. Ridge was certain that a treaty would soon be concluded at the American capital and that the Cherokee would move as one to the west.

Nevertheless, Jackson had sent John F. Schermerhorn, a retired minister from Utica, New York, to finalize the details of a treaty in the Cherokee Nation. It wasn't enough for Sharp Knife that John Ross had finally come to the bargaining table. Consistent with his iron will, Jackson applied pressure equally in New Echota as well as in Washington.

Ridge detested Schermerhorn's thunderous voice, bombastic mannerisms and intrusive demeanor. Christian Cherokee were shocked by the man's use of profanity and by his blatant sexual advances toward Cherokee women. The reviled lawyer, agent, and treaty commissioner Elisha Chester had been a saint by comparison. Ridge questioned Jackson's judgment in repeatedly sending confrontational and corrosive agents into a volatile situation that called for deft diplomacy and tact. The Cherokee hated the Yankee minister, twisting his name into the Devil's Horn.

Ridge would sooner sleep with a wet bobcat than sit in the same room with this coarse, blustering white man. But there he was, Jackson's authorized deputy, so what choice did Ridge have? The only hope for the Cherokee depended on his coming to terms with such men. If Ridge could not conduct the treaty negotiations in Washington, he could at least facilitate them in the home country with Jackson's henchman.

While this was going on, Ridge received word that President Jackson's tentative understanding with John Ross had unraveled. Ridge kicked himself for expecting any other result. Ross's preposterous twenty-million-dollar figure was the latest in the long series of stalling tactics that had characterized the principal chief's dictatorship. Judging from John Ridge's letters, he had since come to the same conclusion.

Ridge's son remained the loud voice of dissent among the Cherokee delegation. Jackson heard him, and so did Schermerhorn, who reacted angrily to the news of delays on the Washington end of the negotiations. The Ridges knew that the Americans would soon seek satisfaction in another locale. Back in the Nation, Ridge saw the Cherokee people sinking deeper into despair. When the reverend soon came knocking on Ridge's door to demand action, the Man Who Walks the Mountaintops was more than ready to break the stalemate.

"We'll have a treaty signed before year's end," Schermerhorn boasted. "Negotiated at New Echota, capital of the Cherokee."

Schermerhorn seemed ignorant of the fact that the Cherokee had long before moved the capital to Red Clay. Nor did he adhere to Ridge's warning that few Cherokee would attend such unofficial proceedings anyway, let alone the principal chief, who was still in Washington misleading Americans and Cherokee alike.

"President Jackson assured me that you possess the requisite stature among your people to act on their behalf," Schermerhorn said with a prodding eye. "Let's you and I set about to discuss suitable terms for a treaty."

Ridge should have answered that although he was a chief, he was not an elected official. Though he could speak for his family and perhaps a few hundred more, by no stretch of the imagination could he claim to represent the entire Cherokee Nation. Ridge could have refused the overture and that would have been the end of Schermerhorn's game.

But wasn't there an opportunity here? Ridge was known as the most likely headman to give the Americans what they wanted. Jackson, through the scoundrel Schermerhorn, was offering Ridge the power that circumstances and a very shrewd politician had stolen from him. Ridge had a very clear end in view, the same he had tirelessly advocated to no avail for several months. It occurred to him that the means were embodied in a loud, fat New Yorker. Ridge looked that disgusting white man in the eye and said, "I'm ready to finalize negotiations when you are."

Once he had spoken the words, they took on a life of their own. Soon afterward, they overwhelmed him. Schermerhorn, undaunted, plowed ahead with his plans. Ridge, on the other hand, kept to himself and grappled with his misgivings. When Ridge could no longer fight off his own conscience, he sought out a trusted ally.

"What course do you advise?" Ridge asked Boudinot, whose opinion he respected as much as his son's. Ross's Washington negotiations were a sham. An elected Cherokee government no longer existed. The people were mired in chaos. Schermerhorn was preparing an alternative document for Ridge's faction in New Echota, but Ridge wasn't authorized to sign it. What was Ridge to do?

"To advocate a treaty is one thing," Ridge said to his nephew. "To officially agree to it, another."

"We have a moral right, Uncle," Boudinot said quietly. In an earlier day, Ridge's nephew would have been a sage, a civil chief. His learning, like John's, had molded him into something Ridge could not understand yet so admired. He was his blood, however, as calm and steady as John was bright and rebellious. The future, however blighted, belonged to them. "An enlightened minority has the right — the duty — to save a blind and ignorant majority from certain destruction."

"You know the law."

"What is a man worth who would not die for his people?" Elias said. "Which of us would not perish if our nation could be saved?"

"I'm proud of you, Elias," Ridge said. "As much as I am of my own son."

"You must swallow your pride, Uncle," Boudinot said. "There's no place for it here anymore."

And so Ridge gathered himself, saddled his horse, and rode with a handful of followers to New Echota. As he had warned the profane parson, attendance was slim. Four hundred at most filtered into the flats of the capital, most mixed-bloods or whites who had tied the blanket with Cherokee women. Few came from the valley towns of Tennessee, and almost none of the full-bloods from the Blue or Smoky Mountains braved their neighbors' invectives.

Ridge queried the arrivals about the fate of their neighbors. Runners came from the government, they said, begging them not to attend. By the missionary's count, there were only seventy-nine legal voters present. There was little doubt in Ridge's mind that Ross was behind such a pitiful turnout. Ridge had long understood that Ross said one thing and did another. Smoldering, he promised himself he would not be guilty of the same offense. Before these people, he would remain as solid as the river bluffs, John Ross, Reverend Schermerhorn, and Jackson be damned.

The people crammed into the houses, barns, and taverns not owned and inhabited by Americans. Mr. Burke, the fortunate drawer of the supreme courthouse, refused entry to any Cherokee. Those who could not find shelter under a roof slept under the stars. Ridge moved among them, sharing their tobacco, smoked pork, grilled corn ears, and connahany, and distributing government blankets to the children to stave off the winter chill.

After breakfast on December 22, the treaty council convened. Officers were elected on the first day. Schermerhorn spent the second alienating everyone. On the third, the roof of the council house caught fire. The blaze was quickly extinguished, and the council quietly convened. Ridge was the last to speak that afternoon.

"I am one of the native sons of these wild woods," he said. "For more than fifty winters I have hunted deer and turkey in these hills. I fought your battles. I married a woman among you. I raised my family. I was your chief. While I floated the river of life, I have defended your truth and honesty and fair trading. I have always been a friend of honest white men.

"The Georgians have shown a grasping spirit lately. They have extended laws over our country that we cannot understand. They harass our braves and make the children suffer and cry. But I can still do them justice in my heart. They think the Great Father is bound by the compact of 1802 to purchase this country for them, and they justify their conduct with this end in view.

"I know the Cherokee have an older title than theirs. We obtained the land from the living God above. They got theirs from the British. Yet they are strong and we are weak. The Americans will not allow us to remain here in safety and comfort.

"I know we love the graves of our fathers. We can never forget these hills. But an unbending, iron necessity tells us that we must leave them. Know that I, the Man Who

Walks the Mountaintops, would willingly die to preserve our land, but any forcible effort to keep it would cost us not only our lives, but the lives of our innocent children. For the Ridge, that price is too high.

"There is but one path of safety, one road to future existence as a nation. That path is open before you. Make a treaty of cession. Give up these lands and go over beyond the great Father of Waters."

Ridge closed his eyes to prepare for the harangue. Instead, he heard nothing. He looked out to those few people, his people, to hear them grunt their approval with tears in their eyes. The old ones came forth first, grasping for his hand.

"I'm sorry," Ridge told them. "Truly, there is no other way."

"I'll follow you to a new world, Ridge," said Corn Shucker.

"And I," another said.

Ridge held each of their hands until they tugged them away.

"I'm so sorry," he said. "I've done all that I could."

Now, on this cold, still Tuesday night, nineteen Cherokees sat with Schermerhorn, waiting for Ridge to sign the talking leaves they'd hammered out over a week's worth of speeches and backroom arguments. James Starr was there. And Andrew Ross, John Gunter, Cae-te-hee, George Adair, William

Rogers, and, of course, his nephew. All waiting for him.

Ridge listened to the muffled tone of Boudinot's voice as he read over the terms of the treaty. Though pine beams and siding stood between Boudinot's mouth and Ridge's ears, he discerned every word. When at last his nephew finished, Ridge heard only silence within. He looked up at the stars. It was near midnight, as close as he could tell.

Ridge stepped into Boudinot's home. The candles flickered in the slight breeze. Twenty-one men stuffed into the front room of such a small house rendered its atmosphere stale. The Cherokee stood still, smoking their pipes, staring at the talking leaves on the table and the quill dipped in black ink as thick as blood. No one moved to touch them.

"Will you do us the honor of signing first?" John Gunter said to Ridge.

"Don't confuse honor with duty," Ridge said, as he warmed his hands by Boudinot's hearth. "Give me a moment to stave off the chill, my friends. I'll sign the goddamn thing soon enough."

"I'm not afraid," Cae-tee-hee said, and he made his X where Boudinot indicated. Te-gah-e-ske followed. John Gunter signed his name in English characters, as did Robert Rogers, John Bell, Charles Foreman, William Rogers, and George Adair. Boudinot signed his adopted name, and on they went until they came to the thirteenth spot. Ridge took up the quill, dipped it awkwardly into the blotter, and scratched an X beneath the characters Schermerhorn had made. His nephew wrote: *Major Ridge* with the X between the words, and *his mark* above and below them.

Thus the figure Kah-nung-da-tla-geh had drawn was boxed in by words he did not understand, his name as it was known among the Americans who had driven him to this empty place at their dying capital. Six more Cherokee made their marks beneath the Ridge's, with Andrew Ross and William Lofsley the last to sign. It was done. Twenty Cherokee, by Cherokee law, had betrayed their nation.

"I want you to know," Schermerhorn said in a booming voice so loud it shook the white hairs on Ridge's head, "I staunchly admire your leadership, Major Ridge. You're a brave man to have placed yourself in such peril."

"I expect to die for it," Ridge said in awkward English, more for the benefit of the patriots who had signed the treaty along with him, although they had known beforehand what the cost would be. For all practical purposes, they'd all signed the Treaty of New Echota in their own blood.

The ultimate humiliation, as far as Ridge was concerned, was that they'd had to do it under the auspices of such an obnoxious, loudmouthed, insensitive fool. So many Cherokee had died at the hands of such white men. Ridge had no idea how many more Schermerhorn and his kind would claim before the Cherokee were left in peace. How he had struggled to control his anger over these past few winters. Now that he'd done what they always wanted, he saw no reason to harness it anymore.

"Well, I hope it doesn't come to that," Schermerhorn said. "I just want you to know how much I admire you."

"Rest assured it will come to that," he said in Cherokee. "Your treaty is my death warrant. And what a weasel like you thinks of me means nothing. You hold a gun to my head and praise me for running. If it were not for the children I was sworn to protect, I'd spill your guts on this floor and carve the scalp from your head while you watched me do it! Yuh! How easily I, the Man Who Walks the Mountaintops, could steal your life from you, just as you've stolen mine!"

Saliva sprayed from his mouth as he spit the last words, sprinkling the astonished face of Jackson's commissioner.

He felt a hand on his shoulder.

"Please, my uncle," Boudinot said in Cherokee. "What good will this do?"

"None, and that's the problem!" Ridge shouted. "Where does a warrior belong in this world? Not here! Not in the hills where I was born!" Ridge turned back and glared at Schermerhorn, who for the first time since he'd been in Cherokee country was struck speechless. "I'm going back to the wilderness to live as a man for as long as my people will let me. The only joy I'll find there is knowing I'll never have to see your dog face again! From the next dawn hither, look upon the Ridge again with your devil's eyes and I'll snuff them out as payment for your treaty! The Ridge washes his hands of you and all your kind forever!"

He reached down and pinched out the candle between his thumb and finger and stormed out the door, leaving Schermerhorn's half-breed linkster to water down what he had said.

He was shoving his arms through his coat sleeves when he heard hard riders approaching. White Path, covered in mud, his cheek scratched from crashing through briars, rode at the head of a full-blood column. The breath of panting horses vaporized in the night air. White Path leaped off his horse and stood chest-to-chest before him.

He glared at the treaty men, all of whom looked away. "What have you done?" he said.

"What I had to," Ridge said. "I did it for my family and yours."

"I don't believe it," White Path said, and he left him to storm inside and see for himself. Ridge heard him question the linkster and even ruffle the paper that White Path could not read. Elias's voice tried to soothe him. Then Ridge heard Cherokee curses, angry footsteps, a slamming door. Ridge stood with his head bowed, feeling White Path's hot breath on his neck.

When he turned, Ridge saw his friend standing over him, his tomahawk raised above his head. Ridge brushed his coat off his shoulders and yanked the buttons loose from his shirt, exposing his bare chest to White Path. Ridge said nothing. He did nothing. He stood with his arms out and his palms open, waiting for his friend to do what he would.

White Path's arm trembled. His whole body convulsed. Tears ran down his cheeks, dripping on earth that no longer belonged to the Cherokee. White Path stared at him. His arm fell. He let the tomahawk drop to the ground.

"Why?" White Path begged him. "How could you do such a thing?"

"Because no one else would," Ridge said.

"I should kill you," White Path said.

Ridge heard hammers cock behind him. "It doesn't matter what you do," Ridge said. "The Cherokee will still go west." He picked up his coat and draped it around his shoulders. "I'm going home to my wife."

He walked straight through White Path's warriors to his waiting horse and mounted.

"Ridge," White Path said. "This can be undone. Go in there and take back the paper.

Burn it in front of my eyes and I promise you as your friend that no one will know about any of this."

Ridge gathered the reins and prodded the horse forward.

"Ridge!"

He rode for his home and Sehoya, beside whom he would spend his last days in the country of his birth. He left behind his people, wrapped in their stiff government blankets, clanking together their new shiny brass government pots, Jackson's down payment for the sale of their souls. He left White Path and his warriors on his backtrail, also. If they didn't follow it, others soon would. Ridge rode on.

The winter woods echoed with White Path's wailing.

CHAPTER THIRTY-NINE

Ridge watched her from his bed. Sehoya oversaw every detail as the new year of 1837 emerged under a blanket of snow and ice. Not a pot or a thimble escaped her eye once the weather warmed. In a cyclone of activity, she saw to it that the corn, oats, and other grains were sacked. Potatoes, dried peas, onions, and lima beans were stored in wooden bins, their vents covered with fine mesh to allow them to breathe and stave off the spring flies. Honey and yams filled clay crocks. Pickles sloshed about in five-gallon glass jugs. The smokehouses were fed with coals of hickory day and night to cure hams, slabs of bacon, jerked beef, and strips of venison shoulder.

Sehoya supervised the servants as they pounded cord between the planks of the wagon to seal them for the river crossings, and caulked the water barrels and side panels with fresh, acrid pine pitch. She had the casks filled with well water, and woe to the servants if she felt one drop on her impatient fingers. Wagon team rigs were repaired, axles lubed with bear grease, harnesses, halters, and reins oiled, and fresh shoes appended to the horses with box-headed silver nails filed flush against shiny hooves.

Sehoya ordered her furniture wrapped in canvas cloth and her woolen rugs rolled up with juniper boughs to discourage the moths. The china was carefully packed in crates full of sawdust. Neatly folded clothes were stacked in cedar chests. Ridge kept to his bed, nursing a cough and a fever, sipping Sehoya's pokeberry wine to soothe his aching joints.

All summer and fall a heavy stench of rot and decay had hung in Ridge's nostrils. The Cherokee had endured two hard winters in a row, and when the snow and ice finally melted, the rains came. Clouds hung low against the earth, shrouding the hills and eclipsing the Blue Mountains. Sehoya was sure that this spring's crops would be ruined by the relentless rains. No matter, Ridge told her. They would plant somewhere else next year.

There were other difficulties. Once the news of the Treaty of New Echota was out, the Georgians could not wait for the Cherokee to abide by the agreed terms. They swooped down on their country like buzzards to carrion, armed with loaded weapons, cheap whiskey, and hungry eyes, and perched near whatever homes and fields they found attractive.

Hundreds of hungry, homeless Cherokee walked the muddy roads like lost dogs. John indignantly appealed to President Jackson, General Wool, and even Georgia governor Lumpkin to protect the Cherokee people from these scavengers. But no one would risk one drop of white blood to enforce the terms of the treaty, and the politicians abandoned the Cherokee to their suffering.

Ridge threw open his stores of grain and his smokehouses of cured hams and jerked beef to any Indians in need. John did likewise, as did every other "treaty man" of property and resources. Ridge could not abandon the ancient tradition of Cherokee hospitality when his people were destitute. But he was quickly limited in what he could provide them. Soon his own shelves and sheds would be bare.

Ridge looked across the swollen Oostanaula River. A white man tended fields that had once belonged to him. Others would pick the apples, plums, and peaches from his orchards that fall, at least those that survived the late frost of spring. Sehoya had neither pruned the older trees nor planted new saplings. She and her servants uprooted all the trees she could carry to plant in the west.

Ross pursued his policy of shock, outrage, and denial. There had been no treaty, he claimed, at least not one made by the proper Cherokee government. The Ridge had usurped his authority and betrayed their nation. The so-called Treaty of New Echota was a fraud, advanced by a spurious delegation of minority malcontents. Ross held Henry Clay's ear, as well as that of Daniel Webster and Ralph Emerson. Such men delivered Ross's promised public outcry, as Ridge had anticipated. They spoke of scandal. They spoke of shame. But what did their words mean to the Americans? Their actions spoke louder to Ridge.

As Ridge predicted, Jackson would not yield. He presented the treaty before the American Senate with staunch determination. The agreement passed by one vote. A week later, on May 23, the Treaty of New Echota was signed into law. The Cherokee were given two years, two months, and an hour to vacate their homeland from the time Ridge had made his mark. Those who remained would feel the prick of a bayonet in their backs. Ridge knew that there was nothing Ross could do but organize his people to move west. So far, the principal chief had yet to arrive at this conclusion.

The sickness that had plagued Ridge throughout the winter persisted. He burned with fever, his eyes watered, every joint in his body ached, and he awoke almost every night in a cold sweat, thirsting for water. He knew rumors of his illness abounded in the Nation. His enemies lamented that he wouldn't live long enough for the Cherokee to kill him. Ridge watched a Georgian's slaves clear the stumps from land he loved and must leave behind. He felt consumed, exhausted, hollow. He brought his hand before his face and watched his fingers quake from the fever. Maybe the sickness would be merciful and carry him away.

At last, on one Gaga lu'nee morning, their carriage, six wagons, and sixteen slaves were ready to embark for the west. Once the teams were fed and hitched to their wagons, Sehoya came for Ridge with caring eyes, his best winter coat slung over her shoulder.

"We're waiting for you, my love," she said.

Ridge stepped away from the fire and poked his weary arms through the heavy sleeves.

"Where's Sally?" he asked.

"She went on one last ride through the pastures," Sehoya said. "I heard her coming before I came for you."

"She's been acting odd lately, hasn't she? She seems rather happy about all this."

"Everyone has been acting strange of late," she said. "She's young, Ridge. Let her mourn in her own way."

"Of course," he said. "I'm ready, then." He coughed into his fist. Sehoya started to dash out the fire. "No," he said. "Let it burn down to ashes. Let the Americans know the Cherokee were here one day and gone the next."

Sehoya nodded and set down the bucket. She took Ridge by the arm and together they walked out of their magnificent home. Ridge directed his family and slaves into places where he thought they'd be most comfortable. He saved a place inside the carriage for Sally.

"You're not going to ride the lead horse all the way to Arkansas, are you?" Sehoya asked.

"Where else?" he said. "I'm still a man."

Sally rode up in a thunder of hooves and dust. His daughter was thin, sharp-featured, and sinewy like her brother, but her skin was dark like Ridge's, her hair just as black. Sally was a spirited and willful girl. She tested her mother daily, but still Ridge doted on her in the most shameful fashion. The child had a way with horses. The more tempestuous the beast, the tighter they bonded. She had a small, dark-eyed, dark-haired white soldier with her. She remained mounted. The officer stepped down and approached him.

"Chief Ridge," he said. "Mrs. Ridge. I'm George Paschal."

Ridge surveyed the wiry, drawn soldier. He was an aide-de-camp of General Wool, stationed at New Echota to keep order in the Nation, a task they had not nearly accomplished to Ridge's satisfaction. Ridge couldn't fathom why the agent of his persecutors gawked at him with such an oafish grin.

"Our affairs are in order, Lieutenant," Ridge said. "There's nothing to do but go."

The soldier removed his hat and clamped it against his breast as if he were ashamed of his insignias. "I'd like to ask for the hand of your daughter in marriage," he said. "With your blessing, I want to make her my wife."

Ridge felt the blood drain from his skull. He shuddered from the chill that chased out his fever. The only person more shocked than he was his wife, who, for once, was speechless. He looked at Sally, blessed with the natural grace of a deer, sitting there with her blue calico dress spread out over the flank of her horse. There was no mistaking the meaning of the warm smile blossoming on her face.

"Step back, please," Ridge said dryly to Paschal. Then he motioned for his daughter to come near. She jumped down effortlessly from the lathered horse.

"Do you suppose," he said in Cherokee, "that this information might have been useful while we were making our preparations over the last few weeks?"

"I'm sorry for the inconvenience, 'Doda," she said. "He only asked me this morning."

"I see," he said, sniffling. "And what was your answer?"

"I said yes, providing my mother was agreeable." Her face brightened. "He's a good and kind man. A lawyer."

"He's a soldier and a Georgian to boot.

571

Could you not find a member of President Jackson's household to marry?"

"Ssshhh," hissed Sehoya. "What good will your jokes do?"

"Very little, I fear." He ran his fingers through his thick tuft of gray hair. "You know," he said to Sehoya, "I'd always hoped that my daughter would marry a full-blood. Right now, I'll settle for just a Cherokee. Any Cherokee." He looked back at his daughter. "Are there no Ani-yunwi-ya in this world that you find suitable?"

"Look at her face," Sehoya said with far too much enthusiasm. "She's in love with him. What would you have her do?"

"I would have her mix her blood with some race of men other than the one that has cast us out. What, in Selu's name, is the attraction to white people, anyway? John married a white girl. Elias did the same. I'll stick my head in a beehive if Walter ever takes a wife of any kind anywhere." He pointed his finger at his daughter. "But for you, Sally, I had other hopes."

"Yes or no, Father?" Sally demanded, planting her feet.

"Where would you live?"

"He'll come with me to the west."

Sehoya sighed in relief. "Wonderful," she said. She clapped her hands.

"Oh, yes." Ridge moaned. "I'm greatly relieved to hear it. We've gone to some amount of trouble to distance ourselves from the whites. It defeats the purpose somewhat if we up and marry a few thousand of them and drag them along with us."

"Yes or no?" Sehoya said, her face flushed with irritation.

"Why do you defer to me? It's your decision. And even if you said no, the stubborn girl would do it anyway."

"She wants her 'doda's blessing," Sehoya said.

Ridge pulled away from his wife, set his rifle aside, and opened the carriage door. "Out!" he yelled to the slaves. "Unpack everything! Put it all back where it belongs. My daughter is to marry. Prepare my wife's house for a feast and many guests. The Georgians will just have to wait."

"That means yes," Sehoya said to her daughter. Sally threw her head back and squealed in delight.

Ridge took the Georgian by the hand. "Welcome to my deeply troubled family," he said. Ridge studied Paschal's curiously dark features. "You have Indian traits, my friend. Any Cherokee in your family by any chance?"

"Not to my knowledge, sir. I'm of French descent."

"French," Ridge repeated. "Hmmm. Just a tinge of Creek or Choctaw blood, maybe?" Paschal shook his head. "Chickasaw, perhaps?"

"I'm afraid not."

"The fear is all mine, I assure you," Ridge said. Sally ran to him and jumped into his arms. She wrapped all four spindly limbs around him like a spider, her skirt fluttering in the breeze.

"I love you, 'Doda," she said.

"More lies," he said. "Help the servants unpack, won't you?" Ridge said. He kissed her cheek and pried her loose from him. She was heavier than she knew. "You're a wicked, wicked girl," he said.

On the third sun of Una 'la nee, the windy moon, Ridge watched the last of the belongings of his family and friends loaded onto eleven flatboats at Ross's Landing. Sally's marriage had been a welcome distraction. Ridge had been his old self for a few days, rekindling his joy of life. He was as proud of Sally as he was of John. Like her brother, she was quick-witted and resourceful, but her wild spirit most closely matched his own. Ridge spent a fortune on her wedding, and was glad to do it. But once it was over and done with, his melancholy returned like an unwanted houseguest. He couldn't see a day when he'd be free of it.

Close to five hundred Cherokee loyal to Ridge assembled at Ross's Landing. Disheartened, they loaded their things onto the barges in silence. At night, they drank whiskey and quarreled. Today — the day they would float down the Tennessee River for the west — they wept.

Ridge sat with Sehoya among the rest on the flat, exposed decks. Icy winds cut through his blankets. The chills returned first, then the fever. The flotilla traveled thirty miles to Gunther's Landing, where the steamer *Knoxville* waited. Due perhaps to his illness or his prestige, or maybe an extra $100 placed in the proper hand by a guilt-ridden American officer, Ridge was allowed cabin passage. The flatboats were tied to the *Knoxville*'s stern, and the paddle wheel began to churn brown water. That evening, Ridge watched from his berth window as the night claimed Cherokee land. He knew he would never see it again.

Once they reached the Alabama country, it became clear that Muscle Shoals did not possess water enough to draft the *Knoxville*. The soldiers escorted the Cherokee onto the box-shaped cars of the Tuscumbia, Courtland, and Decatur Railroad, the cantankerous, smoke-snorting iron serpent, the first contraption of its kind west of the Smokies and the Blue Ridge. Ridge watched the workers feed split oak to its insatiable belly, their white faces blistered red from the heat. He heard a loud screech, and clouds of white smoke and steam spewed from its chimney, and all at once the big snake began to roll west, the frightened Cherokee clinging to its back.

The steamboat *Newark* awaited them at Tuscumbia. Ridge's people spent the better part of day loading their belongings on the two keelboats moored to the *Newark*'s stern. When all was ready, they followed the Tennessee north, and the people's mood improved once they were underway. The keelboats were clean, well kept, and spacious. The people had a roof over their heads, and cooked their meals in one of the three hearths on deck.

At Paducah, they merged with the broad Ohio River and turned west again until they struck the muddy Mississippi, which flowed south with a strong current. At Montgomery Point, which marked the junction of the Mississippi and Arkansas rivers, a new pilot came aboard to steer the *Newark* upriver against the swirling eddies, yellow sandbars, and drift wood snags. They reached Little Rock on March 21. The *Newark* disengaged, and the lighter, flat-bottomed steamer the *Revenue* tied its thick ropes to the keelboats and on they went, deeper west-northwest. The lazy river was the color of tanned leather, its banks choked with vines, brush, and spring growth. They passed Van Buren and churned beyond Fort Smith. *Enough,* thought Ridge, who had studied his maps and charts relentlessly since they'd reached the Arkansas River.

"We've gone far enough on the rivers," he told Sehoya. "We can walk from here."

Ridge asked the skipper to set them off. He thanked the soldiers for their courtesy, and Dr. Lillybridge for his expertise and kindness. Both he and Sehoya had been down with fevers and the doctor had seen to their every need. He shook their hands, walked down the gangway, and rode into Fort Smith with the agents and guides to buy horses and wagons for the journey north.

Ridge led his party up Line Road, little more than a stumpy path that ran parallel to the border between the Cherokee Nation West and Arkansas, across the dozen branches that fed Barren Fork and under the dark, shaded canopy of towering cottonwoods, white oaks, sycamores, and sweet gums. The dogwoods bloomed white as snow, the redbuds purple, pink, and crimson. The streams ran clear below bleached limestone bluffs that terraced the rich hills. The horses stumbled on shiny flintrock beneath their hooves. Ridge savored the clean, fresh breeze and the sweet smell of churned, raw earth. He sat erect in his saddle and took it in.

He followed the agents' maps to the mouth of Honey Creek, aptly named, for he found bees busy robbing the blossoms all around him. Up from the river bottoms in the low hills stood thickets of maple, hickory, pine, persimmon, ash, wild plum, and juniper, much of it draped by wreaths of wild grape and muscadines. In the rolling hills lay deep, thick prairie grass that would fatten Ridge's pigs and cattle and easily yield to his plow.

Sehoya was alive with youthful vigor. She organized their temporary shelters and immediately made plans to build their new home. Ridge tended to the land. He decided which wooded parcels should be cleared and which were better left wild. The servants looked about them and groaned, knowing Sehoya intended to make a crop that fall. But even they could see that Arkansas was a land of milk and honey.

And not one Cherokee had died on the journey to reach it.

"Does this land please you?" Sehoya asked him at the end of the day's labors.

"Oh, yes," he said, sipping the clear stream water. He let the rest run through his fingers. "I see little sign of white men, too, and that pleases me more."

"Is it what you wanted?"

He reached for her hand. "In truth, no," he said. Her expression clouded. "I wanted what the Americans promised us. But once that became impossible, I'm not unhappy to be here." He smiled for her. "I must admit that I'm encouraged by this country. The west is what I promised our people that it would be — a wilderness, rich in grass and woodlands, game, and soil, blessed with good, clear streams, a home that will welcome the Cherokee. What more can an old man ask?"

He looked at the red sun. It was time to go to water. He picked his way through the brush with Sehoya to perch together on the bank of Honey Creek. How he had come this far without violence was a mystery. Sooner or later, the Cherokee would claim his blood. In the meantime, he would hack a home out of this new country for his wife and family, ensure that his line would thrive beyond the long reach of the Americans and their faithless governments. This was his only goal. The expense of bending this wilderness to their will would be great, both in terms of money and of men. But Ridge swore to see it through as long as his lungs drew breath. He knew the task remained within his power, and now that he'd finally arrived in the west it was within his grasp. There was far more left of him than he expected, and he intended to give it all away to Sehoya and the people who had willingly followed him to this new land.

Set an example, ex-Chief Ridge, he told himself as he waded into the water for his prayers. *Show the Cherokee who you are.*

CHAPTER FORTY

Ridge was busy sorting out his affairs. He'd met the few neighbors who shared the valley with him. Most, like him, were new immigrants and adherents to the Treaty of New Echota who had negotiated with the old settlers to purchase their farms and fields, and then set their minds to build anew. Other than these encounters, Ridge had not seen much of the old settlers, the Cherokee who had followed Tahlonteskee, Black Fox, and Oo-loo-teka nearly twenty-five winters ago.

One autumn day in 1837, six armed riders emerged from out of the thickets and cut through the haze toward his house. Ridge knew they hadn't come to be cordial. Ridge held Sehoya's hand as they closed the distance between Honey Creek and his home. When they were within speaking distance, he bade her to go inside.

"Welcome, brothers," Ridge said in Cherokee. They were older men, though younger than he, turbans wrapped around their heads, pipes dangling between chapped lips, their dark, suspicious eyes watching.

"I'm John Brown," one said stiffly, like a carving of wood. "Principal chief of the Western Cherokee since Beats the Drum's return to his ancestors." He introduced the others — two judges, a sheriff, and the rest minor chiefs and elders, as far as Ridge could tell.

"The people speak well of you," Ridge said, taking them each by the hand. Their accent was strange, the inflection harsher than he was used to. They relied on archaic words he seldom heard in the east. He wondered how just a few years could make such a difference. "I am Kah-nung-da-tla-geh, a new man among you. I offer you all food and drink."

Not a one of them made the first move to dismount.

"We've heard of you, too," the sheriff said. He looked at the others.

"I don't doubt it."

"Where's your son, John Ridge?" Chief Brown asked abruptly.

"In the east," Ridge said, shocked by how terse these westerners were. "He visits his wife's family and is buying supplies to stock our store."

"We've heard he's looking to sell some of our country to the whites."

Ridge shook his head. How far must one go to escape the rumors? "He does no such thing. I beg you, shut your ears to idle gossip. Many Cherokee are coming to this country. My son's gone to buy what they need."

They looked at each other, their faces blank. Chief Brown stared at him. "What designs do the Ridges have toward governing the Western Cherokee?"

"None," Ridge said. "Sixty-six winters rest heavy on my head. For forty of these, I've carried my people's burden. I set it down for good at New Echota. My son's lost his taste for politics, as well. We're busy with our families and our fields. Let us know what you require of us to be good citizens of your nation, Chief Brown. We'll do as we're bidden."

Chief Brown nodded. The other elders concurred, although their expressions remained guarded. "Our government is simple," the chief said. "We have four districts. No written constitution and only a few basic laws."

"Such was the case in my youth," Ridge said. "I was content then. I'll be content now."

The gravity returned to Brown's expression. "Will you challenge me for principal chief?"

"Under no circumstances," Ridge replied abruptly to earn their confidence. He wanted them to know that his words came directly from his heart. "As I've said, I'm done with all that. I've heard so much clamor I can't get the ring out of my ears. I'm a simple farmer now. My son is a merchant and lawyer. My nephew, Elias Boudinot, once editor of the *Cherokee Phoenix,* is busy with the missionary Worcester translating the gospels into our tongue, if you find that sort of thing useful. None of my family maintains any interest in governing anyone. If you want to find the Ridge Walker, come to his home and his fields. He'll be there playing with his grandchildren."

"Respect our traditions and what few laws we have," Chief Brown said. "Be a neighbor and friend to our people. Conduct your affairs honestly, and you'll have no problem with us."

"Fair enough."

"One last thing," Brown said. "I don't know everything that went on in the east between you and Chief Ross. Some say you, Ridge Walker, did what you thought you had to do. None of us doubt that you're a brave man and meant well, but nevertheless most of us feel that what you did was wrong. I wanted you to know that."

"I understand." Ridge had expected as much. At least the westerner was blunt, a welcome change from the politicians in the east. "According to our laws," Ridge said, "all of which I spent a lifetime honoring, what I did was wrong. But like a nightmare, time stood still in the old country, freezing the Cherokee and their leaders. Cornered at last by the whites, squeezed from all quarters, the best among us on both sides of the feud forgot who we were and what laws we lived by. Something had to give to let the waters run again. I made my choice, and I stand by it."

"Oh, my," one of the judges said. "He speaks as well as they say. I enjoyed listening to that." Brown shot the judge an impatient look to remind him they were here on business.

"I thank you for speaking your mind freely, Chief Brown," Ridge said. "I'm not surprised to learn that my name bears the brunt of the blame. This fact pains me beyond consolation. For those of us who lived through it, the torrents of our time were far too murky to see how the river flowed. But history will judge me and my kind, my brother. Let the slow years pass and then see what the Cherokee of our grandsons' grandsons will have to say of the Man Who Walks the Mountaintops. To you, my new chief, I say only that the Ridge picked the straightest path in a crooked valley. He stands ready to answer for his actions before you, John Ross, my clan, my people, and the ancestors who came before me."

Chief Brown appraised him in silence. Ridge couldn't discern a look of forgiveness in his eyes, but he was certain he saw a tinge of pity in there somewhere. "Like I said,"

Brown began, "I wasn't there. I'm not here to judge you, Ridge. I just came for some straight talk. We've done so to my satisfaction." He looked at the others, who nodded. The sheriff smiled. "Well, my brothers," Brown said, "that's enough politics for one day." He sniffed the breeze. "Is that corn mush I smell?"

"It is," Ridge said. "And also fresh-baked sweet-potato bread. Come inside and eat to your heart's content."

Brown kicked his feet out of the stirrups and swung his leg over his horse. When the others hesitated, Brown nodded toward the house. He took Ridge's hand. "You're welcome here, Ridge Walker. May you and all yours thrive."

"And yours, my brother," Ridge said.

"Would you come to our next council and speak of your experiences in the east?" the chief said. "I'd like the elders to know your heart." He started for the house, paused, and looked warmly at Ridge. "They hear things, you know. Wicked things."

"Oh, I know," Ridge said. He wrapped his arm around Chief Brown's shoulder and escorted him into the house. Sehoya was already tying her apron around her waist. Her enthusiasm constantly inspired him. "Meet some friends of ours," he told her.

Her smile greeted the old settlers better

than anything he could have said. "My home is yours," she said.

CHAPTER FORTY-ONE

The Unforgiving

I want you to know how I came to be in this place. You owe it to me to listen to the whole story. You just sit there and keep your goddamn mouth shut. My turn to talk now.

I am Kahn-yah-tah-hee, First to Kill, ani-waya, wolf clan, called Charlie Blue by you godless people. I speak Cherokee and English, but read only Sequoyah's alphabet. I'm certainly a seventh-generation descendant from the family of the first inhabitants of this side of the sea. The *adawehis* told my grandmother that we were once as white as any of you, but our ancestors, being winter people accustomed to the cold, failed to protect themselves from the sun. I am one of very few in the Nation who remember these teachings. I'm a full-blood Ani-yunwi-ya, and despite all you've done to make me think different, I'm proud of it.

This is what happened after what you did:

They came like a pestilence, these whites, herding their sickly wives and skinny children before them, telling the Cherokee that the treaty we signed would make us go. What treaty? we asked them. The Cherokee had signed no treaty. But they came anyway, hundreds in the course of one moon, tobacco dripping from their thin lips just like locusts.

Winter broke early last year, 1838. After the windy moon of March, we had no more freezes, but the clouds were greedy with their tears. In years past, I'd plowed around the stumps and dead logs in my fields. That year I burned them, as well as the brush from my fences and hedgerows, reducing all to ashes, which I tilled into the blood-red soil. Never have my fields stood more ready. I'm told I have a gift for farming. I love the clean smell of fresh earth.

I saw my efforts as a measure of my faith in John Ross. By day, I planted my fields with my wife, Hand Basket. She was also a full-blood, ani-gilohi, long hair or wind clan. (Don't bother to ask the meaning of the clan names. They are ancient and no one knows.) By night, we huddled by the hearth with my three children while my wife read from the Bible. Hand Basket learned to read English at the mission school in Spring Place. I loved to listen to the sound of her voice. When she read it was like a beautiful prayer.

The season was slightly warmer than in

years past, and although I usually planted with the first call of the whippoorwill, I dropped my seed in the ground early. Enough rain fell, though not nearly as much as normal. Soon the corn shoots stood as high as my knee. I was certain this year would be my best.

Our principal chief was not among us. He was in Washington arguing with President Van Buren, who had followed Jackson in that office. Van Buren granted Chief Ross one interview, during which he quietly explained that the Ridge agreement — I won't call it a treaty — would be enforced. After that, all future requests for an audience were denied. Chief Ross took our appeal to the Senate, and when that failed, he took our cause to the American public.

John Ross, in my opinion, is a calm, calculating, logical man. He was never a gifted orator, as were some of the older chiefs, but as the date for enforcement of the treaty neared, his appeals grew more passionate. Henry Clay answered him, as did David Crockett of Tennessee, Edward Everett, Theodore Freylinghuysen, and many others. We were told that President Van Buren was ultimately moved by Ross's eloquence in describing the wrongs that had been done to us by the traitors, the Ridges. He proposed allowing the Cherokee two more years on our soil, treatment he considered generous. But Governor

Gilmer of Georgia answered the president's compassion with a threat. Georgia militia would clash with federal troops on Cherokee soil, and the weight of an American civil war would rest on Van Buren's head. Under such pressure, the president washed his hands of our affairs and that was the last heard from him.

Among our own people, I heard only one thing: We shall never submit.

In July 1836, General John Ellis Wool arrived among our people to police us should we decide to fight back. Soon enough, he learned that the Cherokee intended no such thing. He grew sympathetic to our plight, and I'm told he wrote frequent appeals to Washington on our behalf. In the end, I think he loved us more than he did his own nation. At least, living among us as he did, he came to understand that we had been cheated out of everything by those — Cherokee and white alike — who would sell anything to fill their purses with money. This spring — what many said would be our last — he was suddenly replaced. I suppose he was relieved, for anyone who looked upon his drawn face could see that this good man could never have lived with the shame of forcing a peaceful people from their ancestral homes.

General Winfield Scott arrived with a different view. Almost immediately, Old Fuss and Feathers set his crews to work constructing eleven stockades and dozens of keelboats. One by one, the steamboats moored at our river ports — Ross's Landing and Gunther's Landing on the Tennessee, and the Cherokee Agency on the Hiwassee. General Scott watched over it all, as I did. As we all did.

But the Cherokee were not moved. We did not prepare for a journey. We did not lift a finger to pack our things. We trusted in John Ross, who assured us he could untie the noose the Ridges had dropped around our necks. We spun our cloth. Hoed our fields. At night we read the Bible to our children. We would not submit. Better to be murdered on our soil and put to rest with our beloved ancestors than to die in the soldiers' forts.

In the second week of the planting moon, May, I found a letter nailed to a rotten oak. I tore it loose and carried it home to my wife. She read it to me. I still have it. Why don't you read it for yourself?

MAJOR GENERAL SCOTT, of the United States Army, sends to the Cherokee people, remaining in North Carolina, Georgia, Tennessee, and Alabama, this

ADDRESS

Cherokees! The President of the United States has sent me, with a powerful army, to cause you, in obedience to the Treaty of 1835, to join that part of your people who are already established in prosperity, on the other side of the Mississippi. Unhappily, the two years which were allowed for the purpose, you have suffered to pass away without following, and without making any preparation to follow, and now, or by the time that this solemn address shall reach your distant settlements, the emigration must be commenced in haste, but, I hope, without disorder. I have no power, by granting a further delay, to correct the error that you have committed. The full moon of May is already on the wane, and before another shall have passed away, every Cherokee man, woman, and child, in those States, must be in motion to join their brethren in the far West.

My Friends! This is no sudden determination on the part of the President, whom you and I must now obey. . . .

I am come to carry out that determination. My troops already occupy many positions in this country that you are to abandon, and thousands are approaching, from every quarter, to render resistance and escape alike hopeless. All those troops, regular and militia, are your friends. Receive them and confide in them as such. Obey them when they tell you that you can remain no longer in this country. Soldiers are as kind hearted as brave, and the desire of every one of us is to execute our painful duty in mercy. We are commanded by the President to act towards you in that spirit, and such is also the wish of the whole people of America.

Chiefs, head-men, and warriors! Will you, then, by resistance, compel us to resort to arms? God forbid! Or will you, by flight, seek to hide yourselves in the mountains and forests, and thus oblige us to hunt you down? Remember that, in pursuit, it may be impossible to avoid conflicts. The blood of the white man, or the blood of the red man, may be spilt, and if spilt, however accidentally, it maybe impossible for the discreet and humane among you, or among us to prevent a general war and carnage. Think of this, my Cherokee brethren! I am an old warrior, and have been present at many a scene of slaughter; but spare me, I beseech you, the horror of witnessing the destruction of the Cherokees.

Do not, I invite you, even wait for the close approach of the troops; but make such preparations for emigration as you can, and hasten to this place, the Ross' Landing, Gunther's Landing, where you all will be received in kindness by officers selected for the purpose. You will find food for all, and clothing for the destitute, at either of those places, and thence at your ease, and in comfort, be transported to your new homes according to the terms of the Treaty.

This is the address of a warrior to warriors. May his entreaties be kindly received, and may the God of both prosper the Americans and Cherokees, and preserve them long in peace and friendship with each other!

WINFIELD SCOTT
Cherokee Agency
May 10, 1838

Faced with this letter, we still were not moved. We spun our cloth, hoed our fields, tended our orchards and chestnut groves. We will never submit.

Then, like a bad dream, it began. Even when I saw it with my own eyes, I couldn't believe it was happening. I was in the hills above my home hunting deer when I heard my hounds barking below. I raced through the thickets of pine and juniper, leaped over my fence, dodged my bellowing cattle and squealing pigs to find ten mounted, hard-eyed men in front of my cabin. My oldest son, Luke, stood defiantly in the yard beside his mother. Paul, called Little Wing, and my youngest, Elizabeth, stood on the porch, wailing as only frightened children can do.

When I rounded the corner, I noticed that these were not General Scott's soldiers, but Georgia militia. Their leader was shouting orders at Hand Basket, who stared back at them blankly, her arm wrapped around my son's shoulder. I was out of breath and terrified. I still clutched my rifle in my sweating hands. When the militiamen saw me with the gun, they wheeled their muzzles in my direction. I saw blood in their eyes. I dropped my rifle and held up my hands.

"I mean no harm," I said in English. "Please don't hurt my family."

"That's up to you," their leader said, his bright red hair shining beneath his beaver hat. The Ani-yonegas always looked strange to me. This one was speckled like a chicken egg. He had gray eyes the color of my hunting blade.

"Why have you come?" I asked.

"You know why," he said. "Get your gear. It's time to go."

"Go? Go where?"

"West, brother Cherokee. It's time to go west."

I looked upon the faces of my stunned wife and sobbing children, and back to the grim militiamen. And then up the rise where several other white people had gathered, waiting. They appeared to follow the soldiers wherever they went.

"We need time to pack some things. Can you come back tomorrow?"

"You've had plenty of time to get ready," he said. "You kin take what you kin tote. I'll give y'all five minutes."

He dismounted, as did four or five of his men. Together they walked into the yard and up onto the porch. The planks creaked under the weight. "Times a-wastin'," he said, glancing at his silver pocket watch. He pointed to my rifle. "An' you best leave that smokepole right where she lays."

"I'll need to load the wagon."

"No, sir," he snapped. "What you can tote on your back only. No wagons. No stock."

"We can't live without these things."

"I guess we'll see," he said.

I herded my wife and children into our home. I ripped a blanket from the feather bed and spread it on the floor. My wife threw a few clothes in the middle and I tossed in jerked venison, small sacks of corn and beans, and one pot. By then, other whites had entered our home and began rummaging through our things. "How much for this kettle?" they asked. "What'll you take for them sets of dishes?"

It was difficult to put a price on these things in the middle of such confusion. They were what made our house a home. And yet I heard myself saying five dollars for this thing and one dollar for that. It really didn't matter what I said. They pressed cold silver and wadded banknotes in my hands and took what they wanted. Some took and paid nothing. I watched one white woman drag my grandmother's rocker out the door without a word.

"Time's up," the red-haired man said, snapping his timepiece shut. "Out the fuckin' door."

I handed small bundles to each of my children to carry, save Elizabeth, who had but two winters on her confused head. Hand Basket carried her in her arms and walked out without making eye contact with any of the Georgians. I gathered the corners of the blanket, its middle bulging with our things, and found that despite all my efforts, I could not lift it. One of the militiamen ordered me to drop it on the puncheon floor. When I did, he prodded out the heavier items with the toe of his boot.

"Give her another spin," he said. This time I shouldered my load. The militiamen pointed toward the door, but I walked instead to the mantel, where I kept our Bible. I took it and stepped out onto the porch. We left stew on the fire. Bean bread dumplings boiling in springwater on the coals. Fresh butter in the churn, new blossoms on the fruit trees, my best crop ever standing in the fields. Everything wasted. Try as I might, I could not stem my tears. I was ashamed that my children saw me crying. I wasn't a man anymore.

"May we pray before we go?" I asked, and I could see that the militiamen were somewhat stunned by the request. They hesitated, all of them looking to their leader to answer.

"Hell, I guess so," he said, shrugging his shoulders. "Have at her."

I set down the blanket and gathered my wife and children around me. I calmed them as best I could and asked them to take one another's hands. Hand Basket opened the Bible to the book of Job and read a passage. When she was done, I began reciting the Lord's Prayer in English. To my surprise, half the militiamen and most of the settlers knelt beside us, saying the words with me. We said "Amen" in unison, and then I opened my eyes. This was the first time I saw regret in some of their faces, or any trace of guilt. From this point forward, the soldiers were less insistent in their tone toward us. At least, some of them were. That red-haired bastard never gave an inch in his spite. I knew he was born hating Indians. Anyway, one settler, a middle-aged woman, took our blankets inside the house and left them there. The rocker was dragged back in as silently as it had been taken.

"I'm sorry for my part in this," the white woman said with tears in her eyes. "I won't have no more. May God have mercy on you all."

"And also on you," I told her as she carried

herself, slowly and deliberately, as if her legs were made of lead, back up the draw where her wagon waited.

Hand Basket rose to her feet, managed a smile for the children, and walked quietly into the barn. When she returned, I noticed that her apron was full of corn. She tossed out scratch to the chickens until a soldier took her by the elbow and pulled her through the gate. She broke loose to take Elizabeth in her arms. She pulled back my baby's hair and wiped the tears from her eyes. I hoisted my bundle back over my shoulder and we started down the dirt road.

I looked back to see my home engulfed in flames. The squatters were walking back to their wagons, some with their bounty slung over their shoulders, some with their heads down and empty arms — ashamed, I think, of the prospect that they were low enough to scavenge the things of helpless, honest people. I ask you: Who are the heathens?

My dogs followed us, though I coaxed them several times to turn back. What could I do for them when I couldn't protect my own children from this humiliation? One of the younger militia men threw rocks at them. When that failed, the red-haired son of a bitch shot my bloodhound. My dog yelped and then lay down to die. The rest turned tail for the hills after that.

I thought that, if we got the chance, maybe

we ought to scatter to the huckleberry country high in the hills and let all this blow over. The soldiers would never find us up in the caves I'd played in as a boy. I could survive in this manner, but what about my wife and my children? I could not bear to watch them suffer such deprivations, and soon I put all thought of escape out of my mind.

"No one thought we were serious," the red-haired man said, pouring fresh powder from his horn down the warm barrel. "I reckon y'all know better now."

On we walked, the paths and trails merging with cleared roads like mountain creeks with larger streams, all carrying more Cherokee west. We looked at one another. No one spoke. Once we came across a Cherokee man carrying a deer across his shoulder, no doubt headed home to feed a family he wouldn't find there. Under gunpoint, he dropped the deer and his rifle and joined the weary procession. This was the first time I felt lucky about any of this. I knew where my family was. This poor, distraught soul had no idea what had become of his.

Federal troops — dragoons, I think — leaned back on their sabers alongside the roads, watching the flood of frightened Cherokee pass. I saw an eagle on the brass plates of their bayonet scabbards. In one claw, it grasped arrows. In the other it clutched a branch. In its sharp beak, it should've gripped a Cherokee. That's what we felt walking down that road — like we'd been bitten in half.

At Spring Place we picked up the Federal Pike and forded the Conasauga River and later Cooychutte Creek. We were made to cross the rivers in our clothes. The soldiers would not even allow us to remove our shoes and socks. When the sun went down, chills racked all of us. We crossed the Tennessee Line to reach Brainerd on the Chickamauga. Maybe three hundred of us were herded into the old mission and meetinghouses. As quickly as we could, we stoked the old stoves for warmth and brewed hot sassafras-root tea. Mothers, clutching blue-lipped babes in their arms, pressed forward. Shuddering children wept from hunger and cold. The men and women were too shocked and bitter to speak to each other. The missionaries passed through the guard to distribute boiled corn and fresh-cooked steaks.

"After you hear the drumbeat," an officer told us through his linkster, "do not leave this building until dawn. My soldiers have orders to shoot."

"But, sir," said a missionary, "some are suffering from dysentery.

"Very well, then," the officer said after a moment's hesitation. "Ask permission first, but do not leave the camp's firelight. Any Indian found wandering around in the dark will be shot dead. Am I clear?"

Oh, yes, he was clear. I was too busy stripping the soaked clothing from my children and huddling their naked bodies one against the other to warm them. Exhausted, I lay down on the floor to sleep. When it was dark, I could hear their teeth chatter. Listening to them suffer so, I could not sleep. Already Elizabeth was hot with a fever. Little Wing had a cough. And Hand Basket was too heartbroken to eat.

Before dawn the next day, we were given our field rations. None of the adults moved to touch their share, because any Cherokee would rather die than eat out of his enemy's hand. We begged our children, however, to eat all they could hold to keep up their strength. Summer is the fever season in the Nation, and already the country was suffering from lack of rain. My youngest child was delirious with fever, and all Hand Basket could do was dip her hand into a water bucket and let the drops fall from her fingertips into Elizabeth's mouth.

We walked most of that day until at last we reached the stockade of freshly sharpened pine timbers, many of which bled thick, clear sap. A hundred score of us were piled inside the picketed walls while armed Georgia militia, rifles and smoothbores hoisted against their shoulders, walked in heavy boots outside. The regular soldiers came and went, always bringing more Cherokee with them.

We made fires to warm our families and cook our meals. I, like many others, still refused to eat. The outhouses, sheds with benches and shallow trenches, were quickly filled by those still suffering from what the missionaries called putrid dysentery. We could not get access to the wells. The water drawn from the Tennessee for us to drink and clean ourselves with was foul. The women and children sought shelter under the few sheds and tents. The rest of us slept like pigs in a sty under heavens that had forgotten the Cherokee.

It was long known by the old ones that strange diseases had come and gone among the Cherokee in my grandfather's time. The pox, measles, whooping cough, and others had claimed many of our ancestors. But in my time, we didn't see these much. In the hills we lived cleanly. Our diets were filled with fresh meat and vegetables. The water was clear. We went to the rivers twice a day. We did not live too near our neighbors. But once we were packed into the stockades, these diseases reappeared with a vengeance. The weak — the babes and the old ones — began to die.

On the fourth night in confinement, I was awakened by a horrible wailing. There was nothing uncommon about hearing despair, but this time I recognized the cries of my own wife. I went to her to find her rocking, Elizabeth clutched against her breast. The child's body hung limp in her arms; her eyes were frozen in death. I reached for her, but Hand Basket would not give her up. I stroked her head and softly said, "This one is gone. Care for the others who are still living." I pulled Elizabeth from her arms. She weighed almost nothing. The fever had burned so much moisture from her pale skin that if I pressed my finger against it, it remained indented. I went to the soldiers guarding the gate.

"I need a shovel," I said.

One of the guards spit out a thick, brown stream of tobacco. "What for?"

I held up the body of my youngest child, hatred burning in my eyes for this man, my persecutor. I wanted to kill him. "To bury my daughter."

"Oh, shit," he said. "I feel for ya. Sit tight now, and I'll see if I can't hunt ya one up." He returned with a rusted, hickory-handled spade and leaned it against my shoulder. "Where ya gonna put her?"

I'd been to Ross's Landing before. I knew where the others had been laid to rest. "There's a burial ground yonder," I said.

"You're welcome to bury the child where you like," he said, "but I'll tag along, if'n you don't mind. It's been hell roundin' y'all up. Can't see lettin' ya run off after what all we've been through."

I glared at this boy soldier. He couldn't

have been more than eighteen winters. *After what all we've been through,* he'd said.

"Son, understand me. Everything I care about in this world — everyone I love — is behind your wall. I'll die before I let anything or anyone come between me and them. All I want is to bury my only daughter and then you can rest assured that I'll come back to your fort. But I don't want you, or any of your kind, anywhere around me when I lay this child to rest. What I've got to do is between me, God, and this innocent, dead little girl. If you don't like it, you can just shoot me in the back, just like you did the deaf-mute who didn't hear the instructions being hollered at him when he turned the wrong way. I'm going. And then, when I'm ready, I'll be back."

The boy stepped aside and motioned toward the woods. "I had nothing to do with that man's killin'," he said as I passed.

"Didn't you?"

I went out and dug my daughter's grave. Then I came back and gave that boy his rusty shovel and watched as he slammed the gate shut behind me. I went to the kettle and spooned out wads of corn mush on my plate and ate until I thought my gut would bust. My family needed me to keep up my strength. And I vowed to live through this misery wherever it would lead me, and carry my wife and children through it safely. I swore it when

I shoveled the dirt on little Elizabeth's grave. Nothing the whites could do would touch me as long as my Hand Basket and our sons lived. Nothing!

The weeks wore on. Two or three parties of about a thousand Cherokee each set out on keelboats for the west. The rest of us waited and died. Word got back to us that the early parties met with nothing but misery. The rivers were too low to float the boats, the water was undrinkable, the land too parched to support life on the banks. In June, our chiefs begged General Scott to let the rest of us wait here in the Nation until the weather cooled, until the September rains had come, and we knew the travel would be easier. Say what you want about Scott, but he listened to the chiefs and offered to delay any future expeditions until the fall.

By then Chief Ross was back among us. He also made requests of General Scott, pleading with him to allow the Cherokee to manage our own migration. Again, Scott agreed, possibly because he was weary of caring for us, but most of us believed that he would rather have the blood of the dying Cherokee on Cherokee hands. All the soldiers said the same thing. "You were given two years to go as you pleased. You brought all of this on yourselves."

What did we do, we all wondered, to bring this on ourselves? Did we behave in some fashion to cause the United States to drive us from our homes and fields like cattle? Commit some crime to justify our murders? How did we offend? Who did we threaten? The whites heaped this burden on our shoulders because red men lived on land they wanted! They were to blame, them and the family of a chief I used to love and respect more than my own father. The rest of us, as Ross made plain to General Scott and any others who would listen, were nothing more than victims, lambs led to suffering and slow slaughter.

Ross asked to shepherd his own people west, although he also made it quite clear that our compliance with the Treaty of New Echota in no way meant that the Cherokees agreed to it. Scott should infer that we intended to care for our own and nothing more. Chief Ross promised we would move west — by land — when the temperatures cooled and the skies brought rain. In the meantime, Ross, our chiefs and elders, clan mothers, and even the white missionaries, did everything possible to feed, clothe, and shelter us. The first task was to banish the angel of death that stalked us day and night. Once loosed, however, no one, not even Chief Ross, could stop it.

Little Wing fell to smallpox by the end of August. He had been such a handsome child. By the time the pox took him, his arms, chest, back, and stomach were one infected, oozing sore. Crushed, my wife and I buried him beside his sister. Not one blade of grass had grown on Elizabeth's grave.

By October, after we'd assembled 645 wagons, corralled five thousand horses and hundreds of oxen, stacked kegs of flour and sacks of corn high in the barns of Ross's Landing, the missionary Butler informed us that two thousand Cherokee had died in the camps during that summer of drought and sickness. Two of them were my children.

By the first of the harvest moon, John Benge led the first party of a thousand Cherokee north on the land route toward Nashville. I heard the sound of thunder in the distance while I helped with the preparations, as I did with the eleven parties that followed at intervals of three or four sleeps. I was to go with the thirteenth, the one that was to include Principal Chief Ross and his family and also old Chief White Path of Elijay, who had once been a close friend of the Ridge. After Ridge's betrayal of our people, White Path walked the earth like a shadow. No one could console him.

I knew John Ross would see us through, and I was proud of the honor to cast my lot with his. In the end, however, the principal chief decided to take a group of old, sick, and lame along with the tribal archives by the river route. I set out with the last party in the first week of big trading moon, November.

The drought broke like they always do. Once the rains began again, they never stopped.

We had forty-three wagons and carryalls, and only thirty-six oxen teams to draw them. The rest were pulled by mules or horses. As we felt the first of the winter winds on our necks, we forded the Tennessee near its fork with the Hiwassee at Blythe's Ferry and rose together from the bottoms to the Cumberland Plateau. So many thousands of Cherokee had passed before us that the roads were churned into bogs. The wagons sank to their axles. Weary Cherokee snapped their whips against the backs of exhausted teams and on we went to Pikesville, McMinnville, and finally Nashville, pushing on against the sticky muck of wasted roads. Sick faces, drawn and leached of all coloring, bounced listlessly in the beds of their wagons. Barefooted children walked behind them. We covered ten miles each day.

We met all kinds of Americans on this journey. Some would not allow us to camp on their farms or even use the roads that ran through them. Once, I pitched my family's tent and cut firewood three different times before I was allowed to settle in for the night. Others saw us as potential customers for their costly wares: fifty cents for a dozen freckled apples, a silver dollar for a basket of eggs. Our own Lighthorse Guard chased the whiskey peddlers away. We ignored the trash who insisted we pay them to dig the graves of those who died without any family to bury them. Each day we passed graves, sometimes twenty or more. Death was always out there, stalking us like wolves.

Other whites were more kindhearted. Church congregations took up collections to buy us food and supplies. White women fit their children's shoes onto the bare feet of young Cherokees. Hand Basket was given a leghorn bonnet and a woolen shawl. Luke got a new pair of brogans. They blistered his heels at first, but he never complained. Better to endure the blisters, he said, than frostbite. Some whites even opened their barns, stables, smoke houses, and stores to us. We thanked them as best we could, but I think most of us were confused by this generosity. How could such people persecute us one minute and then take pity on us the next? Nevertheless, by then we were desperate and had no choice but to eat from our tormentors' hands.

During the snow moon the ice storms came. Punishing gusts blew the limbs off trees and scattered the coals of our fires onto our blankets and tents. We had made the decision to wait for rain and cooler weather, for summer travel meant certain death. But even the Provider showed us no mercy. The winter set in quickly with cold as harsh as any I could remember. We walked for hours on the frozen earth, never quite able to shake the chill from our bodies. This is when the coughing sickness came, and everyone's voice became hoarse and their heads became feverish. Pneumonia, the white doctors called it, and the death toll climbed to twice what it had been.

Not a day passed when I didn't dig a grave for a friend or relative, or some miserable wretch I'd never laid eyes on before. At night, I heard my people moaning even above the wailing winter wind. I could not help the dying. I invested all of my food and energy in the lives of my wife and remaining son. I gave them my cloaks and blankets. I built fires for them. I dug a potato or carrot from my stew and dished it onto their tins. I'd like to be able to say that I sacrificed so because I loved them, but I have to admit that I was afraid of being left behind in this world without them. I couldn't imagine living alone.

From Nashville, we turned northwest to Hopkinsville, Kentucky, and on to Golcondo, where we forded the Ohio, and clipped the southern tip of Illinois in a western direction, until we came to Jonesboro and the Father of Waters.

The great river stopped us cold. The ice was too thin for the wagons to cross and too thick for the boats to cut through. In the end, we ferried across a channel cut by men with axes and mauls.

The process was slow and dangerous. The ones who fell through the ice were quickly whisked downriver by the currents. We never found them. At night the river froze over again, and the men began again each day breaking our way through the ice. I did my share, as did my son, Luke. But when we gathered on the western bank of the Great River at Cape Girardeau, I saw that his boots were frozen to his feet. The shivers began, and for the life of me, I could do nothing to stop them.

Hand Basket sank into her own hole. She heaped every stitch of clothing she owned on the boy — save her dress. I admonished her time and time again that I couldn't afford to have her fall sick, too. But after gangrene set in Luke's right foot and she watched the physician saw it off with little more than whiskey to ease the boy's pain, she lost all hope. She spent her days riding beside Luke in our wagon, caring for his every need. But his fever never broke, and the blood poisoning climbed higher up his thigh each day until his stinking stump turned black. Had Luke been a favorite horse, I would've shot him. Instead, I watched him suffer.

Still he never complained.

I found no game to hunt in Missouri. So many Cherokee had passed this way that the hills were stripped of life. We chose an other route west, toward Springfield, where it was thought we could find an occasional deer or elk and then turn due south for Fort Gibson in our new country.

We generally fared better. The weather remained cold, but the skies cleared. We warmed a bit during the day. Our contractor reached us here and there with kegs of flour, salt pork, and pickled corn. I shot a whitetail every other day, which reassured me that our decision to follow a different route was good.

But I could do nothing for Luke and Hand Basket. Two weeks into the hungry moon, I stopped at dusk to prepare our camp. I found my son dead in the wagon, and my wife nearly so, lying naked beside his still body. I cursed her indifference, but it only angered her. "Let me be," she cried, and what else could I do?

I went to the other women for help, and though they were occupied with tragedies of their own, they came and tried to reason with her. She sent them all away. I hacked Luke's grave out of the frozen earth. When it was deep enough, the soil felt warm to the touch. I snatched his body from Hand Basket's grip, telling her she was a fool. I planned to bury my son and then force her to care for herself if it came to that. I'd bind her hands and feet if I had to.

I laid Luke's body into the warm earth in this foreign country. I planned to mark it well and then return in the spring to bury him beside his sister and brother. I promised him I would. And then I decided to get his blowgun and other things he loved to bury with him. When I returned, I found Hand Basket lying naked in the grave with him.

"Bury me with him, husband," she begged me. "I'm already dead."

"Please, woman! Have we not suffered enough?"

"Leave us!" she screamed, crazy from grief, and I didn't know what to do. I only knew I couldn't lie down and die with her.

I know this because I tried.

At dawn, I covered their bodies with soil capped with white frost. I don't know how long Hand Basket lasted. I sat by that grave all night, waiting for her to fall asleep so that I could cover her with every blanket I had. I waited until her eyes were closed and her breathing was deep, and then I gently spread the first blanket over her bare skin. Again and again, she wadded it up and threw it out of the grave before I could reach for another. The one time she didn't was the time it didn't matter anymore. In a blind rage, I shoveled the earth on their grave. I no longer saw a reason to mark it. I'd never return.

I built a roaring fire. Then I slaughtered my roan pony and skewered its flesh on stakes to grill over the coals. I fed every Cherokee that passed my camp that day. If they were walking, I lifted their frail bodies to ride along with me. I had plenty of room. I gave every stitch of clothing to those who needed it. Everything else — any item that reminded me of my wife and children — I left beside the road. Her Bible, I burned. When my wagon was full and the meat was eaten, I joined the procession through the Ozarks. We made good time after that. The journey ended at Fort Gibson.

Now that the trail's over, there's been talk. Some say that Chief Ross should've told us that we would have to go. We could've prepared better for this ordeal. We could've saved the young and the old if we'd only known. Shame on them for saying this. I think John Ross never told us this because he never believed it would happen. He knew when we knew — and by then it was too late.

Now that I'm in this new country, which I hate despite its beauty and similarity to my Georgia hills, I'm expected to start over. I'm young. I'm strong. I have plenty of treaty money jingling in my pocket. The Ridges would be happy to sell me any thing I want. I could build a new home, clear new fields, plant new crops. People who knew me in the old country tell me I was a good husband and father. They say I once had a gift for farming. They wonder why I'm so shiftless; why I spend my days in the ragged tent my family used on the Trail Where They Cried. Why I discovered a new gift — drinking bust-head whiskey.

My neighbor, a kindhearted man, brings me fresh lumber, "Build yourself a house," he says. "You'll feel better when you're under a roof."

Build a house for *who*? I had a wife and three beautiful children. All dead, murdered as far as I'm concerned. What do I need with a house? Who am I feeding with all these crops I'm supposed to plant? What purpose do I have here? Where are my hills? Who said they could take them from me? What good is all this treaty money now that my family is dead? Why couldn't I have lain down beside my wife and died with everything else I ever loved? Why, goddamnit, why?

If John Ross had it to do over again, I think he would've spent those last months organizing the migration rather than wasting his time arguing with Americans who told him nothing but lies anyway. He should've told us that one way or another, the whites would steal our homes. But he didn't have to tell us who was to blame.

Four thousand Cherokee — one quarter of the Nation — dead in a few short months. And I promise you, all of them left this life with one hated name on their lips.

I didn't tell you about the last grave I dug. A week out from Fort Gibson I came across an old man kneeling by the side of a frozen stream. He'd gone out the night before to say his prayers and those were the last words he spoke. His face and hands were frozen, his eyes closed in peaceful slumber. I couldn't straighten his arms and legs. I hacked a round grave out of the earth with a pick and laid White Path to rest with the ancients. I didn't have enough tears left to grieve for him. Only hatred still lived within me.

Just as I once swore I'd see my family safely through this or deal, when it was over and I had failed, I pledged another, single oath over the body of a great chief who had once been Ridge's friend.

"Sleep well, my uncle," I said. "I will avenge you and all of our departed cousins. I swear it over your grave and four thousand others."

I took White Path's silver earring to remind me of my promise. I'm still holding it in my hand. I don't care about anything else.

Leave me now. I have to live with all this. So do you. I don't want to talk about it anymore.

CHAPTER FORTY-TWO

The Ridge trod carefully on the waves of spite that washed over him and his family. June was the moon of Green Corn, a time to rest from the frenzied labors of the planting month just past, a celebration of renewal and expectation. The Cherokee spoke blessings to one another, calling upon gods old and new to smile on their first-tilled fields, sapling or chards, and pastures of grass that had new names. Da Tsalu'nee was a month of hope, and fresh from the Trail Where They Cried in the summer of 1839, Ridge knew the Cherokee had never needed it more.

Ridge felt easiest among his neighbors, most of whom were treaty advocates who had sided with his decision to immigrate west. The old settlers, the Western Cherokee, had begun to warm to him and his family somewhat; at least they no longer judged him harshly for what he had done. John Brown and the other western chiefs and elders had been especially gracious. Ridge now thought of them as forgiving friends.

It was the new arrivals, the ones who had suffered so terribly over the forced march west, who remained bitterly cold toward him at this first joined council of a deeply fractured Cherokee Nation. Ridge could not fault them for their spite. Their wounds were fresh, their hatred bright and burning. Over four thousand of their loved ones dead. How could he blame them?

Although John Ross instigated the festival, Chief Brown officiated over the celebration. For eleven days, the old and new settlers greeted one another, danced and feasted together. Brown insisted that the Ridges take part in this formal union of the long-divided nation. Ridge arrived with his family and friends on the fourteenth day of the Green Corn moon — the last, he was told, of the gathering at Takatoka, Double Springs, council grounds for the swollen Cherokee Nation West.

From the beginning there had been trouble. Integrating several thousand Cherokee among those who had lived in these hills for twenty winters or more proved a confused enterprise. Bickering erupted over prices for land, supplies, seed, and livestock. The old settlers felt crowded, the immigrants unwelcome at the end of a journey that had cost them every thing they loved. There was the question of government. By which set of laws should the people abide? Who should be their chiefs? Who would speak for the Cherokee in Washington?

Ridge understood that John Brown had avoided all of these issues at this first gathering. "Why worry with all this now?" Brown confided in him. "They have their homes to build and their crops to raise. These other matters will work themselves out in time."

At the end of the celebration, Brown and the other western chiefs invited Ridge and John Ross to stand beside them as they bade their people farewell.

"Before we take our leave," Chief Brown said, "let me assure you that the Great Provider again shines on this nation. The Western Cherokee are happy to take our eastern brothers by the hand. Know that you are welcome here. Return to your homes and fields with our blessing."

He took the hand of all the chiefs and elders, with his warmest benediction left for John Ross.

"May we ask," John Ross said loudly, for the benefit of the crowd, "on what specific terms we are to be received?"

Chief Brown appeared daunted. "I've already told them," he replied. "The object of our festival has been accomplished to my mind. We're reunited. We've enjoyed our time together. Your people seem well satisfied."

"The celebration itself, Chief Brown, was

most satisfactory," Ross said. "But it's my strong feeling that the immigrants expect a more explicit, formal reception now that the celebration is at an end. We would be grateful if you could spell out the privileges to which we are entitled."

Chief Brown sighed. He looked to his elders for assistance. He even glanced at Ridge, who shrugged his shoulders. "Very well," he said to Ross, and he turned to address the crowd. "We cordially receive you as brothers. The whole land is before you. You may freely go wherever you choose and select any place for settlement that may please you, with this one restriction: You must make every effort not to interfere with the private rights of individuals. You are lawful voters in whatever of the four districts in which you choose to reside. You are immediately eligible for any office to which you are legally elected. We have these past twenty winters established a government under which our people have lived in peace and prosperity. We expect you to live under these same laws until such time that we, as one nation, see fit to alter, repeal, or amend them. In the meantime, we ask that you strive to establish yourselves as good and peaceable citizens of Cherokee Nation West."

The new settlers halloed and cheered the news. Brown nodded to them one and all, and then turned and graciously bowed to Ross. "They seem satisfied now," he said.

Ridge smiled at Brown's eloquence, but he noticed that John Ross did not share his enthusiasm.

"It's important," Ross said, "that my faction remain as an organized body politic for the purpose of settling our accounts with the United States." Chief Brown's gaze turned skyward as he deliberated how to amend his earlier words. "All right," he said, chewing his lip. "For the settlement of all matters growing out of your removal from the Old Nation, you are freely allowed your own chiefs and council with the name and style of the Eastern Cherokee. Conduct your affairs as you see fit."

Ross mulled over Chief Brown's proposition. Ridge had seen this expression before during the negotiations with Jackson. Ross wanted one thing while he was offered another. He rose again.

"We thank you for your goodwill," he said. "We understand that you mean well. We believe your system of government has been fair and just. But perhaps our present situation is more complex than you realize. We feel strongly that such a loose organization of authority is in no way prepared to deal with the problems we now face together."

Chief Brown stiffened. The crowd grew silent. Warriors studied his face. "Our system of government is modeled after your own, Chief Ross," Brown said. "The laws are the same. Nevertheless, as I stated before, elections will take place in October, at which time you can place your own officials in office who can begin to revise the code and write a constitution that will serve us all." He threw up his hands. "What more could you ask of me?"

"We see no reason to wait for the October elections. We're building more than farms in this country. We came to Double Springs to unite a nation. Let's call a convention and set our delegates to the business of governing the whole of the Cherokee."

"I invited you to dance and you come ready to debate me." Chief Brown drew a deep breath. Ridge could see the anger building in his face. "My people, the old settlers, are busy with their personal affairs. Matters of state, as I'm sure you're aware, always wait until the fall, after the crops have been gathered. Wisdom prevails when the elders' stomachs are full. Your own people are hungry, Chief Ross. I wonder if their time is better spent this first summer tending their families and farms rather than engaging in politics. They know they can't eat a new constitution, so I ask you, who wants this convention?"

He glowered at John Ross before he lowered his voice and addressed the people. "You new settlers outnumber us two to one. If it's power you want, you'll soon have it under the system I've already described, the very same one my people have lived under in peace for twenty winters. For now, however, there's nothing more to do. Summer belongs to the farmers. The politicians among you can wait for the October elections. That's the last word from your brothers, the Western Cherokee. We bid you farewell."

Ross sat blankly before a murmuring crowd, allowing time for John Brown and the others to leave the platform. Once the westerners had cleared out, Ross stood and extended his arms.

"I beg you all to remain with me here," he said. "We have much to discuss."

"I'm sure he does," John Brown said quietly to Ridge once they'd taken a few steps from the platform. "I don't know if you did the right thing for all of your people, but I know for a fact it was wise for you to get away from him. The man is a mule."

"Patience," Ridge said. "His heart is good."

"It's his mouth that causes the trouble," Brown said. "Did you see how quickly his people — my people — turned against me? I gave him what he wanted and they still don't trust me."

"They've suffered so," Ridge said. "They'll come around in time. You're a good man. They'll see that."

"I got the distinct impression they were just about to slip a rope around my neck if I said another word. I'm going home to my family to serve out the rest of my term. After that, Ross can have it. I'd sooner butt heads with a river bluff."

"It'll blow over," Ridge said.

"And who will be alive after it does? I had nothing to do with the Treaty of New Echota, and yet I feel threatened by these angry people. I can't imagine what's going through your mind."

"Yes, you can," Ridge said.

John Brown mounted his horse and gathered the reins in his hands. He paused to look back at the crowd. "I'd think hard about staying here if I were you, Ridge. I know I will."

"I've run as far as I plan to."

"Suit yourself, Ridge Walker." He eyed the assembly again. "Best to pull in the latch string at night, my brother. Keep your family close. A watchman up at night."

"Thank you, brother chief. Safe travel."

John Brown clucked his tongue and pressed his heels against the big bay's flank. Ridge looked at his Cherokee. Almost none of them were listening to John Ross. Instead, they were glaring at him. Ridge made the connection. They saw him conferring privately with Brown, the man who they thought was denying them what John Ross told them they deserved — one nation united under Ross's leadership. Their suffering primed them to view Brown's reasoning as an obstacle between them and their rights. Brown whispered harmless talk in Ridge's ear, but the immigrants saw only plot and intrigue. Ridge was conspiring against them. He saw the blood in their eyes.

Ridge gathered his son, Boudinot, and Stand Watie, and all his treaty neighbors. "Away now, all of you," he said. "There's trouble here."

Without questioning they began to untie their ponies from the string. Stand Watie tightened his cinch and yanked his rifle from its scabbard to check the primer charge. Ridge saw groups of three and four men drift apart from whispering cells of womanless Cherokee, reach under their sashes for pistols and knives, and sink back into the brush to circle them.

"You must go now!" Ridge told them. "Stay together. Keep your families under one roof for a time."

John reached for his father's hand. "And you, Ridge?"

"What do I have to fear from my own people?" he said. "Quickly now." Ridge mounted his horse and stood in the tracks left by his family, waiting to cut off any who would follow them. In the end, only one man, dressed in a black suit, came out to him. Ridge held up his hand.

"Welcome, my chief," he said, when Ross was close enough to hear him.

"I'm glad I caught you, Ridge," Ross said.

"I wanted to speak with you alone."

"Ridge is here to listen," he said. Ridge was amazed that he felt no animosity against him. The new country had freed him from his anger toward John Ross.

"I gather Chief Brown is somewhat reluctant to reorganize."

"When cornered, even the opossum shows its teeth," Ridge said. "He's a good man, just like the chiefs we respected when we were young."

"A bit simple for my liking," Ross said.

"Everything's new here," Ridge said. His voice was tempered. He felt like an adviser again. He also believed Ross would listen. "Try not to push so, John. Remember the old ways as best you can. Soon enough, you'll win them over."

"Chief Brown has the luxury of remaining ignorant. It's not so for us. You and I both know what has to be done to stand against the United States. Our battles are far from over. I may have to step on Chief Brown's toes to prepare."

"I don't think you'll get close enough to Chief Brown's toes to mash them," Ridge said. "Organize as you will. He'll avoid you like the pox."

"And you?" Ross asked, looking down his nose. The principal chief still didn't understand that their personal battle was over.

"I won't avoid you," Ridge said. "But I

won't stand in your way, either. You will soon be principal chief of a united Cherokee Nation. My kin will be honored to obey you."

"I sincerely appreciate your faith in me," he said. "There's little I can do for you, of course. But when our people are settled, I intend to publicly redeem you."

"I don't seek redemption, Chief Ross. I seek peace. I've found it here. My sincerest wish is that you will, too."

Ross swallowed hard and dug at the ground with the toe of his shoe. "I want you to know that what's done is done. I've asked for forbearance toward the signers of the treaty."

"I don't see much forbearance on the faces of the young men."

"Not now, no," Ross said, hands deep in his pockets, solidly in control. "But in due time, perhaps. They've suffered so much."

"Haven't we all?" Ridge said, and he hung his head. This might be his last opportunity to speak to his old friend. His heart told him to say what had gone unspoken between them. "I want you to understand that had I known that over four thousand would die, I would never have put my mark on that treaty."

"I know —"

Ridge held up his hand. "But I want you to know this also. In my heart, I know that it didn't have to happen."

"You see?" Ross said. "We're starting to

agree again already."

"No, you don't see. You don't see at all. Two years passed, and you did nothing for our people but tell them what they wanted to hear."

Ridge saw the anger build in Ross's face. "And what did you do but betray our people and violate our laws?"

Ridge didn't care about Ross's bitter reaction. Had angry words passed between them back when it mattered, many Cherokee would still walk the earth. Now, Ridge would be heard. "There was a higher law than yours, John Ross. I was compelled to obey it. Now the people blame me for this horror. But know that I, the Man Who Walks the Mountaintops, blame you. You would not listen. You could not see. The only choice left me was to defy my people to save them."

"I buried four thousand of those you saved, Ridge."

"Had the Cherokee stayed in the old country, you would have buried them all."

"Not so," Ross said. "Even now, a thousand or more squat in the Blue Ridge in defiance. Because of what you did, we'll never know if the rest of us could've done the same."

"I know the answer to that," Ridge said. "But I predict the stragglers will not lose their hold on the Blue Mountains."

"By what means?" Ross asked.

"By means of the Trail Where They Cried,"

Ridge said. "Even the loudest supporters of Indian removal are outraged by this disaster. The Americans have lost their appetite for killing Cherokee. Those who hid in the eastern hills will keep them. The dead bought a home for the living."

Ross shook his head. "Speak of it no more, Ridge. We won't reach an accord. As I said, between us what's done is done. We have the future to think of now."

"I have no future," Ridge said. "The Blood Law hovers over my head like a buzzard."

Almost immediately Ridge sensed regret in his friend's face. Ross seemed coldly logical to those who didn't know him well. But Ridge had witnessed his warmth many times. The quality of moving from one emotion to the next was what had most endeared Ross to him during their good years together.

"I'll protect you all I can," Ross said.

Ridge laughed. "Now I really am worried."

Ross looked slightly befuddled. One seldom saw it. "I have no idea how you can joke at a time like this," he said.

"Who's joking?" Ridge said. He wheeled his horse, checking the edges of the brush to see if the young warriors were coming. What could Ross do to stop them? He looked earnestly at his principal chief, hoping Ross could recognize that Ridge meant what he was about to say. "I'm worried about Sehoya," he said. "She has a cough along with some many cares. If . . . something . . . were to happen to me, you'll look after her, won't you?"

"You have my word on it, Ridge."

He offered his hand. Ridge grasped it between both of his. "I'm terribly sorry about Quatie, John," he said. "We all loved her."

"She gave her last blanket to a sick child," Ross said, his grief sweeping over him. "I couldn't make her care for herself when so many others were suffering."

Ridge closed his eyes to remember Quatie's smile. Another great one gone. The guilt he felt over Ross's wife was second only to that he felt for White Path. He shook his head to chase away the unbearable image of these good people dying out on the roads.

He squeezed Ross's hand. "We've had our differences, principal chief," Ridge said. "But there was a day when we battled together, side by side. I was proud to be your friend. I was honored to be your servant."

"Servant?" Ross said. "Your memory is short. As a young man, you showed me the way. You were the greatest chief of your time. In another age, I would've followed you anywhere."

"You should've followed me here," he said with a weak grin. "But just the same, we've arrived in this new country. We're bleeding, but we're still alive. We have a future before us. I'll take that one lone consolation to my grave."

"God be with you, Ridge Walker."

"I'll cast my lot with the spirits of my youth," Ridge said. "I walked away from my country, but I never abandoned it. Tonight, I'll bathe in the Neosho, but in my mind's eye, I'll be in the clear waters of the Hiwassee, where I swore a warrior's oath. When the young men come for me, I'll already be home among my ancestors."

"I won't let them kill you."

"You can't stop them from claiming what's theirs," he said. "We came here to save our ancient ways. Abide by them." He scanned the edges of the brush. He had time. Ridge climbed down from his horse and scooped up a handful of soil from the heart of the new council ground and held it before John Ross.

"Tell your children that the Ridge didn't die for this," he said. "The soil was never important. It's the Cherokee who are precious. The Ridge laid down his life to see his people endure."

He pulled his medicine pouch from his sash, opened its thong with his teeth, and allowed the dust to sift through his fingers and mix with the spiritual tokens he'd kept close to his body for a lifetime. Then he remounted his horse.

"Lead my people well, Tsan Usdi," Ridge

said, gripping Ross's moist hand one more time. "You have the blessings of my true heart."

Out of the corner of his eyes he saw them coming. Warriors blocked the road. Ross slapped the hip of Ridge's horse and then walked in front of the killers to delay them. Ridge slammed the reins against his mount's shoulders and the stallion easily jumped the fence. Ridge rode hard for the thickets, and once he'd reached them he bore east for Arkansas.

They couldn't have him yet, he thought. His family needed time to prepare. When Ridge was ready, the Cherokee could settle his account.

CHAPTER FORTY-THREE

The Believer
There is a legend among the Ani-yunwi-ya, the People of Kitu'hwa, as ancient as the Blue Mountains, as the People themselves. I first heard it from Agan'stat'. Now that I'm old I often think of my father. For some reason I don't remember the details of our quarrels all that well or even why I grew to be ashamed of him. I can't tell how deeply I regret that now. My guilt guided my relationships with my children and the people I once served as chief. I hurt my father terribly, but I was a better man because I made this horrible mistake I could never take back. From my suffering came a great good.

My father was once a great war chief, and when I was a boy I followed him everywhere like a puppy. I loved that man so much my heart ached whenever he left us for the war trace or the hunt. I don't know if Agan'stat' heard that I always cried when he went away.

I was born a part of him. I couldn't see myself as a separate person. Without my father near me, I was nothing.

When Agan'stat' returned from his journeys, the first thing he always did was take me to the river. We said our prayers together, and then he sparked a fire and told me stories while we dried our bodies under the stars. I remember the way his dark eyes mirrored the flames, how the river breeze tossed his long, black hair, and how rough his hands felt on my shoulders when he told me how proud he was of me. Those days are gone forever, but I've done my best to pass these stories on to my grandchildren. Among all the myths Agan'stat' told me, this one was my favorite:

Two hunters, no different in appearance or manners from any other Ani-yunwi-ya, arrived at the old town of Kana'sta, asking to speak to their chief. The chief welcomed them, as did the elders and clan mothers, and then the chief, assuming the strangers hailed from one of the western settlements, inquired from whence they came.

"We are of your people," they replied. "Our village is very near to your own, but you've never seen it."

"My friends," the chief said, "this can't be. I know every wood and water within twelve sleeps of this country."

"Mark us well, Uncle," the strangers said. "What we say is true. In your village you have wars and hunger, with enemies on every side. Soon, a stronger enemy comes who will take your country from you and cause your people great suffering. In our village, we are always happy. We know peace and need not think of danger. Our soil is rich with plants, our woods thick with game. We have come to invite you to share our village with us. There is room for all."

"Where is this place?" the chief asked.

The strangers pointed to Tsuwa'tel'da, the great mountain known to the Ani-yonegas as Pilot Knob. "We must go," they said. "But if your people will live with us, let them fast seven sleeps. At dawn on the eighth, bid them go to the rivers and cleanse body and mind in crystal streams, and we will come to take them away from their troubles." After this, they said no more, and headed west for the mountains.

The people of Kana'sta discussed the matter at great length in council, deciding at last that they would like to accept the strangers' invitation. For seven sleeps, they fasted. At dawn on the eighth, they went to the river together to bathe and afterward dressed in their finest skins. Before the sun was high, they saw a multitude of Ani-yunwi-ya coming along the trail from the west, led by the same two hunters who had visited them only days before. The two villages greeted one another warmly, and then the chief said, "I have a friend visiting me from another village who has fasted along with the rest. May he come too?"

"He is welcome," they said, and the strangers took up the people of Kana'sta's burden, and together they walked, west to ward Tsuwa'tel'da.

When the people reached the mountain, they paused at a great rock face. The hunters led them through a sharp, dark crevice wide enough for only one man to pass. Warily, the people of Kana'sta followed their guides into this cave, only to find that it soon opened up like a door to bright light. Once their eyes had adjusted, they saw the country before them as lush and clean as the strangers had first described. In the valley lay the village, with two rows of houses running east and west.

"We live in the south row," the strangers said. "The north row has been prepared for you. Choose any house that suits you."

In no time at all, the people of Kana'sta were settled and happy, content to live with their new friends. But the chief's acquaintance began to long for his family and asked if he could go home. The people of Kana'sta thought he was a fool to leave such a paradise, but the old villagers said, "Let him go if he will. He may tell his friends and family what we have here, and they will be welcome, too."

"I thank you for your kindness," the chief's

friend said. "It is truly beautiful here, and I will return. But you need not trouble to send your people after me. I'll come back on my own."

"Our friend," the strangers said, "we come for you. You cannot come for us. We see you wherever you go and are with you in all your dances and prayers, but you cannot see us unless you fast for seven sleeps. When this is done, we will come and speak to you of your desires. If you want to live with us, you must prepare in the exact manner as the time before, and then we will come and lead you and yours to our home."

Then the strangers led the chief's friend back through the valley, through the open door in the bluff, at last squeezing through the tight crevice on the eastern flank of the mountain. They saw him through and departed.

The chief's friend had taken only a few steps before he realized that he had forgotten his favorite bow. He turned around to go back through the crevice, but all he found was solid rock rising to the clouds. For half a day, he searched for the entrance to the mountain valley, but he could not find it.

The people of Kana'sta were never seen again. Those who watched the mountain saw no cook fires at night. Those who hunted it saw no moccasin tracks on its steep, brushy trails. The Ani-yunwi-ya feared that the mountain was haunted by evil spirits who had lured the people of Kana'sta from their homes and made them slaves and prisoners. But the chief's friend consoled them.

"Worry not for them," he said, "for I know they are happy in their sacred home. There is no place more beautiful and abundant on all of Turtle Island, and when I am old and my children are grown and I'm weary of the cares of this world, I will be pleased to join them as I was promised long ago."

Did you like it? I do. It reminds me of how the Cherokee lived before the whites overran us. It's sad for me to think that what we once were we will never be again. I'm old, but I can still imagine. I can still dream.

I think now that winter is upon me I like that myth for another reason. I have a little white man's blood in my veins, but I've never listened to it. Perhaps because the missionaries knew I was a mixed-blood, they were always after me to accept their religion. In my weakest moments, I thought about letting them have their way. I made many compromises as my river ran its course, but I never yielded in my belief in the Great Provider, the one true God. He's probably the same one the Christians worship. But I could pray to Him in Cherokee, and during a life where I let go of so many things dear to me, I could never bring myself to let go of Him. I don't understand why He let us suffer so, but I still believe He loves the Cherokee. I believe He will honor his promises to us.

After a lifetime of struggle and change, the myth remains special to me. It describes where I'm going when I leave this world, and that curious child who still lives within this withered body can't wait to begin my journey. Now that my people are settled in the west, I'm finished here. I loved a good woman. We raised forthright children to walk in our place. I fought the good fight. Despite all my mistakes, I think I lived my life with honor. I believe that my ancestors have made a place for me in that green and happy valley. I've waited a lifetime to make my peace with Agan'stat'. I want to thank him for the gift of that story. Nothing else save the love of Sehoya has brought me so much comfort.

Worry not for the Man Who Walks the Mountaintops, my friends. For I am old, my children are grown, and I am truly weary of the cares of this world. My ancestors are waiting for me. I will know what it's like to be loved by my people again. I'm not afraid to die.

Chapter Forty-Four:
10:00 A.M., June 22, 1839
Little Branch or White Rock Creek, Arkansas

"Before you stands Kah-nung-da-tla-geh," he said, "the Man Who Walks the Mountaintops, once a chief among you."

Ridge paused to gather himself while he stared at the stream running over twisted roots and smooth white stones, an artery connecting this world with the next. Comforted by the sound of running water, he paused and collected himself. He breathed deeply, drawing strength from his conviction that his executioners owed him one last speech. Ridge had accepted many disappointments, but he still believed that given the opportunity, reason would prevail over rage and revenge. Above all, the Cherokee were a people of heart.

He yelled so loudly that his voice spooked Joseph's horse. He told his unseen killers the whole story of hope and faith, of broken promises and betrayal, all far more complex than they had assumed when they agreed that Ridge should die for his crimes. They allowed him to say everything he wanted without making a move, and Ridge was truly thankful for one last chance to demonstrate why he had once been the voice of a nation.

"The Ridge alone saw the future," he said. "And then, with love in his heart for the Cherokee, he picked their only path."

This was the end of it. He closed his eyes, his arms still spread before him, his palms open, waiting for them to pull the trigger. The unceasing flow of the stream marked the passing of anxious moments.

Silence. He opened his eyes. He thought again of the boy. Ridge smiled at him tersely. "Stand back, Joseph," he said. "They aren't here for you."

"Run, Chief Ridge!" the boy cried.

"No," he said. "You stay back."

He turned back to the bench above him, staring at the place where he'd seen the juniper and mulberry limbs twitch. "Step out," he said. "Let me see your faces. What do you have to fear from an old man?"

One by one they rose from behind their cover. Young, spirited full-bloods all, men who would have been warriors in an earlier time. What they were now, Ridge couldn't say. He recognized the brothers, James and Jefferson Hair, and Bird, the nephew of old Doublehead. Last to emerge was Kahn-yah-tah-hee, First to Kill, called Charlie Blue. There were others, he thought, still hiding behind the rocks. The four warriors raked the brush aside and took a step or two toward him, rifles borne forward, eyes narrow and cold.

"We are ani-waya," James Hair said in a low growl. "Your clan, your blood. We've heard your account. But the fact remains that you broke the law."

"I made the law," Ridge said.

"Then you know the penalty."

"I have exacted the penalty myself." He pointed his finger at Bird Doublehead. "I killed your uncle for the crime of treason and was glad to do it. I've never known a more wretched, corrupt man."

"It gives me great pleasure," the young warrior said, "to have the honor of avenging him this day."

"What are you waiting for, then?" Ridge said, sitting erect in the saddle. "Is your cause not just? Did I not betray my own people to fatten my purse?" Jefferson Hair shouldered his rifle. Ridge, his empty hands still extended, lifted his face skyward and let his eyelids fall.

"I can't do it," he heard Charlie Blue say. "Haven't we lost enough already?"

Ridge opened his eyes to see the rifle fall from Charlie Blue's shoulder. "It's not so easy to kill a Cherokee, is it?" Ridge said. "I did it once. I hope you can live with the guilt better than I."

"Four thousand dead," James Hair said. "What's one more? Especially when it's the bastard who killed them."

"He was our chief!" Charlie Blue said. "I admired him so. I won't have a hand in his death."

"I will," Doublehead's nephew said, and Ridge saw no hesitation in his eyes. "The Ridge's tongue is shrewd. He'll talk us out of it if we wait much longer." Bird spit in contempt and took aim.

"I beg of you one favor," Ridge said.

Bird shook his head and persisted until Charlie Blue shoved his rifle aside. "Are you cruel enough that you'd deny him a last request?" Bird wrestled the barrel away from Charlie Blue.

Ridge spoke quickly. "Let my blood settle the feud," he said. "Don't kill my son or my nephews. They possess arts and knowledge that took years to cultivate. The Nation needs them more than ever. Take my life and forgive theirs."

"It's too late," James Hair sneered. "If they saw the sunrise this morning, they saw little else. Others more deliberate than we attended to their crimes."

Ridge's jaw clamped shut. His fingers clawed his scalp while spasms rocked his body. Wasted! Everything wasted. Tears of rage rolled down his cheeks as John's face flickered in his mind.

"Kill me, then!" Ridge shouted. "Or I'll kill you and any other Cherokee I find with my kinsmen's blood on their hands!" He ripped his tomahawk from its saddle loop. "Mere children speak to me of the Blood Law! I lived by it in a time when the Cherokee were warriors!" His killers, awed, moved back from him, fumbling with their rifles. "I'll die by it today!"

Ridge buried his spurs into the horse's gut. The gelding screamed and reared. Ridge leaned low against its neck, jerked up the reins' slack, forced the horse's head toward the warriors, willing the beast to bear down on his enemies. The stallion violently shook its head against the pinch of the halter. Its teeth clanked against the bit. Then it steadied and blew hard. Ridge felt it cock its hind legs, gathering itself to leap forward. He bellowed his war cry and twirled the tomahawk over his head. Bird would be the first to die.

He felt a small hand grip his arm.

"No, Major Ridge!" Joseph said, trotting up in front of him. "Don't do it!"

Ridge wheeled his horse between the warriors and the young boy. "I told you to stand clear, Joseph! They'll kill you." He glanced over his shoulder at the four warriors and yanked his reins to drive Joseph's horse aside. He felt the hot burn pierce his back, shuddering as if he'd been struck by a blacksmith's hammer. He stiffened when the thunder violently shook him.

The horse screamed in terror and looked back at him. Ridge saw the whites of its rolling eyes. Tufts of white, acrid smoke swept over him like a fog. Blood bubbled from his stomach, soaking his hunting shirt, covering his saddle and his thighs, coating the withers of his horse.

His tomahawk slipped from his grasp. His arms felt heavy. He made one last effort to push Joseph back, and then the dizziness came, followed by a numbness in his torso. His body would no longer obey him. He heard a second rifle crack. The instantaneous blow knocked him from his saddle and he splashed headlong into the running stream.

He struggled for breath. His eyelids fluttered. He shook his head and struggled to focus. The water swirled crimson around him. He watched it roll red over smooth stones and around mossy stumps, rushing down stream and around the bend where he could not see. He closed his eyes, imagining his blood flowing from the Ozark hills to where White Rock Creek merged with Barren Fork, then flowing together to the Illinois River, on to the Arkansas, to the muddy Father of Waters, to the dark Spanish sea.

He heard flint rock rattle beneath slow-moving feet. He opened his eyes, looked toward the warriors descending the cliffs above. Behind them were fifty Cherokee —

no, a hundred — standing calmly at the base of the white bluffs. They smiled at him from beneath their calico turbans and buckskins so supple they glowed white in the morning sun. Their silver earrings shimmered.

"Who are you?" Ridge asked one of their elders.

The killers froze in their tracks, confused. They peered behind them to see who Ridge was talking to. One of the Cherokee with a crop of silver hair on his head stepped forward.

"We are the people of Kana'sta," the old man said, his voice soft, warm, and assuring like a spring breeze. "We've made a place for you, Kah-nung-da-tla-geh."

Ridge smudged the mud from his face with the heel of his hand. "And my son?"

"He waits to greet you on the other side," the old man said. "And your daughter Nancy. Kilakeena, too. Your mother and father. They're all with us."

"I can't leave Sehoya alone."

"Sehoya will come when she's ready, my friend."

The old man motioned to the rock face behind him. Ridge saw the gash in the stone. He hadn't noticed it before. The cave cast off its shadow, its opening brilliant, as if the sun burned through it. Beyond was only bright space.

"We'll carry your burdens from here, Ridge

Walker," the old man said. "Rest easy and prepare for your journey. Peace waits for you."

Ridge pushed himself up on one wobbly arm. Rivulets of bloody water trickled down his sleeve. The stream below his body was so thick with blood he could no longer see the white stones resting in its bed. Bird, lips snarling, stood coldly over him, pulling his pistol from his beaded belt. Ridge looked back toward the bluff. Charlie Blue sobbed into his hands. The ancients waited. The stream ran on with his blood.

Ridge yanked his medicine pouch free and poured his crystal, bird claw, and Uktena scales and a mound of council ground soil into his hand. The blood and water turned it into mud and Ridge clenched it tightly in his fist. He held it high over his head.

"Look!" Ridge cried to the ancients, "I still have it. This time I won't let it go."

"Who are you talking to?" Bird Double-head said. "John Ross ain't here. Ain't no Cherokee gonna help you."

Bird slapped the hip of Joseph's horse, sending the beast bounding out of the craggy draw. "Tell his family justice was done!" he shouted to the frightened boy. Ridge watched the horse climb safely out of the stream bed and race for the hills beyond. The sound of frantic hooves and crashing brush died in the distance.

"The blood feud," Ridge said in thick, slurred gasps, "never ends."

"Shut up!" Bird said. "It's your own blood who judges you. Your clan avenges the thousands lying in unmarked graves along the Trail of Tears. You picked that path for them against their wishes and in defiance of our laws. This day, you pay the price."

Bird looked back at the others. The Hairs stood with him, Charlie Blue apart. He kicked Ridge hard enough to flop him onto his back. Ridge felt the sharp pressure and pain, saw how his blood gushed into the rushing stream, racing downhill, running on. It all begins and ends with the rivers, the conjurer had told him when he was a boy. An oracle. His fate. He put his fist against his heart to protect the soil from the currents. This time, he would not let it go.

Ridge stared at the dead eyes of his killer, who straddled him, cocked his hammer, and pressed the warm bore against his forehead. His finger slipped behind the trigger. There was a moment of hesitation, the slightest inkling of uncertainty and regret that falls upon the righteous whenever they commit themselves to revenge. Ridge read the pain in the young man's angry face, and he knew his executioner bore witness to a horror that would never leave him, from which he would never be free.

"I forgive you," Ridge said with no voice.

"If I saw the world as you do, I would have done the same thing. Know you are forgiven. Know that I'll always love the Cherokee."

The hammer snapped against the pan, and then Ridge heard nothing more. The flint sparked and that was the last of the light. Ridge was instantly released from all heat and all hatred. He loved. He felt as if he were floating, gripped by a warm, powerful current, of being gently cast deeper into the void. His spirit merged with that of the water, relentlessly accelerating together, until they were hurled as one toward the welcoming embrace of an ever-expanding ocean. Blood and water rolling on, rushing onward, forever forward, farther and farther away. Absorbed. United. Free.

To the streams, to the muddy rivers. To the dark, fathomless, infinite sea. He knew only the sense of belonging.

AUTHOR'S NOTE

"I fought through the Civil War and have seen men shot to pieces and slaughtered by the thousands, but the Cherokee removal was the cruelest work I ever knew."
— A CONFEDERATE COLONEL WHO SERVED WITH THE GEORGIA VOLUNTEERS

They walk unseen among us. In the 2000 census, 299,862 citizens of the United States identified themselves as Cherokee, which means they constitute the largest North American Indian tribe now existing. Unlike the Navajo, Pueblo, Cheyenne, Lakota, and all other western nations, the Cherokee faced white men from the first moment Europeans set foot on this continent, yet they thrive in numbers far beyond that of any of the surviving American Indian nations. The Cherokee deliver our mail, heal us when we're sick, sit on our juries, work in our factories, run in our elections, teach in our schools, represent us in our courts, and fight our wars. They are

651

with us forever.

Not too long ago, I conducted a book signing in my hometown in Arkansas. One of the women I had known as a child asked about my former wife. I mentioned, at some point, that we'd recently learned that she was one-quarter Cherokee. "It's a good mix," the woman said without hesitation. I couldn't agree more. Cherokee blood has been blended with ours in this intricate, crucial, improbable experiment that we call America, just as the most enlightened of our Founding Fathers had hoped that it some day would. One of Ridge's direct descendants is a blond-haired, blue-eyed senior technical writer who lives outside Dallas, Texas. I can't help but believe that Major Ridge would savor her successful acclimation into a culture that had turned him away.

Even more astonishing is that one can sit in a restaurant owned by the Cherokee Nation in Tahlequah, Oklahoma, and order up a steak next to a full-blood Cherokee. In that person's body runs the unyielding, unbroken stream from our time all the way back to the murky depths of prehistoric humanity. The full weight of the modern world crashed down upon generations of this person's ancestors, and yet there he sits, in quiet, absolute defiance of a society that spent the last three hundred years trying to destroy him by every means at its disposal.

One doesn't hear much about Major Ridge anymore, though the weary Ross-Ridge feud still smolders. Accusations flew back and forth via a few curiously vehement e-mails while I was writing this book. Apparently an argument erupted between Ross and Ridge adherents when the Chieftains Museum opened back in 1971 in Rome, Georgia. After yelling insults at each other, squabblers were led by the museum staff to separate buses for the long journey home to Oklahoma.

The editors of a Web site dedicated to the heritage of northern Georgia listed Major Ridge first in their list of "ten most influential people" of that region. Some ancestors of Ridge's enemies have reached through the veil of time to admire and honor his struggles, while contemporary Cherokee may prefer to remember him as the chief who sold their souls to Andrew Jackson, the contemptible turncoat who drove them from their ancestral homes, the man most responsible for the debacle of the Trail of Tears.

On the beautiful grounds of the Cherokee Heritage Center in Tahlequah, there stand impressive busts and memorials dedicated to the memory of John Ross, Admiral Jocko Clark, and even Elias Boudinot. There are none to Major Ridge. Sequoyah's name and alphabet are rightfully celebrated everywhere around Tahlequah. You won't find any trace of Major Ridge. The mention of Will Rogers brings a smile to their faces. Ridge, if anything, might summon a disappointed frown.

These days most Western Cherokee, like all Americans, tend to celebrate their celebrities, like singer/songwriter Rita Coolidge, or the actors James Earl Jones and the immensely talented full-blood Wes Studi. When it comes to homegrown politicians, Wilma Mankiller still stands tall, as does the current principal chief of the Cherokee Nation, the handsome, charismatic young attorney Chad Smith. For writers, they need look no further than their prolific, award-winning neighbor, Robert J. Conley. There are plenty of flesh and blood heroes in every facet of modern life for the Oklahoma Cherokee to admire.

Major Ridge's name probably won't come up unless one is in search of an argument, and even then the most inflammatory comment will probably be met by an uninterested Cherokee shrug. Most Western Cherokee have far better things to worry about than the reasons why 160 years ago, an aging, ill, and beleaguered man chose the lesser of two unjust evils, and died for his decision. They just know Major Ridge did what he did. They accept it, along with the host of other past indignities suffered at the hands of the dominant culture that overwhelmed them, and move on to the challenges that lie ahead.

But if they look hard at the past, they'll see themselves as a uniquely American miracle.

If they cast their long stares to their Oklahoma hills, they might catch a glimpse of Ridge's defiant spirit as it moves among them. Like the hills, he's still there, still hoping, still urging them to endure.

In fact, despite all odds the Cherokee have endured in the exact manner the illiterate Major Ridge hoped they would when he scratched his mark on the Treaty of New Echota. Though ignorant of the Americans' written language, he understood American minds well enough to know they meant to wipe the Cherokee from the face of the earth. He understood what the document meant, and even more, what he hoped it would accomplish. The stakes, in his view, were all or nothing, with the fate of his nation hanging in the balance. Ridge, born to lead his people, looked far beyond them before he tipped the scales with a reluctant hand.

In the short run, his vision failed him. Just as John Ross predicted, the Americans would come knocking again. Ridge could not save a sovereign Cherokee Nation independent of the United States. History has since proven that no Western Cherokee — not even John Ross — could. But he believed that if he sacrificed himself by forcing his people west beyond the reach of the Americans, he might buy time enough to preserve their culture and heritage — more valuable to him than their land — and let the rivers roll on.

In this one ambition, Major Ridge has succeeded beyond his most imaginative dreams. Today, that full-blood in Tahlequah can do what he pleases, and what pleases him is to remain Cherokee. Whether he realizes it or not, he has, in part, the Man Who Walks the Mountaintops to thank for the opportunity to do so.

The Oklahoma Cherokee have not gone, and they will not go. Major Ridge's monument lies unseen in their living hearts, and this one is the most glorious of them all.

— David Marion Wilkinson
Austin, Texas
February 1998 — August 2001

Major Ridge staunchly believed that education would be the Cherokee's salvation. Honor his memory by continuing his legacy. Please send your tax-deductible contribution to the Cherokee Nation Education Corporation and help young Cherokee scholars achieve their dreams.

Cherokee Nation Education Corporation
P.O. Box 948
Tahlequah, OK 74465
(918) 456-0671, ext. 2420
mraymond@cherokee.org /
www.cherokee.org

ACKNOWLEDGMENTS

A novelist friend of mine once wrote, "A biographical novel is a hybrid creature of fact and fabrication, in which authenticity becomes a dubious virtue." The same is particularly true in the case of *Oblivion's Altar*. I made every attempt to portray Major Ridge and his times as accurately as I could. However, many of the facts of Ridge's life are, in truth, lost to time and flawed memory. Much of Cherokee history and culture was unfortunately recorded by white men who were passionate about their subject, but could not possibly have understood it. Two very likely primary Cherokee sources — John Ridge and Elias Boudinot — both of formidable intellect and education, fully steeped in the tradition of their fathers while they were also eyewitnesses to the events leading to the Treaty of New Echota, were executed in 1839. No one of their ability stepped forward in their time to fill their tragic void. Nevertheless, fragmented accounts from primary sources survived. There is also a paper trail — articles from the *Phoenix,* Congressional and War Department records, and extensive articulate letters penned by John Ridge, Elias Boudinot, Stand Watie, John Ross, and many others who lived through these times. Historians have meticulously documented many of the events of Major Ridge's life and even the verbatim text of some of his speeches. I gladly included these elements in the novel wherever I could to enable a reader to get close to this man, but even these were contaminated by my perspective. In addition, many scenes depicted in *Oblivion's Altar* admittedly occurred only in my imagination. I wrote a novel. Major Ridge lived a real life. Please bear in mind that these two events are by nature incompatible. The best that I can claim is that I was faithful to what is known.

I climbed on the backs of others. First and foremost, I acknowledge my debt to the late Thurman Wilkins. His *Cherokee Tragedy: The Ridge Family and the Decimation of a People* remains the definitive text about the Ridge's life, and especially about the events leading to the infamous Treaty of New Echota. Beautifully written and meticulously researched, I highly recommend *Cherokee Tragedy* for those who wish to read the true history of Ridge's struggles. Another excellent one-volume source of the Cherokee during this era is Marion L. Starkey's *The Cherokee Nation.* Though the book was written in the 1940s, Ms. Starkey's voice is timeless. I borrowed heavily upon the scholarship and craft of John Ehle's *Trail of Tears: The Rise and Fall of the Cherokee Nation.* Mr. Ehle, a lifelong resident of North Carolina, is intimate with his subject and renders a fresh, passionate account. I owe a debt to William G. McLoughlin, Cherokee scholar, professor of history at Brown University, and author of *Cherokee Renascence in the New Republic.* I wove in elements of his fascinating work wherever I could.

I also relied upon Anthony F. C. Wallace's *The Long, Bitter Trail* and *Jefferson and the Indians,* Pulitzer Prize winner Marquis James's *The Life of Andrew Jackson,* Grace Steele Woodward's *The Cherokees,* Gary E. Moulton's *John Ross: Cherokee Chief,* Thomas E. Mails's *The Cherokee People,* Joseph J. Ellis's *Founding Brothers: The Revolutionary Generation,* Gloria Jahoda's *The Trail of Tears,* Robert V. Remini's *The Life of Andrew Jackson,* Theda Perdue's *The Cherokee* and *Cherokee Editor: The Writings of Elias Boudinot,* William L. Anderson's collection of academic essays, *Cherokee Removal: Before and After,* John Sugden's recent biography *Tecumseh: A Life,* Marc McCutcheon's *Everyday Life in the 1800s,* H. S. Halbert and T. H.

Ball's *The Creek War of1813 and 1814,* and Dr. David Stewart and Dr. Ray Knox's account of the apocalyptic New Madrid event, *The Earthquake America Forgot.* I'm pleased to mention the influence of Lucia St. Clair Robson's *Walk In My Soul,* an imaginative novel so richly researched and detailed I used it as a primary source. A copy of *James Mooney's History, Myths, and Sacred Formulas of the Cherokee* was always near me.

The missionaries remain one of the best observers of day-to-day life among the Cherokee before and during the years of the Cherokee Republic. I consulted *The Brainerd Journal: A Mission to the Cherokees, 1817-1823,* and Rowena McClinton's unpublished 1996 dissertation, *The Moravian Mission among the Cherokee at Spring Place, Georgia.* I came across Dr. B. B. Edwards's 1833 *Memoir of the Rev. Elias Cornelius.* Reverend Cornelius visited the Cherokee and left us with his impressions in this obscure volume. Ain't Ebay great!

I'd like to thank Bonnie Haegele and Roy Gene Rhineheart, schoolmates and lifelong residents of Cane Hill, Arkansas, who spent the better part of a day searching for the place where Ridge met his end. More than thirty years had passed between Professor Wilkins's visit and mine. No map, expert, or historian I consulted recollected the Military Highway, the Old Line Road, or even White Rock Creek, called Little Branch. Ms. Haegele and Mr. Rhineheart knocked on several screen doors until we located the landmarks Professor Wilkins described in his 1970 book. Mr. Rhineheart stood where a little-used dirt road crossed a stream below a limestone bluff in the southern Ozark hills, exactly one mile east of the Arkansas-Oklahoma Line. "If it didn't happen right where I'm standing," Roy Gene said, "it happened within a hundred feet." I believed him. Thanks to you both for your courtesy and the sacrifice of your time. Through them, I was able to return alone and stand in Ridge's tracks at the exact time in the morning 160 years to the day of his death. Thanks to Steven Law, the force behind www.readwest.com, for getting us in touch with one another and also for publishing an excerpt of this novel on his monthly e-zine.

Special thanks to Mary King, curator of the Chieftain's Museum in Rome, Georgia, for spending most of a day with me. The Chieftain's Museum is actually the Ridge and Sehoya's home at the time of removal, which still stands near a place marked "Ridge's Ferry" in Rome, Georgia. It was wonderful to walk Ridge's old haunts on an autumn day with the leaves just turning. I'm also grateful to Ranger Julia Autry of the Chief Vann House for sharing her extensive knowledge of this era with me. We talked for two hours until her duties pulled her away. Built in 1804, the Vann House stands as a magnificent example of Cherokee initiative and style. Thanks also to the rangers at New Echota State Park. Boudinot's home is gone, but water still stood in his well on the day of my visit. Missionary Samuel Worcester's house still stands in its original location, and it's an exact copy of the home constructed by his dear friend, Elias Boudinot. Go to New Echota and get a feel for how the Cherokee used to live.

I'm grateful to my readers: Jeanne Jard, Chandler Ford, Barbara Minton, John Holmgreen, Andy Barham, Lynn McFarland, Todd Allen, Mike Pugh, Corinne J. Brown, Lisa Minton, Aline Jordan, Tommy King, and Mack and Pat Barham. Thanks to Dr. John Trimble for his suggestions on the Author's Note. Special thanks to my old friend and teacher Dr. William J. Scheick for reading and commenting on early drafts of the manuscript despite a formidable workload. I owe a debt to award-winning author Ms. Sarah Nawrocki, who edited the first draft with her usual expertise. Special thanks to actor, screenwriter, and producer Todd Allen, whose keen sense of story always fascinates and inspires me. Thanks also to Cyndi Hughes for lending her expertise to later drafts, and to Elizabeth Lyon, who taught me more about the craft than I can ever repay.

I'm especially pleased to acknowledge the assistance and support of many Ridge/Watie family descendants. Thanks to Elias Boudinot's descendant, Ms. Helen Currie Davis, Ms. Nancy Brown, descendant of Flora Ridge and W. D. Poison, and all the other Ridge/Watie relatives who took the time to answer e-mail queries about their forebears. I'm especially grateful for the support, encouragement, and interest of Ridge's fourth great-granddaughter, Ms. Dorothy "Dottie" Doyen Ridenour (directly descended from Ridge and Sehoya's youngest daughter, Sarah or Sally) and her husband, Paul. The Ridenours spent countless hours discussing elements of this novel with me, circulated e-mails throughout the family on those rare occasions when they didn't know the answers themselves, connected me to family, friends, and experts in at least four states, and read and commented on early drafts of the novel. Dottie even meticulously proofread final drafts. Thank you both. It meant the world to me to have you two looking over my shoulder.

I owe a great debt to Cherokee academic and author Mr. Charles Brashear, for reading and commenting on an early draft. But most of all, I owe a sincere word of gratitude to gifted Cherokee novelist and three-time Silver Spur winner Robert J. Conley, author of *Real People* series and numerous other titles, for his encouragement and support while this book was being written. Bob answered a barrage of e-mails with his typical intelligence, sensitivity, grit, and humor, and even served as my tour guide when I visited Tahlequah, Oklahoma. Bob showed me that the old religion still lives in the Oklahoma hills. I'm grateful for the honor of calling him my friend. Charlie and Bob did their utmost to guide me through the difficult journey of wedding fact and fiction, but they (and the Ridenours, for that matter) are in no way responsible for my interpretation of Cherokee and American history as presented in *Oblivion's Altar.* This burden lies with me alone.

I'm fortunate to live in a community where so many writers thrive. Thanks to my many Austin friends for your continued interest and encouragement. Special thanks to Jesse Sublett, Sarah Bird, Carol Dawson, Suzy Spencer, Marion Winik, Mike Blakely, Jan Reid, Kip Stratton, Jim Kunetka, Christopher Cook, literary critics Clay Smith and Don Graham, and literary agent Jim Hornfischer. Thanks to my out-of-town friends, Cindy Bonner, Johnny D. Boggs, and Sandra Scofield, all of whom are exceptional writers. Thanks also to my many friends at Western Writers of America, a superb organization for any author interested in the American West and the pioneer era. The friend I quoted in the first paragraph is gifted historical novelist

Elizabeth Crook.

I remain grateful to my original publishers, Tom Southern and Elizabeth Vahlsing, of Boaz Publications, Inc. Thanks to my former agents, Mary Alice Kier and Anna Cottle of Cine/Lit Representation, for believing in the project when it was just a dream. I'm very grateful for the efforts of Penguin Putnam editors John Paine and Tiffany Yates. Special thanks to Penguin Putnam senior editor Daniel B. Slater. Dan plucked *Not Between Brothers* from regional obscurity and introduced the novel to a national audience, and a friendship began. The "Tonto from Toronto" was an advocate of *Oblivion's Altar* from the time it was just an outline up until the novel was in its final form, always offering encouragement, guidance, and an immense amount of red ink. I can't thank you enough, my friend.

Last, I am so very grateful to Steven Anderson and Brenda Bradshaw and the entire Goldminds team for re-publishing the novel in its finest edition yet. It's been a joy and a privilege to work with all of you. I thank you from the bottom of my heart.

— David Marion Wilkinson
Austin, Texas
April 2001 / May 2013